THE AMISH BONNET SISTERS SERIES: 3 BOOKS-IN-1: AMISH MERCY: AMISH HONOR: A SIMPLE KISS

AMISH ROMANCE

SAMANTHA PRICE

AMISH MERCY

THE AMISH BONNET SISTERS BOOK 1

CHAPTER 1

FLORENCE BAKER RELEASED her foot from the pedal of her sewing machine and looked out the window with longing. Today, her fresh-air wander through the apple trees would have to wait.

"Florence! Why are you staring out the window?" Mercy looked over her shoulder. "My dress is nowhere near done. Can't you sew faster?"

Mercy's voice grated on Florence's nerves. She turned away from the half-made dress and glared at Mercy. *"Nee.* Leave me be. *Dat* always said children shouldn't see things half done."

"I'm not a child. I'm eighteen." Mercy put her hands on her hips.

"Numbers don't always tell the story. You act like a child." Florence turned back to her machine. "I don't know why *Mamm* thinks you're mature enough to marry."

"I am mature. You're only being mean to me because *Mamm's* in the kitchen and can't hear you."

Florence huffed and looked back at Mercy. "If *Gott* wants you to marry, the man will appear from wherever he is and find you. He'll bring the two of you together somehow."

"He won't have to because *Mamm's* helping me." A smirk hinted around Mercy's perfect bow-shaped lips. She always had an answer for everything.

"I don't like all this deception surrounding this man coming to dinner. I'd say he doesn't know people have conspired against him."

"The Bergers said their nephew could help with the harvest this season and they would've told him about me too, I'm sure." Mercy poked out her tongue. "So there."

Florence shook her head in complete disgust and knew this nonsense wouldn't be happening if their father were alive. "You expect to fall in love and live happily ever after and never have any problems because your love will be sufficient? Is that right?"

"Jah." Mercy laughed. "You'll see. I'll be happy and have three *bopplis* before you even think about getting married. Oh, wait. You'll still be here at home with *Mamm,* doing the same old thing."

"Someone has to keep everything running." Florence turned back to her machine and put her foot down, hoping the hum would put a stop to Mercy's talking or drown out her whining.

Florence wasn't sure how it had all come about that Ada Berger was convinced her sister's son was the perfect man for Mercy. All she knew was that *Mamm* and Ada had gotten their heads together and now Mercy believed Ada's nephew was her husband-to-be.

Mercy had moved right next to her and when Florence caught sight of her out of the corner of her eye, she jumped. Her sister looked annoyed. "What?" asked Florence, thoroughly exasperated.

"I'm goin' to marry Stephen Wilkes and I don't care what you say."

"You can't say that for certain. What if you don't like him when you meet him?"

"I'm still going to marry him just to get away from here." She lowered her head and moved closer to Florence. "And to get away from you."

Florence gasped, more than a little hurt by the comment. "Why would you say that? Haven't I looked after you well enough? I've done the best I could to make you and your sisters happy."

"That was my job as the eldest, but I've never been able to be the eldest because of you." Mercy planted her fists on her hips. "I want to be in charge of something and when I'm married, I'll be boss of my own *haus*." She stomped away.

Since nobody was around, Florence allowed her tears to flow. Nothing had been the same since her father had died. Her stepmother was good to her, kind and loving, but still there was a gaping hole in her heart.

Mercy wasn't grateful for all Florence had given up for the family. She could've gone to the young people's events looking for a husband. Instead, she'd worked hard in the orchard while delaying any plans of having a family of her own.

Mamm came hurrying out of the kitchen with a dust rag in her hands. "Were you two squabbling?"

"Not really." Florence wiped her eyes and moved the fabric slightly so it would sit tighter under the needle.

"You're upset."

"I'm okay." Florence didn't want to bother her stepmother with anything that would worry her, so she did what she always did when she was upset; she kept working.

When *Mamm* was dusting the mantle over the fireplace, Mercy came back into the room. "My dress should be finished by now, *Mamm*. I want it perfect for tomorrow night and she's not finished it."

"If Florence says it'll be done, then it'll be done," *Mamm* said.

"Jah, but I want it done today and not tomorrow. What if I want to make some changes? She always makes them too long."

"That's easily solved." Florence swung around to face her. "You can do the hem once I've finished."

"Be grateful she's sewing your dress at all, Mercy," *Mamm* said. "It's a special treat and I've taken money out of our savings for it."

"Denke, Mamm. I do appreciate it, I do, but she's always sewing and won't let me have a go."

Florence had taught all her sisters to sew, but she ignored that comment not wanting to get into an argument. "It will be ready." Florence didn't even look up when she added, "Now go away and leave me to concentrate!"

"Humph. Rude!" Mercy said. "Did you hear how she spoke to me, *Mamm?*"

Mamm had moved on to dusting the wide wooden arm rests of the couch. She always went into a cleaning frenzy when they were having special guests for dinner. There was one guest in particular she was hoping to impress, on behalf of Mercy.

"Mamm, will you answer me?" Mercy asked.

Mamm reacted to the frequent arguments of her daughters by ignoring them completely. It was often up to Florence to step in, but this time Florence was involved. While Florence turned her attention to the sewing, *Mamm* finally spoke. "She's the best seamstress out of the lot of you. Do you want to look pretty tomorrow night or not?"

Mercy pouted. "I do but … Hey, wait. Did you just say I'm not as good at sewing as Florence?"

When *Mamm* hesitated, Florence said, "I'm better only because I've been doing it longer."

"Only because you're always on the sewing machine and I don't get a chance."

"Keep cleaning, Mercy. Do you want Stephen to think we have a dirty *haus*? He'll think you'll make a dreadful *fraa*."

"It's fine. It's good enough already."

"Help me clean. Get a rag from the kitchen."

When Mercy was out of the room, Florence stopped the machine. "Does Stephen even want to get married, *Mamm?*"

"He would. Why wouldn't he? I also know he hasn't got a girl-friend. Ada told me so much about him. He's her older *shweschder's* middle son. She has three and none of them is married."

"Why aren't they trying to marry off the oldest one?" Right now, Florence wasn't the least bit concerned about Ada's nephews. What she'd asked was meant as a big hint to *Mamm*, since *Mamm* wasn't the least concerned about finding a husband for her. It also made it worse because she, not Mercy, was the eldest of the girls.

"She didn't say why. She recommended Stephen instead. I guess she likes him better."

Florence frowned, not liking the hurtful implications of that answer. *Mamm* kept dusting, unaware of what she'd just said and how it related to Florence and Mercy. Adding to Florence's upset was the fact that the conversations she'd overheard between Wilma and Ada were all about finding a nice man for Mercy, whom *Mamm* had referred to as "my eldest."

At first, Florence had tried not to think about it, but it had festered in her mind like a forgotten piece of bread left in the back of a cupboard. She'd always thought of Wilma as her mother and had called her *Mamm* since she was four. Didn't Wilma see her as one of her daughters? Florence turned away from the machine and said, "So is the older *bruder* a stepson?"

There was no chance for her stepmother to even hear her question, much less to answer it, because loud screams rang from outside. It was Florence's two youngest half-sisters hollering at the top of their lungs. "Florence! Florence, the Graingers' cows are out again!" she heard Cherish yelling.

"Ach nee! Not again. Florence, will you see about that?" *Mamm* asked.

Florence was always the one sent to talk with people, whether it was the Graingers from next door or people who came to the door of their home. The cows had gotten out just weeks ago, and Doug Grainger had promised to fix the fence and make it stronger.

Florence bounded to her feet. "Okay." She left the dress draped over the sewing table and headed out of the house. She was glad her stepmother hadn't heard that last question. She'd regretted the words as quickly as they'd flown off her tongue. Of course, *Mamm* preferred her own children to her stepdaughter, but she shouldn't make it so obvious.

When Florence stepped outside onto the porch, she was faced with her two youngest half-sisters. Each carried a bucket of windfall apples. It was one of their chores to pick up the apples that fell before the harvest.

Florence walked closer and looked in the buckets to see they hadn't gathered many. They had hundreds of apple trees and picking up those apples from the floor of the orchard was an important job. "Is that all you got?"

Favor held up the bucket as she shook her head. "There are more."

"We haven't finished yet," Cherish added.

"Sort those and then get the rest while I talk to Mr. Grainger," she told the girls.

The apples they'd collected were to be divided into three groups —eating apples, apples suitable for cooking or making into cider, and apples that were good for nothing but to be thrown into the compost heap.

"Can I come too?" Cherish, the youngest called out. "I want to hear what you say to him."

Florence turned around. *"Nee.* You do your chores and then see what *Mamm* wants you to do in the *haus.* We've guests coming tomorrow for dinner." They all knew that meant everything had to be spotless.

"We wanna come too," Favor said in a whine much like Mercy's.

"Nee. Stay here." Florence glared at them, almost daring them to defy her. She had to be stern with all the girls or they'd do

whatever they liked. They'd already stopped listening to *Mamm* because she wasn't firm enough.

When Florence was a distance from the house, she heard Favor call out, "Say hello to old Mr. Grainger." Then she heard Cherish giggling along with Favor. Mr. Grainger was gruff and they knew Florence didn't like speaking with him.

She yelled back, "Just get the rest of those windfalls picked up. On my way back, I'm going to check you've gotten them all." Florence kept walking. Each day she tried to get away and be alone amongst the trees. It was where she felt close to her father. He'd loved his apple trees and perhaps that was why she loved being amongst them. Out here in the fresh air, the breeze blew her troubles away, and the trees smelled like happiness and comfort.

She stopped and touched a ripe red Fuji apple, and memories of her father introducing that variety to the orchard jumped into her mind. He'd told her it was a variety developed in Japan—a cross between the Red Delicious and the Ralls Janet apples. They had a reputation for being good for both eating and baking, along with the added bonus that they stored well.

There was another reason Florence felt good in the orchard. She was surrounded by history. Not only the history of her own family, but the early American settlers who had grown their apples from seeds after traveling from their home countries. Her father's passion had been collecting those early varieties, the ones that still had the same properties and lineage as those from the early days. They were dying out as the more popular hybrid varieties took over. When she got some spare time, she intended to search out some of those rare varieties herself.

With her fingers still wrapped around the Fuji apple, she twisted it off the branch. She held it in the air and admired how perfect it was with the tiny stem still attached.

Her mouth watered. It'd been ages since breakfast and there was nothing like a fresh apple plucked from the tree. She polished it on her apron and then sank her teeth into it as she started walking again. The Graingers didn't have too many cows, and hopefully Doug Grainger had heard the girls screaming and was already moving the cows back to his own property.

Still worried about her sister rushing into marriage, she dragged her feet. There was nothing she could do. *Mamm* approved of it and Mercy had her mind made up. What upset her most was she herself was twenty-four, a good six years older than Mercy. Did her stepmother hope to keep her around to run the place? Is that why *Mamm* wasn't bothering to find her a husband? Actually, she could think of nothing worse than being set up. Love would happen if it was meant to be. That was what she'd told Mercy, and that was what she believed.

Once she'd finished the apple, she placed the core at the base of a tree so she could collect it on her way home.

When she came to the border of the two properties, she walked past three cows happily eating the fallen Red Delicious apples. As she got closer to the Grainger's house, her foot caught on a rock and it caused her to trip. Instinctively, her hands flew up in front to save her face from smacking into the dirt. The day was getting worse by the second.

She picked herself up, looked at her grazed and stinging palms, and then dusted the dirt from her white apron with her fingertips. It was then she noticed her *kapp* on the ground. Embarrassed, and afraid someone might see her without it, she snatched it up and popped it back on her head. As she tied the long strings under her chin to prevent it coming off again, she noticed someone walking toward her. Someone far too handsome to be Mr. Grainger.

CHAPTER 2

"Hello," the man called out. He was tall. His slim fitting jeans, loose white button-up shirt, and short-cropped dark hair let her know that, just like the Graingers, he was an *Englischer*.

She fixed a smile on her face and wondered if he was minding the house while the Graingers were away. "Hello," she replied when he got a little closer. "I'm looking for Doug Grainger."

She stared up into his dark hazel eyes, admiring how they were fringed with long dark lashes. Suddenly she was nervous because this man was a dream-come-true even with his two-days' growth of beard.

He thoughtfully shook his finger at her, and then briefly pointed at her. "You're one of the bonnet sisters."

She stared at him, wondering what he was talking about. "No."

"You've got the most incredible blue eyes."

She did her best to hide the pleasure she felt from his compliment. She got so few of those ... Especially with her attractive half-sisters always close by.

When she didn't speak, he asked, "Are they real?"

It was an odd thing to ask but the absence of a smile told her he wasn't joking. She tilted her head. "Whatever do you mean?"

"Are they colored contact lenses?"

"Oh. No. They're my very own eyes."

"They're beautiful." He stood staring at her and smiling.

"Um, 'bonnet sisters,' you said?"

"I see you all going past in your buggies and you've all got those white bonnets, and you're all sisters. The Graingers told me a little about you girls. I've found myself calling you the bonnet sisters—just talking to myself, that's all." He looked pleased for a reason Florence couldn't understand especially since he freely admitted talking to himself.

Suddenly, he lost all appeal and she was jolted back to the reason she was here—the cows! "Where are the Graingers?"

"They've gone. Moved away. They sold this place to me."

"Oh. That's a surprise. Then these are your cows?" She glanced over at the intruders happily munching on her family's income.

"I guess so."

She sighed. If he was their new neighbor, she wasn't going to stand for the 'bonnet sisters' nonsense. Putting aside the issue of the cows that suddenly didn't seem as important as checking him on his rudeness, she touched her *kapp* with her fingertips. "These are prayer *kapps*."

"*Kapps*, bonnets … they're all the same to me."

Now she knew he was just an ignorant man, and he might as well stay that way. "I'm here about the cows, not our head-coverings."

"Do you want to buy them? I'll sell them to you. The Graingers left them with the farm."

"'Buy them?'" Now she knew they weren't going to get along with this man any better than they had with the former neighbors.

He nodded. "I'll take a reasonable sum. I don't want to rob anyone."

"Oh, well, that's good to know. But why would I buy them? They're eating my apples."

"So that's a no?"

"Yes that's a no. Can you get them away from the apples before they devour them all? We use the dropped ones too, and soon your cows will start pulling the lower-hanging fruit from the trees." She wasn't normally unfriendly, but the upset with Mercy and then the fall had caused her to lose patience. Now to find the Graingers had sold, without even offering to sell the land back to them, had further upset her. She gently rubbed her sore palms. "Can you move the cows please?" She noticed an expensive-looking white SUV parked close to the house. Surely the man understood economics. "We need to sell the apples because they're our livelihood. Unless you'd like to buy this year's produce to feed your cows?"

He frowned and rubbed his stubbly square chin. "I don't think so. That sounds costly."

"Then fix the fence. Or I'll have to charge you for what they've eaten."

"I can fix it."

Looking him up and down, she sincerely doubted he could fix a fence or had ever done any kind of manual labor. "Thanks," she said in reference to him saying he'd fix the fence.

"I'll do my best with the fence. Something like that shouldn't be too hard."

"My father had an agreement with Doug before he sold him the place that Doug would always keep the fence in good order." Had her father known the Graingers' would bring bothersome cows to their property, he might've thought twice about selling them the parcel of land. At the time, though, they'd needed the money—they'd had three poor-producing seasons in a row. It was a rough patch and it came in the years directly following her father's marriage to Wilma. There were more mouths to feed and at that time Florence's two older brothers were too young to find work to help out the family.

"Your father owned the place before Doug?"

"That's right. Didn't Doug tell you about the importance of maintaining the fences?"

"No, but I will do everything I can to keep the horses out of the orchard."

"They're cows."

"I meant cows." He chuckled and then scratched his head. "I'm just not sure how to get the cows back here. How would I get them to do what I say?"

"You herd them. They're cows."

"I'm well aware they're cows. Even though I accidentally said 'horses' a minute ago. I know that much."

Florence sighed. It was either offer to help, or go back and finish sewing the horribly-ungrateful Mercy's dress while listening to her nag and whine. Either choice was as unappealing as the other. If she helped the new neighbor, at least she'd be out in the fresh air for longer. "Would you like me to help?"

A smile spread over his face. "I'd appreciate it. I have no idea what to do."

She looked him up and down once more. "Neither do I really, but I probably have a better idea than you. I just hope my hands hold out." She looked at her palms that were now red. The skin hadn't broken so she was pleased about that.

"You've hurt yourself?" He put out his hands for her to show him, but she pulled her hands back against herself.

"They'll be okay. Let's get this done, shall we? I've got lots of other things I need to do today."

Together they pulled back the fallen down fence so the cows would have a wider area to move through. Then Florence had a brainstorm. "Do you have hay?"

"Plenty of it stored up for the winter. And it'll be winter soon."

She nodded. "Bring some and put it on your side of the fence."

"Hmm, hay or apples. Which would they prefer?"

"Hopefully the hay. You get all the hay you can carry and then I'll try to move them away from the apples and herd them back through the fence. Once they're through and onto your land, we can fix the fence."

"Okay."

CHAPTER 3

IT ONLY TOOK fifteen minutes to get the cows back on his side of the fence. When the cows paid little attention to the hay, Florence had lured them back to their own property with handfuls of apples.

When they had pulled the broken fence mostly closed, he said, "Thanks, I couldn't have done this without you."

She stood close to the small gap in the fence, on his side, knowing that everyone back home would be wondering what had taken her so long. Mercy would be annoyed she wasn't finishing off the dress, but all of that seemed so far away as the sun danced on her skin while a cool breeze tickled her face.

He picked up one of the apples from the ground and then straightened up while he stared at it. "Delicious, right?"

"Yes, that's right. They're a variety that's less popular than it was once. The Fuji and the Honeycrisps have taken over–at least for us. The Granny Smiths have always stayed a firm favorite."

He chuckled. "Sounds like a sales pitch."

"It's not. And we need to truly fix the fence, now."

"I saw wire in the barn."

"Fetch it, and pliers."

WITH THE NEIGHBOR'S pliers and some wire he'd found in his barn, Florence fixed the fence the best she could with her sore hands.

Looking at her handiwork, she said, "It'll do for the moment, but since they've tasted my apples, I know they'll try it again. The fence needs to be strengthened all along this side, and as I said before—"

"I know. Your father sold it to the previous owner with the understanding he'd look after the fence. Even though my contract had nothing of the kind on it, I'll honor that original agreement. I'll trust you're not making up stories."

"I'm not. Trust me." She smiled. "Anyway, thank you. Before you interrupted me, though, I was going to say you could run barbed wire across the top or electric tape. Both things work well, I'm told."

"I'll look into them."

His gaze traveled to her mid-section.

She looked down to see her soiled dress and apron. "Look at my clothes."

He grimaced. "I'm trying not to."

"They're ruined." It was incredible that his white shirt had remained crisp and clean, despite having carried hay and fencing wire.

"I'm sorry. Let me pay for it."

"It's not the money. It's the time it takes to sew." She cleared her throat, shocked at how much her whining tone reminded her of one of her younger sisters. "Thanks anyway. It's an old dress and I'm sure the stains will come out adequately with a good soak. I'm surprised Doug didn't tell you about the fence agreement." She frowned at him. "Are you a city man?"

"How can you tell?"

"Believe me it wasn't difficult."

He looked over at the apple trees. "They do look tasty. No wonder the cows want to eat them."

"We start picking on Monday, officially." She thought she'd be neighborly. It was the right thing to do. "I can bring you some. We grow a few different varieties. One for everyone's tastes."

"No, that's okay."

"I will. I'll bring you a bucketful. Some are good for eating and we've got others better for cooking. The Granny Smiths are wonderful in pies and you can do all kinds of other cooking with them. We sell our apple goods, too, and cider in our shop at the front of our house near the road."

"I've seen the shop. When do you open that?"

"Monday. I'm cleaning it tomorrow so it's ready for opening day."

"I wouldn't mind half a dozen apples. Eating ones. I don't do that sort of cooking. And I'll strengthen that fence even more tomorrow. Is it a deal?" He put his hand out, above the fence, and she showed him her grazed palms and he put his hand back down by his side.

"It's a deal," she said.

He held her gaze and she stared across the fence into his dark hazel eyes. Her former attraction was sparked once more. It was a shame he didn't know what he was doing on a farm. Uselessness was such an unattractive trait in a man. It was an even greater shame he was an off limits *Englisher*.

"Goodbye, Mr. …"

"I'm Carter."

"Hello, Mr. Carter. I'm Florence Baker."

He laughed. "I'm sorry. Forgive me for laughing. Carter's my first name. I'm Carter Braithwaite. I didn't think folks would be so formal around here." He placed his hands casually on his hips. "We are neighbors after all. Seems you called the previous owner by his first name."

"We hardly spoke to him because he kept his cows in. Well, most of the time he did. They got out a few weeks ago."

He smiled at her and for a second, she wondered if he was attracted to her, and then he ruined the moment by saying, "I'm pleased to meet one of the bonnet sisters at last."

She grimaced. Even though he was handsome, he was offensive. Just when she was contemplating telling him so, he spoke again.

"How many sisters do you have?"

"Six. Plus me. I'm the eldest."

"I see. I thought you might be."

"And why's that?" Did she look so old? She was only twenty-four, but everyone always thought she was much older.

"You've got an air of authority about you. Like you're running the show."

"Hmm." She didn't know how to take that. "I've got two older brothers. Technically, I'm not the eldest, but I'm the eldest living at home. Also, the eldest girl." She was the youngest child of her late mother, but she didn't need to tell him too much.

"Why didn't your father come to tell me about the cows?"

"That would be a challenge. He died a couple of years ago."

"Oh," he said with raised eyebrows. "I'm sorry to hear that."

"My older brothers have left home. One got married and lives quite close but the other moved to Ohio soon after our father died."

"You're running an orchard and there are no men at home?"

"Yes. We're fine. We have seasonal workers who help."

He tipped his head to one side. "Who's managing the place?"

"Me and my mother, mostly. My stepmother."

"And your mother?"

"She died when I was quite small." She hadn't wanted to tell him all that since they'd only just met. "And what about you?"

"Me?" he asked.

"Do you have family? It's your turn to tell me. It's only fair."

He chuckled. "Are you trying to find out if I'm married?"

She inhaled deeply. "No. I didn't even think …"

"Oh. I'm so unappealing you thought no one would marry me?" He looked down at the ground.

"Are you … married?" she asked.

He looked back at her and smiled. "No."

"That's what I thought."

He laughed. "Why's that?"

"For one thing, I don't see a woman around."

"Hmm. Did you ever stop to think she might be out working to help support me and these cows?"

Florence couldn't help but giggle. "I wouldn't believe that. You'd be the one working if you were married, wouldn't you? Your wife would stay at home, or she could work too, but she wouldn't work while you just laze about the place."

He laughed again. "I'm not lazing about. I was busy with something before you interrupted me this morning and, just so you know, it's just me alone in the world."

"Sometimes being alone is a good thing."

"Spoken like someone who's never *had* to be alone."

They smiled at one another, until she said, "I better get back to—"

"Back to your bonnet sisters?"

She opened her mouth in shock. Didn't he know how derogatory that sounded? "Please don't call us that."

He grinned and instantly became disturbingly more handsome. "And I have to get back to my chess game."

She scrunched her brows and glanced over at his house. "I thought you lived alone."

"I do."

"Doesn't it take two people to play chess?"

"Not when you have a computer."

"Ah, you play against the computer? That is your opponent?"

"That's right."

"Wouldn't it win every time?"

He chuckled. "I could be a chess genius for all you know. Actually, it has different skill levels. I'm not that good, but I'm learning."

It seemed like a complete waste of one's time. "Goodbye," she uttered before she turned and hurried away.

The brief exchange with the *Englisher* had made her feel lighter inside, which surprised her considering how different he was from any man she'd met before.

CHAPTER 4

MERCY WANTED to give herself the best chance of marrying the man coming to dinner tomorrow night. A brand-new dress might've seemed a small thing, but she desperately wanted to make a good first impression and every detail had to be perfect. That included her appearance. Many people had told her she was attractive with her reddish-brown hair and greenish-blue eyes, but she wouldn't be that attractive in an old black hand-me-down dress. That was why she'd talked *Mamm* into allowing her to have a new one.

For years, she'd dreamed of having her own home and raising her own *kinner*. Apart from getting out from under the shadow Florence cast, she'd be the one to make all the decisions and look after everything and everyone. Best of all, she wouldn't have Florence telling her what to do all day every day. Florence had always been better at everything—in fact, she was more like a second mother than an older sister.

While her younger sisters were busy in the kitchen making the midday meal, Mercy picked up the half-finished dress that Florence had left near the sewing machine. *"Mamm,* she hasn't even finished it. It's taking so long." Her mother was sitting on the couch and had been just about to put her teacup to her lips.

She lowered her cup back to the saucer and placed it on the coffee table in front of her. "There's other things she's had on her mind. Anyway, you don't need it to be finished until tomorrow evening. Have some patience for once in your life. She's making it out of the kindness of her heart."

"I wanted to do it. I want to make sure it's perfect." What she really wanted was to sit down and finish it herself, but she knew Florence was a *wunderbaar* seamstress. That was, when Florence put her mind to it and wasn't distracted with other things.

Mamm continued, "Florence has always done a good job with dresses for you girls."

Mercy sighed. "I know. Where is she anyway? Hasn't she been gone for an awfully long time?"

"Why don't you go look for her if you're worried?" Wilma picked up her cup once more and settled back into the couch and sipped her hot tea.

Mercy spun on her heel. "I will." She walked out the door, jumped down the three front porch steps in one go, and when she looked up she saw Florence walking back to the house. "About time," she mumbled under her breath. Then she hurried to meet her to find out what had taken so long. When she got closer, she saw Florence's clothes were filthy. "What happened to you?"

Florence rolled her eyes. "We have a new neighbor. He didn't know how to get the cows back, so I had to help him. He had no idea about fencing, either, so I had to make a temporary fence repair too."

"That's awful."

She glanced down at her clothes. "I fell in the dirt as well."

"Mr. and Mrs. Grainger aren't there anymore?"

"*Nee.*"

"That's weird."

"I know. I would've expected them to tell us they were going, or at least say goodbye. The new neighbor's interesting."

"In what way?"

"He's an *Englischer* and he's living there by himself. He knows nothing about cows—and from the looks of him, nothing about much else."

Mercy put her hand over her mouth and giggled. "He can't be as cranky as old Mr. Grainger. Anyway, are you going to keep working on my dress?"

"Of course. I'll clean up and have something to eat and then I'll finish it. I know it doesn't look it, but it's nearly done. You can do the hem, can't you?"

"I can."

"Good."

Mercy knew there was something different about Florence. She didn't seem quite so disagreeable. Did it have something to do with the *Englischer?* "Was he handsome?"

Florence glanced over at her as the pair walked side-by-side. "Who?"

"The new neighbor."

"He was a bit rude. Well, not so much rude, he was ... *different.*"

"Keep away from *Englischers*. He's handsome and you liked him. I can tell. Don't tell Joy you like him or she'll give you a lecture about—"

"He is handsome, but I've no interest in him as a man. I would never get involved with an *Englischer.*"

"Is he living there by himself? Just him and the cows?"

"Enough about him. I can't wait for us all to meet Stephen tomorrow night."

Mercy was happy to talk about her husband-to-be.

DURING THE MIDDAY MEAL, the conversation between *Mamm* and the girls was all about Stephen and Mercy's upcoming marriage. Florence was horrified and had to say something to stop the nonsense. If only *Dat* was around to caution Mercy on falling in love with a man she'd never spoken with, or even so much as exchanged letters with.

"Just be careful, Mercy. You need to choose a husband wisely." Florence's best friend had married in haste some years ago and she'd confided in Florence that she regretted it daily.

"I'm sure he's the one. If he doesn't suit me I can change him into the man I want him to be."

"I don't think it works like that." Florence shook her head and wished she could give Liza's unhappiness as a real-life example, but her friend had sworn her to secrecy.

"Oh, coming from someone who hasn't even had a boyfriend. Have you ever even liked anyone?" Joy asked, snatching up the last piece of bread that Florence was reaching for.

With all the bread gone, Florence picked up the dish of boiled potatoes and spooned two onto her plate. *"Nee,* but it's common sense. You don't want to end up living apart from your husband."

"Like Ira and Mary Schwartz?" Joy asked.

"Jah, like them." They were another example besides Florence's friend.

Joy said, "Everyone knows they just don't get along anymore."

"Not every marriage within the faith is going to work as well as you might think. You can't rush into it and you can't marry just anyone. You've got to have things in common and … and all that."

"We'll have *Gott* and our beliefs in common, and if he looks okay I'm going to marry him." When Florence heaved a sigh, Mercy patted Florence's shoulder. "It'll be okay. I've prayed about it. I asked *Gott* to bring me a *gut* man and the day after that *Mamm* started talking about Stephen. I knew he was the one for me."

Florence looked over at her stepmother who'd stayed silent all this time. That was what she did when things got difficult. Wilma didn't even see there was a problem, so Florence had to be the voice of reason. "I just don't want you to be disappointed, or feel you have to marry him because Ada and *Mamm* think you should."

Mamm looked down at the table and kept silent.

"No one's going to influence me. You'll see. Stephen and I will get along better than you've ever seen two people get along. We'll go together like pepper and salt, apple pie and ice-cream, peanut butter and jelly."

Florence looked down at her plate. "I hope so."

Then *Mamm* lifted her head. "Stop worrying so, Florence. *Gott* wants people to marry. It's His intention that everyone find someone."

"Jah," Joy said, "In Proverbs it says, *Whoso findeth a wife findeth a good thing, and obtaineth favour of the Lord.* It would be the same as for a woman. If you find a husband, Mercy, you'll be finding a good thing. Don't listen to Florence." Joy stared at Florence almost defiantly, and all *Mamm* did was smile.

"*Gut* girl, Joy," Wilma said, "You've been reading again."

"*Jah.* I have." Joy, the third oldest of Wilma's daughters, often quoted from the Bible and rarely let anyone get away with anything without telling them what the Word said.

Mercy, who was sitting next to Florence, looped her arm through hers. "And when I'm married, I'll find one of Stephen's older friends for you. We can all sit around the table having dinners together just the four of us."

Florence giggled and gave up her quest, for now. "That would be nice. And we'll all live close so things here will never have to change. We'll keep working on the orchard."

Mercy let go of Florence's arm and straightened in her chair. "I don't know if I'll stick around here. I'll have to go wherever my husband wants, and Stephen lives in Connecticut."

"*Jah,* she'll have to be an obedient wife," Joy added.

Florence ignored Joy. "Mercy, don't you think he'll willingly listen to your opinion and you'll decide together where you'll live?"

"I don't want you to move away," *Mamm* added somberly, as though she hadn't thought about that until now.

"I might not move, but I'll be out from this *haus.*" Mercy smiled. "Who'll miss me when I get married?"

"Everyone will," Honor said.

Hope added, "It'll be one less pair of hands around here."

Mercy's mouth turned down at the corners. "Is that all I am to you all? Just an extra pair of hands?"

"Sometimes," Florence said, "Especially when you're mean to me like you were this morning."

"I'm sorry."

"It's okay. I know how important your dress is to you. I'll start sewing again shortly and won't stop until it's done. Then I'll pin the hem for you."

"Denke, Florence. You're the best."

"I know. I'm the best older sister you'll ever have."

Mercy frowned. "What?"

"That's a joke, Mercy," Honor said.

Favor giggled, "Don't worry, Mercy."

Florence had forgotten that Mercy had no sense of humor.

Mamm pushed herself out of her chair and stood up. "Who's going to clean up in here while Florence sews? She can't do everything."

"I'll do it," Mercy said, "since Florence is finishing my dress."

"I'll help you," said Honor.

"Gut. And the rest of you girls can wash the floors, sweep the porch and pull weeds out of the front garden before our guests come tomorrow."

The younger girls groaned.

CHAPTER 5

JUST BEFORE THE Baker family's guests were due to arrive for dinner on Thursday night, Mercy waited in her upstairs bedroom. Wearing her new dress, she felt confident. With her palms, she smoothed her violet dress down enjoying how the fabric was cool and smooth against her fingertips. It was a nice change from the normal dark heavy fabric all their everyday dresses were made from. They'd worn clothes made from that material since they were young. To make matters worse, hers had all been Florence's hand-me-downs, and they went on down the line until they reached Cherish or were worn out.

Honor rushed into Mercy's bedroom. "They're here."

Mercy hurried to the window and looked out. From her window she could see from the house to the barn and beyond, with a clear view of who was coming and going.

Joy suddenly joined them in looking out the window. "Is that him?" asked Joy just as a young man stepped out of the buggy and looked around.

"*Jah* it is." Mercy's eyes were glued to her future husband examining his every movement.

"How do you know? You've never met him before."

"There's no one else coming. It must be him." Mercy stared at the tall and slim young man as he adjusted his hat and then straightened his jacket. He looked skinnier than most men, which wasn't too appealing, but she figured he'd fill out with the passing of time. "I think he's very handsome. He'll suit me nicely."

Joy giggled.

Mercy didn't care what anyone else thought. This was her decision to make and hers alone. "We'll marry before the end of the year." Mercy stared at him from the high bedroom window, watching him walk toward the house between his aunt and uncle.

"But what if he doesn't like you?" Honor asked.

"Of course he will. Why wouldn't he?" Mercy stared back and forth between her sisters.

Honor opened her mouth and ended up shaking her head instead. "I don't know."

"Just make sure no one chatters too much throughout the meal, and tell the others the same. I want him to be talking only to me. Okay?"

"*Jah.*" Joy nodded. "You can talk as much as you want and we won't say anything."

"Don't make it weird. Just be normal. Tell the others."

"I wonder what Ada said about you?" Honor asked as the girls stared back at their guests.

"She would've said a lot of nice things."

Joy turned her attention to Mercy. "Your dress looks nice."

Mercy looked down at her dress. "*Jah,* it turned out good. You two stay here. I want to meet him first." Mercy left her sisters and hurried out of the bedroom to meet her future beloved.

WITH HER STEPMOTHER busy finishing off the gravy in the kitchen, Florence opened the front door and a ruddy-faced young man stepped forward. "Mrs. Baker, I've heard so much about you and your *dochders.* It's nice to meet you." He smiled and offered his hand.

Florence was devastated, although she did her best not to show it. He thought she was Wilma. Did she really look old enough to have six teenage daughters? Even if she'd married young and had a child at eighteen that would have to put her around thirty-six or thirty-seven, allowing for the nine months of pregnancy. Did this young man think she looked more than twelve years older than she actually was? It was an insult to the highest degree, but she could tell by the anxiousness in the poor young man's large green eyes that he was horribly nervous.

Ada stepped forward and filled in the silence. "This is Florence, Stephen. Mrs. Baker's step-*dochder*." Florence hated how Ada emphasized the word "step."

His shoulders drooped and he stared sheepishly at Florence. "Oh, forgive me! I'm so sorry. I didn't even look at you very closely. You're obviously not old enough."

He wasn't the first person to think she was older than her years. She never gave much thought to her appearance, but every now and again she wondered what it would be like to have people—men—look at her the way they looked at Mercy. Florence laughed it off. "It's fine. Welcome. Come inside and meet everyone."

"I'm really, really sorry," he said as he took off his hat to reveal a mop of sandy-colored hair.

"Forget it. Here, I'll take that from you." She took Ada's coat and the men's hats and jackets, hanging them on pegs near the door. All the while Stephen kept apologizing.

"I don't know how I could've made such a mistake," he said once more.

Ada patted his shoulder soothingly as she said, "It was the light and the shadows. It's just on dark and the light plays tricks."

"It's easily done. Don't worry," Florence assured all of them. The more they went on about it the worse she felt.

Florence was saved by Wilma who hurried out of the kitchen to meet Stephen and greet her friends.

MEANWHILE, Mercy was halfway down the stairs when she saw Stephen. He looked up at her and their eyes locked. It was as though they both knew they were meant for one another. His gaze left hers when Ada introduced him to *Mamm.* Mercy hurried over to be included in the introductions.

As soon as she was close, her mother grabbed her arm and pulled her forward. "And this is my eldest, Mercy. That is if you don't count Florence, my step-*dochder.*"

"Nice to meet you, Mercy. I'm Stephen Wilkes."

"Hello, Stephen." He was even more handsome up close with his unusual green eyes, and he was tall.

"My other girls are around here somewhere. Upstairs most likely. They'll be down soon. Florence, take everyone through to the living room while Mercy and I finish off in the kitchen."

Florence did what she was asked, and when Mercy was alone in the kitchen with *Mamm,* she whispered, "What do you think, *Mamm?*"

"He looks like he'd match you nicely. I can see the two of you together. I can picture it in my mind."

"I knew it. And he was polite and everything and he's handsome too, don't you think, *Mamm?*"

"He is. Ada and even Samuel had good things to say about him, so I was expecting him to be well-suited. Ada hasn't ever let me down when making a recommendation."

CHAPTER 6

WHEN EVERYONE WAS GATHERED around the table and had said their prayers of thanks for the food, Samuel asked, "When does the fruit picking start?"

"On Monday," Florence said. "We've got lots of work to get through before then."

"Florence has arranged for the girls to bake pies and make a supply of other items for the shop." *Mamm* turned to Stephen and explained that at harvest time they sold goods from the small building that stood at the edge of their property alongside the road. Year around, they had a roadside stall where they sold vegetables, jams, jellies, apple-butter, and pickles along with other goodies.

As Ada helped herself to some roast chicken, she said, "I told Stephen all about the store and what you sell there."

"It sounds interesting. I'd like to see it."

"There'll be taffy apples, applesauce, apple relish and butter, and of course the freshly pickled apples. Oh, and cider. Do you have use of a buggy while you're here, Stephen?" *Mamm* asked barely drawing a breath.

"I do. *Onkel* Samuel's allowing me the use of one of his."

Mamm leaned forward and stared at Stephen with her pale brown eyes nearly boring through him. "Perhaps you'd like Mercy to show you around tomorrow? That is, if you're not busy doing something else?"

"I'd like that." He gave Mercy a big smile. "What do you say, Mercy?"

"I'd be okay with that." Mercy was grateful her sisters didn't start giggling. She knew from their faces they were trying hard not to.

"Good. Shall I collect you at nine?" he asked.

"*Jah*. Perfect."

"Have you picked apples before, Stephen?" Hope asked, smiling.

"Not apples, but I've picked other fruit. I've traveled south to pick oranges with one of my brothers."

"It's quite hard work," Honor said.

He nodded. "Don't I know it. The first time I picked fruit I was about ten. It was the hardest work I'd done. Since then I've done a lot harder work. I've done all kinds. I've done construction, I helped out our blacksmith, and I've dug holes for fencing. I'm sure I'll be able to handle picking apples without too much bother."

"We have a race to see who can pick the most buckets by the end of the day. We make a game out of it," Favor told him.

Florence frowned. "I don't like that *game* because there's a risk of the fruit being damaged by rough handling. The Honeycrisps are especially vulnerable to bruising, but we have customers who come back specifically for them every year. We can't sell damaged apples. Once they're bruised they'll go bad and contaminate the apples around them. We won't even be able to use them in the cider or the vinegar."

"I'll be careful. Do all you girls help out in the orchard?" Stephen asked, while looking directly at Mercy.

Cherish said, *"Mamm* doesn't allow me to go outside much."

"She misses out on the fun," Honor told the visitors. "She's spoiled." Honor giggled loudly and Mercy glared at her. She'd told them not to draw attention away from her, and talking about Cherish was doing just that.

Stephen didn't seem to notice what anyone was talking about because his gaze was firmly fixed on Mercy. When Mercy saw Stephen smiling at her, she looked down and cleared her throat. In an effort to show herself to be a good conversationalist, she then said, "We had trouble with cows in the orchard today."

"You have cows as well?" Stephen asked.

"Nee, they're from next door." Florence answered before Mercy had a chance. *"Mamm,* I haven't told you yet. We have a new

neighbor, an *Englischer*."

"The Graingers sold?" *Mamm* asked.

"*Jah.*"

"How did the cows get out?" Honor asked.

"The cows broke the fence down by pushing on a weak spot."

Mamm frowned as she buttered a piece of bread. "Did he fix it properly?"

"I had to help him. He seemed a bit useless. He's a city man."

Mamm sighed. "You would think they would've told us they were moving."

"Did the new neighbor bring the cows?" Samuel asked.

"Seems the Graingers left them there, almost like they were part of the barn." Florence giggled. "He didn't tell me so, but maybe he got there, ready to move in, and saw the cows. He mightn't even have known the Graingers were going to leave them."

Stephen cleared his throat. "That reminds me of a joke." Everyone looked at him, and he continued, "Who wants to hear it?"

Hope was quick to say, "I do."

"*Jah,* tell us a joke, Stephen," *Mamm* said, smiling.

"Why did the cow cross the road?"

"Why?" *Mamm* asked.

"To get to the *udder* side."

Everyone grinned or laughed except for Mercy.

"You mean to get to the *other* side," Mercy stated.

Hope, who was seated next to Mercy, dug her in the ribs. "It's a joke, Mercy. Get it? Udder—other?"

Mercy shook her head, unsure why everyone was laughing. He used a wrong word ... so, how was that funny?

"I've got another one." Stephen's face was beaming. "What would you call a cow when it's eating grass?" When everyone just looked at him, he gave the answer. "A lawn moo-er."

Once again everyone but Mercy laughed.

Then he told yet another. "Here's a good one. What do you call a sleeping bull?" He paused a moment. "A bull dozer."

Giggles rang out while Mercy sat in silence.

"Tell us more," Cherish said.

He shook his head. "I think that's enough, especially at dinner."

As soon as all was quiet. Mercy giggled, trying to please Stephen, and everyone looked at her.

"What are you laughing at?" Joy asked her. "No one said anything."

"Just the jokes." Then Mercy looked across the table at Stephen and they shared a secret smile.

CHAPTER 7

W H E N T H E V I S I T O R S L E F T, the five younger girls were sent to bed leaving Mercy in the kitchen with Florence and *Mamm*. "What did you think of him, Florence?" Mercy asked, anxious to know her sister's opinion.

"I think he's lovely. Very nice, but it's more important what you think of him."

"I'll still marry him even if I don't understand his jokes."

"And that's okay," *Mamm* said, "You don't have to understand him to have a happy marriage. Sometimes you don't want to marry someone too much like yourself. You'll have a lifetime to learn about him."

"You liked him too, *Mamm?*" Mercy asked.

"I did and it was clear how much he liked you."

Florence giggled. "*Jah,* it was because of the dress I sewed."

"Oh, Florence, the dress was good, but it was Mercy's personality and her pretty face he was drawn to."

"Er, I know that *Mamm,*" Florence said. It seemed Mercy wasn't the only one who didn't catch it when someone said something as a joke.

Mercy started clearing dishes off the table. "You have to say that just because you're my *mudder.*"

"I'm not telling fibs. It's true. Just don't get prideful."

Mercy sighed. "I won't. Tonight was okay because everyone else was around. What if we have nothing to talk about tomorrow? I'm a little nervous to be alone with him."

"Then you won't marry him and you'll find someone else who suits you better." Florence thought that was a perfectly normal thing to say, but Wilma didn't agree.

"Florence, if you don't have anything nice to say, don't say anything at all. You can see Mercy has her heart set on marrying Stephen."

"I know that, but surely she won't marry him if he's unsuitable."

"He will be suitable. I mean, he is. Ada said he's perfectly fine and she recommends him. She's known him since he was a little *bu.*"

Florence shook her head. "Okay. I'll keep out of it then."

"Good. I think Mercy was talking to me anyway, not you."

"Nee, Mamm, I'm interested in what Florence has to say because she's sensible."

Florence was pleased Mercy was willing to listen to her advice. "We can talk later, Mercy. Why don't you two talk in the living room while I clean up in here?"

Mamm nodded and then Mercy said, "You can't do all this by yourself, Florence. And you've got the store to clean tomorrow."

"It won't be much work. I'll just be doing a bit of this and that. It won't be too hard."

"Nee, I'll help you in here. You go to bed, *Mamm.* I'll bring you up a nice hot cup of tea."

"You're so sweet, Mercy. I'd really like that."

When their mother was gone, Mercy made and delivered the tea. Then she helped Florence finish clearing the dishes. There was a large area off from the kitchen with a table that seated twelve. It was where they ate all their meals.

"I'm pleased *Mamm* likes him and I know you're cautious. I'm stuck between the two of you." She giggled. "I'll find out more about him tomorrow and then I'll make my final decision. Now that she's gone, you can tell me what you really think about Stephen."

Florence gathered the dishes and walked them over to the sink ready for washing, and while she walked, she said, "I *really think* he's very nice from what we've seen of him tonight, but you have to really get to know a person. You just can't go on meeting them once. Everyone is on their best behavior when they're meeting someone for the first time. You ought to see him in different situations. See how he interacts with his family and his friends. See him in different stressful situations to know how he acts in a crisis."

Mercy stared at her. "You've really got finding a husband all figured out."

Florence laughed. "If that were true, I'd be married by now."

"You've been thinking a lot about it. You must've been. I mean, look how old you are. Haven't you been thinking and hoping you'll marry?"

"I do like to daydream."

"So, you do want to get married?"

"I do. I never said I didn't."

"That's good."

Five minutes later, when the plates were rinsed and stacked and ready to be washed, Mercy said, in almost a whisper, "You'll find someone, Florence. Someday, someone will come for you."

"I know it," Florence said, wanting to sound positive, because deep down that was her secret hope. The Bible talked a lot about hope and it was important to have some. If she hoped, it would increase her faith and God might reward her with the desires of her heart.

. . .

WHEN FLORENCE WAS in bed that night she tossed and turned; she couldn't stop thinking about love. Mercy had said someone would come for her and just as those words echoed in her mind, an image of the neighbor next door jumped into Florence's mind. He wasn't the strong Amish man that God had for her somewhere, but she had been attracted to him and she'd never had those feelings before. It made sense he was a sign for her, sent from God. A sign not to give up and that there *was* someone for her. Florence fell asleep comforted that she wouldn't be alone forever.

CHAPTER 8

ON FRIDAY MORNING, Mercy was so nervous about going out with Stephen that she knew she'd have to force herself to eat breakfast. Her younger sisters weren't helping matters with their constant chatter while they waited for Florence to finish cooking the pancakes.

"What will you talk about with him?" Honor, the next-younger sister, asked just as Mercy sipped hot black tea with a little mint added to settle her tummy.

That was the very thing Mercy was worried about, but she wasn't going to admit it to any of her sisters. "I don't know. Whatever he wants to talk about, I guess."

"Now it's time for our prayer of thanks," Florence announced. She was always the one to tell the girls what to do while their mother sat there almost unaware of what was going on.

They all bowed their heads and each said a silent prayer the same way they did before they began every meal. As soon as they had all opened their eyes, the questions for Mercy started again. This time it was Cherish's turn. "Where are you going with him?"

"I'm not sure yet. I suppose I'll have to—"

Honor interrupted, "Don't you think you should plan what you're going to say? That's what I'd do. That time I had to stand in front of the class and say what we did the weekend just gone, I had to plan it a little—otherwise I would've stood there not knowing what to say."

Mamm said, "That was years ago."

"It's still on my mind."

"*Nee,* Honor, I'll let the conversation flow naturally. You're making me nervous. Zip your lips."

The other sisters giggled and even *Mamm's* mouth turned upward.

Honor didn't find it funny. "But what if it doesn't flow? He didn't say much last night. All he did was tell those dreadful jokes."

"That will be enough," *Mamm* reprimanded her.

"They weren't dreadful. You're saying that because you have no sense of humor," Florence said. "Anyway, I saw you laughing too."

"I didn't laugh, and neither did she." Cherish pointed at Mercy.

"Cherish, go to your room now," Florence said.

"Do I have to, *Mamm?*"

When *Mamm* just sat there, Florence said, "One thing *Dat* always disliked was people saying rude things about others. I won't have it in this *haus.*"

"You're right, Florence. You'd better go to your room, Cherish."

Cherish looked horrified. This was probably the first time *Mamm* had agreed with Florence about punishing her. Normally, Cherish could do no wrong in *Mamm's* eyes. She stood up and knocked her chair over in the process. Florence, who'd been sitting next to her, picked it up while Cherish picked up the bottom of her dress in both fists and strode out of the room. They all sat in silence listening to her stomping up the stairs.

"That girl's got a temper. I don't know where she gets it," *Mamm* said shaking her head.

"From the devil." Everyone gasped at Joy's words. Joy was taken aback by their reactions. "I'm sorry, but where else would she get the temper? All good things come from *Gott,* so where else but the devil do you think the other things come from?"

Florence shifted uncomfortably in her chair. It wasn't the pleasant start to the day for which she'd hoped. In her experience, the breakfast always set the tone for the girls for the remainder of the day. "Let's just eat, shall we?"

They ate the rest of their meal in silence, Mercy's nerves apparent as she picked at her pancakes.

AN HOUR LATER, Mercy was pretty much done getting ready when she looked out the window and saw Stephen coming up the driveway. She couldn't wait to get away from the house. She finished tying the strings of her prayer *kapp* and then took hold of her black shawl, raced out the bedroom door and ran down the stairs taking them two at a time. "Bye," she called out to everyone before she pulled open the front door. When she stepped out into the daylight, Stephen was out of his buggy and heading toward the house.

"How are you this fine morning?" His face beamed with a smile.

"I'm good. And, how are you?"

"Great. I'm just going to say hello to everyone before we start."

"No need. They're all busy anyway."

He looked up at the house. "Are you sure?"

"*Jah*. Come on." She started walking toward the buggy hoping he'd follow and he did.

"Where are we going?" he asked.

"Where would you like to go?"

He smiled at her and repeated, "Where would *you* like to go?"

Then she remembered what her mother had said over dinner. "Would you like me to show you the town?"

"I'd like that."

"Okay, let's go."

Before they had a chance to get into the buggy her sister's dog ran at Stephen and jumped up at him.

"Stop it, Caramel! I'm so sorry. This is my sister's dog and she hasn't bothered to train him."

Stephen laughed, crouched down and gave the dog a few pats. "It's okay. I love dogs. I've got Buster. He looks a little similar to this one, but he's bigger. I miss him already. I had him since he was six weeks old. I could hold him in the palm of my hand. Caramel's an unusual name."

"It's Cherish's dog. She loves candy and caramel is her favorite flavor. It's a dumb name I know."

Cherish came running out of the house. "There he is. I'm sorry." She grabbed Caramel's collar and then picked him up.

"Train him," Mercy said.

"He is trained. He can sit."

"Yeah, well train him to come to you, *jah?*"

Cherish simply frowned at her and walked away with the dog.

Mercy told Stephen, "She's the youngest and a little bit spoiled. She wasn't well when she was younger and that's when she got the dog. That's a whole other story."

"It must've worked for her. I hope Buster's not missing me too much."

"I'm sure he'll be fine. Let's go." Mercy walked over to the buggy and Stephen followed.

CHAPTER 9

AFTER MERCY HAD LEFT on her important date with Stephen, Florence escaped to her sanctuary, the log cabin shop her father had built close to the road.

Florence placed the large black key in the lock and turned it to the left. This would be the first time she'd been in the place for many months. It'd only need one day to give it a good cleaning and she much preferred to do that away from her giggling noisy sisters. Pushing open the door, she inhaled the aroma of wood mixed with the sweet smell of beeswax from the candles she'd lit at dusk to add up the takings on the last day she had worked there—several months ago.

Soon the place would be bustling with tourists, as well as locals who came back every year for the fresh apple pies, pickles and chutneys. The shelves were already stocked with jarred and canned goods and the boxed crates of apple cider vinegar bottles were full to the brim. They'd need more as the season progressed but with this supply it was a good start.

The place would need a good dusting and then everything would have to be washed down. Realizing she'd forgotten her cleaning items, she spun around intending to fetch them when she faced a large silhouette in the doorway. She gasped in fright at the unexpected sight.

It was Carter from next door. "You want to inspect the fence?" he asked.

Her hand moved to her chest. "You scared me half to death. What were you doing sneaking up on me?"

"You said you'd be here."

"Did I?" She couldn't recall she'd told him anything of the kind.

"How are your hands today?"

She looked down at them. "Much better thanks. Good enough for me to use them today."

"That's great to hear. Do you want to inspect the fence? I strengthened it."

"I'm sure it's fine. As long as it keeps the cows out of the orchard, it'll be good enough."

"It will, but I wanted to show it to you to get your feedback. This is the first fence I've ever repaired."

She didn't have time to waste today. "I'm sure it'll be fine, and I'm busy at the moment."

"With what?"

"Trying to get the store ready. If you don't mind, I've got a lot of work to do and I work best when I'm alone." She was surprised when she heard herself sound so abrupt, but he didn't seem to notice.

He walked further into the shop. "It's not much fun being alone."

Fun? She couldn't remember the last time she'd had anything that resembled fun. Not with all her responsibilities. This man obviously didn't have a care in the world and for some reason that irritated her. "I don't want to look at the fence. Just keep the cows out next time, okay? Then we can live in peace next door to each other."

He didn't seem to notice her irritation as he walked over and picked up a bottle of apple cider vinegar. He read out the label, and then asked, "What do people use this for?"

"It's apple cider vinegar."

"I know that. I can read even though I'm not good with cows. What do people *use* it for?"

"A lot of women buy it for beauty products. It's good for the hair and skin, they tell me."

"Putting it on the outside or drinking it?"

"Both. It also helps to ward off colds and has many other health benefits. Too many to name, and possibly more too that no one's discovered yet." She reached under the countertop and pulled out a leaflet. "Here. Read this." He stood there looking it over. "You can keep it. Take it with you,"

"Thanks." He put the bottle back, folded the leaflet and slipped it into the back pocket of his jeans, and then dusted off his hands. He looked at her and then nodded to the bottles of vinegar. "You might want to dust those."

"I'm getting to that. Come back on Monday and the whole place will be spotless. That's when we're officially open."

"Am I annoying you?"

"I've only got one day to clean this place. So, to answer your question, you're not annoying me, but you are in my way."

He laughed. "I like an honest woman."

"I hope you find one. There must be another one out there somewhere."

He frowned at her. "I'm sorry."

She stepped out from behind the counter. "For what?"

"For wasting your time. I won't do it again." She stared at him and he raised both hands, palms facing her. "Okay, I know when I'm not wanted." He walked out of the one-room building and she was glad.

It took a few seconds for her to regret her rudeness, but by then it was too late. Stepping out the door, she looked for him. When she spotted him, he was a tiny figure in the distance disappearing behind a clump of trees. "At least you won't bother me again," she muttered under her breath.

. . .

SHE WALKED BACK to the house and saw some of her sisters were still there and they hadn't begun collecting the apples from the ground. "Who's working the stall today?"

"You didn't tell us we were doing the stall."

"We do the stall every day. We can't afford to lose the money we make." Florence could feel her heart rate gallop as she tried to keep calm. "Joy and Honor can do the stall and they better hurry. Hope, gather the girls and tell them what's happening. Favor and Cherish can start getting those apples together, *jah?*"

Hope shrugged her shoulders as she sat on the couch staring into space holding onto a white coffee mug. "It won't take long. We'll do it later."

"*Jah*, we'll do it when Mercy comes back," said Honor, who was sitting on the opposite couch. "Why should I work the stall when Mercy has a day off. That's why I thought we weren't doing the stall today, Florence. You didn't say who was going to replace Mercy."

"Can't anyone around here think for themselves?" Florence yelled.

Mamm came rushing out of the kitchen. "Florence, what's wrong?"

"No one's organized the stall. Just because Mercy has a day off everyone thinks they can have one."

"*Jah,* well they can't, can they?"

"Nee, Mamm. They need to move now and get that wagon to the road and set up that stall!" Florence put her hand over her chest and felt her heart pumping. She was so angry with everyone.

Mamm licked her lips and looked at the girls lazing on the couch. "All of you do what Florence tells you."

Florence knew it was hard for *Mamm* to say that and she was grateful. "I don't care who does it but two of you need to set up that stall and get moving NOW!"

Joy fixed her eyes on her. "What are *you* going to do?"

"I'm cleaning out the store and it'll take me all day. We talked about this last night."

"Do what she says, girls. Joy and Honor, you do the stall today."

"I'll finish my *kaffe,*" Joy said.

"Nee you won't!" *Mamm* told her. "You're already late, so you'll go without. Set it down now and get in that wagon."

Her stepmother backing Florence up took a lot of pressure off her shoulders.

Begrudgingly, the two girls stood and started moving. Florence didn't wait to see what happened next. She headed to the back of the house to collect the mop, bucket and the cleaning rags while hoping *Mamm* would keep the pressure on the girls to do what they were asked. They had a way of getting out of things— if they whined persistently enough *Mamm* often gave in to them rather than disciplining them.

As she walked back to the store, the girls were hurrying to get the horse hitched to the wagon. The wagon was already pre-loaded with the goods for the roadside stall.

Once she was back in the store, Florence took a deep breath in and let it out slowly, slowly, relishing the silence. *Refrigerator first, or shelves? Hmmm ... shelves, I think.* She started from the top and worked down, wiping the jars as she took them off the shelves, and then scrubbing the wooden shelves until the rinsed rag came up clean.

When she was on the second shelf, her mind drifted to Mercy and she hoped she was having a good time getting to know Stephen. The last thing she wanted was for her sister to get into a bad marriage, but Mercy and Stephen seemed like a good match, and that had surprised her. It had always been the Amish way to marry young, and she knew that was what Mercy wanted.

CHAPTER 10

"How do you like it here so far?" Mercy smiled at Stephen as he drove the buggy.

He momentarily drew his eyes away from the road. "I like it here—a lot."

She felt all aglow when he smiled at her the way he had just now. He was even more handsome when he smiled.

"Aunt Ada said I should come here not only to help with picking the apples but also to meet you."

It was just as she'd thought. He had come to dinner knowing it was all a setup. The first thing she'd tell Florence when she got home was that she had been right and Florence was wrong. "Did she say that?"

He nodded and then turned his attention back to the road. "Ada likes you. She likes you a lot."

"My *mudder* and Ada are best friends. I think they've been best friends forever."

"The last time I was here I was five. I came with my whole family for my grandfather's funeral."

"That would be too far back for me to remember anything."

"Me too. I barely recall it. Mostly just so many people that I didn't know."

They traveled along the quiet country road in silence for a few minutes. She hoped he liked the area and the community enough to stay here after they married. Then she could be around her family rather than a bunch of people she'd have to get to know.

"I'm pleased you like it here." She couldn't think of anything to say and she regretted not listening to Honor's advice.

"I like it a lot."

"That's good. And you'll get to meet everybody on Sunday and everybody is so nice."

"Good. I'm looking forward to it."

"Do you think you might like to maybe live here one day?"

"It's not totally out of the question. The community I come from is very small. I prefer to be around more people. That way it's livelier, and there'd be more things to do and more folks to visit."

Mercy smiled, imagining them with a large family. She wondered if he would talk about marriage today or whether it would take him a little longer. They both knew that was why he was there even though neither of them had said the word 'marriage.'

"Did you have breakfast?" she asked.

"Sure did. Ada filled me up with pancakes and some kind of sausage with a white cheese sauce."

"Oh, that sounds interesting. I'll have to get the recipe from her. I love cooking."

"Are you a good cook?"

"I like to think so. I do most of the cooking at home so obviously you'd have to ask the family how good I am."

"If they keep letting you back into the kitchen, you cannot be too bad." He laughed. "Have you ever traveled around to other communities?"

She shook her head. *"Nee.* Oh, we did a little before *Dat* died. We went to a few of our cousins' weddings and things like that but after he died we haven't been anywhere. We're too busy with the orchard and *Mamm* says it's too much trouble to go anywhere."

"I imagine that would keep you busy."

"I know a place that makes nice food."

"Around here?"

"Not too far.

"Maybe we could go there for lunch. If you can stay with me for that long?"

She was pleased he wanted to spend more than a couple of hours with her. "I can. I have the whole day free from chores and from the stall. I normally do Fridays on the stall but I got out of it today."

"Good. Your family is nice for letting you off your chores to spend the day with me."

"Of course they would. They like you. Especially after all the nice things Ada said about you."

"So, Ada did talk about me?" he asked.

"Of course. Is there anything that I should know about you that she wouldn't know?"

"Nothing that I can think of. I haven't done anything bad." He looked over at her and asked, "Have you?"

She put a hand up to her mouth and giggled. "Sometimes I tell one of my little sisters it's their turn to wipe the dishes and they can't remember whether it is so they do it anyway."

He gasped. "That's very wicked."

She felt dreadful. "Do you think so?"

He laughed. "Relax. I'm only joking."

"Oh." She giggled.

"Your secret's safe with me. I hope you're not going to be awful like that with me."

"If I knew you thought it was awful I wouldn't have confessed just now."

"Hmm. Smart as well as pretty." He glanced over at her and she felt the heat rise in her cheeks. "You must have a lot of men stopping by the house to see you."

"I don't." She shook her head vigorously hoping he didn't think he'd have to wait to marry her or be in competition with anybody else. "There's no one else, truly."

"I find that very hard to believe."

"It's true. It's totally true."

"You're the prettiest girl I've seen since ... Well, since forever."

"That can't be right." She giggled with embarrassment and also a small amount of delight.

"It is. I wouldn't lie. I'm blessed you're going out with me today. I know looks aren't everything and it's what's inside that counts, but it's *wunderbaar* when you can have both in one woman. Are you with me today just because your mother asked you to last night?"

"*Nee.* I wanted to go out with you."

"You did?"

"*Jah.*" She looked up at the road ahead. "Now turn left at this intersection."

"Yes ma'am. Where are we going?"

"Keep going along here. I'm taking you to a covered bridge. We've several of them around here and this one is really pretty and the trees are so nice. And the stream that runs alongside it is so nice at this time of year."

"Good. Then can we stop the buggy and take a little walk?"

"Sure, if you'd like to."

He leaned forward and looked up at the sky. "It's a beautiful day. And I love to walk."

"Do you?"

He nodded. "I do."

"I love how the sky looks this time of year."

"Me too."

"The trees are all kinds of colors. So pretty."

"I've got some jokes about trees. Do you want to hear 'em?"

She didn't, but she had to be polite if she wanted him to like her. "Sure, go ahead."

"Did you know I'm so good at cutting down trees I can do it just by looking at them?"

She frowned at him, wondering what she was supposed to say.

Then he said, "I *saw* them with my own eyes."

She had to be honest. "If that's a joke, I don't get it."

"I *saw* them with my own eyes. Get it? Saw. You cut down trees with a saw." When she shook her head, he said, "I'll have to work on my delivery. It was a tricky one. How about this one? What kind of tree can you fit in your hand?"

"A very small one?"

"No. A palm tree." He chuckled.

"I don't understand that. You couldn't fit it in your hand if it was a large palm tree, but you could fit any young tree in your hand if it was small enough."

He drew his eyebrows together and lifted up his hand. "Palm and palm tree. It's a kind of a play on words."

"I see. I realize that. It just doesn't work." Even with his jokes, she liked being with him.

"Okay, last one of the day. I'm sure you'll think this one's funny. How do you know if a tree is a dogwood tree?"

"I don't know."

"By the bark." He laughed. "Get it?"

"*Jah,* I do. Dogs bark and trees have bark." She forced a giggle and that seemed to make him happy. Thankfully, he'd said it was the last joke of the day. A few miles along they drove around a bend and there it was—the bridge. "There, what do you think of it? It's very old. I'm sure there's a story attached to it somewhere, but I don't know it."

"It is indeed lovely. We could make up our own story about it."

A giggle escaped her lips at the look of wonder on his face. "We can drive through it and then to the left is a parking area and there just might even be a walking trail."

"Do you happen to know there's a trail for certain?"

"You'll have to wait and see."

"You haven't taken another man here, have you?"

She gasped at the idea. "Oh no. You're the first man I've ever been alone with in a buggy."

He shook his head. "I still can't believe you haven't got men knocking on your door every single day."

She loved his attention and the constant compliments he gave. It was a magical moment as they drove through the darkness of the covered bridge and came through into the bright sunlight on the other side. With slight pressure on the reins, he moved the buggy off the road and into the parking area. Once he had stopped the buggy, they both jumped out at the same time and then he secured his horse.

"I can see a path," he said when he walked over to join her.

"Let's go." Feeling playful, she started running toward the trail and he ran after her.

"Wait for me," he called out.

CHAPTER 11

WHEN FLORENCE HAD FINISHED MOST of her cleaning, she regretted how rude she'd been to Carter. Hoping to make it up to him, she bundled together some canned apples into a box along with two bottles of apple cider vinegar. She looked around the store and was happy with how much she'd gotten done already. All she had left was to mop the floor and then it would be ready for the grand opening on Monday.

Several minutes later, after she'd picked some apples from one of the trees, she knocked on Carter's door holding the box of goodies close to herself. The door was slightly open and she found it strange when he didn't answer. His SUV was there so she knew he was home. She walked over to the window and saw him on the couch with a computer in his lap and earphones in his ears. His head was bobbing up and down like he was listening to music.

She contemplated leaving the goods by the front door but she wanted to apologize in person, so holding the box in one hand she tapped on the window with the other.

He looked up and she gave him a wave. He pulled out his earphones, set his computer down on the coffee table and leaped to his feet. He met her at the door, clean shaven and looking far more handsome than she remembered.

"This is a surprise and an unexpected one. Did you get all your work done?" he asked.

She resisted the temptation to tell him that surprises generally *were* unexpected and that was the nature of them. "Most of it, yes. I said I'd bring you some apples and here they are." She held the box out to him. "And I brought you some of the apple cider vinegar you seemed so intrigued about."

"That's very kind of you. How much do I owe you?"

She laughed. "Nothing of course."

"I have to give you something."

"No you don't."

He pulled a wallet out of his back pocket, opened it, pulled out a hundred dollar bill and held it out to her. "Take it."

"No!" She leaned back. "I just came here to—"

"Take it."

"No, I won't. It's a gift."

He shook his head while placing the money back in his wallet. As he did so she noticed he had many other notes in his wallet and they all looked like the first one. While he shoved it in his back pocket, he stepped back slightly. "Come in."

"I shouldn't. I've still got some work to do back at the shop."

"Surely you can have a five-minute break? Come in and I'll show you what I've done with this old place."

Just to be neighborly, she agreed. "All right, just for a couple of minutes. What were you doing just now?"

"Playing chess."

"Oh, that's right. Playing chess by yourself against the computer."

He frowned a little. "That's right."

She looked around the sparsely furnished place. The walls were blue at the top and the bottom half of the walls were covered with varnished wooden boards. In one corner of the room was a staircase. There was a small table with a single chair in one area of the L-shaped room and one two-seater couch and one coffee table in the other. A small TV sat on a wooden crate. The impression was the house of a person without much money, but then there was his car and what looked like an abundance of cash. She spun around to face him. "What is it you do when you're not playing chess?"

He laughed. "I know you think I'm just some lazy person who's not good with cows and sits on his computer all day, but Amish people aren't the only ones who work hard."

"I wasn't saying that."

His lips widened into a grin. "Come here."

She followed him through to the kitchen. It looked like a bomb had exploded and smelled stale—like years of dust had been unearthed. "This is a kitchen?"

"It was once. I've taken the cabinetry out and I'm about to redo it. There was a lot of wood and a lot of blue and the layout was wrong. All the cupboards were blue. The same shade as the living room."

She'd been there before when she was young and it looked a lot smaller than she'd remembered. "How long will it take for you to build a new kitchen?"

"I'm not going to do the actual construction of it. I've got others doing it. I was pleased with myself for taking the old one out. I thought you'd be impressed."

She couldn't help smiling. "You want to impress me?"

"Only to make up for the cows."

"Yes, I'm not happy about the cows. Which reminds me, what are you going to do with the cows?"

"In what way?"

"Do you intend to keep them here forever or will you send them to the butcher?"

He frowned at her and rubbed his chin. "Eat them?"

Then she remembered he knew nothing about farming. "They're not dairy cows."

"Do I have to *do* something with them?" He leaned against the wall. "Can't they just stay here to eat the grass and do what they please?"

"You want to keep them as pets?" She giggled not expecting his next answer.

"Yes." When she kept laughing, he added, "Is there a law against it?"

"No, but it's crazy." She stared at him and wondered how this chess-playing man who lived alone ran his life. "Most people have a cat or a dog if they want a pet. They're much easier. They're also smaller and far less trouble. You don't have to worry about fences so much." When he shook his head, she asked, "A guinea pig or a bird?"

He shook his head once more. "A dog would be the best choice."

"Yes, good. Get a dog. Leave cows to farmers."

Raising his eyebrows, he asked, "What pets do you have?"

He was trying to draw her into conversation, but she had to get back to the shop. That floor wasn't going to wash itself. She inched toward the door. "We have two cats that live in the barn. They sleep all day and they're not very friendly at all. One of my sisters has a small dog. It was supposed to be a golden lab but it never grew. I'm not sure what kind of dog it is. A mixed breed of sorts."

"You have no pets yourself?" he asked.

"I guess my trees are my pets."

He laughed. "You're an extraordinary woman."

She didn't know how to take that but decided he didn't mean it in a flattering way. "Have you done any other work on the house?" she asked walking to the door.

"I have. I've pulled out the bathroom too. Come back in a few days to check on my progress if you like."

"When will it be finished?"

"I'm not sure. I figured I might paint the place too."

"Sure, I'll come back and have a look … someday." She backed away. "Enjoy your apples." She misjudged where the doorway of the kitchen was and bumped into a wall.

She was shocked and embarrassed—even more so when he smiled at her. "Careful, this is a construction site."

"More like a de-struction site."

He chuckled and sent tingles through her when he put his hand on her shoulder. "Let me walk you out before you do some real damage." When they were at the front door, he said, "Thanks again for your generosity."

"You're welcome."

"And you said the store will be open on Monday?"

"That's right."

"I might have to sample some of your apple pies."

She gave him a smile. "I might see you then … then." After that, she hurried away. She didn't want him to come back to the store. Neither did she want to bring him a pie since that would mean she'd have to see him again. The best thing she could do was to keep away from him completely.

When she was halfway through the orchard, she suddenly came to a halt when she realized he'd never answered her question about what he did. She resumed walking and to keep him out of her mind she thought about all they had to do the next day. It was going to be their busiest cooking day of the year.

CHAPTER 12

MEANWHILE, Stephen had caught up with Mercy and they were ambling along the walking trail while autumn leaves gently fell about them.

Stephen had been doing most of the talking, so now it was her turn. "When I get married and have my own *haus* I'm going to have my bedroom on the top floor where I can see the whole countryside. It'll be built on a hill. My bedroom now is above the doorway and I can see everything from there."

He gave her a big smile. "That's what I want."

"And when I have that home, I'm going to open all the blinds during the day. *Mamm* prefers the place dark and for every blind to be pulled down. It's always so gloomy and depressing. I think the light makes me happy."

"I like a well-lit *haus* too."

She giggled. "We have a lot in common."

"I didn't notice your place was so dark. I guess that's because I was there at night."

Mercy sighed. "The only sunlight comes from the living room, the window in front of Florence's sewing machine. The machine was her mother's and that's the only one we have. If she won't allow us to use it we have to hand-sew everything." Florence had so many privileges that it annoyed Mercy most of the time. *Mamm* always allowed Florence to do whatever she liked. It was normally Florence who reprimanded them while *Mamm* sat there without saying a word.

"She won't allow you to use it?"

"She does, when she feels like it and only when she's not sewing."

"Is sewing by hand that bad?" Stephen inquired.

"*Nee*. I don't mind it. It's just that sometimes it's so much quicker to use the machine. Especially for doing long straight seams." When she thought he looked bored, she tried to think of something interesting to say. "Are you getting a little hungry yet?"

He smiled. "A little."

"We should go to the diner I was telling you about."

"Okay."

"Let's go back."

They spun around and started their way back to the buggy. Just as they did, a breeze swept up through the trees and sent a flurry of golden leaves down on them.

WHEN THEY REACHED THE DINER, Mercy told Stephen she was too nervous to sit inside amongst the *Englischers* who might stare at her.

Stephen shrugged agreeably. "So, what do you want to eat?"

"Their fried chicken is *wunderbaar*. It's their signature dish."

"Sounds great to me," Stephen said with a grin, heading inside to buy take-out for them.

When he returned with a bag full of delicious smells, they drove back and found a spot by the river. They sat at a table eating fried chicken, creamy coleslaw, and fresh-baked rolls while admiring the water.

Stephen was perfect for her, Mercy mused, except for his jokes. She had never understood jokes and didn't see why people thought such things were funny. It bothered her a little but not enough to stop her marrying him. Everything else about him appealed to her and she hoped he felt the same about her. On the way back, Stephen let out a yell that made her jump and turn toward him.

"What is it?"

"That man walking up ahead—I know him. That's my brother."

She turned forward to see an Amish man with a knapsack slung casually over his shoulder.

Stephen pulled the buggy over to one side and jumped out. The young men spoke for a moment and then she watched them both heading back to the buggy. They were similar in appearance except for his brother being a little taller and not quite as thin, and—she guessed—a little older. Stephen then introduced his brother, Jonathon, who wore a big smile. Stephen got into the buggy while Jonathon, still on the ground outside the buggy, shook Mercy's hand.

"Pleased to meet you, Mercy."

"It's nice to meet you, too. This is a surprise. I certainly wasn't expecting to meet Stephen's brother today."

He jumped in the back and then leaned over and said to Stephen. "And this is the woman Aunt Ada's been talking about at such great length?" Stephen laughed, and then Jonathon told Mercy, "I'm here to help with picking the apples. Aunt Ada made it sound exciting and I didn't want Stephen to have all the fun. I'm going to work for free."

"Me too," said Stephen. "I couldn't take money from you, Mercy, or your family."

"*Nee,* you must. *Mamm* won't allow anyone to work for nothing. Only the local families who help us every year, but we supply them with apples. All the other workers will be paid. *Mamm* won't like it any other way."

"I'll talk her into it. I have a way of getting everything I want."

"It's true. He does," Stephen admitted. "And, *bruder* Jonathon, were you hitchhiking?"

"There's nothing wrong with that. It's the easiest way to get around."

"I'm sorry for this interruption to our day, Mercy," Stephen said.

"She won't be sorry. You're probably boring and tedious. Now I'm here to liven things up."

Stephen smiled as he moved his horse forward. "One thing you'll learn after you get to know my brother is, never believe a thing he says."

"I see I came just in time before you spread rumors about me."

"They aren't rumors if they're true."

Mercy stayed quiet, unsure of what to say while the brothers' banter went back and forth. She guessed they were teasing, but that was as incomprehensible to her as Stephen's jokes had been. When they got to her house she stepped down from the buggy. "Goodbye, Jonathon."

"See you around, Mercy."

Stephen was quick to get out of the buggy. "I'll walk you in."

"*Denke.*"

Then Jonathon got out, and said, "I'll come in and meet everyone. I'll tell your *Mamm* I'm working for free."

Stephen turned around. "Not today, Jonathon. They've had a busy day. You can meet them all at the meeting on Sunday."

"Okay." He didn't seem to mind and slipped into the driver's seat.

When they were away from the buggy a little ways, Stephen said, "I'm really sorry our day out was ruined. Well, the end of it was."

"Nee, it wasn't ruined. Just interrupted. I had a good day. It was the best one I've ever had in my whole entire life, in all my born days." She smiled at him. The day *had* been ruined by his brother, but she wouldn't tell Stephen so. They'd missed out on talking privately in those last fifteen minutes. In her daydreams, he'd proposed within days and she had secretly hoped he would have done so today.

"Me too. Does that mean you'll come out again with me sometime?"

"I'd like that."

"Can I see you tomorrow?"

She stopped walking and he stopped too and faced her. *"Nee. Mamm* will have a heart attack and so will Florence. We have to spend the whole day making apple pies and things for the shop."

"All of you? Won't that be a little crowded in the kitchen?"

"Yeah, it will, but if I'm not doing that she'll have other things for me to do." She saw from his downturned mouth how upset he was. "I had a really good time today."

"Me too. You won't change your mind about going out with me again, will you?"

"I won't." When she stared into his eyes, peace and fulfilment welled within her. This was the man she was going to marry and she knew it. "I'll see you on Sunday, Stephen."

"I won't be able to wait."

She giggled. "Me either. Bye, Stephen."

"Bye, Mercy." She hurried to the house while he walked back to the buggy.

CHAPTER 13

WHEN FLORENCE HAD FINISHED WASHING the floor of the shop, she walked back to the house with the mop and bucket in one hand, and all the other cleaning equipment in a basket on her opposite hip. When she was still a distance from the house, she smelled dinner cooking and remembered she'd forgotten to eat lunch. It seemed if she didn't organize things, even things as simple as a meal, no one else bothered.

Mercy ran out of the house to meet her. "You'll never guess what happened today."

"He proposed already?" Florence asked teasing her.

"*Nee*. His *bruder*, Jonathon, is here too, and he's helping us with the harvest."

"*Gut*. Many hands make the load lighter. Have you met him?"

"I did. Stephen wasn't even expecting him. We caught up to him walking along the road when we were coming back here. He'd been hitchhiking to Ada and Samuel's. He said he'd work for free, and then Stephen said he's doing the same."

"Ach, nee. I won't hear of that. We always pay our workers."

"I know. We're not taking handouts because we're not in need, and I told them so. I'm just telling you what he said."

"What's he like?"

"He seems nice. He's older than Stephen and nearly as handsome." Mercy took the basket of cleaning items from Florence as they continued toward the house.

"Denke. I'm happy you get along with Stephen. It was just like you thought."

"I know. I told you he's the right man for me. And, he did know he was coming here specifically to meet me, like I thought—no truth to your worry about a secret conspiracy."

DURING THEIR DINNER of pork chops, mashed potatoes, beets, carrots, Brussels sprouts, and asparagus, Honor asked Mercy about her date. The girls were excited because Mercy was the first of the girls to go anywhere alone with a man. "Did you find enough to talk with him about, Mercy?"

"It was hard at first, and I remember thinking, I wish I'd listened to Honor, and then we just started talking about anything and everything. He's so easy to talk with."

"*Gut.*"

"We talked about seventy things at least. And I really like him. He's nice and he's kind and ... and he stopped joking after a while."

"Just ask him to stop joking," Joy told her.

"I don't know about that," said Florence. "She could hurt his feelings if she did that."

Mercy bit her lip. "I don't want to do that."

"Is it something you can't look past?" *Mamm* asked.

"It doesn't bother me."

Honor leaned closer to Mercy. "Would you marry him if he asked you?"

"Of course I will, and I'm sure he'll ask me. I just don't know when."

"After dinner, Florence has organized for us to stew the apples so they're ready for tomorrow's pie baking," Honor told Mercy.

"I never get a chance to roll out the pastry. Can you show me how to do that tomorrow, *Mamm?*" asked Joy.

"Okay. I've shown you all how to do it before, but I'll show you again."

"Then what will I do?" Honor asked.

"There'll be plenty for us all to do."

Florence could sense some arguments brewing in the air. "I'll make up a timetable and assign each of us some chores in a rotation."

"As long as it's fair," Joy said with a pout.

"Everyone will have equal work and get to do a bit of everything, and that way it'll be fair, plus it will help us keep on track for the work." Florence looked at everyone in turn until they agreed.

CHAPTER 14

O<small>N</small> S<small>ATURDAY</small> <small>MORNING</small>, everyone woke at five except for Cherish, the youngest. *Mamm* allowed her to sleep in for no good reason, which had made the other girls grumble. Cherish's health had been fragile as a young child, but she had been fine for the past several years.

Florence had made everybody scrambled eggs and sausages for breakfast. It was important they have a hearty breakfast so they could have energy for their big day in the kitchen.

Mamm was the best pastry maker in their whole community, and as much as Florence tried, she could never match Wilma's skills. Wilma had said she was too heavy-handed, so the skill had passed over Florence and now Honor was the best out of the girls.

As Florence started on her morning coffee, she was entertained by watching her stepmother roll out the first batch of pastry.

Skilfully and ever so lightly, she rolled out the dough with her old wooden rolling pin and then dusted her hands with flour and sprinkled some on the pastry. Then she rolled some more. When it was the right consistency and thickness, she lined one of several waiting pie dishes and sliced the leftovers with a sharp knife.

Honor was doing exactly the same as she worked side-by-side with *Mamm*, but it seemed she didn't have her mind on the job. "Why's Cherish asleep still? She should be working with the rest of us."

"She's younger than you," *Mamm* said. "There'll be plenty for her to do later. She won't be missing out. We've too much to do today to have any of you complaining or worrying about what others are doing. Just keep your mind on what you're doing."

"It's weird that you give her special treatment. I've noticed you've never even shown her how to roll out pastry."

Her mother looked at her in shock. "I have, Honor, I'm sure. Anyway, she was awake late last night not feeling well."

"Here I am."

Everyone looked up at Cherish, who was still in her nightgown.

"Sit down," Florence said. "I'll get you some breakfast."

Mamm told Honor. "When we finish up these ones, you can start on the taffy for the candied apples and Cherish can do the rest of these with me."

"Who's doing the stall today?"

"Joy and Hope."

They had already loaded the wagon with a table and their goods to travel to the usual spot three miles along where there was more passing traffic.

Florence wasn't very happy about Cherish being allowed to help with the pie pastry. Everybody loved their apple pies and came from far and wide. What if her sister didn't do a good job? She didn't seem to pay too much attention to anything she did. Where she cleaned in the house would always have to be cleaned again by someone else. She had the attitude that 'near enough was good enough,' but in Florence's book it wasn't. And *Mamm* never made Cherish redo her own poor-quality work.

"Watch her closely, *Mamm,*" said Honor echoing the thoughts in Florence's mind.

A smile touched Cherish's lips. "It'll be fun. I've always wanted to have a go. I've watched *Mamm* do it so much—that's why I know it'll be easy for me."

FOUR HOURS LATER, the table and all the counter tops were filled with baked apple pies. Many years ago, *Dat* had installed two large ovens into their large kitchen. They'd loaded both of those ovens with pies, while Honor used one of the stovetops for cooking up the taffy. Favor had been given the task of inserting a stick into each of the dozens of apples that were soon to be dipped into the warm taffy.

Mercy walked into the room after pinning out the washing. "I love the way the pies smell when they're baking. This is what I'll remember home smelling like."

Cherish had just sat down at the kitchen table. "You mean this is the way you'll remember it when you marry Stephen?"

Before Mercy could comment, *Mamm* said, "I hope you'll make apple pies for Stephen when you marry, so your home will have this smell, too."

"Of course I will."

"And for all your *kinner.*" Cherish giggled.

Mercy joined in with her laughter unsure of whether Cherish was teasing her. It didn't matter. She would have many children with Stephen and she would bake them all pies.

Mamm said, "Mercy, you must remember to try to get him to move here rather than you move away."

Cherish butted in, "Why, just so you'll have more people to help in the orchard?"

"*Nee,* that's not what I was thinking! We'll miss you when you go, Mercy. I won't be able to bear it."

Joy and Hope walked into the kitchen just then, back from working the stall. Joy said, "We might all move out of this area when we marry, *Mamm. Therefore shall a man leave his father and his mother, and shall cleave unto his wife.*"

"We don't need to keep being reminded what it says in the Bible. We have eyes and we can read for ourselves." Honor said.

"Besides, that verse seems to say the husband should go where the wife is from."

"Stop it, girls. Can't we just have a nice day of baking without squabbles? Just one time?"

"It wasn't me," Joy said. "I was just talking about the word of God. What's wrong with that? Maybe if we all spent a little more time reading it, I wouldn't have to keep telling people what God's word says."

"I know and it's good that you read so much, it is. But sometimes it seems to be the only thing you say."

Honor lifted her chin. *"Jah,* people want to know what *you* think not what you think the Bible says."

Joy's mouth fell open in shock. "What I think is what the Bible says. Because—"

"That's enough. No one say another word." Florence said firmly, feeling a headache coming on. "Why are you both back so soon? Did you make so much money on the stall you thought you could come home?"

"There was no one around. I think it's a public holiday or something."

"Is it? I'm not sure. Wouldn't that mean more people would be about?"

"Believe me," Joy said, "I wouldn't lie."

"Everyone can have some free time now, when the taffy apples are finished," said *Mamm."* Then lunch, and then it'll be more pies."

"Can I make you a cup of tea, *Mamm?*" Florence asked.

"That would be nice, *denke*. I'll wait in the living room."

Florence set about making the tea and put two cookies on a plate along with a frosted doughnut. Her mother always liked to have her tea with something sweet.

Once Florence had the girls organized with fixing lunch, Florence took the tea to her stepmother. *"Denke,* Florence. Sit with me a moment?"

Florence sat down next to her.

"She has to go where God leads her ..." She sipped on her hot tea.

Florence assumed Wilma was talking about Mercy.

Mamm continued, "but she might live a day's journey away and that means I'll hardly see her." Her mouth turned down slightly at the corners.

"That would be hard."

"I'd prefer her to live close by but who would she marry if she stayed here? There's really only the Johnson boy or one of the Storch brothers."

"There are many more choices than that."

Her mother opened her eyes wide and then blinked rapidly. "I know but she doesn't like any of them."

Florence officially gave up her protests about Mercy's intentions. No one was listening to her words of caution. It seemed as useless as Mercy trying to understand one of Stephen's jokes.

"What I am pleased about is she's not going on *rumspringa*."

"I know she doesn't want to. We had a talk about it some months ago and she asked me why I never went."

"Possibly if you had, she would've felt she needed to. You've been a good example for my girls."

Florence smiled because she knew *Mamm* had meant it as a compliment, but it wasn't, not really. By saying it that way, she had made it clear she didn't see Florence as one of 'her girls.' "I'm glad I'm good for something."

Mamm chortled. "You're so good at everything, Florence. We could never do without you." She placed her teacup back onto the coffee table and picked up the frosted doughnut.

When her stepmother fell asleep, full of hot tea, cookies and doughnut, Florence slipped away to her room. There were no mirrors in the house, but she'd purchased her own small mirrored compact years ago. She opened the top drawer of her chest and pulled it out from beneath her underwear.

Then she took it over to the window, sat down and opened it. It had been a good while since the last time. What she saw was a shock. She did look years older, pale and weary with dark circles under her eyes. Since her father had died, she could never get enough sleep and that was evident in the fine feathery lines fanning their way out from the corners of her eyes. The bloom of her youth was fading already. The man God had for her would never see her youthful self, and that was sad. It wasn't how she wanted things to be. She'd come to terms with the fact that life was sometimes harsh, though, and things had rarely gone how she'd wished...

SHE SHUT the double-mirrored compact with a snap. It gave proof she was nowhere near as attractive as her half-sisters.

Her blue eyes, she'd been told were beautiful—some said they were the same shade as the sky on a bright summer's day. She'd gladly trade her shade of eyes for the symmetrical and pretty contours of her younger sisters' faces. Although she wasn't supposed to be concerned about her looks, she couldn't help it. She'd often thought that if God didn't want people to admire beauty, He wouldn't have given them eyes or a heart to appreciate what they saw. Why hadn't He made everyone look the same? Why were some born beautiful and others plain?

Her gaze was drawn back out the window. One thing would make her feel better and that was to walk among her trees. She got off the chair and hid her mirror back in the bottom of her drawer, and slipped out of the house before *Mamm* woke. Yes, there was a lot left to do today, but there was a lot every day. Sometimes, she just needed to be alone to feel better.

The fresh aroma of the trees wafting on the cool air revived her somewhat. *Gott* had blessed the orchard with good weather and good crops for the last few seasons. He'd smiled upon her family and in so doing had increased their savings. Florence gave Him thanks every morning for looking after them. Her father would've been pleased. In her mind, she saw *Dat's* smiling face. Happiness was to feel him near.

During her walk, she found her legs were taking her close to Carter's house. It was a good opportunity to look at the fence situation, she told herself.

Once she saw all was fine with his fencing reinforcement, and that the cows were on their side, she glanced over at the house hoping to catch sight of the intriguing and mysterious new neighbor. The white SUV that had been parked near the house was gone. Pushing him from her mind, she turned and walked back through the orchard.

Florence found it hard to relax because of all that still had to be done today. It would be easier if she wasn't in charge, but just as well she was or nothing would ever get done. With tomorrow being their day of rest, they'd have to work late into the night tonight to get things ready for Monday. Still, many hands made light work and between her and *Mamm* and all of her sisters, they had many hands. The baked goods would have to be taken out to the shop and placed into the huge commercial refrigerator, which was powered by an old generator. Before that though, she'd have to go out and start the often-finicky machine to get the refrigerator chilled down. A new generator was on the list of things they'd need to get before too long. *Before next season,* she told herself.

CHAPTER 15

THE NEXT MORNING, a weary Florence drove everyone to the Sunday meeting. She got down from the driver's seat and secured her horse.

When Florence looked up, the girls and Wilma were halfway to the house and no one had waited to walk with her. Feeling a little upset and very tired, she patted her horse, Chester, wishing she could've had the luxury of a sleep-in. Chester nuzzled his nose against her giving her sympathy. "You understand me, don't you, Chester? You would've waited for me if you were a person, wouldn't you?"

She left her horse and then noticed her heavily-pregnant friend, Liza, making her way toward her. "You haven't had the baby yet I see." Florence laughed sympathetically at the uncomfortable-looking way Liza was walking.

"Nee, but it can't be too far away. I hope. You'll be the first to know. Simon has instructions to call you first."

"I'm pleased to hear it."

Liza placed both hands over her belly. "Sometimes I feel I've been pregnant for years."

Florence giggled. "The *boppli* can't stay in there forever. It'll have to come out sooner or later." She noticed Liza's eyes were rimmed with redness. "Are you all right? You look like you've been crying."

"I'm just upset. We had another fight, last night."

"Not another argument?"

"Jah."

"Ach nee. A serious one?"

"We argued about what to call the *boppli.* I feel like I should give up and let him call the *boppli* whatever he wants, but it's my *boppli* too so I should have a say. I didn't give in and because of that it ended in a row."

"Did you tell Simon how you feel?"

"Nee because he'd blow up."

"You could put your favorite names into a hat and draw them out."

"We might have to. If he'll agree to that." As they strolled toward the house, Liza said, "I'm often sorry I'm not having a child with a man I'm truly in love with. Now I'm stuck with

Simon. If only we were in love—really in love. It'd make all the difference."

Florence looked down at the pale gray compacted dirt that made up the driveway. She knew her friend needed somebody to talk with, but it was often a burden to hear such things. "You can only do your best," she mumbled.

"I know. I'm trying."

When they walked into the house, they found a spare bench on the women's side and sat down. When Florence saw Mercy was seated directly in front, she wondered if she should warn her once again not to enter into a hasty marriage. Anyone can get along on a couple of dates, but it took a whole lot more than that to make a marriage work.

Liza whispered, "I'm sorry I told you that just now, but I don't have anyone else to talk to."

"That's okay. I'm always here. That's what friends are for."

"And you'll never breathe a word to anyone?"

"Of course not. Never. You know me better than that."

Liza's lips curved into a smile, while Florence was more worried about Mercy.

WHEN THE MEETING WAS OVER, Mercy walked outside hoping she'd get to talk with Stephen. But with so many people wanting to meet him and Jonathon, she knew she might only have time to say a few brief words to Stephen today.

She was working at the food table to assist the ladies when all of a sudden someone walked up to her. Looking up from handing out plates to people, she first thought it was Stephen and then saw it was Jonathon. And then, as though it had been planned to the second, they were suddenly alone.

He gave her a big smile. "Hello."

"Hello again." She looked around. "Where's Stephen?"

Jonathon sniggered. "You don't want to worry about him. What you need is a man like me."

She stared at him wondering if he was joking. Stephen joked all the time so maybe Jonathon was the same. Just in case, she gave a little laugh.

"Come sit with me. Stephen said he'll be over in a minute."

"Did he?"

"That's right. Come on."

She looked at the other helpers and figured there were enough workers to allow her to slip away. She followed him to one of the empty tables that had been set up in the Fishers' yard and they sat down.

"What made you decide to come here?" she asked.

"I start a new job in another month, so it's a way for me to fill in my time and keep Stephen out of trouble."

Cherish suddenly sat down with them. "Hello. I'm Cherish, and you must be Jonathon."

"This is just my youngest *schweschder*," Mercy told him. "He isn't in any trouble, is he?"

Jonathon's face lit up when he looked at Cherish. "Hello."

Mercy bit her lip. The last thing she wanted was to marry a man who was in some kind of trouble. "Is he in any trouble?" Mercy repeated.

"Not yet, but there are all kinds of trouble he could get into especially if he's dating someone as pretty as you."

Cherish giggled and Mercy felt uncomfortable and looked around for Stephen. "There he is."

"*Jah*, he's talking to the bishop now, and he's telling Stephen to behave and be good."

"Has he been in trouble before?" Cherish asked joining in the conversation.

A smile beamed across Jonathon's face. "Could've been. I can't say."

"Jonathon, you must tell me if he's been in trouble before." Mercy rubbed at her throat feeling a nerve rash coming on. If something made her upset, her neck on one side would turn beet red.

The smile left his face and he frowned a little. "I was just having a little fun—joking."

She immediately relaxed and repositioned herself on the wooden bench.

"That's a problem she has. Mercy never knows when people are joking or not."

Jonathon smiled at Cherish, then he looked back at Mercy. "That's going to be hard for you. My family always jokes around with each other. That's what we do—how we relate to each other."

Mercy looked back at Stephen and was pleased he'd finished talking to the bishop. Their eyes locked and they smiled at one another and then he walked her way. "Here he comes now."

Jonathon placed his elbows on the table. "You really like him, don't you?"

"I do. I think he's very nice."

"Nice? Yes, that's how I described him, too—nice." He sniggered.

"Boring!" Cherish said.

Mercy wished Cherish would go away. She looked at Jonathon's face to see whether he was joking again, but he didn't seem like he was.

As soon as Stephen sat down with them, Jonathon said, "Who was that lady you were talking with before you spoke to the bishop?"

"No one. I can't think who it was."

"She was very attractive, but so are all the girls around here." He grinned.

Cherish giggled again, while Stephen leaned over to Mercy. "Ignore him. I wasn't talking with anyone. Has he been terrorizing you?"

"A little." She smiled knowing that was meant as a joke.

"That's rude. All I was doing was looking after her for you. Come with me, Stephen, and we'll get some food."

Both men stood, and Stephen said to Mercy, "We'll be back in a minute."

"I'll come with you," Cherish said half standing up.

"No! You stay with Mercy and mind our seats," Jonathon told her.

"We'll bring food back for you," Stephen said with a smile.

Mercy sat there and watched them walk to the food table, talking all the while, and she wondered what Jonathon was saying about her. She would have to develop a sense of humor the same as Stephen, but she wasn't quite sure how to do it.

"He's so handsome," Cherish said staring after them.

"I know."

Cherish scowled at Mercy. "Not Stephen. I'm talking about Jonathon."

"He looks all right, but you're far too young for Jonathon or anyone. He'd never take you seriously."

"He likes me already, I can tell."

After a few minutes, Stephen came back alone balancing three plates.

"Where's Jonathon?" Cherish asked once Stephen put a plate in front of her.

"He got distracted when he met some girls."

Mercy looked around and saw Jonathon sitting with two of the Yoder sisters.

"Excuse me," Cherish said taking hold of her plate.

Once Cherish left, Stephen smiled at Mercy. "I hope you'll stay for the singing. I'll drive you home if you're staying."

"I'd love that. We all stay for the singing normally."

"I'm looking forward to having you all to myself again."

She giggled and cut a portion of roast chicken and popped it into her mouth. All the while she knew Stephen was staring at her and she loved the attention. Then she noticed Cherish had sat down with Jonathon and the Yoder sisters.

CHAPTER 16

LATER IN THE DAY, Mercy felt sorry for Florence. Florence had wanted to stay on for the singing and *Mamm* had wanted to go home. Her older sister had no choice but to take *Mamm* home.

As she waved goodbye to Florence and her mother, Mercy realized just how much Florence did around the house and in the orchard. It wasn't always easy being the oldest. Florence had a lot of unpleasant stuff to do, along with the good, and she carried so much responsibility. She looked around for Stephen and couldn't see him.

Jonathon caught her eye and walked over. "Are you sure you won't change your mind?"

"Quite sure. I've already told Stephen he can take me home. But …" He leaned closer with expectation dancing on his face, until she said, "My sisters need a ride home."

He stepped back and his face contorted into a grimace. "I've met Cherish. How many more of them are there?"

"Five. I mean, four more besides Cherish."

"Sure, I guess so. I'll take *Onkel* Samuel and Aunt Ada home and come back."

She smiled at his sad face. He would much prefer taking home a special young lady, that much was obvious. *"Denke,* Jonathon, I appreciate that. I'll tell them you're taking them home and I'll tell them who you are. I should've introduced you to *Mamm."*

"I met her. I told her who I was and I also met Florence."

"Ah good."

After Jonathon left her, she was walking over to her friends when Stephen walked up to her. "There you are. We were just talking about you. Joy was telling me a little more about you since you haven't told me very much about yourself."

She giggled. "I have too."

"You haven't. Not very much."

"I thought I did. We talked a lot on Saturday."

"There's talking and then there's talking. You don't talk very much. You didn't tell me much about yourself."

She put her hands behind her back. "What is it you'd like to know?"

"I'd like to know everything about you."

She gave a girlish giggle. "Everything?"

"Every single little thing. I want to know everything you did today from the time you woke up."

"That's a little boring. I woke up and had breakfast and then came here."

"It might be boring to you but it's interesting to me. For instance, what was for breakfast?"

She smiled and was pleased how everything was going so well between them. She'd marry him right now if he asked her. "Granola. We make our own granola from rolled oats and other grains, and add nuts and dried fruits. It's really good, and it's filling."

"See? That's interesting, and it sounds really good. Tell me honestly, now. Jonathon wasn't giving you any trouble, was he?"

"*Nee.*"

"What was he saying to you?"

"Nothing. I asked him to drive my sisters home. *Mamm* and Florence left already."

He rubbed his chin. "That leaves you and me alone, truly alone?"

"That's right."

"My prayers have been answered. I can't wait to drive you home tonight."

"Me too."

At that moment, it was announced that the singing was just about to start.

"We'd better take our places," she said.

"I'll be counting every moment every word and every song until we can be back together."

She couldn't help smiling at his wonderfully romantic words. He was exactly what she wanted in a man. God had heard her prayers. She sat on the wooden bench between Joy and Honor and then the singing began. From her back-row position, she could barely see Stephen. He was sitting in the second row from the front. Every now and again, when Jacob Hostetler moved his head just right, she caught a glimpse of Stephen. Throughout the next hour, she noticed between songs he turned around to catch a glimpse of her and she pretended not to notice he was looking at her.

After the singing was over, she gathered the girls together and told them, "Jonathon's taking you girls home."

"I wanna go with you and Stephen," Favor whined.

"Don't be stupid. You can't go with her, they want to be alone," Joy said.

It was rare that she and Joy agreed on anything.

"They spent all day Friday together. What could they possibly have left to talk about?" Favor grumbled.

"You'll know when you're older," Joy told her.

"I'll see you when you get home, Mercy," said Honor.

"Denke, Honor."

Honor and Joy shuffled the other three sisters off in Jonathon's direction and when they'd all introduced themselves, Mercy saw Jonathon's smiling face. She guessed he hadn't expected for all her sisters to be so attractive.

Before it was time to go home, though, there were the refreshments. While soda and cookies were being devoured by all, Mercy and Stephen decided to have an early start and they grabbed a few cookies and slipped away.

Once the buggy was out on the road, Mercy asked, "Did you enjoy the singing?"

"It was good. It's better than at home. There aren't enough good singers at home to sing loud enough to drown out the ones who can't sing."

She giggled.

"You find that funny but not my jokes?"

"I know what it's like when people can't sing and it can sound really off. Sometimes it even hurts my ears."

"That's how it sounds at home all the time. None of 'em can hold a tune and I'm the same, I'm sorry to say. That's why I sing quietly and, just between you and me, sometimes I just mouth the words."

She laughed again pleased he'd said something she found funny. From the look on his face it made him happy too.

When they were on the dark lonely road under the moonlight, driving down the road and finally alone, he turned to her and said, "I honestly didn't think that my visit here would be anything like this."

"But your aunt told you about me."

"Do you really believe all the things she said about you? Someone like that would've surely been too good to be true, I told myself, but then here you are and you're real. You're *wunderbaar*."

She held her breath, waiting, just waiting for him to propose. Then there was silence. She finally broke it. "You are the first person to have said that—even my mother hasn't said something so nice about me."

"I can't see why."

"Me either," she said and they both shared a little laugh.

After twenty minutes of driving around, they decided it was time for Mercy to go home. As much as she was enjoying being close to him, she was disappointed he hadn't taken a perfectly good opportunity to propose. She wanted to have a unique story to tell her *kinner* of how their *vadder* had proposed on the night of their first official buggy ride, but now she didn't have that. Her future story was ruined. Even though he'd said all those nice things to her, wasn't she good enough? What was he waiting for? "It looked like your *bruder* was enjoying himself tonight," she said only to fill the silence.

"He was happy because he was taking your sisters home."

"He didn't sound too pleased when I asked him."

"He can be grumpy sometimes. He says he's looking for a wife, so he'd be pleased with as much female companionship as he can get."

"My sisters are far too young to marry."

He glanced over at her. "Then how old are you?"

"I thought Ada would've told you?"

"No."

"I'm eighteen, and then my sisters are one year apart from each other. Honor is one year younger, then the next one's a year younger than her and so on. It goes like this, Me, Honor, Joy, Hope, Favor, and then Cherish—she's just turned thirteen. Then there's Florence, my older half-*schweschder* from *Dat's* first marriage, and I have two older half-*bruders,* Earl and Mark. You'll meet Mark, but Earl has moved away."

"I thought it was bad enough remembering the ages of my two brothers."

She smiled, but wondered if he was looking for a wife. Surely he was. He'd mentioned Jonathon was looking for a wife as though he himself wasn't.

When they arrived back at the Bakers' house, they saw Jonathon walking out of the door with Cherish giggling by his side.

"Looks like he had a good time."

"It does." She stepped out of the buggy and then Stephen got out and ran around the back of the buggy to meet her. "Thank you for a lovely time tonight, Mercy. Can I see you again real soon?"

His sincere question gladdened her heart. He did want to see her again. "Sure, any time."

"What about tomorrow?"

"Tomorrow? Isn't that too soon?" She tried to think what work Florence had lined up for her the next day and whether she was supposed to be at the roadside stall. "No, I'm sure that'll be all right. What about tomorrow afternoon? Wait, I forgot all about the harvest."

He laughed. "Me too. We'll be seeing each other early tomorrow, and every day." He took off his hat and ran a hand through his hair. "That's what I'm here for—the harvest."

She didn't want him to go. All she wanted was to put her head on his shoulder and for him to encircle her within his strong arms. Maybe he might give her a quick kiss or try to hold her hand.

"I'll see you tomorrow, Mercy."

"Okay."

He turned and got into his buggy and left even before Jonathon had gotten into his.

CHAPTER 17

WHEN SHE WALKED INSIDE, the girls were all lined up waiting to hear about her romantic date. How she wished she could tell them that he'd proposed. It would've been a dream come true. Instead, she had to tell them that nothing of the sort had happened.

The younger girls went to bed while *Mamm* went into the kitchen. Needing some parental advice, Mercy joined her mother.

"What am I going to do, *Mamm?* When will he propose? I thought he'd do it on Friday and then I hoped he'd do it tonight."

"*Nee,* Mercy. He wouldn't be a responsible man to ask you that quickly. He has to get to know you first."

"What *Mamm* means is, he'd be a fool to marry you." Cherish giggled.

"I thought you'd gone to bed."

"I'm getting a drink of water. Why don't you marry Jonathon? *Nee,* he's probably too choosy."

"Stop it. Don't let her say things like that to me, *Mamm."*

Mamm just stared at her and then Florence walked into the kitchen. "Just relax about it all Mercy. It will happen if it's meant to happen."

Mercy gasped "I can't help it. I'm not doing it deliberately. That's just how I feel."

Her mother held her head. "You lot will be the death of me. Now I have a dreadful headache and I'll have to go to bed. I can't take any of you any longer. It's just too much." *Mamm* walked out of the room.

"I always get the blame." Mercy pushed out her chair and ran away crying and reached the stairs before her mother. Florence watched as Mercy took the stairs two at a time.

Cherish got herself a glass of water, took a mouthful and tipped the rest down the sink. Florence guessed she had just wanted to hear what her sister was going to talk about with their mother.

"Gut nacht, Cherish. Unless you want to help me clean up?"

Cherish pretended to yawn as she stretched her hands above her head. "Nah, I'm too tired." She walked out of the room.

It was then that Florence knew she'd be stuck with the washing up and the cleaning of the kitchen. At least it had only been the two of them for the Sunday dinner of leftovers. After a few minutes, Mercy was back and sat down at the kitchen table.

Florence wiped her hands on a hand towel and sat down beside her. The only reason she'd be back was to talk. "Don't be upset."

She looked up at her through misty eyes. "How can I not be? I need guidance from my *mudder* and she … says nothing."

"I know. Don't mind *Mamm*."

"Does he think I'm not good enough?"

"If he does, he has no taste at all."

"We get along so well. He's said so many lovely things to me and we talked about how we wanted our houses to be and everything."

"Are you in love with him?"

"I'm sure I am, but the only thing is he jokes all the time. I don't find it funny and I don't understand any of it. I'm not a joking person."

Florence didn't know what to say about that. Stephen did like telling his jokes. "Maybe he jokes because he's nervous and thinks he has to fill in the silent moments with telling funny stories."

"*Jah,* that could be it. That must be it. *Denke,* Florence."

"Mind you, I'm not saying you should jump into marrying anyone without serious consideration and knowing him fully.

The way I think about that is you must observe them over a period of time."

"You'll make a good *mudder* someday, Florence."

Florence smiled. "Maybe … someday."

CHAPTER 18

IT WAS the first day of their official apple harvest and they were up before daybreak. Even Cherish was awake. Florence's plan was to get everyone organized early, and then leave for her store at eight.

As they were finishing an early breakfast, three buggy loads of people pulled up outside the house. "Come on girls, let's go. You don't want to be late."

They greeted the usual families that came to help out on the first day of harvest. Today they'd have to abandon their roadside stall because it was 'all hands in the orchard.'

Wasting no time, everyone grabbed buckets and ladders and headed out to the orchard. Since there were no newcomers apart from Jonathon and Stephen, she let the others go on ahead while she gave the young men their instructions.

After she made sure all was going according to plan, she headed to her store. She opened the door and was pleased to see everything looked nice and everything was in its place. Forty-two pies were lined up ready, and taffy-apples in ranks by the dozen. It was the pies, she guessed, that would sell out first.

Just when she was congratulating herself that everything was running smoothly, she saw the signs propped against the wall. She was supposed to have gotten two of her sisters to put those signs out to direct people to the shop. That was how the locals knew the shop was now open and that was how the tourists found them.

Looking at the clock on the wall, she saw it was still early. Early enough for her to walk to put the signs out and make it back in enough time to open the shop. She took hold of the stakes attached to the two signs, grabbed the hammer and headed off. It was half a mile one way and half a mile the other.

Just when she was calculating whether she should go back and hitch the wagon, she heard a car. It was the white 4x4.

Carter slowed and opened his window. "Hello."

She seized the opportunity. "Could you do me a favor—if you're not in a hurry?"

"Sure, what is it?

"I have to put one of these signs up this way," she said as she gestured, "and one back that way. Would you mind driving me and my signs to do that?"

"Sure, jump in." He got out of the vehicle and put the signs and hammer in the back.

Once he was back inside, she clipped on her seat belt. "Thanks for doing this."

As he drove off he said, "You look a little flustered."

"It's just that my sisters usually do this and with everything being such a rush this morning, it being a Monday, and being our first day of harvest ... I completely forgot."

"You said your sisters usually did it."

"They do, but I forgot to remind them."

"I see. It's your first day of harvest? That's right, you told me it was Monday."

She directed him where to stop. He got out and insisted on hammering in the sign, and then he did the same in the other direction. When he got back into the car with her, she felt a little awful for having been so mean to him "I really appreciate you doing this."

"Sure, it's no problem."

"Where are you heading to today?"

"I'm just heading to town to get a few supplies."

She couldn't help smiling because he sounded like he was camping. And that's what he might've thought since he was a city-folk man and now he was living out in the country.

When he stopped the car at her shop, she said, "You've saved me so much time."

"Good, I'm glad."

"Stay here a minute." She went back inside and got two apple pies and took them out to the car. "Take these as a part of your supplies."

"No, I couldn't."

"Please take them."

"Can't I do a simple favor for you?"

"I'm grateful."

"At least let me pay you for them."

"I really appreciate your help."

"Thank you, Florence. Would you have time after you finish here to stop by and taste one of these with me?"

She was taken aback by the question and didn't want to be alone with him again. "We usually have a bit of a thing on the first night of harvest with the people who've helped. We make a big bonfire and cook over it. You're welcome to join us."

"Maybe I will."

She nodded. "Thanks again."

He smiled at her and then backed his car onto the road, and drove away.

. . .

Soon she had the first customers. A few hours later, she noticed her brother, Mark, and his wife, Christina, traveling up the driveway in their buggy.

They had helped with the harvest last year but with them having just opened their saddlery store she'd thought they weren't coming. Apart from that, Christina didn't get along very well with anybody.

Going from the timetable Florence had written out, Honor came to take over at one in the afternoon to give her a break.

Florence was starving and was very much in need of a break. She walked into the kitchen and found *Mamm* making more apple pies. "I'm so pleased you're making more because we'll definitely need them for tomorrow."

"I thought you might."

And then she saw Cherish sitting down at the table staring into space. "Cherish, why aren't you out helping the others?"

"I didn't feel too good."

"Well I don't feel good most days, but it doesn't stop me doing anything."

"You're stronger than she is," *Mamm* said.

"I don't think that's true anymore. I just push myself and work through things when I'm not feeling well—like today and yesterday. I woke up with a headache and I started work and now I feel a little better."

Cherish scowled at her. "I do feel sick, Florence. And, I made everyone sandwiches just now and there was a mountain of them."

"Now you've upset her," *Mamm* frowned at Florence.

"That's good she made sandwiches. And if she's well enough to sit up, she could be peeling apples, or doing something to help."

"Why aren't you in the shop?" Cherish asked peevishly.

"I've been there all morning. I'm just having something to eat." Florence buried her annoyance and opened the gas-powered fridge and pulled out some leftover meatloaf from days ago. It smelled okay, so she made herself a sandwich. When she sat down in front of Cherish, she took a bite.

"You didn't make me one."

"I thought you would've eaten by now. Didn't you eat with the others?"

"*Nee*, I was too busy making them sandwiches. I haven't been doing nothing."

"Well, you could've made me one, too. Anyway, I've got to rush back to the store. Do you want to come with me and help?"

"You're mean. I'm going to bed so you'll believe I'm sick." Cherish stomped out of the room.

Mamm didn't say anything. She was too busy putting the top crusts on the apple pies. Then *Mamm* smiled, seemingly unaware of Cherish's recent outburst. "Did you see Mark and Christina are here?"

With a mouthful, Florence could only nod. When she swallowed, she said, *"Jah,* I saw them and I hope they stay for the bonfire tonight."

"They said they would."

"Good. We're going to have a *gut* season this year."

"It would be nice if your *vadder* could see what a good job you're doing with the orchard, Florence."

Florence smiled. It was rare *Mamm* said something nice like that. "I couldn't do it without everybody's help. We all help each other and that's how we get things done, but that'll change in a few years as everyone gets married. Unless … unless they marry local men and then their husbands can help in the orchard too at harvest time. *Jah,* that would be so *gut."* Florence finished the last mouthful of her sandwich.

"There's no one for us to marry here."

Cherish was back.

Florence looked at her scowling face. "Well, you might change your mind about the boys you know when they turn into men. Time changes people a lot especially during those years."

"Yeah, well what are you going to do, *Mamm,* when we all leave? It'll be just you and Florence."

"Denke. I'll be here forever, will I?" Florence asked, feeling more on-the-shelf than ever.

"*Jah.*"

Mamm stopped decorating the edges of the pies and stared at Cherish. Instead of reprimanding Cherish for being rude, she simply whimpered, "I don't want any of you girls to move away."

Florence couldn't work it out. "*Mamm,* you do know where Stephen lives, *jah?* He lives in Connecticut. You won't see Mercy every day if they get married."

"Didn't you think about that?" Cherish asked her mother.

"Don't worry. They might not get married," Florence said trying to make Wilma feel better. "She might marry someone from around here."

Mamm placed her hands on her hips. "I don't know why you're against her marrying Stephen. Don't you want her to be happy?"

Florence dusted off her hands. "She's happy now." It seemed like whatever she said was the wrong thing so it was best to keep her mouth well shut and not say any more. She got up from the table, rinsed off her plate and left it in the sink. "I'm going back to the store."

"Aren't you going to wash your plate properly, dry it and put it away?" Cherish asked.

"You do it," Florence said. "Your tongue is well enough to talk, so put that energy into your hands."

Florence walked past her youngest half-sister and then slipped out of the house. All the while she could hear Cherish complaining about her. Florence didn't mind, she was pleased her stepmother had acknowledged all the hard work she did around the place.

THAT NIGHT, while the Baker family and their workers toasted apple fritters over the bonfire, Florence kept looking around for Carter. She hadn't told Wilma or anybody else that he might be coming and she wondered how they would feel about an *Englischer* joining in with their celebrations. She would simply do some fast talking and tell them he was their new neighbor. It was only right that they should meet him anyway since he was their closest neighbor. The first few hours Florence spent hoping Carter wouldn't show and as the time slipped by, she found herself sitting on the edges of the group hoping he'd come.

Christina, her sister-in-law walked over to her and sat next to her. "You've been quiet all night, Florence. Why's that?"

"We've been very busy these last days and I'm a little tired. That might be why. *Denke* for coming. I know you're busy at your store these days."

"It's not my choice. We had to pay workers to cover for us so we could come here. I said to Mark that it didn't make sense for us to work for free here and then we have to pay our workers."

Florence didn't know what to say. *"Denke,* it was kind of you."

"It was kind of Mark. He's always looking after others."

"Why don't you and Mark come for dinner next week sometime? *Mamm* and the girls would love that. We don't see much of you these days."

"Why don't you all come to my place?" she asked.

"Denke, but it's so hard to get all the girls out of the *haus.* It'll be much easier if you and Mark can come here."

"It's easier for me if I stay where I am, too."

Florence smiled at her and wished she could forever ignore her completely, but she couldn't. "The invitation is always there."

"And the same to you."

"You're welcome." Florence wasn't sure why she said you're welcome. From Christina's reaction, neither did she. She gave Florence a smile that was more of a grimace, stood, and then headed back to her husband.

Hopefully Earl will marry a girl I get along with.

Then she looked back in the direction of Carter's house. There was still no sign of him and people were standing up looking like they were about to leave. She still hadn't gotten around to each and every one of them to thank them, so she hurried to do just that.

CHAPTER 19

SEVERAL DAYS LATER, the harvest was nearly over. All the apples had been picked and sorted. Mercy had asked Florence if she and Stephen could make some apple cider alone, without any of her sisters interrupting. Florence had said that she'd do her best to keep them away.

The cider apples were in the shed and ready to be processed when Stephen and Mercy walked in.

"It smells nice in here, like perfume. It smells a little like cider already."

"These are mostly scraps and windfall apples, not the eating apples."

He nodded. "I know that. I helped sort them."

"Firstly, we have to wash them because most of them are covered with dirt."

He looked closer, *"Jah,* I can see that."

"After we wash them we grind them. Also, we make sure to pull out any rotten ones that we missed before."

"Don't get ahead of me. We wash 'em first, yeah? Then get out the rotten ones and then grind 'em."

"That's right. I'll show you."

They spread the apples into an old bathtub that they used for washing them, and blasted the apples with water. They threw the no-good ones into a bucket, and then put the others into the grinder and turned the handle. Out flowed the cider into the bucket below.

He laughed as he saw it come out. "Can we drink it now?"

"Sure." She lifted the heavy bucket and poured cider into a glass and gave it to him.

He blew off the froth and drank it. When he finished he had a froth mustache.

She held her stomach and laughed at him.

"This is so good. Hey, why are you laughing?"

"You have froth on your face." He scooped froth out of the bucket and tried to put it on her face. She squealed and ran away. "I'll stop chasing when you've got it on your face as well." He caught up with her and dabbed some on each cheek.

"Unfair," she said as she squealed with laughter.

Then he wiped it off for her with his fingertips, before he held her hand and led her back to the shed. "You drink some now."

"Okay."

He poured her some and she made sure she got rid of all the froth before she drank it.

When she stopped drinking, she looked at him. "There. How's that. Have I got any on me?"

He shook his head. "Not a bit. You've done this before."

"Once or twice. Come on. We have to make more and then we have to bottle it. Maybe tomorrow I'll show you how to make apple cider vinegar."

"Okay. As long as I can be with you, I don't care what we do."

"It's my job to make it. Everyone has their jobs to do around here. Florence has the place well-organized. She runs the orchard and the *haus*."

"What about your mother?"

She shook her head. "Not so much. Florence does most things around here."

As they made more cider, she explained how to make apple cider vinegar, and then added, "Nothing goes to waste. We use the cores and the peels."

"I like the idea of nothing going to waste. How many apple trees do you have here exactly?"

"Hundreds. I can't tell you exactly."

"Can you guess what my favorite food is?"

She giggled. "What is it? Wait, let me guess. I think you would like roast chicken, and cooked ham while it's hot?"

He shook his head.

"Roast potatoes?"

He frowned and shook his head again.

"I give up."

"Apple fritters."

"I didn't know that. You would've enjoyed them the other night then."

"I did. I mentioned they were my favorite and I thought you would've remembered."

She smiled at him. "I thought you were just being polite."

"What's the food you like best?"

"The ones I just named. I hoped we'd like exactly the same."

"I do like all those things too. I like most food."

"You're easy to please."

"I know. I am very easy to please." He looked down at the apple cider that was flowing once again. "It's nice to learn new things."

"Now we have to bottle all this."

Once they were finished with the bottling process, they headed to the house carrying some of the bottles.

"I hope you're enjoying your stay," Mercy said.

"I am and I knew I would."

She loved him saying nice things to her. "When did you know you would enjoy your stay here?"

"The day I saw you on the stairs. I knew you were the woman for me."

"Really?"

He nodded. "There's no doubt in my mind." He stood still and she stopped as well.

Their romantic moment was interrupted by her sister's dog running toward them at great speed. Now Mercy was annoyed. She wasn't annoyed at the dog; it wasn't his fault. Cherish wasn't far behind Caramel.

"You can't have him running at people like this, Cherish. You're going to have to train him."

"I will."

"Nah, he's fine," Stephen said as he put the bottles on the ground and bent down to pet the dog.

Cherish picked Caramel up. "I'm sorry. I had him tied up while I was watering the vegetables, but somehow, he got off."

"That's fine. I love dogs. This guy makes me miss Buster."

"You've got a dog?" Cherish asked.

"Yeah." He stood up. "He's my best friend. We've been through a lot together." He chuckled.

Cherish was smiling at Stephen a little too much so Mercy had to do something about that. "Take him back to the house. Can't you see we've got bottles?"

"I'm sorry, Mercy."

Cherish turned around and hurried away with her dog.

"She's a sweet girl."

"Sweet? You don't know her."

"Oh, really?"

"She's a bit of a troublemaker."

"I wouldn't have thought that, but I believe everything that comes out of your mouth. Mercy, I don't want to leave tonight to go back to my aunt's. I don't want to wait until tomorrow."

"It's not long."

They stood together talking not far from the house. "It's too long. Meet me tonight?"

"I can't go out at night. Florence would never allow it."

"I'm talking about me coming here without anyone knowing."

She gasped.

"Which window's yours?" He looked up at the house. "You said it was above the door but there are two virtually on either side of the door.

Pleased he remembered everything she said, she answered, "The one to the right. The other one is Florence's."

"Come with me." He walked over to the barn. "It'll be a full moon tonight so it'll be light. If I stand here, you'll be able to see me from your bedroom window. Then sneak out."

Should she do that? She'd get into dreadful trouble from Florence if she found out. She might even be grounded and not allowed to see Stephen ever again. When she stared into his green eyes, she found extra confidence. "What time?"

"I dunno. Late. Between midnight and two."

"What excuse will you give Samuel for taking the buggy? He'll want to know where you're going so late. It'll be a little weird."

"I'll walk."

"You can't do that. It's way too far.'

"It's not. I'll run to see you. I walk long distances at home and when I get bored walking, I run."

"Okay, but we'll get in the biggest trouble if anyone finds out."

"We'll just be talking. We never get enough time together and I'm due to go home soon. Please, Mercy. I love being with you."

She nodded. "Once everyone goes to sleep, I'll be looking out my window. You will come, won't you? I don't want to wait up all night for nothing."

"I'll be here. I give you my word."

CHAPTER 20

WHILE FLORENCE WAS WALKING in the late afternoon, she wasn't thinking about her neighbor until she happened to be on that side of the orchard. She saw him walk out of his house. He looked up at her and waved, and when she waved back he started walking over to her. She headed to meet him and they both stopped when they reached the fence line.

"What are you doing?" he asked.

"Just walking. I try to do it every day."

"Don't you get enough exercise picking the apples to last you for a while?"

"I like to keep an eye on the trees and it's peaceful and I feel close to God."

He smiled and shook his head. "I know nothing about your God."

"He's everyone's God."

Raising his dark eyebrows, he said, "He's not if you don't believe."

She didn't want to get into a pointless argument, but she was convinced *Gott* believed in Carter.

"Got nothing to say?" he asked.

"Not today. I'd rather not." She looked up at the sky, then she noticed the cows. "Still got the cows I see."

"I do. I haven't eaten them yet. I'm thinking of becoming a vegetarian."

"Because of your pet cows?"

He gave a nod. "Maybe I'll just stop eating red meat."

That made her giggle.

"Anyway, I'm sorry I didn't make it over the other night when you invited me. I was nearly going, but I thought I'd be out of place."

She admired his honesty and it gave her a small insight into his character. "My family could've met you."

"I'll meet them soon enough. I still haven't been to get more of your food. Your pies were delicious."

"I'm pleased you liked them."

"I've got the new kitchen in already. I paid them overtime to get it in faster. Come and have a look."

"Not today." She stared at him and there was just something about him that appealed to her. It was as though he had some magnetic device attached to him and she was being pulled toward him. Yet, they were from two different worlds. Neither of them would fit into the other's. "I should keep going."

When she turned away, she knew she had to stay away for good. It would be easy to spend time with him and get to know him better, but sometimes the easy things were the worst things to do.

CHAPTER 21

MERCY WAS SHOCKED when she looked out the window after everyone had gone to bed. Stephen was there already! She wasn't certain if Florence was asleep yet and, as usual, she'd been the last one of them to go to her bedroom.

She waved at him, unsure if he could see her, but he could because he waved back. Then she grabbed her shawl, tucked it under her arm, and slowly opened her door. Her heart beat hard as she slowly walked past Florence's door to get to the stairs. The floor creaked a couple of times.

"Is that you, Mercy?"

"*Jah.* I'm just getting a glass of water. Do you want one too?"

"*Nee,* I'm fine. *Gut nacht.*"

"*Gut nacht.*"

She kept walking and hoped Florence wouldn't wait to hear her go back to her bedroom. Instead of going out the front door, she went out the back and then she hurried to meet him glad that the night was so bright. He saw her and came to meet her. Then he grabbed her hand and without saying a word pulled her into the barn.

Once they were in the barn, he closed the door and they both laughed.

"I can't believe you agreed to this," he said to Mercy.

"Me? I can't believe you asked … and did you run?"

"I walked some and then I ran. Can we sit down somewhere in here?"

"*Jah*, we've got hay bales over here." In the darkness, they found their way to the hay and sat down. Then they ended up sitting on the dirt floor and leaning against the hay.

"I'm so happy you agreed to meet me."

"Me too. I want to spend more time with you too."

He put his arm around her and she sank her head against his shoulder. She closed her eyes and it felt right to be there with him even though she'd had to sneak out of the house.

"I'm pretty sure I'm falling in love with you, Mercy."

"I feel the same."

"I never want to leave your side."

150

She held her breath and thought she'd pass out. Was he going to propose? This was what she wanted and what she'd waited for. "I'd like that."

"I want to hold hands and walk in the moonlight, but someone might see us."

"Florence is still awake."

"Really?"

"*Jah.*"

He breathed out heavily. "That's not good. You should go back. I don't want you to get into any trouble."

"But we've hardly had any time together."

"There'll be other nights. I'll come again tomorrow night and every single night after."

"Will you?"

"*Jah.*"

"But it's so far for you to walk."

"It's worth it to spend more time with you. I'd walk that distance to spend one extra minute with you."

She giggled. "You would?"

"I surely would." He stood up and then pulled her to her feet. Once they were out of the barn, he took her into his arms and they hugged. She felt safe and protected wrapped in his strong arms. And then he stepped back. "You better go."

"Okay. I'll see you tomorrow, *jah?*"

"Of course. Your *mamm* and Florence are finding loads of work for Jonathon and me."

"Night, Stephen."

"I'll see you tomorrow. I'll be counting the minutes."

She hurried back to the house. Once she was in the kitchen, she filled up a glass with water and walked up the stairs. When she got to the top, Florence was standing there. "There you are. I didn't hear you come back to bed and I was just about to look for you."

"I had a snack too while I was there."

"You've not changed out of your clothes yet."

Mercy looked down at her dress and apron. *"Nee,* I was just about to now. I fell asleep in my clothes."

Florence seemed to believe her because she smiled and then put her arm around her and gave her a squeeze before she went back into her bedroom.

Mercy walked to her bedroom and looked out the window. Stephen was nowhere to be seen. She placed her water on the nightstand and changed into her nightdress before slipping between the covers. It was awful, lying to Florence just now, but if she hadn't both Stephen and she would've been in big trouble.

CHAPTER 22

THREE MORE DAYS had passed and each night Stephen had met her in the barn. It was their secret time together. They talked of what they wanted for their futures, but still, he hadn't proposed and Mercy was deeply troubled. He'd said all the right things to let her know he was in love, but he wasn't saying the one thing she wanted to hear.

On Thursday when they were boxing the apples to take to the roadside stall, Stephen suddenly disappeared. She assumed he had just gone to the bathroom, but when she saw Jonathon heading toward her instead of Stephen she wondered what was going on.

"Where's Stephen?"

"Wilma asked him to go to the markets for her."

"Oh, I would've gone with him. I can't imagine what she would've needed." They rarely went to the markets because they were fairly self-sufficient and what they lacked, they traded for with nearby farms.

"Will you come out somewhere with me on Saturday? We could do anything you want."

"*Nee.* I've already told Stephen I'd go out with him."

He dismissed the idea with a wave of his hand. "Yeah, but I'm sure you'd rather go out with me, wouldn't you?"

She didn't want to hurt his feelings but neither did she want to agree with him. It seemed he liked her, but the feelings weren't returned. "Sorry, Jonathon, but I like your *bruder.*"

"You're kidding, right?"

"*Jah,* I mean, no, I'm not kidding—we've grown very close. Extremely close."

He shook his head and scratched the back of his neck. "I can't figure out how he gets all the girls. He's got you and …"

Her heart froze. "And what? I mean, who?"

"Nothing."

"You must tell me. Does he have another girlfriend?"

"No, but he does have someone very interested in him. I thought they were close, but then he came here. They have the same sense of humor."

"Oh. I didn't know."

"Of course you wouldn't know. He's not going to tell you about the competition."

That was something she hadn't wanted to hear.

"Never fear. I can help you. I can help you if you want him."

She stared at him and everything clicked into place. That was why Stephen hadn't proposed and most likely that was why he was keen to spend so much time with her. He was deciding between her and another girl. "How can you help me?"

"For starters, he needs to know you've got a sense of humor. I notice you never laugh at his jokes. The other girl back home appreciates his jokes. He'd find you more suited if you joked a little with him."

She sighed. "I don't know any jokes. I only know the one's he's said."

"What I've got in mind is really funny. I'm not talking about telling a joke, I'm thinking that you should *play* a joke on him."

"Play a joke?"

He nodded.

"Okay. What do I do?"

He stepped closer and whispered, "It would be funny to tell him Buster died."

She stepped back. "His dog?"

Jonathon nodded.

"What are you two talking about?" In typical Cherish-fashion, she had appeared out of nowhere.

Jonathon smiled at her. "I'm just helping out two people in love. You go back into the barn and I'll come help you in a minute."

"I want to hear."

Jonathon shook his head. "Go now." He pointed at the barn, and Mercy was shocked when Cherish did what she was asked.

"Did you say to tell him his dog died?"

"That's right."

"That's cruel and horrible. Who would do such a thing? He's told me about Buster and he loves him."

"Ah, it would be horrible if it were true, but it won't be true. It'll be a joke. After you tell him about Buster's demise, tell him you were joking."

"Really?" She rubbed her forehead trying to figure out this joking stuff. None of it made sense. "I don't know."

"It's not a regular joke. It's called a practical joke and he'll be relieved that Buster's not really dead."

"I know he'd be relieved but I don't see how it's funny at all."

He frowned at her. "Has he asked you to marry him yet?"

That question got to her. He should've by now and he hadn't mentioned the word 'marriage' in all the time they'd spent together. "Well … no."

"This might make the difference for you. He jokes around all the time and he'll feel happy he's found a woman who's the same."

"Do you think so?"

"I know so."

"Okay. Are you sure this is going to work?"

"Trust me. He'll think it's funny."

"I don't know if I can do it. He'll be upset if I tell him."

She couldn't see it, but neither did she see any joke as funny and she so badly wanted Stephen to think she was the one for him. If he left and married that other girl, she didn't know how she'd cope. "Okay. I'll do it. Tell me exactly what to say."

After he went over exactly how to word the joke, they parted and Mercy went back to doing what she had been doing and waited for Stephen to return.

Then she saw him coming back in the wagon with Florence. She waited until Florence was gone, and then she headed over to him.

"Stephen. Hello."

He walked over to her smiling, until he saw her face. She was sick in the tummy for what she was about to say. "Is all okay?"

She swallowed hard and told herself she had to do it. She had to be brave if she wanted to be Stephen's wife. "Everything is okay, but …" She hesitated. If it was going to be funny about Buster, perhaps it would be funny and an even better joke if she substituted for Buster. "Our phone in the barn rang just now. It was news for you from home."

He frowned. "Who would know to call here?"

"Someone called about your parents."

His eyes opened wide. "Are they okay?"

"I'm sorry to tell you this … they're both dead."

CHAPTER 23

ALL COLOR DRAINED from Stephen's face on hearing the shocking news about the death of his parents. Grief and anguish caused him to throw himself on the ground. He wailed, writhing around on the pebbled driveway. "No. It can't be." He looked up at her. "How? How did it happen?" Before she could answer, he pounded the ground with his fist.

He was taking it really bad and she knew she had to put an end to his heartbreak. "It's not true, Stephen. What I said just now was a joke. It's just a joke."

He stopped crying, sat up and wiped his eyes. "Are my parents dead?"

"*Nee.*"

"They're alive?"

"*Jah,* as far as I know."

He put one hand over his mouth. "Why did you just say they died?"

She smiled and hoped he'd join her in a laugh. "It was just a joke."

He put his hand to his chest and took a couple of deep breaths. "Who told you they died?"

"No one. I just made it up. It's a joke." When she saw him glaring at her, she knew it wasn't funny. Then it clicked in her mind that Jonathon had lied to her. *"Ach nee!* It was supposed to be funny. I thought you'd laugh." She crouched down on the ground with him and put her hand out to touch his hand, but he pulled it away.

"You'd thought it'd be funny to hear my folks were dead?"

"Nee, after that. When you found out it was all a joke."

"You refuse to help me collect the new generator just now and Florence had to come with me, and now this." He slowly picked himself off the ground, and dusted off his trousers. "You must hate me."

"Wait a minute."

He turned away from her and walked to his buggy.

"I didn't know you were going to get a generator. I heard you were going to the markets."

"It doesn't matter where, does it? Nothing matters now." He picked up his pace and she ran after him.

"Wait. Where are you going?"

"Home to Connecticut to see my parents. If they're still there."

In shock, she froze. She was losing him. While he got his horse out of the yard and hitched it to his buggy, she begged him to listen to her. "Stephen, I'm so sorry. I thought it would be a funny joke. Don't go."

He said nothing the whole time and when he had finished buckling the last strap, he jumped into the buggy. "Goodbye, Mercy," he said without even looking at her. The buggy started moving and she ran alongside it.

"I'm sorry, Stephen." He didn't answer and he didn't even look at her. "Can't we start this day over? I take it all back. I'm sorry." His gaze was fixed straight ahead. Then the horse broke into a trot and she could no longer keep up. "Will you be back tomorrow?" she called after him. There was no answer and then he was gone.

She turned to walk back up the driveway and saw Jonathon coming toward her. "He's gone, Jonathon. It didn't work."

Jonathon shook his head. "I saw it. I didn't think he'd take it like that."

"I didn't tell him Buster died."

He tilted his head to one side. "What joke did you tell him?"

"I told him his parents died."

His eyes opened wide and his mouth dropped open. It took a couple of moments before he spoke. "You what?"

"Told him your folks had died. I thought it would be funnier for some reason. If Buster dying was funny, I kind of thought it would be even more funny about his parents—hilarious even."

"Don't worry. It shows what kind of person he is to drive off like that. He's an unreliable character. There's still work to do here and he couldn't care less."

"None of it was funny, was it, Jonathon? You lied to me."

"Hey, don't blame me. I didn't tell you to say what you said. What did you think he'd do? Now it's home time and I'll have to walk back to *Onkel* Samuel's." He shook his head and walked down the driveway. Then he turned and came running back. "Hey, forget him. He left you. I'll be back tomorrow." He gave her a big smile and then walked down the driveway.

Mercy stood there in shock trying to take everything in.

What had just happened?

"Wait, Jonathon." Cherish ran to catch up with him.

Tears stung in the back of Mercy's eyes and she ran all the way to the house.

She flung the back door open and Florence stood there in front of her. "What's upset you?"

"Oh Florence. It was terrible and too embarrassing to tell anybody what I did. I can't even believe it. I'm in a bad dream. A horribly bad dream and one I can't wake up from."

Florence gasped and took hold of her by the arm. "Sit down, Mercy."

She took a deep breath and sat down at the kitchen table, while Florence pushed some freshly ironed clothing to one side.

"It can't be that bad." Florence wore a sympathetic smile as she sat beside her.

"I told Stephen his parents died."

Florence's jaw dropped. "How?"

"Nee they didn't!"

"I don't understand. They're not dead?"

Mercy shook her head.

"Why would you tell him they died when they didn't?"

Mercy told Florence the whole story of what Jonathon had suggested she do. "I don't know why I thought it would be funnier to tell him … what I told him. I can't even say the words now."

"Where's Jonathon now?"

"Walking home. Well, walking back to Ada and Samuel's place."

"Apologize to Stephen and tell him truthfully what happened."

"I can't. I mean, I think I did. He'll never talk to me again."

"He'll calm down."

"When he does, he'll be all the way back in Connecticut. He'll never look at me the same again."

"It's all life experience. You can learn a lesson."

Mercy sobbed on Florence's shoulder and Florence put her arms around her and let her cry. Mercy didn't want to learn a lesson if it meant losing the man she loved.

Florence said, "Don't listen to others when your heart and your head are telling you something else."

"It wouldn't have been funny about the dog either. Right? Why would Jonathon do that, Florence? He must've known Stephen wouldn't think it was funny."

"I don't know. The only reason could be if he likes you and he was trying to split you and Stephen apart."

"I thought that too, but that's horrible if he did that. It's an awful thing to do."

"You should tell Stephen the truth. You were trying to impress him and Jonathon told you to tell him his dog had died and then—"

"I can't. I can't tell him something like that about Jonathon. Then he'll be mad at Jonathon too."

"You can't go too badly wrong with the truth." Florence handed her a handkerchief that sat atop the ironed clothes.

"*Denke.*" Mercy blew her nose. "*Mamm* said you don't tell the truth when it is going to hurt someone's feelings."

"*Jah,* but if you think you could marry this man it might be a slightly different thing. He's not just anybody."

"Oh, Florence, why is everything so hard? Will love always be so elusive for me?"

Florence couldn't help laughing. "You're young and you've got some years ahead of you before you start complaining about love."

"Some people don't care about being married, but I wanted to be a young *mudder*. I want to have ten *kinner* by the time I'm thirty."

"Don't give up on Stephen just yet."

Mercy wiped her eyes. "Do you still think there's a chance?"

"There's always hope. Pray, and then leave it in *Gott's* hands and let Him sort it out, okay?"

"I guess I have to. There's really no other choice."

"No other good choice, anyway."

"What will I say if *Mamm* asks why he left so early? I don't know what to say. She'll ask questions when he doesn't arrive tomorrow."

"Say you had a little disagreement."

"Will you tell her for me?"

"Of course." Florence gave her another hug. "Will you be okay now? I've got some things to take care of."

"I'll be fine."

. . .

FLORENCE WALKED out of the house and hitched the buggy. The only thing she had on her mind was talking with Jonathon and telling him exactly what she thought of him.

Then she'd tell him that the right thing to do would be to tell his brother exactly what he'd done. If Jonathon confessed then Mercy wouldn't have to be the one to tell Stephen what happened.

Florence found him about a mile from the house and the worst thing of all was that Cherish was walking with him. She pulled the buggy over to the side of the road a little way in front of them. She got down and walked back to them. "Cherish, turn around and go home."

"Why? I'm just having a walk. You go for a walk every day, so why can't I?"

"Do as she says, Cherish," Jonathon said softly.

"When will I see you again?"

He rubbed the side of his face and looked over at Florence. "It's hard to say. Soon I hope. Go on. You don't want to get into trouble."

"I'm going." Cherish turned and walked back slowly, dragging her feet.

Florence turned her attention to Jonathon. What she felt like doing was slapping him hard, but she managed to control herself. It was no surprise he didn't look too happy. "Can I have a talk with you for a moment, Jonathon?"

He hunched his shoulders. "Look, I know what you're goin' to say. You think it was all my fault."

"And wasn't it?"

"Wait. What are we talking about here?"

"We're talking about how you talked Mercy into telling that dreadful joke. Only it was no joke."

He took off his hat and ruffled his dark hair in an agitated manner. "I didn't say to tell him that our folks had died."

"I know exactly what you said. She told me. It was bad advice from the beginning, and you knew it was going to drive a wedge between her and Stephen."

"I guess so." Jonathon put his hat back on his head.

"You admit it?"

"Yeah. It's not fair. All the girls like him." He looked back at Cherish and at that moment, she'd turned to look at him and she waved. His hand raised a little, and then he turned back to face Florence.

"Do the right thing, Jonathon. You have to tell Stephen what you've done. Tell him what you said to Mercy and leave him to straighten this whole thing out."

"I can't do that."

"You can and you will. Otherwise, I'll tell him myself. Also, everyone will learn of it. What about your folks?"

He took a step closer and stared into her eyes. "You wouldn't."

She stepped even closer until there were only two inches between them. "You might think you know me and the kind of person I am, but you know *nothing*. I'll tell everyone and I'd enjoy the telling."

He took a step back. "It'd make Mercy look stupid."

She took a step forward. "I'm not bothered by that. She did listen to you so …"

He rolled his eyes and took another step back "Okay. I'll tell him."

"Good. And do it right now, just as soon as you get back to Ada's, so he has a chance to straighten things out with Mercy. She likes him a lot. You could be standing in the way of them having a life together."

"He'll hate me forever but if that's what you want."

"I can't control his reaction and you have to take accountability for what you've done. Just be sure to tell him. All of it, too. Exactly what was said and how it happened. It's better for all concerned if you make this confession on your own." Florence walked back to the buggy feeling good that she'd been able to help. Then she hurried back to him. "Get in the buggy. I'm taking you to Ada's right now so you can tell Stephen sooner. I'll let you out near the *haus* so no one sees me."

Reluctantly, he agreed.

.   .   .

Florence had driven slowly to Ada's place lecturing Jonathon all the way there. She was convinced by what he said that he would confess all. When she got back home, she was unhitching the buggy and deliberating whether or not to tell Mercy about her talk with Jonathon, when Cherish ran over to her. She thought Cherish was going to ask her about Jonathon and she, in turn, was going to tell her to keep away from him because she was making a fool of herself.

"Someone needs you!" Cherish said.

"What? Is everything all right?" From the look on Cherish's face, she wondered if someone had started a fire in the kitchen by burning something, or if someone had burned themselves or been otherwise injured.

"It's Liza; she's had the *boppli* and she's asking for you."

"Is she okay?"

"Yeah, she just said she wants to see you. Well, she didn't. Simon called here and I was near the barn and I answered the phone and that's what he told me to tell you."

She buckled up the side pieces of the harness she'd just undone. "I don't know what time I'll be back, but can you make sure there's dinner for everyone and a meal set aside for me?"

"Sure."

"That would be *wunderbaar, denke.*"

On the way there, she wondered what her friend would've wanted to see her about. Liza had her sister and her sister-in-law both there as birth helpers and Ruth, the midwife, lived less than a mile away. She half thought Liza would've wanted her at the birth as well since they were the best of friends, but Liza had never asked.

Liza's house was five miles away so the trip didn't take very long, but it felt halfway to forever because she was so eager to get there.

After she finally arrived, she secured her horse, and Simon, Liza's husband, came out to meet her with a grin that reached from ear to ear. "We have a *boppli*."

"So I heard. I'm so happy for you."

He walked up to her and hugged her. The man had normally acted gruff and standoffish, and it was so out of character for him to act this friendly or excited. In the back of her mind, Florence hoped it would be a lasting change.

"How's Liza?"

"They're both good. C'mon inside—I'll take you up to her. She's been asking for you."

"I can't wait to see her and the *boppli*."

"He's big they tell me. He's just shy of ten pounds."

"That is big."

"Can you wash your hands first? Do you mind?"

"*Jah,* of course. I wouldn't dream of being near the *boppli* with dirty hands."

He took her coat and over-bonnet and she walked into the washroom. When her hands had been scrubbed, they walked up the stairs and she found Liza alone in the bedroom. Simon left her there and went back downstairs. The new mother's eyes were glued to the baby she cradled in her arms.

A weary-looking Liza turned to look at her with a smile. *"Denke* for coming. I've sent my birth-helpers and the midwife into the kitchen to get me something to eat. I've worked up a good appetite. I wanted to talk to you alone."

Florence edged closer, feeling a little nervous about getting her first peek at the baby. "Give me a good look at him." She saw he was sleeping. "He looks a little like Simon. He's not wrinkled at all like other new *bopplis."*

"I know. Ruth said he looks as though he's a few weeks old already. I can't believe that he's here and I made him."

Florence giggled. "Not just *you* made him."

Liza joined in with her laughter. "Simon might have helped a little."

"I can honestly say I don't think I've ever seen Simon so happy. He's like a new person."

"That's what I want to talk to you about. Forget all those things I said about him. He's been so good through the birth and I think … I know it was just me complaining about him for no good reason. Probably because I was feeling a little frustrated and letting myself be dissatisfied with life. Now that's all changed. I've got a purpose now. Simon and I can share our love with this little one."

"I can understand that. Don't worry, I would never ever have said anything to anyone anyway."

"But I don't want you to even think anything bad about him."

"*Nee,* I won't." She swiped a hand through the air. "All bad thoughts are gone, just like that."

"*Denke.* I want you to be one of the first to hold him."

Florence leaned down, lifted the baby and cradled him in her arms, carefully minding his neck. He opened his eyes, and she was sure he looked right at her before going back to sleep. "My, he is a *big* little *bu!* What have you called him?"

"Malachi, after Simon's *vadder.*"

"That's a nice strong name." Florence guessed Simon had won the name battle, or Liza had relented to save the peace. "He's so precious. I hope to have my own one day."

"Of course you will. It'll happen. You just have to be patient."

Florence smiled at her friend. It was such an easy thing to say for someone who already had a family of her own to love and to care for.

She smiled again and then kissed the baby's bald head. He smelled so good. "His skin is so soft. Don't worry I washed my hands. That's the first thing Simon asked me to do."

"He's going to be a *gut vadder.*"

"I'm pleased. I didn't even know you were in labor."

"Things happened pretty fast. My helpers were only here for an hour or so before he arrived. Oh, how was your harvest?"

"Really good. We had so many helpers this year, and loads of great apples, and the shop's been quite busy."

"That's just your side business isn't it? The shop, I mean. You make most of the money selling apples?"

"True, but the earnings from the shop and the roadside stall help a lot."

Liza yawned.

"You must be tired."

"I feel okay, not too bad for birthing such a big baby, and I'll recover."

Staring at Liza she wondered how painful childbirth was. "I'm so happy for you. I feel as though something good has happened for me too."

"Of course. You're his Aunt Florence."

"I like the sound of that. It's my first time to be an aunt."

"How's Mercy doing with that new boy?"

Florence pulled a face. "Long story—I'll save it for another day. Can I do anything for you? Get you anything?"

"*Nee,* they're bringing me up some soup."

She passed the baby back. "I'll go now, but I'll visit you again soon. Is that okay?"

"Always! Please do."

She left Liza's house amazed at how relationships could change. Perhaps if two people who were once so at odds could reunite, then there was hope for Mercy and Stephen.

Simon and Liza's house, once full of arguments, was now filled with peace and love.

On her drive home, she drove past Carter's house and found herself smiling at his 'pet' cows grazing in the fields.

CHAPTER 24

MERCY HAD STAYED AWAKE all night praying. After breakfast, she was washing up the dishes when she saw Stephen's buggy coming to the house. She asked Honor to finish the dishes for her while she hurried out to meet him.

She waited until he pulled up and then walked over to meet him. Judging from his smiling face, she knew he was ready to forgive her. "Stephen, you're back."

He got out of the buggy. "I never left to go back home."

"I'm so sorry."

"It's okay. I'll just let the horse into the yard and then we can talk." When he'd done that, he turned to face her and then said, "I know what happened. Jonathon told me everything."

SAMANTHA PRICE

"It was a horrible thing to do. I wanted you to think I was funny and for some twisted reason I thought it would be funny and you'd like me more."

He chuckled. "You've got a *funny* way of showing your feelings. I know my brother's part in it. He also told me he said I liked some other girl, but I don't. Why didn't you tell me all that yesterday?"

She shook her head. "I didn't want to tell you what he said. He's your *bruder.* I didn't want to cause bad feeling between the two of you."

"I understand, and that makes me like you all the more."

She studied his face. "Can things be back to normal?"

"Yeah. All is forgiven. Let's forget it ever happened."

She put her hand over her heart. "I'm so relieved. I don't think I'll forget it, though, or the lesson I've learned."

He wagged his finger at her. "Just never do it again."

"I won't. I'll never do anything like that again."

"Good. Now, what has your *Mamm* lined up for us to do today?"

"I don't know, but she said you could stay for dinner tonight if you want and then she said you could help me with the goodie bags for the school kids after dinner." As they walked, she explained, "We've got a group of children coming tomorrow to see how the orchard works and what we grow, and what we produce. We give each of them a bag with goodies in it to take home."

"That's a nice idea. I'd love to help."

She smiled at him.

"Does your mother know about what happened yesterday afternoon?" he asked.

"Nee. She has no idea. I guess I would've had to tell her if you didn't come today. I'm glad you came back. Is Jonathon coming today?"

"I'd rather not talk about him for a while."

"That suits me just fine." She stared at him and wondered what their children would look like. With his green eyes and her bluish-green ones, they'd have to have green eyes for sure—at least some of them. Their hair would be light and maybe tinged with gold, and maybe darken as teenagers to match her reddish-brown. It was fun to imagine.

AFTER A BUSY DAY of delivering apples to three different markets, Stephen stayed on and had dinner with the Baker family. He got along well with everyone and Mercy knew all her sisters liked him, even Florence. After the dishes were done, Stephen and Mercy were left alone in the kitchen to prepare the bags for tomorrow's visitors.

"You like children a lot, don't you?" Stephen asked her.

"Of course I do. I like them very much."

"Me too. I could tell. Would you like to have your own soon?"

"I really would." She smiled at the thought as she tied a bow on another one of the bags.

"That would mean you'd have to get married."

She looked up at him, pleased they were talking about marriage. "Of course. I wouldn't have children without being married."

He laughed. "I didn't think that you would."

"I'll get married, and then have children."

After he looked around, he spoke again. "Would you consider …" He gulped. "Would you consider marrying me?"

She looked into his eyes. This was the moment she'd dreamed of. "For real?"

"Yeah, for real."

"You want me to marry you?"

"Yeah, I wouldn't ask if I didn't want it to happen."

"I will marry you, Stephen Wilkes."

He smiled. "I like how you said my full name."

"And I like everything about you. You'll make a *gut vadder* and a *gut* husband."

"You'll make a *gut fraa*." He stood and held out his hands. She stood up and put her hands in his.

She stared up into his eyes and then his head slowly moved closer and he stared at her lips. She closed her eyes ready for her very first kiss. Before their lips met, she heard a squeal.

They jumped apart and she looked over to see Cherish in the doorway of the kitchen. "What is it, Cherish?"

"Mamm wants to see you."

"Right now?"

"Jah, right now."

"Can Stephen come too?"

"I guess."

Cherish disappeared, and then Mercy looked at Stephen, but the moment was gone.

"We better see what she wants," Stephen said.

"It better be important," she said under her breath as she headed out of the kitchen.

Stephen followed her and they found *Mamm* in the living room working on her cross stitch sampler. She was only awake this late because of their visitor. The other girls had gone to bed. Even Florence, who normally stayed up late. She had been working so hard lately she'd told them she was too tired to push through it tonight.

"What is it that can't wait, *Mamm?"*

Mamm looked up at her. "What do you mean?"

"You wanted to see me."

She shook her head. *"Nee."*

"Cherish said you want to see me about something."

"I don't think so."

Why did she constantly allow people to trick her? If Stephen hadn't been there she'd have found Cherish and told her exactly what she thought of her.

"Shall we tell her our news now?" he whispered.

"Okay with me, but do you think we should?"

He nodded and then they both looked at *Mamm* who was staring at them.

"What's going on?"

"Stephen has asked me to marry him."

Mamm squealed, tossed her sampler into the air and ran to hug Mercy. She paused, pushed her out to arm's-length and looked her in the eyes. "You did say, 'Yes,' didn't you?"

Mercy laughed as she answered, "Of course, *Mamm*."

Mamm chuckled and folded Mercy into a warm hug. Then she hugged Stephen. "This is the best news I've had in my life. I'll be a *grossmammi* soon."

Stephen raised his eyebrows. "Not too soon, Mrs. Baker."

"When do you plan on getting married?" *Mamm* asked.

They stared at each other, both waiting for the other to speak. Finally, Mercy said, "We don't know. This has only just happened."

"You'll have to get married here rather than Connecticut because it's a little difficult for all of us to travel all that way."

"I was already thinking of getting married here," Stephen said. "I'm sure my folks won't mind."

"This is so good. Am I the first one to find out?"

"Jah." Mercy giggled.

"You must call your folks and tell them right now, Stephen."

"What? Now?"

"Jah, now. It's still plenty early. Go and call them from the phone in the barn. I won't tell the girls until you tell your parents, Stephen. They should be the very next people you tell. It's only fair."

He rubbed the back of his neck. "I guess so. I hadn't really thought about it."

"I can wait. I'll keep it quiet until you tell them."

"Come with me, Mercy. I'll put you on the phone so you can say hello."

Mercy giggled nervously. "Okay." This wasn't how she'd expected to meet her future in-laws.

CHAPTER 25

MERCY HAD to keep her secret overnight and into the next morning, as Stephen's parents hadn't answered their phone.

Eventually, at midday they answered their phone. They sounded a little hesitant about the news and not nearly as joyful as *Mamm*. It put a bit of a damper on Mercy's excitement, but Stephen assured her it was just that they were surprised. He told her they'd soon be happy for him and eager to meet her.

The next thing Stephen and Mercy did was find her sisters and tell each one.

The last people to tell in Mercy's family were her half-sister and her two older half-brothers. Mercy and Stephen kept an eye on the shop and when the last customer of the day left, they headed to share the news with Florence.

· · ·

WHEN FLORENCE LOOKED up from tallying the day's sales and saw both Stephen and Mercy approaching the doorway wearing grins, she knew they had happy news.

"Guess what? We're getting married," Mercy blurted out as soon as she walked into the shop.

Florence pushed the last of her doubts aside. She had as much chance at stopping the wedding as stopping a runaway buggy. Besides, she didn't want to. She'd gotten to know Stephen a little better when she'd traveled with him to fetch that new generator, and she thought he'd showed wisdom and maturity by forgiving Mercy so wholeheartedly. "I'm so pleased for both of you." She gave them each a hug.

"Are you sure, Florence?"

Florence laughed. "Of course I'm sure. I'm really happy for you."

"*Mamm* wants us to get married here at the *haus* and we want to get married really soon."

"Oh?"

"I'm calling my folks tomorrow and we'll arrange a time. And then we'll have to see if that time's all right with your bishop."

"You haven't told him yet?" Florence asked.

The young couple stared at one another.

"*Nee*. We should go there now, Stephen."

"I guess so. I've never done this before." He rubbed the back of his neck.

All three of them laughed at that, and Florence said, "Best head over there right now and tell him."

When they hurried out of the shop, Florence knew the Bakers were in for a busy time preparing for a wedding. It would take place right here at the house. Although she was pleased everything had worked so well for Mercy, she was a little saddened. She was still alone in spite of being six years older than Mercy. Where was her man?

MERCY GAVE Stephen directions to Bishop Paul's house.

"Will he tell us we haven't known each other long enough?" Stephen wondered.

"*Nee*. I don't think so."

"I hope not. I don't want to have to convince him. I just want to arrange a date when we can get married."

"A Friday. A Friday before Christmas would be what would suit me. Early December."

He screwed up his nose. "That's over a month away."

She giggled, pleased he wanted to marry her quickly. "There's a lot of preparation that goes into a wedding. There's the food and the clothes and people have to know a long way ahead so they can plan to come."

"I guess."

"And it's our special day and I want everything to be perfect."

"It will be."

When they arrived at the bishop's house, he was just getting into his buggy. Bishop Paul stepped down when he saw them. They got out too, and met him halfway.

He smiled at them and his long gray beard moved upward on his face and then he adjusted his thick black glasses. Stephen said, "Are you heading off somewhere, Bishop Paul?"

"It's nothing that can't wait. I have to collect Hannah from her friend's *haus*, but she won't mind staying a little longer. I was early anyway." He then eyed them carefully. "Have you come to see me?"

"*Jah.*"

The bishop smiled again, as though he knew why they'd come. "Come into the *haus* and we can sit. But you'd best secure your horse first."

Once they were sitting on the couch in the bishop's living room, Mercy felt her throat constrict. At that moment, it all became real and she realized the enormity of the decision they were about to make official.

"We want to marry," Stephen began.

"Okay ... and you've both had a good long think and you've talked about whether it's right? You haven't been here long, Stephen."

"I know my own mind and we're both of age."

"That's right." He rubbed his beard. "From the looks on both your faces I'd guess you want to marry without too much delay?"

"First Friday in December," Mercy blurted out, fighting against her light-headedness. Stephen suited her perfectly and there was no doubt in her mind.

The bishop calmly rose from his chair and picked up a large black book that had been on a wooden chair by the fireplace. He also picked up a pen that had been underneath the book. When he sat down again, he said, "This is my wedding appointment book. First Friday in December is the fifth. And it's available."

"Perfect," Mercy said.

Stephen gulped and Mercy could see how nervous he was. "Can we marry on the fifth, then?"

"I don't see anything that would stand in your way. Your parents are all in agreement?"

"*Jah*, both are," Mercy said.

"Let's write you in for that date." The bishop asked for their full names and birth dates, and then told them what else needed to be done. Including, he reminded them, that they'd both need to be baptized into the Amish faith prior to marriage, which is something they'd clean forgotten. They also made a date with him for that.

Minutes later, they drove away from Bishop Paul's, elated. "It was so easy," Stephen said.

"I knew it would be. There was no need to be so nervous."

"I just didn't want anything to go wrong."

She took hold of his hand pulling it away from the reins. "Nothing will. Meet me tonight outside the *haus* at midnight?

"Sure."

"We can talk more about our future."

He squeezed her hand tighter.

THAT NIGHT, Florence had stayed up late sewing. When she found herself nodding off, she folded up her sewing and crept up the stairs. As she did so, she met Mercy tiptoeing down the stairs. Mercy jumped when she saw her. "I thought you'd be asleep," Florence said, looking her up and down. Mercy was still in her day clothes.

"Nee, I'm just getting a glass of water."

"You drink an awful lot of water at night. Perhaps you should drink more throughout the day?"

"Sure. I'll give that a try. *Gut nacht.*"

"Gut nacht, Mercy."

. . .

MERCY POURED herself a glass of water so she wouldn't be lying to Florence—not so much, anyway, and then hurried out to meet Stephen. She'd seen him from her window and he was waiting in the usual spot.

CHAPTER 26

IT WAS FRIDAY, December 5, and Florence Baker sat in her living room along with a crowd of people, waiting for Mercy to marry Stephen Wilkes.

Sitting beside her was her stepmother, who bumped Florence's shoulder, and then leaned in and whispered, "I don't know why I encouraged this wedding."

"It's too late for regrets."

"I know."

Florence was the only one who'd been against Mercy marrying a man she barely knew, but Florence was more confident now she'd gotten to know Stephen a little better. "They're perfectly suited. Don't you think so?"

Mamm sniffled and dabbed at the corners of her eyes with a white handkerchief.

With little sympathy to offer, Florence faced the front. If anyone should be crying it was she—watching her six-years-younger half-sister get married before her. However ... to get married she needed a man, and there was no one in whom she was remotely interested.

From her back-row position, she cast her gaze over the crowd, looking at the single men. It was a futile scan; none were her age. Then there were the older widowers, all of whom had seen their better days—and they all sported long graying beards. Not the kind of man she saw herself with. Even if *Gott* placed the perfect man in front of her, he'd have to be pretty open-minded. She couldn't leave her beloved apple orchard. Her situation was hopeless, but she'd always have her apple trees.

After two hymns, a reading and a long talk given by Bishop Paul, Mercy and Stephen were pronounced married. When everyone rushed to congratulate them, Florence stayed in her seat worrying about her remaining five half-sisters. What if Mercy marrying young had set a trend her sisters thought they should follow? It wouldn't do to have them all rushing into marriage. They were all easily led except for Joy and she was a different case altogether. Joy was an abrupt and no-nonsense kind of person, who took after their maiden-aunt, Dagmar. Florence expected the same outcome for Joy.

Florence then looked over at her friend Liza, two rows in front, happily holding her sleeping baby. Now that Liza had a child, she insisted her marriage was happy. Florence hoped that it was so, and suspected Liza regretted confiding in her over the years. The things Liza had said made Florence think twice about marriage. Well, they would've done so if she'd ever even come close to it.

Reminding herself there was work to be done, Florence rose to her feet and headed to the kitchen to take charge of serving the food. *Mamm* had left her to arrange the food for the roughly three hundred and fifty guests that were expected. The number of people coming to a wedding was always an unknown, as no invitations were sent. Word went out that there was to be a wedding and people would travel for miles to attend. There were always hundreds of guests.

As well as planning the menu, ordering the food, and arranging for the women to cook, Florence had also sewed the wedding clothes for the bride and groom and all their attendants. In all, that was three dresses, capes, aprons, and *kapps,* and three suits for the men. The men all had their own black bowties and shirts, so it was a saving that she didn't have to sew those. Because of the extra workload of Mercy's wedding as well as running the apple orchard, Florence had hardly been out of the house for several weeks.

Back in the kitchen as they put the food into serving dishes to be taken out to the tables, squeals rang out as *Mamm* and her best friend, Ada, had only just realized that since Stephen was Ada's nephew, *Mamm* and she were now relatives of a sort.

Once most of the work was done, Florence said to *Mamm,* "Why don't you sit down outside and enjoy the wedding? I've got enough helpers in here." To seat everyone, an annex had been set up in the yard with tables, and there was a special bride and groom's table at the front. Large gas heaters either side kept the guests warm.

"Are you sure? You always work so hard."

"Go on. It's Mercy's wedding. Celebrate with her."

"Denke, Florence." *Mamm* hurried out and Florence looked out the kitchen window to see *Mamm* sitting down next to Earl at the closest table to Mercy's. Earl was Florence's older brother who'd moved to Ohio. This was the first time he'd been back in over two years. He'd left not long after their father had died. She made a mental note to speak with him as soon as she could. He'd arranged to stay with a friend rather than at the family home, so she'd best use this opportunity. She missed him, but he never got on too well with Mamm, which was the reason he'd moved away.

The groom's parents and his younger brother couldn't make it to the wedding, but they'd sent their apologies by letter and added that they were eagerly awaiting the newly married couple, excited to welcome them into their home. Of course, Jonathon, the trouble-making older brother was in attendance today.

She looked at Jonathon and then noticed her youngest half-sister walk over to him. She'd told Cherish many a time to keep away from him. It was staggering to Florence that Jonathon and Stephen were so different. They were similar in looks but poles apart in personality. She was keeping a close eye on Jonathon.

What is Cherish up to?

Florence found someone to take over her job in the kitchen and moved closer to Cherish and Jonathon to hear what they were saying.

"I happen to know you've been invited to Honor's birthday dinner next week."

"That's right." Jonathon smiled at her and then looked around. "I'm looking forward to it. Seems funny my younger *bruder* has married your older *schweschder*."

Cherish pouted. "That's hardly fair that they got married and we have to wait."

He laughed. "It's just how things have turned out. That wouldn't have been a problem if you were the second oldest *dochder* instead of the youngest."

"It's my fault? Hey, wait. What do you mean second oldest?"

He chuckled. "By that I mean I like Honor. She's the second oldest if you don't count Florence.""

"You're not serious, are you? She's deadly boring."

"I'm deadly serious and she's not boring. Not to me anyway. She could be to you."

"I—"

Having heard enough, Florence walked over to them. "There you are, Cherish. I've been looking for you to help in the kitchen. We all have to take a turn."

"I will soon." She looked up into Jonathon's eyes and said, "I'm talking to Jonathon right now."

Annoyed by her dismissiveness, Florence stepped forward and took hold of Cherish's arm. "Jonathon, would you mind if I steal her away from you?"

"That's fine."

Florence steered Cherish across the yard.

"Don't you know it's rude to interrupt?" Cherish said trying to free herself from Florence's grasp.

"I heard what you were saying and I saved you from making an idiot out of yourself. Remember, you're only thirteen." Then they were in the kitchen and Florence told one of the ladies to give Cherish a job. She was given the job of scraping food off the plates and stacking them for washing.

Once Florence was satisfied Cherish wasn't going to talk her way out of the kitchen, she put the irritation of Cherish out of her mind and helped herself to a plate of creamed chicken with broccoli. She walked outside and sat down with Liza and her husband, Simon. Liza was busy jiggling her baby up and down to stop him whimpering.

Florence ate a quick mouthful and looked around to see Jonathon now talking with Honor. They seemed engaged in a serious conversation. This wasn't good.

When baby Malachi opened his mouth and yelled, Liza's husband got up and cheerfully took him from Liza to walk him around.

Florence leaned over and whispered to Liza, "What could Jonathon possibly have in common with Honor? She's so lovely and quiet and he's a bit of a schemer. I know for a fact that he likes her."

"How do you know?"

"I just overheard him saying it."

Liza looked where Florence was staring. "Are they dating?"

"Not that I know of." Florence nibbled on the end of a fingernail. "I don't like it."

"Relax. I don't think she's interested in him."

"I hope you're right." Florence blew out a deep breath and then looked around for her stepmother. She was talking and laughing with Levi Bruner as though she didn't have a care in the world. Everything always fell on Florence's shoulders.

"Why are you so worried? I had loads of crushes on all kinds of unsuitable men when I was her age or thereabouts."

"I don't trust him. He concocted a plan to break Mercy and Stephen up because he wanted Mercy for himself. At least I think that was his reason. Either that or he just wanted to be mean to his *bruder*."

"Why didn't you tell me?"

"I don't know. I think Malachi was only just born—the very day, now that I think about it, and I didn't want to tell you any worrisome things."

"You should tell me these things." Liza looked back over at Jonathon and Honor. "It's hard to say. They're only talking."

"Jah, at the exclusion of everyone else and they've been like that for several minutes."

"Should you say something?"

"Like what?" Florence asked, no longer interested in the food.

"Just go over there and talk to them."

"I guess I should."

Florence picked up her glass of soda and headed over to them. When she was halfway there, Jonathon whispered something to Honor and by the time she reached them he was gone. She faced a glum-looking Honor.

Honor frowned at her. "Why did he leave when he saw you coming?"

"You'd have to ask Jonathon that. I don't see what you have in common with him. He's so much older."

"I like him."

Florence's heart sank. *"Jah,* well just remember your age."

"Age means nothing."

"It does. You're a child, technically, and he's a man. I'm going to tell him to keep away from you." She turned to walk away and Honor reached out and took ahold of her arm nearly spilling her soda. Florence looked down at the strong grip Honor had on her. She'd never realized she was so strong.

"Don't say anything. Please, Florence."

Florence took hold of her soda with her other hand and then pulled her arm away. "I'll say anything I please. What do you think *Dat* would say about you liking Jonathon?"

"He'd be pleased I found someone."

"Found someone? You've got years ahead of you to think about that. Worry about that when you reach my age."

"I won't be as old as you and still living at home. I'll have my own family way before then."

She looked into her sister's radiant and youthful face. Didn't she know life wasn't so simple? In life, there were struggles and pain, not to mention disappointments. She didn't want any of her sisters to regret choosing a man in a giddy moment to then face a life of hardship when she found him unsuited to her. There was no divorce—no way out. Marriage was binding and final.

"Nothing to say?" Honor asked lifting her chin slightly.

"I don't want to be still living at home either, but there's worse out there." She stared into her sister's blue-green eyes and it struck her that her own life was so pitiful that Honor was looking to escape the same fate. Suddenly, her sisters finding someone by the time they were eighteen didn't seem so young. "You'll find someone when you're older. When you're Mercy's age, and until then I won't have you even thinking about boys. Well, boys, but not men and ... and not men like Jonathon Wilkes."

Honor lifted her chin again and folded her arms across her chest. "I like him and I'm only one year younger than Mercy. Honestly, you can't stop me from seeing him. You're not my *mudder*."

None of the girls had talked to Florence like that before and that was worrisome. She was losing control and she wondered what her father would've done. She summoned all her strength and took a step closer. "You'll do what you're told. Once you're older you can do as you please. I'm going to talk with Jonathon right now to tell him to stay away from you."

"You wouldn't."

"Watch me." She turned away and found Jonathon at one of the food tables heaping food onto a plate. "Jonathon, we need to talk."

He looked around at her. "Sure. What is it?"

"It's Honor."

"What about her? She's the *schweschder* next oldest after Mercy, right?"

"Jah, the one you've spent the last half hour talking with."

"I thought so. There are a lot of you. Anyway, what about her?"

He was making this very difficult. "Stay away from her."

He drew his dark eyebrows together and his face contorted into confusion. "Why?"

"She has a childish crush on you and … well, it'd be better for her if you stayed away."

"Sure. Does that mean no more dinner invites?"

Florence nodded. "Until she gets over it."

"No problems. I'll keep away." He chuckled. "Are you sure she has a crush?"

It sickened her to her stomach that he found it amusing. "It's not funny."

"It's kind of flattering."

"Not really. She's only turning seventeen in a few days." She was pleased she got that in, and she also noticed he swallowed hard.

"I'll do as you say. I have no interest in her, I can assure you of that. Just so you know."

Florence laughed. "Of course you wouldn't, not at her age. I didn't think you did, but it'd be best for all concerned if you keep your distance."

"Okay sure. I can do that."

"*Denke.*" Unconvinced, Florence headed back to Liza and sat down.

"You're brave. I saw you talking to him. What did you say?"

"I told him how old she was."

"He would've known."

"He should've, but I drove the point home and asked him to stay away."

Liza looked over at Wilma. "Your *mudder* didn't even notice."

"She wouldn't. She lives in her own little bubble coasting over the surface of life." Florence poured herself a soda from the jug and took a mouthful. It was hard being the disciplinarian in the family.

"In other words, she has no backbone," Liza said.

"*Nee,* it's not that so much. She can't cope with anything. She was far harder on the girls when *Dat* was alive."

"She might've taken his death harder than she lets on."

"*Jah,* maybe. Now she's upset Mercy will be gone for a year."

"Are Mercy and Stephen staying at your place tonight?"

"*Nee.* They're staying at Ada and Samuel's house and then they're leaving in the morning. We'll all miss her." She looked over at the happy couple. "I haven't even congratulated them yet. I'll do that now."

On the way to congratulate the newly-married-couple, she saw Earl sitting alone. She took the opportunity to talk with him. He smiled when he saw her walking toward him.

"How are you?" she said when she'd sat next to him.

He pulled her into a one-armed hug. "Pretty much the same. I had thought I'd be coming back here for your wedding, not Mercy's."

She rolled her eyes. "Don't *you* start. *Nee,* there's no one who suits. What about you?"

"There are a couple of ladies, who might be contenders."

She giggled. *"Gut.* I'm happy to hear it. You must write to me more."

He nodded. "I will. I've missed you."

"And I've missed you dreadfully." They stared at each other for a moment, both missing their father and neither wanting to mention him. Earl would also be missing their mother. He'd have memories of her, and Florence was sure that was why he'd never gotten over their father marrying again.

"I should congratulate our *schweschder* and our new *bruder*-in-law."

"I'll be leaving tomorrow," Earl said.

"Nee. Can't you stay awhile longer?"

"I need to get back for work. It was all I could do to take a couple of days."

She sighed and nodded. "Well, don't you dare leave without saying goodbye."

"I'll find you and say goodbye tonight because I leave first thing, early tomorrow morning."

Florence nodded.

CHAPTER 27

IN THE EARLY hours of the next morning, all the girls and *Mamm* crammed themselves into one buggy to travel to Ada and Samuel's to say goodbye to Mercy and Stephen. It was most likely the last time they'd see them for a year, until they moved back.

When the horse and buggy traveled up Ada and Samuel's driveway, they saw the taxi. *Mamm* started weeping at the sight. Stephen was helping the driver put their luggage in the trunk while Mercy was on the porch saying goodbye to Ada and Samuel.

Then Mercy ran to the buggy. "You're late. You nearly missed us."

"You know what it's like to get all of us anywhere on time," Florence said as she stepped down from the buggy.

The girls got to Mercy first and then *Mamm* got out of the buggy and Mercy wrapped her arms around her. "I'm going to miss you so much."

"We'll all miss you too."

Florence threw the reins over the post and joined in with the farewells.

"Bye, Florence," Mercy hugged her. *"Denke* for everything. I know it was hard work sewing all those clothes, but you did them just right."

"Jah, well I wasn't game to make a mistake."

Mercy smiled. "I know I haven't been the easiest person to live with leading up to the wedding, but I'll make it up to everyone when I get back home."

"Have *bopplis* soon," Cherish called out.

"Jah, we want to be aunts, don't we, Cherish," Favor said with a giggle.

"Jah."

"Hush, girls," *Mamm* said, frowning.

Then Stephen walked up beside Mercy and said goodbye to everyone in turn. Ada and Samuel stepped off the porch and stood with the Baker family and watched Mercy and Stephen get into the taxi.

Stephen and Mercy waved to them all as the taxi slowly drove away.

Mamm burst into tears. "She's gone."

Ada put her arm around her. "Why don't you stay here—if Florence can fetch you later?"

Mamm looked at Florence through tear-filled eyes and Florence nodded. "Sure, I'll do that."

After Florence's half-sisters said goodbye to their mother, they all got back into the buggy.

WHEN THEY CAME BACK HOME, Florence told Hope and Joy to unhitch the buggy and tend to the horse. "Then you can all have a couple of hours off," Florence announced.

"Yay, free time," squealed Honor.

"*Jah,* but then there's the cleaning up to do. The only ones who'll get out of that are the two who are going to the markets today."

"It's Hope and me," Joy said. "We'll take the buggy and go now, if that's okay."

"No stock to take with you?"

"*Nee.*"

"Okay. Take the buggy."

Three girls headed into the house, two got back into the buggy, and Florence finally had a tiny bit of freedom. There was no more wedding sewing and no more wedding organization. Normally, she loved to sew, but sewing to a deadline—and in

SAMANTHA PRICE

such quantity—was too much pressure. Adding to that, Mercy wasn't the easiest person to sew for. She'd had exact ideas how she wanted everything to be and mostly told Florence about it after she'd done it differently. There had been hours of picking out stitches, but thankfully the younger girls had done that job.

It was finally time for Florence to think about herself for a moment and take that walk for which she'd been longing. It was one of the few things that calmed her. The other was a hot bath, but it was rare that she could linger in a tub without one of her sisters banging on the door saying they needed to use the bathroom.

She'd been longing for this stroll through the orchard—her sanctuary. She'd only been walking twice in the last several weeks and both times she'd noticed her mysterious *Englisch* neighbor, Carter Braithwaite, hadn't been home and his house had seemed closed up. Had he decided country life wasn't for him and he'd headed back to the city?

WALKING along the orchard with the apple trees either side of her, she was away from all annoyances. She walked on and on allowing the icy wind to blow her worries away while the weak winter sun moved higher into the sky.

When she was near the southern fence-line, she heard whistling and her heartrate increased. That had to mean Carter was there, but she couldn't see him anywhere. The whistling got a little louder and then she saw him walking around from the side of his house. She couldn't resist walking closer. When he looked up and saw her, he stopped whistling. His hand shot up in the air and he smiled and waved. Then he jogged over and they met at the fence.

She felt different when she saw him this time. Her life could've been made easier if he'd been born an Amish man, but had that been so, he'd probably have been married by now—to someone else.

"I haven't seen you for a few weeks." She wished she could've taken that back. Now he knew she noticed he'd been gone.

"I had to leave for a while and take care of something."

Take care of what exactly? she wondered. That reminded her that she still didn't know what he did for a living. The *Englisch* world was a bit of a mystery, but she was certain no one would pay him to play chess against his computer. By his own admission, he wasn't even a good player. That was the only thing he'd told her about himself apart from the fact he was overseeing house renovations and he was from the city.

A big smile covered his face. "I've got my new bathroom and kitchen installed. Would you like to see them?"

"Some other time, thanks. I've got so much to do back at the house."

"I thought you could rest up now that your harvest's over."

With that comment, his appeal lessened. It irritated her when people thought that having an orchard was a breeze. It was hard work and the work didn't stop just because the harvest had finished. "Is that what you think? You think we just have apple trees and only work a few weeks of the year?"

"No." He shook his head. "I know that's not right. You have the stall that your sisters run down by the main road. I've seen them there—driven past. I even bought some pickles from them once."

"We work all year around in the orchard. The girls just do the roadside stall for extra income. The orchard is hard work the entire year, throughout all the seasons."

"I'm sorry. I didn't know." He shifted his weight from one foot to the other. "What do you do at this time of year? There's no fruit on the trees, so ..."

"We all still work in the kitchen, canning and making preserves. As for the trees, we prune them and check regularly for any health issues."

His gaze traveled to the orchard behind her. "The trees look dead to me."

She frowned and then remembered he was from the city, so she kept things simple for him and launched into the spiel she gave the school children on their yearly tours. "They aren't dead. They're still working hard." *Never resting, much like myself,* she thought. "They're gathering nutrients from the soil to be ready for the next growing season. You see, they lose their leaves so they don't have to waste the nutrients on the leaves. They store everything through the colder weather, and the colder it is, the better the apples the tree produces."

"They need the cold. I see, well that makes sense."

"Good." Could he have been married and he was recovering from a divorce? Maybe his wife died in a tragic accident. He folded his arms over his chest and she found herself looking at his left hand for a wedding ring or a sign that one had been there. There was nothing.

"You're certainly passionate about your trees. It seems like they're your life."

"Every orchard owner's the same. Taking care of trees is time consuming and sometimes all consuming."

He scratched his neck. "Seems so. Were you having some kind of an event yesterday at your house?"

"Yes. My sister's wedding."

"One of the bonnet sisters got married?"

"Please don't call us that. Or … or I'll call you the … the hatless man with no siblings."

His lips twitched. "Hmm. That would be quite a mouthful. I'm surprised that *you* didn't get married. Aren't you the oldest?"

She didn't need to be reminded. "I am, but there's no law that says the oldest has to marry first."

"No, but I thought your family was traditional, and I would've thought they'd want the oldest to marry first. And then each one down the line."

"Not at all. You're wrong."

He grinned. "It's possible. I thought I was wrong once before … but I was mistaken."

She frowned at the cheekiness of his grin. They stared at one another and there was some kind of moment between them; she was sure he felt the same. "I have to go."

He stepped forward nearly stabbing his chest on the high barbed wire that ran on the top of the fence between them. "Will you be walking again tomorrow?"

"I try to walk every day, but sometimes I don't get the chance."

"I'll keep an eye out for you." He beamed her a smile. "Just in case."

She gave him a little nod, then turned and headed back to the safety of her trees.

He wasn't going to see her tomorrow or any other day. She had to keep away from him and, somehow, she had to stop thinking about him.

As she walked on, she wondered about the differences between the Amish and the *Englisch*. Then she thought about her community and all the different personalities of everyone she knew. There was Jonathon who'd tricked Mercy into unknowingly doing something unkind. Thankfully, Stephen forgave her and they were reunited. Then there was Wilma, who lived off in the clouds somewhere leaving Florence to step in and do her job of keeping the girls in line. Then there were all the differing personalities of her half-sisters.

Why aren't people more like apple trees? she muttered. She stopped and put her arms around the trunk of one of her trees, resting her head on a low branch. It was the unpredictability of people that made them disagreeable and difficult. With apple trees, you always knew what you were going to get. They fruited in the summer and fall, dropped their leaves in the winter, and then came to life again in the spring.

Florence wanted to keep walking and be with her trees, but in her heart, she knew the girls wouldn't start cleaning until she got home. She'd have to further encourage them by saying it would be a surprise for their mother if the place was spotless on her return.

CHAPTER 28

THAT AFTERNOON, Florence went back to Ada's and collected a happier Wilma. They arrived home and all the girls fussed over *Mamm* and made sure she was comfortable as she sat working on her sampler while Florence reheated wedding leftovers for dinner.

When they all sat down to eat, Florence saw *Mamm* staring at Mercy's empty chair and considered removing it, but that might've made *Mamm* even sadder.

Once they said their silent prayers of thanks for their food, Honor said, "When can I marry? Seventeen? I don't have to wait until I'm eighteen, do I?"

"*Nee,* with permission, but you won't be marrying Jonathon because he's so much older and unsuited."

Honor frowned at Florence while Cherish was too busy playing tug-o-war with the chicken wishbone with Favor to notice Florence had mentioned her unlikely crush, Jonathon.

"How do you know Jonathon's the one I like?" Honor asked. "I could be talking about Isaac, Christina's *bruder.* He's moved in with Mark and Christina you know."

Mamm tipped her head to one side. "Then, who were you talking about? Jonathon, did you say? Or Isaac?"

Cherish interrupted, "Did someone say Jonathon?"

"Nee," Florence snapped. "Who do you like, Honor?"

"Christina's *bruder,* Isaac, I'd reckon," Cherish said. "He would suit you perfectly."

"Oh him. I met him at Christina and Mark's wedding too," *Mamm* said. "He's nice. But isn't Jonathon staying with Mark and Christina?" *Mamm* asked. "That's what I heard from Mark's own mouth."

Florence added, "It'll be awfully crowded in their tiny place."

"Nee, Mamm. Not exactly. Jonathon is staying in their barn. It's got living quarters there. Isaac is staying in their actual *haus,"* Honor said.

"And when can I marry?" Cherish asked. "How old do I have to be?"

"A lot, lot older than you are now. That is for certain," Florence said.

"I was asking *Mamm,* not you." Cherish looked over at *Mamm.*

"Florence is right. You're still too young for such talk."

Cherish pulled a face. "You two always stick together."

Honor stared at Cherish and said, "What is unfair is that you're continually talking about boys when you're too young to even go on a buggy ride."

"We need a rest from weddings for the moment and any talk of weddings," *Mamm* said.

"Jonathon likes me and I like him. Our love will find a way. I love him more than you do, Honor," Cherish said.

FLORENCE STARED AT CHERISH. "LOVE?" That was exactly what Florence had feared. "I don't think he takes anything seriously, Cherish. Perhaps he's the kind of man who loves everyone? That's what I think, so just be mindful of that."

"Nee, he's not. He stayed with me the whole day yesterday and there were lots of other girls there."

Florence sighed knowing that if Jonathon had been talking with Cherish it was only to get closer to Honor.

"Jonathon likes me not you," Honor told Cherish. "I'm not meaning to be rude or nasty, but you're far too young for him to even think about liking you."

Cherish's face screwed up as though she was going to cry. "You are being mean."

"Excuse me. I'm no longer hungry." Florence headed out of the kitchen leaving her dinner and leaving *Mamm* to cope with the girls. She could be the disciplinarian for once. There were problems ahead with both Honor and Cherish liking Jonathon and she couldn't think of someone worse for one of her half-sisters to like.

With the background chatter of the girls, Florence sat down at the desk in the corner of the living room. In need of more lighting, she lit the lamp that stood atop the desk and then pulled the financial ledgers out of the drawer.

Florence sighed. Keeping the books was a burden she wished was someone else's, but there was no one good with numbers like she was. Without even referring to the books she knew they were doing okay financially, but if they had one bad season they'd be in trouble.

They'd made a lot of money in the last few months, but that had to last for the entire year. With the colder weather, she'd told the girls to stop the roadside stall until the weather was more favorable. She didn't want them freezing to death on the side of the road. The income from the daily stall was sorely missed.

"What's wrong?"

Florence turned to see Honor beside her. "Ah, just looking at how we're doing."

"We're doing okay, aren't we?"

"We always get by. I'd like to have more to put away. You're too young to remember, but we had three bad seasons in a row and had to sell some of our land. And we had to sell it for less than it was really worth. There weren't any buyers around. Anyway, *Dat* selling the land to the Graingers got us out of trouble and then we were okay after that. The next season was good and we've been okay ever since."

"I wondered why he sold off that land and those buildings."

"Buildings? There's only a cottage and the barn."

"There's the smaller house too at the back of the property. I saw it once. I haven't noticed it lately. Maybe it got pulled down or fell over in a storm."

"I vaguely remember that now. Was it made from stone?"

"I'm not sure. So, you'd like enough in the bank in case something bad happens?"

"*Jah*. That new generator set us back. There's always something going wrong or something that needs fixing."

"I guess the wedding cost a lot too."

Florence grimaced. The food for the wedding and the fabric for the clothes had added up to a small fortune. "I didn't want to say, because I'm really happy for Mercy and Stephen, but *jah*."

"We really should keep selling anything we can to keep the money rolling in. I'll probably get married in a year or two."

"I know." Florence nodded, not wanting to face that until it was upon her. "It's no use thinking of the roadside stall. There are so few buyers around right now, so it's not just the possibility of you girls freezing to death."

"We'll hope and pray that nothing goes wrong with the weather and all that."

"That's best, but *Gott* gave us a brain to use and I believe He wants us to be practical and do all we can."

"How about I get you a hot cup of tea while you look at those books?"

Florence relaxed her shoulders. "That would be nice. It's just what I feel like. I had to get out of the kitchen though." She whispered. "I couldn't listen to Cherish one moment longer. And … Jonathon of all people. I'm sorry, but you know I don't like him. Not one little bit because of the prank he pulled on his *bruder* and Mercy."

"I heard about it and he's truly sorry. He just made one mistake. *Gott* says to forgive."

Florence chuckled. "That might take me some time. I can forgive him, but that doesn't mean I want him anywhere near you."

"You'll get used to him. When you get to know him better you'll like him. I'll bring you a cup of hot tea."

"Denke, Honor." Florence knew Honor had been won over by Jonathon's charming personality. He knew all the right things to say to win her heart and that was a worrisome thing. At the same time, Florence knew there was most likely very little she

could do about the situation and what's more, if she forbade her to see him that would make her want him all the more.

Florence was delighted when Honor brought the remainder of her dinner out to her along with a cup of hot tea.

CHAPTER 29

WHEN THE GIRLS had all gone to bed, Florence sat with Wilma in the living room. They were in their nightgowns and ready for bed, but they both decided they'd stay up for a little while. Wilma worked on her cross stitch sampler and Florence crocheted squares for a blanket.

"I can't believe Mercy is all grown up and married. Even more unbelievable that she chose him before she met him. It was as though God had whispered in her ear and told her Stephen was the one. I can tell you I was worried. She was so determined to marry him before she'd met him. That could've gone horribly wrong for her."

"I know what you mean." Wilma said smiling, most likely thinking of the grandchildren she'd have.

While Florence was pondering love, she wondered how much of it was determined by *Gott* and how much of it was the choices that He allowed people to make. She'd previously thought the ones who'd rushed into things were the ones with unhappy marriages. Maybe she was wrong about that theory. There was so much she'd asked *Gott*, but He still hadn't answered. Why did some women find their husbands young while others had to wait? Some, like her *Dat's* older *schweschder* Aunt Dagmar, never found anyone at all.

She was too old now to find young love like Mercy, and she definitely didn't want to end up alone like Aunt Dagmar, who had an austere and slightly unpleasant demeanor. She'd come to visit once and found fault with everything and everyone of her sisters. When she left, her stepmother had told her Aunt Dagmar was bitter because she had never married.

Florence looked over at her stepmother who was now nodding off with the needle in her hand. "Careful you don't stick yourself with the needle."

Wilma opened her eyes and blinked rapidly.

"Perhaps it's time for bed," Florence suggested.

"Already?" Wilma looked over at her. "It's nice to sit here without constant chatter and I was enjoying your company."

Florence was pleased to hear it. "All right. I'll stay up a little longer if you can stay awake. I can't stop thinking how well-suited Stephen and Mercy are."

"*Jah. Gott* has blessed us and them."

"He has. *Mamm*, why were you so set on finding a man for Mercy?"

"Because getting married was all she could talk about, and she's the oldest."

"She's not, though. I am."

"Florence, that has nothing to do with it. She's the oldest born to me, but you are every bit my *dochder*. I didn't think you were interested."

"I am interested." It was nice to hear those words from *Mamm's* mouth. Wilma was the only mother she remembered other than a couple of very hazy and happy memories of her birth-mother. *Dat* and other people had told her she resembled her mother, but she had no way of knowing because photographs were never taken among the Amish.

"I always thought you would stay on here and help with the orchard. This is the income for us all. It was a harsh blow to us all when Mark left, and then Earl too."

"Maybe, just maybe, I'll want to marry one day."

"Yeah, and you should." Her stepmother opened her mouth to say something else, but no words came out. Then she closed her lips.

"Don't worry about it."

"Do you want me to help you find a husband like I helped Mercy?"

Florence chuckled. *"Nee.* I can find my own. Not that I'm going to look. It'll happen if it's meant to."

"Of course it will. I thought you might've met someone at your *schweschder's* wedding."

"I didn't." Florence had thought the same at every wedding she'd gone to from the time she'd been a teenager.

"I hoped having the wedding here might've encouraged Stephen to stay in our community. What did you think?"

"There's no use talking about that now. She's gone for a year, but they both said they'd be back. Stephen was a tremendous help to us in the orchard." They could certainly use Stephen's help on his return and not just at harvest time.

"It would've been nice if your *vadder* had been here for the wedding. I miss him."

"Me too." Florence couldn't look at Wilma because she knew they'd both cry. She missed her father unbelievably. After her mother died, it had been just the four of them—her and her two older brothers and *Dat*, but not for long. She was four when *Dat* married Wilma. Earl had come for Mercy's wedding, but hadn't even stayed with them and she'd barely gotten to talk with him. Ever since Mark married Christina, they hardly saw either of them. Seeing Mark meant she had to see Christina and that was often a chore.

Several minutes later, Florence looked over at Wilma and saw her eyes closed and her mouth wide open. She giggled to herself. As she decided to call it a night, she wrapped up her crochet project and put it on the small side table next to the couch. Then she very carefully lifted the cross stitch fabric from her stepmother's lap, inserted the needle, and laid it on the table, too.

"Gut nacht," Florence whispered to her sleeping stepmother before she headed upstairs for bed. She unbraided her thigh-length hair and pulled her brush through it thinking about her half-sisters. Honor wanted to marry Jonathon, that was no secret, but it was troubling how Cherish was already interested in love at such a young age. If one of her *bruders* were still at home, she might not have had to be so strict. She placed her brush back onto her chest of drawers.

As she slipped between the cool sheets, she wondered if she'd ever marry.

She turned off the gas lamp on her nightstand, and then buried her head in her pillow, thinking about Carter Braithwaite. He'd never suit her, but she was certain God was using him as a sign. A sign that there was a good Amish man out there for her somewhere. If Mercy had found a man so suddenly, one who was so perfectly suited, there was definite hope for her.

"Bonnet sisters—humph," she murmured as she pulled her quilt higher around her shoulders.

AMISH HONOR

THE AMISH BONNET SISTERS BOOK 2

CHAPTER 1

FLORENCE BAKER WOKE UP EXHAUSTED. She'd just gotten over all the sewing, the organizing, and the cooking for Mercy's wedding, and tomorrow was Honor's birthday. Her throat was dry from breathing the chilly air so she pulled the covers over her head to keep out the cold. Normally when Florence woke, she hurried downstairs to put more logs on the embers from last night's fire and then she'd have a quiet mug of coffee before the rest of the household woke. Today, though, she was weary—weary in body and mind.

Besides doing much of the cooking today for the birthday dinner tomorrow, Florence was determined to come up with a way to make more income in the winter months.

OVER BREAKFAST, Florence asked her family to think hard on what they could do.

"You see, it's important we put money aside for bad seasons. That's why *Dat* had to sell the five acres next door to the Graingers." Florence shook her head. If they still owned that land, and the house that sat on it, they could've had the money from leasing it. The Graingers had since sold to Carter Braithwaite. Florence's father had always hoped to buy back the land, and that was now one of her dreams.

"Any ideas anyone?" *Mamm* asked.

Florence looked at each of her half-sisters, and all of them had blank looks on their faces. All of them, that was, except for Honor.

"I have an idea and, if I can take the buggy, I'll look into it further."

Florence narrowed her eyes at Honor. "Well, what is it?"

HONOR DIDN'T RESPOND. She wasn't only concerned about money for the family. Her idea would also help her to see more of Jonathon Wilkes without anyone looking over her shoulder. The trouble was, Florence didn't like Jonathon, and her youngest sister Cherish had a huge crush on him. Two reasons why she couldn't have him visit at the house.

"What is it, Honor?" *Mamm* finally asked when Honor hadn't answered.

"I'd rather not say until I know if it's a real possibility. All I need is to use the buggy for half a day."

"She just wants to get out of chores," Cherish said.

Joy shook her head at their youngest sister. "That's what you'd do. You can't judge other people like that. In fact, you shouldn't judge people at all."

"You just did."

Joy looked at Favor. "I'd never …"

"You just judged Cherish by saying that's what she'd do."

Florence groaned. "Stop it, all of you. Okay, take one of the buggies, Honor. You can do your chores once you get home."

"Denke, Florence. Of course I will." Honor looked over and saw Cherish staring at her, and Honor knew what she was thinking. Cherish thought she was sneaking off to spend time with Jonathon Wilkes. She wasn't totally wrong. Her plan did involve Jonathon. If she had a job—say, at the markets—she'd see more of Jonathon with no one knowing.

As soon as Honor arrived at the markets, she headed over to Warren, one of their large customers for apples. He was an *Englischer* who worked with his father in the largest fruit and vegetable stall there.

"Hi, Warren."

"Hello. What are you doing out this way?"

She looked over at Warren's father busy serving some customers. "I'm thinking of looking into having a stall here where we could sell our small goods. We won't sell apples because we don't want to compete with you or our other customers."

"It wouldn't matter if you did," said Warren. "You need to speak with Lionel Pettigrew about getting a stall. He's the manager. I'll put a good word in for you."

"Thank you. That would be appreciated. Where would I find him?"

"I saw him heading out to the parking lot a few minutes ago. I'll see if I can catch him. Stay here."

"Thanks so much."

Warren called out to his father telling him where he was heading. Less than two minutes later, Warren came back with Mr. Pettigrew, a short chubby-cheeked balding man.

Once Warren introduced them, Mr. Pettigrew smiled and said, "Warren tells me that you want to sell apples here."

"No. We have an apple orchard, but we want to sell small goods —canned goods, baked goods, pickles and chutneys. Also, apple pies and such."

He nodded. "Come with me and I'll show you one or two spots we might be able to squeeze you in. I'll give you an idea of pricing too."

"Okay, thank you." Before she walked away with the manager, she gave Warren a smile and a nod.

After Mr. Pettigrew had taken her on a tour, showing her where she could set up, he told her the prices. She was pleasantly surprised that they were low in comparison to what she had thought they'd be.

"Is that per week or per month?" she inquired.

"Per month. Is it too much for you?"

"No, not at all."

"And then we have one closer to the front, but that's more than double the size and double the price."

"Would we be able to start with the small one and see how we do?"

"By all means. When would you like to start?"

"We could start tomorrow if that's not too soon."

"That's fine by me. Come with me to my car. I don't have an office at the moment while it's being repainted. I'm reduced to working out of my car. I'll give you some paperwork to sign and bring back tomorrow."

When they got to the car, he pulled some paperwork out of a well-worn leather briefcase and scribbled some figures on it. "Here it is. Read through it and if you agree, bring this with you and be here tomorrow. On the last page, you'll see where to make the weekly payment."

She stared at it to see he'd written a figure even lower than he'd quoted her. "Are you sure?"

"Yes."

"Do we pay at the start of the week or the end?"

"At the start."

"Oh." She wondered what *Mamm* would say about that. "I'll have to get my mother to agree to this first. Don't worry, I'm sure she will. We run a roadside stand in the warmer months, but it makes so much more sense to be here."

He smiled. "The end of the week is fine if that'll make your mother happier. We all have to keep our mothers happy." He pulled more sheets of paper out of his briefcase. "This is a list of rules." He chuckled. "It's nothing too strange. Operating hours and what not."

She nodded.

"Is it a deal? Assuming your mother agrees?" He put out his hand and she shook it.

"It's a deal." She felt grown-up making a big decision like this with a proper businessman. Now, she just had to get Florence and *Mamm* to agree. Her idea wasn't a new one. Florence had wanted to do it before but *Mamm* had squashed the idea. *Mamm's* main objection had been the cost. Setting up on the roadside was free. In spite of how much a stall was to lease, Honor reckoned they'd make more money there than sitting at home not selling anything. In the springtime they'd have to decide about the roadside stand.

．　．　．

AS SHE TRAVELED TOWARD HOME, she knew Florence would be okay with the idea and she'd help *Mamm* see it was a good one. The girls could all take it in turns, just like they did with the roadside stand, while Florence stayed home and ran the orchard business.

To put her mother in a good mood, she stopped at their favorite coffee shop and bought her a fancy take out coffee. *Mamm* liked hers with hazelnut-flavored syrup and plenty of chocolate sprinkles. For Florence, she got an oversized chocolate marshmallow cookie to satisfy her sweet tooth.

When she arrived home, Florence was waiting for her on the porch, with her arms folded and looking none too happy. As soon as Honor stopped the buggy, Florence strode out to meet her.

"You've been gone plenty long enough, and your chores are still waiting."

"*Jah,* I know, but it's my birthday tomorrow and I thought you'd be able to do without me for a little bit. I did something." She stepped down from the buggy. "I committed us to taking out a stall at the markets. I negotiated that we pay at the end of every week and it's not really that much money."

"What markets?"

"The main one in town."

Florence gasped. "The farmers market?"

Honor nodded.

"How much is that going to cost? You didn't sign anything, did you?"

"Not yet. I'll show you." From the passenger side of the buggy, she grabbed the agreement and showed her the figures Mr. Pettigrew had written in.

Florence took the paper and held it up. "That's a lot less than I thought it'd be. Are you sure it's right?"

"*Jah.* I asked him the same question. He wrote it in himself. What do you think?"

Florence narrowed her eyes at her. "You had this idea all by yourself?"

"*Jah,* because we can't stand by the roadside freezing, and what else are we going to do when it's so cold? And how will we make money?"

"We'll get by."

"Yeah, well ... now we can get by better—hopefully. What do you think? Also, we didn't have to commit to a lengthy lease or anything. If we want to stop, we just give one week's notice. It says so right there." She pointed at the rules paperwork that she'd skimmed through on the way home.

Florence wiped away a tear. "You've lightened my load. If I didn't have so much to think about I would've thought of this."

"I remembered you wanted to do it a couple of years ago."

"*Jah,* but *Mamm* didn't like the idea."

"Will she allow us to do it now?"

Florence smiled. "You said you've committed us to it."

Honor giggled. "I did. Oh, wait, did I? I don't think so. We shook hands, but nothing is signed."

"Let's unhitch Morgan and then we can tell her together."

"Okay."

"When do we start?" Florence asked.

"He said we can start tomorrow."

"Wunderbaar."

"I got *Mamm* a hazelnut coffee and I got you a great big cookie."

"Ach, denke. I love those giant cookies and the coffee will make *Mamm* happy. Good idea—let's go tell her now."

WHEN THEY WALKED into the kitchen, the girls were all there. They heard what Honor had done while she told their mother. "What do you think, *Mamm?"*

"It's up to Florence. Do you think it's a good idea?"

Florence couldn't hold back her enthusiasm. "I think it's a *wunderbaar* idea. We don't have much to lose and we have enough goods to sell."

Joy nodded. "We do now, but what if we sell out?"

"Then we'll make more," Favor said. "Like we always do, even if we have to stay up into the night."

"Ach nee! The nights are too cold to stay up," said Cherish. "I'd much rather be warm and toasty in bed."

"Honor, why don't you make up a schedule for the girls for the first couple of weeks and also figure out what stock we've got and how long you think it'll last?"

"Okay."

"Can I help?" Hope asked. "I'll get the pens and paper."

"Sure."

"You don't want to work on your birthday, do you, Honor?" *Mamm* asked. "Make sure not to put yourself down to work on your birthday."

"I don't mind."

"Before you do your schedule, stay still for one moment and let's talk about your birthday," *Mamm* said.

"I don't want a fuss. A dinner is fine and I don't want presents."

"Ach, you're easily pleased," said Cherish. "I like loads of presents. Don't tell people you don't want gifts and you can give 'em all to me." Cherish giggled.

"I'd just like a dinner like I always have, but with a couple more people invited. Jonathon, and Isaac too, since they're both staying with Mark and Christina. It would be rude not to include him."

"Jonathon's coming already," Cherish chimed in. When everyone stared at her, she said, "He's our *bruder*-in-law now that Mercy's married Stephen, and he's also staying with Mark and Christina. Mercy might've even married him if she'd met him first. Anyway, I happen to have overheard *Mamm* inviting the four of them."

Mamm nodded. "I did. And there's Ada and Samuel, who'll come too."

Mamm's best friend Ada and her husband were just like family and came to all the girls' birthday dinners.

Florence asked, "Anyone else you'd like to include, Honor, since it's your birthday? Any friends?"

"I'll see my friends through the day, if I'm not going to be working at the market stall. I'll take the buggy and go see them. No need to invite them for dinner. So, just those four will be fine."

"Six." *Mamm* corrected her.

"I meant six. *Gut.*" Honor nodded.

ONCE ALL THE girls had left the kitchen, Florence had a quiet moment alone with *Mamm*. "It's not a good idea for Jonathon to come to Honor's birthday. He should be keeping away from Cherish. You know she's got a crush on him and also I think that Honor likes him."

Mamm shook her head. "We can't leave him out. Besides, I already invited him. He's your *bruder*-in-law now."

"Not really. I don't believe he'd be technically classed as my in-law. He's Mercy's *bruder*-in-law, but he's not mine."

"Besides that, Christina and Mark are coming as well as Isaac, and Jonathon is living on the same property. It would be rude to leave him out."

Florence wasn't happy to hear that. "I'm just trying to stop problems before they start."

"Florence, you're just like your *vadder*—overly cautious."

"Well …. That's a good way to be."

"Not if it's going to upset people and ruin Honor's birthday. Jonathon's coming to Honor's birthday and that's final."

She stared into *Mamm's* eyes. Once her stepmother had made up her mind it was always final. It was rare for her to be firm like she'd been just now, so Florence chose to go along with it. "Okay, but I'm wary of him."

"Why ever for?"

Mamm had never learned how Jonathon had tried to drive a wedge between Mercy and Stephen. Florence had chosen to keep that quiet. She wasn't sure why. "Never mind." It was too long a story to tell and now that Mercy and Stephen were married, *Mamm* would most likely shrug it off.

CHAPTER 2

HONOR SAT down to breakfast on her birthday, missing her older sister. "My first birthday without Mercy. It won't be the same. Why do people have to die and why do people have to leave?"

"*Jah*, it's so unfair," said Cherish. "I want *Dat* to still be here. I miss him. I was his favorite. Now Earl and Mark have gone too."

"We hardly see them either."

"I was *Dat's* favorite," repeated Cherish.

"He didn't have any favorites." Florence had waited for *Mamm* to say that, but since she hadn't, Florence had to stop the back and forth that was inevitable.

Joy said, "Everyone dies. Life's a cycle. We live, and then we grow old and die. Just as the apple tree blossoms, then the blossoms die and the fruit grows, then the fruit shrivels up and it dies too."

Hope screwed up her face. "I don't like the sound of that."

"Yeah, how long did it take you to think of that sad story, *Joy?*" Cherish asked with a scowl.

"I'm just simplifying it for all of you."

"We're not dumb," Cherish said. "You think you know everything."

Joy wrinkled her nose. "I do. I know more than you because I read more."

"Hope and Joy, you're on the stall today, *jah?*"

"That's right. We're going as soon as we finish eating," Hope said.

"Good, some peace today," said Cherish, who didn't get along at all well with Joy.

Thankfully, Joy ignored her as she finished the last of her scrambled egg.

HONOR HAD a day off from the markets since it was her birthday. She helped her *Mamm* in the kitchen while Hope and Joy went to work the market stall and the rest of her sisters cleaned the house.

. . .

HONOR WAS happy with herself that she'd made Florence so pleased about opening the stall at the markets. It was the sensible thing to do, she'd been sure, and now everyone could see it. She was even happier that Jonathon was coming to her birthday dinner. She'd helped her mother with the main meal and watched how her mother had made her favorite German dark-chocolate cherry cake.

Florence and her mother were busy in the kitchen when their guests arrived. Cherish pushed Honor out of the way and opened the door to both Isaac and Jonathon who'd come in one buggy. Honor was disappointed about that because it meant they'd have to go home at the same time. It had been her secret hope that Jonathon might stay longer than everyone else so they could talk. Preferably after her younger sisters had gone upstairs to bed.

"Happy birthday, Honor," Isaac said in his large voice that matched his large frame.

"*Denke.*"

"*Jah,* happy birthday," Jonathon said ignoring Cherish and pushing forward with a huge basket of pink roses.

"Ah, Jonathon. They're beautiful."

Cherish turned and walked away with Isaac while Honor admired the different shades of pink amongst the roses. "I said no birthday presents."

Jonathon leaned forward and whispered, "Maybe it's not a birthday gift."

She giggled. That meant he had brought her flowers. No one had ever given her flowers. *"Denke.* We better join the others." When they sat down, Honor placed the flowers on the low table to the side of the couch.

"Hope, can you tell *Mamm* our guests have arrived?"

"They haven't yet. Ada and Samuel are coming, aren't they? Also, Christina and Mark?"

"They won't be far behind us," Isaac said.

Honor was annoyed with Hope because she never did what she was told until she had argued about it first. She thought she knew better than everyone else and questioned absolutely everything she was asked to do, but Honor couldn't say anything to her about it now in front of the guests.

"Go on, Hope. Just tell her Jonathon and Isaac are here."

"Say please?"

She rolled her eyes. It wasn't worth an argument. "Please?"

"Fine." Hope flounced into the kitchen.

"Is that what she's like all the time?" Jonathon leaned over and whispered to her.

"You don't know the half of it."

Having overheard them, Isaac said quietly, "I'm glad my sister isn't like that."

Honor wondered what Christina was like to Isaac—or had been when she'd been younger. She wasn't very nice to her and her sisters but her half-brother, Mark, didn't seem to notice. Otherwise, he wouldn't have married her.

When Hope came out of the kitchen there was a knock on the door, so she walked over and pulled it open. Honor hurried over to greet the guests. It *was* her birthday, after all.

Christina and Mark had arrived along with Ada and Samuel. "Happy birthday!" they all said at once. Then Mark handed her a gift wrapped in white paper with a red ribbon. She moved away from the doorway so they could move through.

"Mark, I said no gifts."

He chuckled. "I mustn't have heard that part."

"He insisted," Christina said with a rare smile.

"Do I have to open it now?"

"Isn't it your birthday today?" Mark asked.

"You know it is."

"Open it now, then."

Honor was a little embarrassed to open the gift in front of everybody. She never knew how surprised or delighted to look. And what if she hated it? She wasn't good at lying and being false. That was why she preferred no gifts at all. Besides, she didn't need anything. She sat on the couch and carefully unwrapped the parcel while feeling all eyes on her. The first thing she saw was white fabric. Then she lifted it to reveal a beautifully made prayer *kapp* fashioned from sheer organza. She held it up high. "It's beautiful. It's the most *wunderbaar* thing I've ever seen."

"I'm making them," Christina said. "I'm making ones like that to sell."

"I think you'll do very well, but how do you find the time with the new saddlery store?"

"I'm working in the store now remember?" Jonathon said.

"That's right. So, he's working there to give you more free time, Christina?"

Christina nodded and Mark beamed a smile at his wife. "Christina always likes to keep busy."

"It reminds me of the industrious woman from the Bible," Joy said, and then she quoted the entire passage from Proverbs 31 from memory in German.

Sitting back on the couch, Honor whispered to Jonathon, "Joy likes to remind us what it says in the Bible at least five times a day."

He rolled his eyes while shaking his head.

Honor giggled. It seemed as though they thought the same about things.

"That would be extremely annoying," Jonathon whispered back. "I'm not against hearing what the Word says, not at all, but …"

"I know. I mean, once in a while it would be all right, but it's too much. I don't know why she's like that."

He shrugged his shoulders. "Some people are just like that, I guess."

"I guess so."

Florence and *Mamm* came out from the kitchen to greet the guests and then announced that the birthday dinner was ready.

"Before we eat, I want to show both of you what Christina made for me." Honor showed *Mamm* and Florence the prayer *kapp,* and they loved it, praising Christina's workmanship.

When Honor walked into the dining area, which was off from the kitchen, Favor said, "Surprise! I made everyone paper hats and, everyone *has* to wear them."

The hats were in front of everyone's place setting at the table. Once everyone was seated they placed them on their heads with a fair bit of giggling, including the older folk, Samuel and Ada, who looked especially funny. The women placed the paper hats over their prayer *kapps*. Honor loved the idea and was pleased her sister had gone to the trouble.

When everyone's silent prayer of thanks for the food had been said, Jonathon asked if he could say a special prayer. *Mamm* nodded telling him he could. He prayed for *Gott's* blessings over the Baker family and especially the birthday girl. Then he hesitated and asked for a safe trip for everyone on their way home when the night was over. Then he ended with, "Amen."

"Amen," Samuel and Mark echoed.

For dinner, they were eating roasted chicken and roasted vegetables, with plenty of gravy and mashed potatoes.

"Mrs. Baker, I heard there's volleyball on tomorrow night at the Yoders' *haus* and I'm hoping you'll allow me to take Honor."

Mamm looked over at Honor and then looked back at Jonathon. "Of course, if she wants to go."

"Jah, I do."

"I'll bring her home and take her there. You won't have to do a thing."

"I suppose it'll be all right if you take her there and bring her straight back once it's over."

"I will. You can trust me."

"Does that mean you'll be borrowing our spare buggy again?" Christina asked.

"If that's okay?"

Christina nodded.

"I told you it's yours to use when you want," Mark said.

Honor saw Cherish fidgeting in her chair and knew she was going to ask if she could go to the volleyball too. A short sharp kick under the table and a glare from Honor was enough to stop that from happening.

Joy said, "Let me get something straight in my head. Jonathon, you're working in Mark's saddlery and living in Mark's barn?"

"That's almost right, Joy," said Mark. "It's not a barn. It's off from the stables and it was originally built as living space for workers. It's quite comfortable."

Without commenting on what Mark said, Joy then looked over at Isaac. "And, Isaac, you're Christina's *bruder,* you have no job and you're living with Mark and Christina inside their small *haus?*"

Christina leaned forward. "It's not that small. It's perfect for us and a guest."

Joy raised her eyebrows. "I heard that it was small."

"Not at all." Christina's lips pressed together firmly.

Joy said, "If we'd ever seen it, we could judge for ourselves."

Samuel gave an embarrassed laugh. "What's big to some is small to others."

"It does the job for the both of us." Mark smiled, then added, "The two of us and one guest. Isaac doesn't plan to be with us forever and then it'll be just the two of us again."

"It's not going to be the two of you for long." Cherish giggled.

"This is not a conversation to have over dinner, girls," Florence said frowning at Cherish and Joy.

"I was just asking," Joy said. "And I was going to ask Isaac and Jonathon why they've both moved here. Is that okay or do I have to be someone other than who I am with my own family?"

"Please be someone else," said Hope. "It'd be a nice change."

Favor sniggered.

The night was going downhill fast and Florence sat there tired and exhausted. She couldn't believe Joy's rudeness, but was too weary to reprimand her. Then she was pleased when *Mamm* quickly changed the subject. "We have cake for dessert."

"*Jah*, it's my favorite," Honor said. "*Mamm* always makes it every birthday."

"What kind is it?" Jonathon asked, his gaze fixed on Honor.

"German dark chocolate cherry cake."

"I don't think I've ever tried that before."

Ada said, "Wilma makes it so well."

"*Jah*, she does. I've been meaning to get the recipe from you, Wilma," Christina added.

"I'll write it down for you. It came with my *mudder's* family from the Old Country," said *Mamm*, "so sometimes I have to substitute for ingredients I can't get here."

By now it was obvious to everyone that Honor and Jonathon liked one another and Florence wasn't okay with that. Neither was she okay with Cherish's crush on Jonathon. Cherish was far too young to know she was making a fool of herself. Florence looked at *Mamm* to see if she might've noticed what was going on, but she was busily talking with Ada.

When Christina interrupted them and started talking about her prayer *kapps*, Florence was surprised. Whenever Christina had been there for a meal she'd sat at their dinner table looking glum and hardly saying anything at all.

Florence took hold of her glass, raised it to her lips and took a mouthful of water, observing everyone as though she was an outsider. Christina became even livelier when Ada said she might order a *kapp*.

AFTER DINNER when the guests sat in the living room to wait for coffee and chocolate cake, Honor noticed Jonathon making faces at her. He was trying to tell her something. Then he nodded to his hand and she saw a slip of paper. He had a note to give her. He stood up and she walked close to him and the note was slipped into her hand without anyone seeing.

She slipped the note down the front of her apron as she went past him and on into the kitchen. She tried to help to prepare the dessert, until she was shooed out of the kitchen because it was her special day.

When they were all seated with coffee and hot teas, Caramel, Cherish's dog, rushed downstairs. He jumped on Isaac, sending his coffee flying all over the rug.

"Bad dog." Cherish grabbed his collar and put him outside.

Isaac stood, stunned, and looked down at the coffee. Florence told him not to worry about it.

"I'm so sorry, Mrs. Baker."

"That's okay. It wasn't your fault."

"Caramel doesn't usually behave like that. He just doesn't like you," Jonathon said to Isaac, and everyone laughed.

"Seems so," Isaac replied with a grin.

"Sorry, Isaac. I've got no idea why he did that. He takes a liking to some people and not others," Cherish said.

Isaac sat down again. "Does that mean he likes me?"

"*Nee,* he doesn't. He likes Jonathon, though." Cherish smiled at Jonathon.

Jonathon said to Cherish, "Are you going to leave him out there all night?"

"*Nee.* I'll get him now and put him back in my room."

Honor was pleased to see that Jonathon liked animals.

It wasn't until all the guests left that night that Honor sat in her bedroom along with her gift of pink roses to read Jonathon's note.

Meet me tomorrow night outside your house. I'll be there at midnight. I'll throw three tiny pebbles at your window then you climb out your window onto the tree and I'll be waiting for you. Now destroy this note, my love.

She ripped the note into tiny pieces and placed it in the water under the roses so no one would find it. Then she opened her window and looked out. He knew which bedroom window was hers, because she'd pointed it out at Mercy's wedding. He must've noticed that big tree that grew in front of the window alongside the house. *Jah,* she could easily step onto the tree and climb down. In their younger years, she and her sisters had been expert tree climbers. There was little else to do on summer afternoons in the orchard.

CHAPTER 3

JONATHON LOOKED over at Honor as his horse clip-clopped along the road under the amber glow of the sinking sun.

"Why did you give me that note when you knew you were seeing me tonight?" The question had been bugging her since the previous night.

"I just wanted to pass you a note." He smiled at her and she giggled. "You'll never be bored with me," he said.

"I'm learning that."

"You will meet me tonight, won't you? When everyone's asleep?"

"I'd like that."

"Good."

He settled back into his seat. "Isn't night-time volleyball a crazy thing?"

Honor didn't care two hoots about volleyball. Any excuse would've done to be alone with Jonathon. She'd liked him ever since she met him at the harvest, but she had been too shy to say much to him. Things were different now. "The Yoders have night volleyball quite a bit. We stop as soon as it gets too dark, and then we eat and sit around talking."

"Eating and talking are two of my favorite things to do."

Honor giggled. She stared at Jonathon as he concentrated on the road. Against the backdrop of the golden sun she noticed tiny pinpoints of freckles covering his nose and cheeks. It made him look younger than his twenty-three years. "How are you settling in at Mark and Christina's place?"

"Fine. I don't want to be there forever. I need to make a plan to move out. I was talking to Isaac about moving out with me but he seems quite happy doing what he's doing."

"Living with his sister while you're living in the stable, you mean?"

"It's not the stables exactly."

She giggled. "I know. I was only teasing. We heard all about that at my birthday dinner."

"That's right. It's off from the stable, and it's like my own little apartment."

"It sounds cozy. I'd reckon that Isaac's sorry he didn't get to live there."

He chuckled. "He missed it by a day, along with the job at their saddlery store. They'd already promised it to me before they knew Isaac wanted to move here. That's why I feel bad. I figured if Isaac wanted to move out with me, it'd be cheaper with the two of us and we could get a better place."

"Maybe he'll move out soon. When he gets a job."

"I don't think he's going anywhere. I've got an idea he likes someone, but he won't say who. That's why he moved here. I'm not going home that's for certain. It's going to be too crowded there with Mercy and Stephen. At least I've got somewhere to stay and I can stick around here and be close to you."

When he smiled at her she was so happy it felt like one million tiny butterflies had been set loose inside her chest, and all were flapping their wings hard.

"How was your day at the markets?" he asked.

"It was fine, but we're way down toward the back. I'm going to see if we can be moved forward. That might mean we have to pay extra. I don't know how much. We did make more money than at the roadside stand, though."

"It sounds like it was a good move then. It was your idea, wasn't it?"

"It was, this time around. Florence wanted to do it a while ago, but *Mamm* said no back then. But it just makes sense in the cold weather. It'll also be better in the hotter weather if we get to stay there."

BY NOW, people knew Honor and Jonathon liked each other, and there was also an implied understanding between them. Even though no words had been spoken, they were boyfriend and girlfriend.

When they stopped at the Yoder's house they were surprised there were no buggies out front. "Are we early?" Honor asked.

"A little late if anything."

Brett Yoder opened the front door of his house and slowly walked over to them. "Hi, you two. I didn't think anyone was coming so I called it off."

"I said I was coming," Honor told him.

Brett shrugged his shoulders. "Yeah, well I thought you said you *might* come. I'm sorry."

"No harm done," Jonathon said.

"Stay for dinner? It's not ready yet and *Mamm* will love it if you do."

"*Nee,* we couldn't."

"*Jah,* stay. I'll just tell *Mamm* we've got two more people for dinner. She won't mind, she always cooks plenty."

Honor stepped forward. "*Nee* don't. It's okay. We've got somewhere else we can be since the volleyball's not on."

"Are you sure?"

"Quite sure."

"I'm sorry. Everyone else said it's too cold for volleyball now. I can't see why. Volleyball would warm everyone up."

"The days are shorter." Jonathon looked up into the sky. "I think there's only about half an hour of daylight left."

"I guess so. But we didn't have to do volleyball. I'll have to think of something else we can do in the wintertime."

"*Jah,* think up something else, and we'll come to that. Just let us know."

Brett nodded.

"Bye, Brett." Honor was happy since she realized she could have secret time alone with Jonathon. Everyone at home thought she was at volleyball. They could take their time getting back.

"See ya later." Brett stood there, and lifted his hand in a half-hearted wave.

Jonathon gave him a nod and then Honor walked back to the buggy. Jonathon had to hurry to keep up with her. "What's the rush?"

"I'm trying to get away so his *mudder* doesn't see us and make us stay for dinner. If she knows we're here she'll also tell *Mamm* we didn't stay. Oh, unless … you're not taking me home right now, are you?"

"Not until I have to."

She smiled as they climbed into the buggy at the same time.

He took hold of the reins and clicked his horse onward. "We'll take the time to have some alone time, the two of us. Is that what you had in mind too?"

She looked at him and nodded. "I'd like nothing more. I was hoping we'd be able to sneak away from the volleyball anyway." She gave a little giggle.

"It suits me just fine. Where do you want to go?"

"Anywhere, I don't care."

"Where can we go so none of your family will pass us and know we're not at the Yoder's house?"

She directed him down a quiet road and then suggested he pull over to the side. "Now we can be alone to talk."

He looked over at her as he looped the reins over one hand. "Good. What do you want to do in life? Where do you see your life headed?"

"I want to help in the orchard with Florence and *Mamm*."

"I like it around here too. I've liked it here ever since I first arrived."

"What do you remember about me from when you first arrived?"

He chuckled. "Just that there were a bunch of Baker sisters."

"So, you don't remember me?"

"I do. I just didn't want to say it."

That pleased her even more.

"I must admit I feel awful about the fuss that happened with Mercy and Stephen. I was just having a bit of fun with both of them. I didn't know she'd take it the extra step. It made me look like a real cad."

"I know. I think Florence is still mad. She's been so protective over all of us since *Dat* died, and *Mamm's* gone the other way."

"It must be hard to have a parent die."

"It's so hard. *Dat* wasn't even there to see Mark and Christina get married, the first of his *kinner,* or Mercy, and he won't see any of us get married, either. I find it sad."

"Maybe he can see everything from where he is."

She shrugged her shoulders. "I'd like to know if that's right. I don't think we'll ever know."

Slowly he nodded. "I'll tell you something."

"What is it?"

He ruffled his hair. "I don't know if I should've done it but I had a talk with Mark and told him Isaac could have the job."

"What did he say?"

"He wouldn't hear of it. He said I got the job and he's not going to give the job to Isaac just because he's his *bruder*-in-law."

"That was nice of you."

"Or stupid." He chuckled. "At least I still have a job. It's four days a week but it's still a job. I'm not going anywhere now. Now that I've found you I never want to leave."

CHAPTER 4

LATER THAT NIGHT Jonathon brought Honor home at a reasonable hour to keep *Mamm* and Florence happy. After that, when everyone had gone to bed, Honor sat up waiting for Jonathon. When she heard the three tiny pebbles hit the window, she flew into action.

She pulled on two extra pairs of thick stockings, threw a shawl over her shoulders, and slipped into a coat. Then she opened her window slightly. The chilly night air swept into the room and in that moment she had second thoughts about the adventure looming ahead. Spurred on by the thought of seeing Jonathon, she looked out the window. It was a long way down, but aided by the large tree she knew she could easily make it to the ground.

Jonathon's idea had been for her to step out and hang onto the tree and climb down it. That was something she'd never attempted before. Climbing up trees yes, and then back down, but never before had she stepped onto a tree from a height.

When she opened the window further, she sat on the windowsill and looked around for Jonathon. She couldn't see him anywhere. He had to be there somewhere, keeping out of sight. Once she sat on the window frame, she pulled the window down as much as she could, fearing the wind would whistle under her door and through the house and someone would come to find where the cold air was getting in. Now she sat with the window pulled down on her legs.

She took hold of a branch and slipped her legs out of the house until her feet reached a branch. Once she was out, she slid along closer to the tree trunk. Branch by branch she lowered herself, but when she put her foot on the lowest branch, she heard a cracking sound.

Instantly, she knew she was in trouble. The branch gave way beneath her feet, leaving her hanging by her hands. She looked down at the ground. It was too far to jump, but she had no choice. Then the strength in her arms failed, leaving her crashing to the hard ground below.

Pain shot through her foot. She had twisted it when she'd landed on it. She called out in pain. Her sisters or her mother hearing her cries was the last thing on her mind.

Where was Jonathon? Now she was worried that he hadn't tossed those pebbles on the window. Maybe he wasn't there at all. While she was envisioning herself yelling for help at the top of her lungs and having to tell her family she'd fallen out the window, she heard rustling in the nearby bushes. Was it a bear or a wolf?

"Honor, are you okay?" she heard Jonathon whisper as he rushed toward her.

"Do I look like I'm okay?" she snapped.

"I don't know. I can't see you in the dark."

"I fell out of that darn tree when the last branch snapped, and broke my foot," she hissed.

"For real?"

"*Jah*. Where were you?"

"I was waiting for you where we arranged to meet."

"Your note said you'd be waiting when I climbed out of the tree. Weren't you watching?"

"I wasn't. I was trying to find a spot where we could talk."

"That doesn't make sense."

He sighed. "I was answering the call of nature if you must know."

"Don't tell me that!"

"Well, you kept asking. Put your arm around my neck."

She reached her arm up and hung onto him. He lifted her up and carried her a distance from the tree and laid her down on soft grass. Then, when she straightened her leg, he took off one shoe.

"It's the other foot," she whispered.

"Sorry." Slowly, he eased off the other shoe while she groaned in pain. Once it was off, he asked, "Can you wiggle your toes?"

"I can, but it hurts."

"I don't think it's broken."

"Is that right?" she snapped. "Since when did you become a doctor?"

"I'm only trying to help you, Honor."

"Well you're not helping. It was your idea to meet at night, so it's all your fault."

"Are you blaming me for you falling out of the tree?"

"Yeah. It was your idea." Honor sobbed and he put his arm around her and patted her back. "What am I going to do now? I can't walk inside because everybody will see me and then they'll know I've been out with you. And I'll be grounded for the rest of my entire life and I won't be allowed out until I'm thirty."

He looked up at the tree. "Yeah, it's pretty high up to your bedroom. You might have to sneak back into the *haus.*"

"I won't even make it up the stairs."

"It won't be as bad as you're saying."

"It will. If only *Dat* was still alive. I hate it here now." She sobbed into her hands. Her whole life had changed since her father died. It wasn't the happy home she'd once had.

"Do you?" he asked.

"Jah, and now I'm going to be stuck here until I'm thirty because of this—because of you."

In the moonlight she saw him smiling at her. "That won't happen. I'll wait for you."

"You will?" She was starting to forgive him a little.

"Of course."

"You'd wait until I was thirty and ignore every other woman in the world?"

"I'd wait forever for you. Forever and a day."

She found herself smiling and then tried to move her foot a little. "Oh, it still hurts."

"Don't move it for a while. Give it a rest. Let's talk to take your mind off it. How was your day?"

"We've talked about today just hours ago."

"Let's pretend this is the first time we've seen each other today."

She was willing to do anything to take her mind off her leg. "Fine. I was looking forward to seeing you all day."

He gave a low chuckle. "Me too. I was looking forward to seeing you. I'm so sorry you hurt your foot. You don't blame me, do you?"

"Jah, I do. If I hadn't been coming out to see you then I wouldn't have broken my foot."

"I said I don't think it's broken."

"I'll listen to your medical opinion when you become a doctor. Right now, you can stop telling me it's not broken when it is. It's obvious."

He was silent for a moment. "I've heard that if you have a broken leg you can't wiggle your toes."

"It might be all right, but I won't be able to get back up that tree. Anyway, it's my foot that's broken and not my leg."

"Let's not keep saying the same things. That gets boring real fast."

"Shh. Keep your voice down."

"You, shh."

"Jonathon Wilkes, don't you ever shush me. I don't like the way you speak to me sometimes. I won't take it."

"I'm sorry. I won't do it again."

"I hate being in pain. I haven't been sick for years. Never even had a cold. I'm sorry for being so mean to you, but I'm thinking of how much trouble I'm going to get into and ..."

"Yeah, I know. Florence already hates me and she'll stop us seeing one another. I know, but I have the answer."

"What?"

"I'll carry you up the tree on my back."

"Don't be stupid."

"There's no other way apart from knocking on the front door and you don't want to do that."

She looked over at the tree and wondered if he could possibly do it. It would take great strength. "What if we both fall?"

"Then I'll have a soft landing."

She slapped him on his shoulder. "I'd rather fall on you. That would be fairer."

"Then you carry me up."

She huffed. "We could give it a try. I'm heavier than I look."

"I doubt it. You'd weigh the same as a feather. Let's do it." He leaned over and scooped her into his arms.

"This isn't going to work!"

"It will. Have a little faith." He smiled and then placed her carefully back down onto her feet. Then he crouched down. "Get on my back and hang on. Don't let go for anything."

"I won't and if you drop me, I'll never talk to you again." She leaned forward and placed her arms around his neck and then he started his climb up the tree.

He made gagging sounds. "You're choking me," he whispered.

"I'm sorry." She eased the grip around his neck.

"Hold onto my shoulders instead."

"Okay."

"No! Hold onto me around my neck but try not to cut off my airway."

"I'll try." She readjusted her arms. "Is that better?"

"Jah." He reached up and grabbed hold of the branch, but then he couldn't get further. "It's no use like this. It'll work if I had something to stand on to get me started."

"There's a chair in the barn. Would that work?"

"Where in the barn?"

"Just to the left as you go in."

"You stay here, I'll fetch it." He leaned over and she put her feet onto the ground and then he carefully lowered her.

"Just don't let anyone see you," she whispered.

"I'll do my best." A couple of minutes later he was back with a chair. "I'll get up first, and then you stand on the chair. Get on my back when I tell you."

"Okay."

He stepped onto the chair. "Come on."

She hobbled over and then with him holding onto the branch with one hand and the other under her arm, he hoisted her onto the chair.

"Now hang on."

She jumped onto his back and he groaned.

"Told you I was heavy."

"Don't let go." Inch by inch he made his way up the tree while she ducked her head around the branches. By the time they got to the top, she was relieved. While he stood on a branch that was level with the window, he pulled up her window and turned around so she could move herself in.

Once she was inside, he slipped through the window after her.

"You can't be in here!" she whispered.

"I need to check on your foot."

She hobbled over to the bed and sat down. "I think it's getting swollen."

He looked at it in the warm glow of the kerosene lamp on her nightstand. "It's not too bad."

"It hurts."

"Go to sleep and it might be better by morning." He pulled back the covers for her and she took off her shawl and, still fully clothed, she got into bed. Then he pulled the covers up over her. He kneeled down beside her bed. "When can I see you again?"

"I don't want to go to the markets tomorrow, but I know Florence will force me. She makes us work when we're sick and she won't care about my foot. I'll have to say I jumped out of bed the wrong way." She sighed, not wanting to lie.

"Will you meet me there at the markets?"

"Won't someone see us together?" she asked.

"I don't care. I have to see you."

"*Jah,* me too," she whispered back. "I'll be working on the stall with one of my sisters."

"Is there one of them you can trust?"

"*Nee,* not one. Mercy would've kept my secret, but she was the only one."

"That's too bad. Keep an eye out for me at the markets, then when you see me tell your sister you have to go to the bathroom. By then I would've come up with a plan for us to meet regularly."

"You sure?"

"*Jah,* I can't not see you."

She whispered, "Me too."

"*Gut nacht,* my sweet." He leaned down and kissed her softly on her forehead.

"*Gut nacht,* my love."

He got to the window and once he'd gotten a hold of the tree, he slowly closed her window.

The way he'd taken care of her convinced her Florence was wrong. He was a good person and so patient when she'd been so mean. That was just the kind of man she wanted for a husband. She recalled Mercy saying that when you're in love with someone you just know it's right. That's how she felt about Jonathon. She just knew it was right.

CHAPTER 5

THE NEXT MORNING, no one could get Honor out of bed. She was whining about a sore foot and when she didn't get sympathy over that, it had swiftly traveled from her foot to her head. Now she was complaining of a headache.

Finally, she got out of bed and left for the markets with Favor, complaining all the while about what Florence knew was a fake sore foot, and a fake headache.

Once Favor and Honor left and the remainder of the girls were consumed with baking bread, Florence took the opportunity to sit down to have a restful cup of hot tea with *Mamm*. She liked these quiet moments when she got *Mamm* to herself.

"I'm worried about Honor," *Mamm* said. "She's never sick. She's always been the strong one out of them all."

"She was only pretending to get out of work. It's cold and she wants to stay in bed, that's all. I suppose I don't blame her in a way. It's nice to have a break sometimes. It is surprising because I've always seen Honor as the sensible one."

"I know." *Mamm* slowly nodded. "I wouldn't have thought she'd be the one who wouldn't want to go. The market stall was all her idea."

"Well, you *have* spoiled her. That's why she thinks she's entitled to stay in. She doesn't realize the value of hard work."

Mamm looked over at Florence. "You think I've spoiled her?"

"*Jah*." Florence laughed. "I think you spoil them all, but Cherish more so. Possibly because she's the youngest."

"It's only because she was so ill when she was younger and I'm so grateful to have her still here with us."

Before Florence could reply, they heard a horse coming to the house. At first Florence was worried that it was the girls back from the markets, but when the sound got louder, Florence knew it was a buggy rather than a wagon.

Mamm looked out the window. "It's Levi Bruner. Whatever is he doing here?" *Mamm* looked very pleased and then Florence recalled that the two of them had been talking a lot at Mercy's wedding.

Levi was a widower with three older children. Two of them had moved communities to marry and the third one, Bliss, was a friend of Favor and Hope's.

Florence walked to the door with Wilma and when they opened it, they saw Levi with a horse tethered to the back of his buggy.

He walked over to them smiling and took off his hat. After he nodded to Florence, he said to Wilma, "I have a spare horse and I thought with all your *dochders* you might be able to use an extra buggy horse. They could go out more and you wouldn't have to drive them everywhere."

Mamm stepped forward. "You're giving us a horse?"

"*Jah*. Do you like him?" He pointed to the tall bay horse with long black glossy mane and tail.

"He's beautiful, isn't he Florence?"

"He surely is, but we can't accept something like this Levi. Honestly, we can't."

Levi wasn't offended; he simply chuckled. "I don't see why. He's an extra horse for me and one I don't need. I bought him at an auction on impulse." He looked back at the tall bay horse and then turned and smiled at Wilma. "He was the last horse in the program and I reckon everyone had already bought. I got him and I don't use him. I thought you might be able to use him."

"*Jah*, I think we could use him. *Denke*. The girls will be pleased."

Florence frowned wondering why a man would want the girls to go out more and, anyway, where would they go? "*Denke*, Levi, that's very kind. We were just having some hot tea. Would you like to join us?"

"*Jah*, I would. Where shall I put the horse?"

Florence pointed to the front paddock. "There's a gate just near where you stopped your buggy."

He turned around. "I see it. I'll put the horse there."

"Very well." Florence and *Mamm* moved back inside the house.

"Why did you say we'd have the horse?"

"It's a gift and it's rude not to accept a gift."

"Do you believe that story he just told?"

A smile hinted around *Mamm's* lips. "I have no reason not to."

"I think he likes you. He might be thinking of making you his next *fraa*."

Mamm laughed. "Don't be ridiculous, Florence. I'm too old for that now."

Wilma wasn't too old. She was only in her mid-forties and that wasn't old at all. Florence wasn't sure how old Levi was, but she was certain he was somewhere around sixty.

Florence headed to the kitchen to re-boil the kettle and her sisters were still there, busy with bread making. They'd overheard the whole thing and couldn't stop giggling. Florence told them all to keep the noise down and stay in the kitchen until their visitor left. One thing was for certain, Florence was not going to be polite and leave *Mamm* and Levi alone together.

CHAPTER 6

WHILE THE THREE of them sat down in the living room drinking hot tea, there were many awkward silences. Levi kept glancing sideways at Florence most likely wishing she'd leave so he could be alone with Wilma, but Florence stayed.

"What's the horse's name?" Florence asked.

The man stared at her for a while until he finally answered. "Wilbur."

Florence couldn't help being amused. He'd made up that name right then and it was suspiciously close in sound to Wilma. He had probably come straight from the auction with the horse to give to *Mamm*. And why give Wilma a horse? That was something Florence couldn't figure out. Perhaps because a horse was a costly purchase and he wanted to show Wilma his feelings were real.

Florence looked over at her stepmother as Levi talked. There was no hint on Wilma's facial expressions or in her eyes that she liked Levi as anything more than a friend.

"Wilma, why don't you and I try the horse out now?" Levi smiled hopefully at Wilma.

There it was—a possible reason, albeit a very extravagant one to get *Mamm* alone in a buggy with him.

Wilma was silent for a moment, and then said, "Any other time I would, but Honor isn't feeling too well."

Florence raised her eyebrows. She'd never known Wilma to lie or even exaggerate. It wasn't a lie exactly, but Levi would've definitely got the impression that Honor was upstairs sick in bed.

"Might Florence be able to watch her?"

Mamm shook her head.

Florence helped her out. "I'm not the most tolerant or sympathetic person with the sick. I'm used to trees. If I have a sick tree, I cut off a branch or cut it down altogether. Then I burn—"

Wilma cleared her throat. "We get your point, Florence."

"I'm sorry." Florence had been getting carried away. When Levi nodded and just sat there, Florence felt slightly sorry for him. "I'll be happy to take a ride with you if you'd like, Levi?"

Levi blinked rapidly, and then said, "I just remembered I have an appointment in town. I'm sorry, Florence. It went clean out of my mind."

"That's perfectly all right. What I might do then is take Wilbur out myself. He's fully trained and everything, isn't he?"

"Yeah, he's a *wunderbaar* buggy horse."

"We're so grateful for him. We really appreciate it don't we, *Mamm?*"

Wilma nodded vigorously. "We do appreciate it. *Denke* for thinking of our family, Levi."

Levi stood. "I'm happy to help since my two boys have moved out and it's only me and Bliss at home now. Her cooking's not too good since her *mudder* went home to God when she was small. She hasn't had good training."

Florence tried to stop smiling, certain he was angling for a dinner invite.

Wilma didn't seem to notice. "I'm looking forward to Florence telling me how the horse travels. I'm sure he's a *wunderbaar* horse. *Denke* again, Levi."

They both walked him outside. Then they watched him get into his buggy, turn the horse and buggy around and head back down the driveway.

Florence turned to her stepmother. "He likes you a lot."

"*Ach nee!*" Wilma giggled covering her mouth with her hand. "Do you think so?"

They walked back into the house. "Why else would he give you a horse? And he wanted to go on a buggy ride with you too. Did you see his face when I suggested I go with him to try out the horse? And *Wilbur?* Do you really think that was the horse's name? He had your name on his mind. Wilbur is so close to Wilma it's not funny. Or maybe it is..."

The girls came out of the kitchen and asked their mother what was going on. Florence knew from their smiling faces they'd overheard the whole thing. Now that Florence's quiet time with her stepmother was ruined, she figured she'd try out the new horse. "I'll go for that drive, *Mamm.*"

"Good idea."

Florence left the house and walked over to the horse with a quarter of an apple in her hand. Wilbur looked over at her as soon as she opened the gate. Then he walked over to her and politely took the apple out of her hand and she took the opportunity to slip a lead around his neck.

He didn't so much as flinch when she put the harness on and he even backed nicely into the buggy.

Pleased about the idea of a nice ride alone, Florence set off. She'd only just gotten out of the driveway when a silver car came toward her, a hand waving out the window.

"What now?" she muttered as she looked in the rear view mirror and pulled her horse to a stop. When the car got closer, she saw it was Carter from next door.

He stopped his car beside her.

"Is that another car?" This was a sedan, and the only one she'd seen before was the white SUV.

"It's a new one. I got tired of the old one."

She smiled and wondered if he might get bored with people just as easily. Is that why he was alone? Wilbur snorted. "This is a new horse. His name is Wilbur."

"That's a coincidence. That's also the name of my car."

She had to laugh at the ridiculous look on his face. He was making fun of her and she was in a good mood and didn't mind playing along. "That's an unusual name for a car. Do you normally name your cars?"

"Just this one. What do you think of her ... I mean him?"

"Beautiful, but I think your last one was a little more practical for the country lifestyle, don't you?"

He smiled and wagged a finger at her. "You and I both know that I'm not very country."

"I knew it, but I didn't .... I wasn't sure if you did."

He chuckled. "Where are you headed?"

"Nowhere, really. I'm just trying out the new horse."

He turned his head and looked at the horse. "You never did see my new bathroom and kitchen."

"I will one day."

"Would you like to? I don't want you to feel I'm forcing you."

"Yes. I'd like to see what it looks like now."

"Don't get too excited. The rest of it's the same as the day I moved in."

She nodded not knowing what else to say. One thing she knew was that she didn't want to spend too much time talking with him, but it was hard not to when he was so friendly.

"What about tomorrow?" he asked.

She gulped not expecting him to set a time. "Tomorrow isn't a good day because— "

"The day after?"

She laughed. "You're getting too far ahead of me. What I was trying to say is that we're busy now with the new stall at the farmers market. We have to keep up the supply of things to sell and I have to help the girls in the kitchen."

He pulled his mouth to one side. "What about your bonnet sisters? Couldn't they do without you? There are enough of them."

She rolled her eyes, hating it when he called them that. "I have to supervise."

"Ah, you have to crack the whip?"

"Basically."

His deep hazel eyes stared at her while his head tilted slightly to the side. "Do you really have to work as hard as you do?"

"It's good to work hard."

"No, it's not. Not if you never have any fun and you're not enjoying life. What's the point of living if every day is dull and the same as the one before?"

"My life's not dull." *It wouldn't matter if it was,* she thought. He didn't understand that she didn't live for this life. This life was like the blink of an eye. She looked around to see if any cars or buggies were coming so she'd have an excuse to drive away. "I'm not enjoying life. I mean… What I meant to say was that I am enjoying life."

"Is that right?"

She smiled. "Yes."

"What do you do for fun?" He held up his hand. "Without telling me anything about your apple trees. Other than the orchard, which you'd probably tell me is fun, what do you do?" He lowered his hand.

"I like to sew."

"And?"

She sighed and thought hard about what she'd do if she had unlimited time all to herself. "When I have time at some point, I'm interested in finding early varieties of apples. Ones that are hundreds of years old. My father was trying to do that before he died."

He rested his arm on the window and stuck his head out further. "Is that so?"

She nodded.

"Is that what you want to do, or you want to do it because your father wanted to?"

"I want to do it for myself."

"Tell me about these apples. I never knew they existed. I thought an apple was just an apple. Other than there are green ones and red ones, I know nothing."

She had hoped her enthusiasm for rare apple varieties would bore him, but he seemed more interested. "They do exist, and there are a handful of growers around now trying to get their hands on these varieties."

"Interesting ... and do these particular apples have names?"

She thought for a moment. It had been a while since she'd read her father's journals. "The Narragansett and the Blake."

"And they're hard to find?"

"They are. My father traveled to his cousin's wedding a few years ago and drove past a Blake apple tree in someone's backyard. They let him take a branch for grafting. They didn't know what it was, but my father knew. I was so excited when he brought it home. He'd been talking about wanting to get one of those trees ever since I can remember."

"There's more to you than I first thought."

She laughed. "I'm not sure if that's a compliment."

"It is, and please take it as one."

Wilbur stomped his hoof on the ground a couple of times while snorting. Florence giggled. "That's my signal to move on."

"Hey, Wilbur, you'll have to cut that out. I wasn't finished talking yet." He revved his car. "Now your Wilbur has given my Wilbur a bad example."

She laughed again. "I might see you outside your house one day and I'll come and look at that new kitchen and bathroom."

"Please do." He gave her a smile then put his hand out the window and patted his car door. "Come on, Wilbur, let's go home." Then without so much as a smile or a backward glance, he drove away.

Laughing once more, she moved her horse onward, happier for having seen him.

CHAPTER 7

MEANWHILE AT THE MARKETS, Honor was excited that Jonathon came to see her. She left Favor there and limped away so her sister wouldn't hear them talk.

"I didn't think you'd be here."

"I said I'd be here." He looked down. "How's your foot?"

"It's okay. It's not broken. It's getting better. I can walk on it."

"Just as well for me or you'd never let me forget it."

She giggled.

"Christina asked me to ask you something."

"What is it?"

"Would you come to their place for dinner?"

Honor was more than a little shocked. "Me?"

He smiled and nodded. "That's right. I'll be there too, of course."

"To dinner?" she squeaked.

He chuckled. "Why are you talking like that?"

"In the whole time she's been married, I've never known her to invite anybody over for dinner. Not even *Mamm.*"

"She's invited you."

"And who else?"

He shrugged his shoulders. "I'm not sure."

"Isaac?"

"*Nee,* he won't be with us tomorrow night."

"She's invited me for dinner tomorrow night?"

"That's right. And … what shall I tell her?"

"Tell her yes, of course."

He smiled. "It's another way for us to see each other. I'll collect you, and bring you back to your place when the dinner is over."

"Did you ask her to invite me?"

He shook his head. "She just offered. Maybe because they came to your birthday dinner?"

"*Nee.* It couldn't be that. They come to all our birthday dinners and she's never felt obligated to repay that in any way."

"Maybe she's got a new recipe she's trying out."

"Or, she might've changed. She was nicer at my birthday than I've ever seen her and she made me that *kapp*. Do you think I should wear it to her place for dinner?"

"That would be a way of showing your appreciation, I reckon."

"Okay." She hoped she hadn't said too much. She was talking as though Christina was a mean person. "I hope you don't think anything bad about Christina. I like her and everything, it's just that the dinner thing is a bit out of character."

"People can change. Look at me."

"What do you mean?"

"I've become a better person because of you. Same with Isaac. He tells me there's someone he likes. I can see him growing softer and growing up a bit."

"You've only known him a week."

"Sometimes that's all it takes," he said with a grin.

"I wonder who he likes?" Honor tapped her chin with her finger.

"I got the feeling it was one of your sisters."

"*Nee,* it couldn't be. He's not been near the *haus* other than at the wedding."

He shrugged his shoulders. "Maybe I'm wrong, but he arrived here for Mercy's wedding and now he's stayed on. Only because he's met someone, that's my guess. What about Joy? She's the next oldest to you, isn't she?"

"It wouldn't be her. I don't think anyone would be good enough for Joy unless they could recite the Bible backwards and forwards and then backwards again."

He chuckled. "We've talked a fair bit and he hasn't offered the information about exactly who he likes, so I was polite enough not to ask."

Honor nodded. "Since you've talked, does Isaac ever tell you what Christina was like when they were growing up?"

"He said they went their separate ways most of the time. She's older and they weren't really that close, but he likes Mark. He said he's been a *gut bruder*-in-law."

"In what way? They didn't even give him a job at the saddlery." She was teasing him and she was glad he didn't take it seriously.

"He would've been a bit disappointed to hear he missed the job by about one day. But it wasn't meant to be and something else will turn up for him. Probably something he's better suited for. I didn't know if I could be confined within four walls of a store all the daylong. I like to be out in the fresh air doing things with my hands, but I've coped well. It's a good job and the business is doing well, so the job's secure."

"I hope so."

Suddenly Honor felt someone pull her arm. She turned to see it was Favor. "I need help back there."

"I'm coming. I was just talking to Jonathon. Go back. I'll be there in a minute."

Favor clamped her lips together in a clearly dissatisfied manner, and then turned and walked away.

"I have to go."

"Yeah, me too," he said.

They smiled at one another before they went their separate ways.

WHEN HONOR ARRIVED HOME, she told everybody Christina had invited her to dinner—everybody was just as shocked as she'd been.

"Why are you going there for dinner?" Joy asked.

"I'm not sure, but Jonathon told me Christina invited me."

"Us too?" Cherish asked.

"*Nee.*"

"What about me?" Joy asked.

"She just said none of us," Favor said. "She especially wouldn't want to ask you."

Joy's mouth fell open. "Stop being so mean."

"Stop it all of you!" *Mamm* said. "You girls will be the death of me one day, the way you argue all the time."

Joy said, "it's not me, it's her." She pointed at Favor. "You should do something about her, *Mamm.* She's so disrespectful."

Florence said, "All of you be quiet and that includes you, Joy. You heard *Mamm.*" Florence looked over at Honor. "When are you going for this dinner?"

"Tomorrow night."

"She must want you to marry Jonathon," Hope said with a giggle.

"There's no need to rush into anything, Honor," *Mamm* said.

"I'm not going to get married any time soon, don't worry about that." Honor smiled.

"I didn't know how much I would miss Mercy, and I'm in no hurry to lose any more of you."

"You should've thought of that before you had Stephen to dinner, *Mamm,*" Favor said.

"And had him help with the harvest," added Joy.

Cherish said, "It wasn't *Mamm's* idea, it was Ada's. She said it was planned all along to marry off her nephew."

Florence held her head. All of this chatter was making it ache.

CHAPTER 8

ON FRIDAY, Jonathon brought Honor to Christina and Mark's house for dinner. They stood at the closed front door and smiled at one another for a moment before Jonathon lifted his hand to knock.

The door swung open and Christina smiled immediately. "*Ach,* Honor, you're wearing my prayer *kapp*."

Honor touched the strings of the carefully made *kapp*. "I am and I love it."

Christina grinned. "Be sure to tell everyone where you got it. That'll help me sell a few more."

"Sure, I'll do that. It would be nice to be able to sew as good as you."

"There's no reason why you can't. It's only being shown what to do and then doing it over and over again. Hasn't Florence shown you how?"

"*Jah,* but we've only got one sewing machine and it belongs to Florence. It's one of those treadle ones. It can be converted to use a gas-powered motor, but mostly we don't do that."

"Same as mine. I would offer you to come over here and sew, but I'll be on my machine most of the time."

"*Denke* anyway."

Christina then smiled and laughed as she stepped aside to allow them through. "Sorry to leave you standing at the door in the cold. I was just so pleased to see you wearing my *kapp*, Honor."

"Well, it's hers now," Jonathon said.

Christina laughed. This was a different Christina from the one Honor knew. She was being extra nice and friendly. Both Christina and Mark got along well with Jonathon, so perhaps he'd told Christina his feelings and she was helping the two of them develop their relationship. Having both Christina and Mark approve of Jonathon reinforced her feelings for him. It made things difficult with Florence being so against him.

Christina sat them down with Mark in the living room.

After they greeted Mark, Jonathon said, "Tell us how you two met."

Mark chuckled and looked over at Christina. "We were both on *rumspringa* when we met. Being from different communities, I didn't even know she was Amish. We returned and got married and she moved here. Then we wanted to open a business together and that's when we heard about the saddlery being for sale."

"Ah, a real romance story," Jonathon said.

"Can I help you with anything in the kitchen?" Honor asked Christina when she stood up.

"*Nee*, I'm fine. Everything is fine."

Honor sat down next to Mark and the conversation drifted into work.

When there was a pause, Honor asked, "Where is Isaac tonight?"

"We don't see him much anymore. He comes and goes when he pleases. He doesn't need to check in with us."

"I realize that, but I just thought he might have said where he was going." When they both stared at her she realized it sounded like she cared too much where Isaac was. She coughed. "It's just that someone had asked me if he'd be here tonight, that's all."

"Has an admirer, does he?" Mark chuckled.

"Hardly, he's a bit old for that."

"But that doesn't stop one of your sisters having a crush on him," Jonathon pointed out mischievously.

"Dinner is ready now," Christina called out.

They all moved to the kitchen. When they all sat around the cramped table with barely room for four people, Honor realized why they rarely invited people to the house. There was simply no room unless some of the people sat on the couch with their dinner on their laps. Then as Mark sat down, Honor's gaze swept over the food. There was a large dish of something that looked like bologna, and a green salad, potato salad, cooked ham and gravy.

Once all of them were seated, they each bowed their heads and gave a silent prayer of thanks for the food.

When Honor opened her eyes, she looked again at the food. "This all looks so good."

"So long as it tastes good," Christina said. Christina then stood and dished out the food onto everybody's plates.

After that, everyone was quiet for a while as they ate the first couple of mouthfuls. Then Honor thought it was best to compliment Christina on the food, even though it wasn't that great. That's what their dinner guests did at home, but they probably meant it. "Mmm, this is nice, Christina."

"Denke."

"Jah, it is. The wedding went well the other day," Mark said to Honor.

"It did. It was the first one in *Mamm's* house. Since you got married in Christina's community at her parents' *haus."*

"I'd reckon *Mamm's* still talking about that, is she?" Mark asked.

Christina smiled. "She wasn't too happy about that."

"Wasn't she?" Jonathon asked.

Mark shook his head. "I can't say I don't understand. She would've wanted me to get married here. Since we had planned on living here after we were married, I should've got married surrounded by her friends in the community where I was raised. She didn't exactly say that, but that's a roundabout way of saying what she thought."

Honor recalled all the fuss at the time. It wasn't long after *Dat* died and *Mamm* insisted it was too far to travel and too much trouble to go to Mark's wedding. Was that why Christina was a little frosty with *Mamm* and acted standoffish with the rest of the family?

Of course, there were two sides to everything and Honor hadn't heard *Mamm's,* but she wasn't going to ask. "What's it like to have your *bruder* around all the time, Christina?"

"Good. I've really missed him these last couple of years. I still don't see him much because he's out of the house most of the time looking for work."

"Are you missing Mercy?" Mark asked Honor.

"I am. We were always together. Now I'm closest with Hope."

"What about Joy?" Christina asked.

"Joy's a loner. She prefers to stay in her room and read. She reads for hours a day whenever she's not doing chores."

"What does she read? The Bible all the time?"

SAMANTHA PRICE

"*Jah.* She must've read it through three times by now. If you say a verse she'll tell you where it is in the Bible and sometimes the exact chapter and verse."

"Isn't that a good thing?" Christina asked.

"*Jah,* I'm not saying it's bad. Of course, it's good." Honor looked down at her food and then she looked up at everybody. Jonathon was smiling at her and she knew they both thought Joy was annoying. They could communicate without the exchange of words.

CHAPTER 9

THREE HOURS LATER, after dinner and two cups of coffee, Honor was delighted to climb into Jonathon's buggy to be taken home.

When Jonathon sat next to her, he whispered, "I thought the night would never end."

"Me too."

He chuckled and moved the horse forward. "I didn't know there was so much to do with prayer *kapps.*" He shook his head. Christina had spent a lot of time talking about them. "Are there different designs or something? I've never noticed."

"There are different ways of making them. Just ask your *schweschder,* she'll tell you."

"*Nee denke.* And I have no *schweschder* to ask. Plus I've heard more than enough about them to last me a lifetime. I already know more about them than most men know. Except for Mark."

THEY BOTH LAUGHED as he turned the buggy onto the road.

"Honor, what do you think your family would think about us marrying?"

"They'd say I'm too young. Far too young and now with Mercy having moved away, *Mamm* misses her. They'll be against it."

"That's hard. I'd marry you tomorrow if you were older."

"Would you?"

He looked over at her. "For sure."

"We'll have to wait."

He sighed. "I've never been good at waiting."

"Me neither."

"Meet me tomorrow at the markets? I'll try to get there to see you as soon as I can get away from work. Sometimes Mark sends me on errands."

"Sure. I'll keep a look-out for you.

FLORENCE STARED out the window when Jonathon brought Honor home. Everyone else had gone to bed and it had been up to her to wait up. She pulled the curtain aside and waited while tapping her foot on the floorboards. It was too dark to see inside the buggy.

After a couple of minutes, Honor still hadn't gotten out of the buggy and Florence was seeing red. She stomped to the front door, swung it wide open not caring the least about the cold air that would whistle into the house, and she got to the buggy door just as Honor was getting out.

"Get to the *haus!*" Florence hissed.

"What's the matter with you?"

Through gritted teeth, she said, "Just do it."

Honor hurried into the house and then Jonathon said, "Good evening, Florence."

Florence glanced over her shoulder to see Honor inside and then she turned back to Jonathon. "Why don't you leave her alone and find someone more like yourself?"

He frowned at her. "I want to marry Honor. It's a matter of timing."

Florence recoiled. "You can say that again. 'Timing' is right though, because there's no time in this world that I'll ever allow you to marry Honor. I'll tell her that trick you played on Mercy."

"She knows all about it. We tell each other everything."

"I'm sure the way you tell it and the way I will tell it will be vastly different. Jonathon, why don't you go back home?"

He stared at her looking hurt and Florence turned her back on him and stomped back to the *haus*.

As soon as Florence got into the *haus*, Honor was standing there. "What did you say to him?"

"I told him how things would be from now on."

"Why do you care so much about him? You're acting like he's horrible and he's not. He's a decent person. Even Mark and Christina like him. Doesn't that say something? Your own *bruder* has him working in his business."

"Having him working and having him marry someone close to you are two very different things."

Honor shook her head. "I'm going to bed. Can we talk about this another time?"

"*Jah*, tomorrow."

"I'm going to the markets early. Can we talk when I get home?"

Florence nodded. "Sure." Honor walked upstairs and Florence was pleased that Honor was taking everything so well. She'd expected a big argument.

CHAPTER 10

THE NEXT DAY, Honor went to the markets, taking her turn with Joy.

The first customers of the day had only begun to wander through the markets when Honor looked up from straightening the stock and saw Jonathon. She told Joy she needed to go to the bathroom.

She headed off in the direction of the ladies room and then with a quick look over her shoulder to make sure Joy wasn't looking, she took a detour toward Jonathon. She met with Jonathon behind a stall displaying tall hanging rugs.

"You're early," was the first thing she said. "Now I've got nothing to look forward to for the rest of the day except finishing time."

He touched her shoulder lightly and then his fingers traveled down her arm to take hold of her hand. "I couldn't wait another minute to see you."

"How did you get out of work? Did Mark have an errand for you?"

"I told Mark I needed to post an urgent letter, so I don't have long. I'll have to get back."

"I have to be quick too. I'm sorry about Florence last night. She's so protective she's ridiculous sometimes."

"You've got nothing to be sorry about. Her being against us is going to make things even harder for us."

Honor rolled her eyes. "Don't say that."

"I've been thinking. I've got an idea, but it'll be a big risk."

"What is it?"

"What if we run away together?"

She gasped. "Could we do that?"

"I don't see why not. The way Florence spoke to me last night, I don't see we have any other choice."

Honor was upset at Florence interfering, acting like her mother. "Where would we go?"

Jonathon looked around. "Back home. I know some people about ten miles from my folks' home and I reckon I could find a job with them pretty easy. I had a job lined up, but I threw it in when I moved here. If I don't get a job there I've got other ideas."

"Doing what?"

"It doesn't matter what I'm doing. As long as we can stay together I'd get a job doing anything."

"We can't get married until I'm eighteen." She sighed. "It's no use."

"We can be together until we marry. I'd rent us a place. We'd have to pretend to be *Englischers* and once we're married, we can go back to the community. Maybe a community where no one knows us. We can get baptized and be proper members and all that."

"I'd rather it not be like that."

"I know, I'd rather a lot of things, but sometimes life doesn't work out how we'd like it and we have to work out other ways around things." He moved some strands of hair away from her forehead. "Don't pout."

"I'm not pouting."

His eyebrows drew together. "Until we're married we'd have two rooms of course, if that's what you're worried about. If we can only afford a one bedroom place I'll sleep on the couch."

"Do you mean it?"

"*Jah.* Everyone thinks I'm a bad person and I have done some pretty rotten things, but I don't want to be like that anymore. I've changed since I've met you."

She giggled. "Can I trust you?"

"Can I trust you?" he asked sporting a crooked smile.

"*Jah.* I want everything to be proper."

"I can live with that. It won't be proper in one way, but I get where you're coming from."

"Okay let's do it."

"What, run away?"

"*Jah.*"

A smile beamed across his face. "Do you mean it?"

She giggled. "I do." She stepped out from behind one of the rugs on a stand and saw her sister back at the stall serving two people at once. "I better get back to work and help Joy."

"Can you arrange to come here tomorrow as well? I could meet you at lunchtime and by then I'll have our escape plan figured out."

"Sure. Wait. Tomorrow is Sunday and the meeting is on at the Fishers' *haus.*"

He chuckled. "So it is. I'll see you there and we'll have to find each other during the meal."

"Okay."

He smiled and gave her a nod. "I should go."

"Okay." She turned and hurried back to help her sister. What they were planning was wrong, but she couldn't see any other way.

"Where have you been?" Joy asked when the customers were gone.

"I wasn't sure where the toilets were."

Joy frowned at her. "You've been to them before."

"I found them eventually."

"Don't take that long again. I was swamped with customers."

"You must've sold a lot then."

"I did. But sometimes people don't want to wait to be served, and they just leave. We need to sell as much as we can to keep Florence happy."

"All right. I'm sorry." Honor shrugged her shoulders.

THE NEXT DAY, Honor briefly saw Jonathon after the meeting. There was a family visiting from another community, so people were preoccupied with them. That left Honor and Jonathon to talk unnoticed.

"I've booked us tickets. At five in the morning, meet me outside your place on the corner. I'll be in a taxi waiting."

"Tomorrow morning?"

"*Jah.* Only bring a small bag of things with you. I'm bringing one bag, and I already bought some *Englisch* clothes for you, so I'll bring them with me. Write a letter and leave it in your room telling everyone you've gone somewhere and not to worry. Otherwise, they'll think you've been kidnapped."

"*Jah,* okay, and what time did you say?"

"Five in the morning and, what did I say for you to bring? Repeat it so I'll know you'll remember."

She giggled. "I'm not to bring much, and you said you'll bring clothes for me."

"And?"

"Write a letter so they don't think I've been kidnapped."

"Good. I'll see you tomorrow and whatever you do, don't be late or we'll miss the bus."

"Got it."

"You won't change your mind, will you?"

She shook her head. "Never."

He looked around and then said, "We'll be a long way from your home, and I mean a long way."

"I don't care as long as I'm with you."

They exchanged smiles and went their separate ways.

CHAPTER 11

THE NEXT MORNING, Florence was making breakfast when Favor rushed into the room. "*Mamm,* Hope and I can't find Honor anywhere and she's not in her room."

Mamm, who was sitting at the breakfast table, put down her mug of coffee. "Well she'd better hurry or you'll be late for the markets."

Joy walked into the kitchen. "She didn't want to go the other day, and now she's pulled this stunt to get out of it."

"She wouldn't do that," *Mamm* said. "She was the one who wanted us to have the stall."

Hope held her hands in the air. "She's nowhere in the *haus*— we've looked everywhere."

"I'll help you look outside," Joy said. "Maybe she's helping in the barn getting the wagon ready."

"*Nee,*" Hope said. "She'd wait for me to help her do it."

"I'll help," Florence said. "Everyone, look for Honor."

All the girls left what they were doing and searched through the house, and then went outside, through the gardens, calling out everywhere.

"Is she in the orchard?" Favor asked.

"Could be," Florence said, "We'll have to split up and have a look."

The girls went through the orchard hollering for Honor at the top of their lungs, but still there was no reply.

"I don't know what to do," said Favor. "We should be leaving right now. "

"Joy, you go with Favor today. I'll take the buggy and go looking for her."

"I should stay with *Mamm* and Hope should stay too. Cherish and Favor can go to the markets. They're quite capable of going on their own."

Florence shook her head. "They aren't old enough."

"I'll drive them there and back. I really think I should be here with *Mamm.*"

"Okay."

"She's done this deliberately to get out of it," Cherish grumbled.

"*Nee*, she's not getting out of anything. She'll be punished with extra chores. She'll be every day at the markets for the next two weeks running." Florence was worried because Honor was usually the sensible one.

Joy rolled her eyes. "We'll take the buggy."

"Okay, but hurry," Florence urged.

While Favor and Cherish were outside hitching the buggy, Joy sat on the couch giving Caramel a final pat. "I'm going to look for Honor after I take the girls to the markets, *Mamm*."

Mamm was now sitting on the couch next to Hope, and she looked up at her. "Where will you go?"

"I don't know."

"I'll come too," said Hope bounding to her feet.

"*Nee*, you stay with *Mamm*." She hurried out the door and then heard the front door open and looked over her shoulder to see Hope hurrying after her. She stopped until Hope caught up.

"I want to come too."

"You can't. Can't you see how upset *Mamm* is?"

"She's okay."

"*Nee* she's distraught, or will be as soon as she realizes Honor hasn't gone for a walk."

"Okay. I'll stay. Where are you going?"

"I'm stopping by all her friends' places." She wasn't, but she couldn't tell Hope she was going to see Isaac.

"Okay."

"Go back inside and sit with *Mamm.*"

"I'm going."

ONCE CHERISH AND Favor left with Joy, Florence had another look through the house. Honor knew that when one girl stopped working it put pressure on all the others. That's why it was surprising that she would go somewhere without telling anyone.

She walked upstairs and, once more, looked in all the bedrooms, under everybody's beds, and then in all the closets. Then she had an idea—the attic. She lit a lantern and climbed up into the attic. She held out the lantern to light all the corners and there was no Honor. The attic was where her late mother's possessions were boxed. One day when she had time, she'd go through them again and be reminded of what was there. It would have to be when everyone was out and that was something that hardly ever happened.

Now, she was starting to get seriously worried about Honor. She went back to the kitchen to see how Wilma was doing.

"Have you found her?" *Mamm* asked.

"*Nee.* When did you last see her?"

"Last night. She'll turn up. I finished making the breakfast," *Mamm* said.

Florence had clean forgotten the breakfast she'd been making. The girls had also gone to the markets with no breakfast. Honor had a lot to answer for when she got back. Florence looked down at the eggs and bacon. *"Denke, Mamm."* She sat down to eat. "Are you eating?"

"We already had something while you were in the attic."

Her mother didn't seem too concerned, or if she was, she was covering it up pretty well.

Mamm's calmness helped to soothe Florence a little, and thinking she might need her strength later, she ate breakfast.

When breakfast was finished and Honor still hadn't shown up, Florence announced she was going to hitch the buggy and go out looking.

"Okay. I thought she'd come home once it was too late to leave for the markets. She didn't." Now, *Mamm* was starting to worry.

"I'm sure she won't be far. You know what? She's probably out visiting someone."

"Who would she possibly be visiting at the crack of dawn?"

"Do you want me to come with you?" Hope asked.

"*Nee*, I'll go alone. You stay home with *Mamm*, and when Honor shows up, tell her how much trouble she'll be in when I get back."

"Gladly." Hope giggled.

She led Wilbur out of his stall that was connected to his paddock. He looked a little dismayed that she'd brought no tasty morsel with her today. "I'm sorry, boy, but this is an emergency." She patted his neck. "I'll give you an apple when we get back—a whole one."

A dark gloominess weighed upon Florence as a heavy feeling of foreboding settled in. She tried not to let bad thoughts gnaw at her tummy and cloud her judgment. While she hitched the buggy, she planned her search. There was no wavering in her mind over where her first stop was. She had to make sure Jonathon was where he was supposed to be.

CHAPTER 12

MARK AND CHRISTINA'S house was closer than the saddlery store where Jonathon worked, so Florence stopped there first. She jumped out of the buggy and knocked on the door. As soon as Christina opened it, Florence blurted out, "Do you know where Jonathon is? Is he here?"

Christina lifted up her chin in a surprised manner. "He's gone."

"What do you mean, 'he's gone?'" Florence's throat constricted and she could hardly say the words.

"He was supposed to travel to the store with Mark today. He didn't meet Mark at the buggy so he went to Jonathon's room and he wasn't there. All his stuff has gone too. He left without saying anything."

Florence sank to the cold boards of the porch while Christina kept talking.

"He was supposed to work today because Mark and I had somewhere important we were supposed to be and he was going to be the only one in the store. He let us down badly." Then Christina repeated, "He's not in his room and all his stuff is gone."

Florence's hand flew to her neck. "Really?"

"You can have a look if you don't believe me."

"I do believe you. I just cannot believe this is happening."

Christina scratched her face. "Why are you here so early in the day? And why are you asking about Jonathon?"

Florence gulped not knowing how much she could say to Christina. If Jonathon and Honor weren't somewhere together, she didn't want Christina knowing that she thought they might be. "I just wanted to know if he could help with something in the orchard."

"*Nee* he can't because he's not here. I'm sorry that Mercy brought him into the family. It's all her fault."

"How's it Mercy's fault?"

"She married Stephen and if she hadn't married Stephen we wouldn't have let Jonathon stay here."

"That's a bit far-fetched to blame Mercy." Florence gathered her strength. She was going to need it.

"It makes sense."

"Anyway, I've got to go. If Jonathon can't help me I need to find someone who can."

Christina eyed her suspiciously. "What did you want him to do?"

"I've got to go."

"*Nee,* wait."

"I'm in a hurry." She climbed into her buggy before her sister-in-law interrogated her further.

Driving away, she was sick to the very pit of her stomach.

Both of them have gone missing.

There was a good chance they'd run away together and Honor wasn't yet eighteen, not for almost an entire year.

FLORENCE HAD no idea what she was going to do next. She headed toward home, but she couldn't tell her stepmother that her daughter had run away with a man in his early twenties. Her mother would surely have a heart attack. And right now, Florence almost felt like she was going to have one. The only thing she could do was find them.

They'd be trying to get out of town.

If they'd run away together they wouldn't stay close by. She drove on into town, passing the local bus stops and hoping to see them, but there was no sign.

It was too much—too much for her to handle on her own. She had to tell her stepmother and together they'd decide what to do next. Her stomach was doing summersaults all the way home.

Just as she was about to turn the buggy into her driveway, she noticed Carter's car on the road coming in her direction.

He has a car!

She stopped her horse, jumped out of the buggy and waved him down. The car would be much faster than a buggy and this was an emergency.

He stopped his car, rolled down his window, and then she hurried over to him. "What are you doing right now for the next few hours?"

"Nothing that can't wait. Why, what's wrong?"

"I'll tell you on the way. Follow me up the driveway, and I'll leave the horse and buggy at home."

"Okay."

She got back into the buggy, and as she said a quick prayer of thanks she headed up the driveway while changing her plans. A minute later, she burst into the kitchen. "*Mamm*, get Hope to unhitch the buggy. I've got something I need to do."

"Is everything alright?"

"Did you find her?" Hope asked.

"*Nee*. Don't forget the buggy. I've got to go."

"I'll do it for you," Hope called out after her as she walked outside.

"*Denke.*" Florence got into the car and as Carter drove away, she looked back and saw both Hope and her stepmother at the front door staring after her.

"They've never seen you in a car before?"

"It's not that. We do travel in cars, we just don't drive them. I didn't tell them where I was going or what I was doing. Or who I was going with."

"You haven't told me where we're going either."

She took a deep breath and tried to calm herself. "My little sister is missing and so is the boy she likes. He's not a boy, he's a man and she's only seventeen."

"Back up a minute. Are you saying that they're together?" He glanced over at her.

"That's my fear." She nibbled on the end of a fingernail.

"That's not good."

"I know that."

"Where are we going?"

"I figure they're trying to get away, so train stations, bus stations, everywhere ... or anywhere they might've gone."

"Hotels?" he asked as he moved the car onto the road.

She frowned at him. "What do you mean, 'hotels?'"

He raised his eyebrows.

"Oh, don't even say that; don't even think that."

"Surely that's what you're thinking?"

"No! My sister's not like that." She gulped when she realized her sister was with a man who probably would try to take every advantage he could. She'd never liked Jonathon and now she was being proved right.

"She's only human. These things happen. You hear about them all the time."

They were wasting time talking. All she wanted to do was get going. "Not my sister. Anyway, we can't knock on all the hotel doors in the county."

"Do you think you should call the police? I mean she's seventeen. I don't know, but isn't that kidnapping?"

"She would've gone willingly." She knew her stepmother would hate the idea of getting outsiders involved. That's why she had to find Honor—and fast. "Maybe, I don't know. Let's just try to find them first."

"Sure." He pushed some buttons on the dashboard of his vehicle. "This will tell us where all the bus stops and train stations are."

"Really?"

He nodded. "It's called technology."

She remained silent.

CHAPTER 13

ONCE JOY HELPED Favor and Cherish set up the stall, she headed back to the buggy wondering where Honor might be. In her heart, she knew she was somewhere with Jonathon. Her first stop would have to be Christina and Mark's house since Jonathon was staying on their property.

If Honor wasn't with Jonathon, then Jonathon would be at work. Rather than raise alarm bells, she hoped Isaac knew something. Jonathon might've confided in him since they both lived on the same property.

When Joy stopped the buggy outside Mark and Christina's house, she hoped Christina would be out. She knocked on the door hoping to see Isaac standing there, but when the door opened it was Christina.

"Joy!" Christina looked over Joy's shoulder.

"I'm here by myself," Joy told her.

"Come in.”

Joy walked through the doorway and then Christina turned around to face her.

“Is Isaac here?"

Christina raised an eyebrow. "Florence was just here looking for Jonathon and now you’re looking for Isaac. What's going on?"

"Florence was here looking for Jonathon?”

“Jah.”

“And, where is he?”

“He’s gone. He’s left without a word. He was supposed to work today, but Mark had to work. Tell me, what is going on? I know something is.”

Joy drew in a deep breath. "Don't say anything to anyone, but Honor is missing and … and I am thinking she might’ve gone somewhere with Jonathon."

Christina frowned. “Where?”

“I don’t know. Do you know where Isaac might be?"

"He’s at a job interview. It should be finished by now."

“Do you know where?"

"At the timber mill. The one down by Old Mill Creek Road."

"I'll see if I can find him and ask him if he knows anything."

"Good idea. You said Honor has gone too?”

"*Jah.*"

"It figures. Jonathon has always struck me as someone who's unreliable. I told Mark, but he saw something in him that I couldn't see. Now this has happened. That'll teach Mark to listen to me."

"I'll have to keep looking for Honor."

"I'll pray you find her quickly."

"*Denke.*"

She hurried out of Mark and Christina's house, got back in the buggy and turned the horse toward Old Mill Creek Road. Just when she was nearly at the timber mill, she was relieved to see Isaac's buggy on the road coming toward her.

He slowed down when she got closer, and then he pulled his buggy over to one side.

He jumped down from the buggy and hurried over to her. When he saw her face, he asked, "What is it?"

She stepped down from her buggy. "It's Honor. She's missing."

"Since when?"

"She was supposed to go to the markets today and when I went to wake her up she wasn't there. She's run away from home."

"Are you sure?"

She nodded. "Jonathon's missing too and she has a huge crush on him. She thinks she's in love with him."

"You think she ran away with Jonathon?"

"*Jah!*" She repeated, "She has a giant crush on him."

He shook his head and looked at the ground.

"If you know anything you must tell me."

He shook his head. "Everyone knew they were in love. Didn't you?"

"I guess, but I didn't know they'd do something stupid like running away together."

"Where would they have gone?" he asked.

"I don't know. We don't even know if they're together for certain. It seems a huge coincidence that they both choose this day to leave without telling anyone where they're going."

"She's only been missing since this morning, right?"

Joy nodded. "Just since this morning. But she's never done this before."

"Did she have an argument with anybody last night?"

"Not that I can think of. Nothing unusual anyway. We're always having small squabbles between ourselves." She thought back to last night. "There were no arguments last night at all. You've spent some time with Jonathon, what do you think?"

He shook his head. "I don't know. I'm a bit shocked. What should we do?"

Joy adjusted her *kapp*. "Apart from drive around the streets looking, or ... I don't know what to do."

Isaac said, "Have you had a good look right around the orchard? What if she's fallen asleep in the barn or something?"

"She's never done that before."

"Let's go back to your place and have a good look around to see if we can find her, *jah?*"

"Okay. And if she's not there we'll have to do something."

He nodded. "Agreed. Let's go."

CHAPTER 14

TWO UNSUCCESSFUL HOURS LATER, Florence felt like she was going to burst with worry. "I just don't know what to do now." She held her throbbing head and longed for the lavender oil she massaged on her temples when she felt this way.

"Maybe we should go to the police?"

"But I'm not sure they're together. If only I had proof then I might go to the police. But I don't know."

"It sounds pretty likely they're together." He looked at his navigation system. "We've got a couple more places to try. They're out of town a bit."

Florence nodded. "Let's go."

Isaac and Joy pulled up at her house. They left their buggies and walked toward each other.

Isaac looked across at the sheds. "Have you been through each and every one of the sheds?"

"I haven't and I don't know about the other girls either. We've called out and she hasn't answered."

"Let's look through them—carefully."

"Okay."

They looked through the shed where they stored the apples, the shed where they made the cider, and the shed where they stored odds and ends that didn't belong in the barn.

Lastly, they came to the barn. Isaac pushed open the double doors of the barn and called out to Honor. There was no reply. They looked in every stall, behind an old buggy that was pushed up to one side, behind all the hay bales, and she was nowhere to be seen.

"What about up there?" He pointed to the unused hayloft.

"I'm not going up there and that ladder hasn't been used in years. It's rickety."

"I'll have to go up and see if she's there."

She stood and watched him climbing the ladder placing each foot carefully on one rung after another. He finally reached far enough so he could view the loft. Then she heard a loud hiss and Isaac yelled out and leaned back nearly falling off the ladder.

"There's a large ginger cat up there." He made his way down the ladder.

Joy giggled. "That's Rochester, one of our barn cats."

"He nearly killed me. Anyway, she's not up there."

"Come down slowly." She held the ladder.

When he put his shoe on the second-to-last rung it went straight through it. Joy jumped forward and tried to steady him, but he was too heavy and they ended up on the floor of the barn together. He laughed and she jumped to her feet.

"Are you okay, Isaac? I'm so sorry. I should've caught you."

"*Nee*. I would've squashed you." He sat up and smiled at her. "I'm fine. No harm done."

"I told you that ladder wasn't safe. No one's used it in years. It's rotted through."

She put out her hands and helped him to his feet. Once he was standing, she pulled her hands away. It could've turned into a time for romance, but not when her sister was missing.

"Have you looked through the *haus?*" he asked.

"Of course we did. We looked in every cupboard, every room, and under every bed. She's just not there, not anywhere."

"What about her friends? Have you checked with them?"

"Florence went to them this morning. If she found her she would've been back by now. Shall we drive around the roads?"

"Yeah, let's do it. Will you come in my buggy?"

"*Jah,* okay. I'll just tell *Mamm* that's where we're going and see if she's heard any news yet."

"That sounds like a good plan. I'll wait in the buggy."

CHAPTER 15

WHEN FLORENCE and Carter arrived at the last bus stop and there was nowhere left to check, the two of them sat in his car in silence. He parked and turned off his engine, and then looked over at Florence. "Well, what should we do now?"

"I don't know what to do. We've run out of places to look."

"Perhaps she's home by now?"

She bit her lip. "I hope so. Can you take me home?"

"Sure."

"If she's there, she's going to be in the biggest trouble."

He chuckled.

She looked over at him. "What's funny?"

"Go easy on her. She's a teenager and sometimes it's hard to adjust to things."

Annoyance welled within Florence. How could he possibly understand what it was like growing up in a large family? Discipline and routine were the threads that held the fabric of family life together. "What things?"

"Life and such. Making mistakes is part of growing up."

Florence didn't say anything because Carter didn't understand their ways, but if Honor had been out somewhere with Jonathon she would be grounded for the rest of her life!

He glanced at her. "You must be hungry by now."

She put a hand over her stomach. "I couldn't eat a thing."

"Are you sure? Because I know this nice little diner where we could get something to eat."

"I can't eat when my sister's missing."

Then Florence felt bad because he had gone to a lot of trouble driving her around and he was probably starving. "Are you hungry?"

He looked over at her and then started his engine. "I'm always hungry."

"We can stop then if you'd like to."

"It's okay. I think I'll be able to last until I get home." He moved his car onto the road.

WHEN HE PULLED up at her house, he said, "Can you do me a favor?"

"What is it?" She opened the door and stayed seated.

"Stop by this afternoon and let me know if she's been found?"

"Sure. I'll do that."

"And let me know if you need me to drive you anywhere else."

"Thank you. I appreciate it. And thank you for what you've done today."

He gave her a nod and then she got out of the car. By the time she got to her front door, his car was already at the end of the driveway. When she pushed the door open and saw Mamm standing in front of her, she knew at once that Honor hadn't returned.

"You didn't find her?" *Mamm* asked.

Florence shook her head and moved further into the house. "Our new neighbor from next door drove me to all the stations – all the bus stations and even the train station. I couldn't see either of them anywhere."

Mamm scrunched her brows and peered into her face. "*Either* of them?"

Florence gulped. She had forgotten Mamm didn't know the full story. "Jonathon is also missing."

Mamm went ashen and hurried over to sit down on the couch. "Do you think they're together?" she asked. "You do, don't you?"

Florence wished she could tell her no. "That is my fear."

"What will we do, Florence?"

"I'm not sure." She looked around. "Where is everyone?"

"Joy is driving around with Isaac trying to find her. Hope is upstairs, I think ... or in the kitchen?"

"Should we tell the bishop what's happened?"

Mamm shook her head. "*Nee,* not yet. We'll wait and see if Isaac and Joy find her."

CHAPTER 16

IT WAS mid-afternoon and Florence was peeling potatoes for dinner when she heard the phone in the barn. She threw down the paring knife and ran as fast as she could to the barn hoping the call would bring news of Honor.

"Hello," she said breathlessly as she held the receiver up to her ear.

"Florence."

"Is this you, Mercy?"

"It's me. You know Honor isn't there?"

"*Jah,* we've been looking everywhere. Have you heard from her?"

"That's why I'm calling. She told me not to let anybody know, but she's run away with Jonathon."

Now that she knew it for sure, Florence felt doubly worse. "That's what I thought had happened. Do you know where they are?"

"I know they're coming here. They were getting on the Greyhound and it stops at Hartford, Connecticut. I only found that out because she was talking to me and I overheard a man telling her they'd missed the bus. She was still talking to me when he told her to stay there and he'd find out when the next bus was leaving. After that, I'm not sure what their immediate plans are, but she told me they were both going to live as *Englischers* until she's old enough to get married. Then they'll come back to the community."

Florence sighed, fearing they might never find them. "Did she say what the expected arrival time of the bus was or when it was leaving?"

"*Nee.* She only called me about half an hour ago, but it took me all this time to find our home phone number. I forgot it. I had to get—"

"Okay, tell me that story later—is there anything else I need to know?"

"I can't think of anything, but I'll call back if I do."

"*Denke,* Mercy." She hung up the receiver and ran back to tell her stepmother what was going on.

Mamm stared at her after she'd told her what Mercy had said. "Can you drive there and try to find them?"

"I could, but do you think we should call the authorities? They'd have a better chance of finding them. I mean, she's only young."

"*Nee.* I don't want anybody else involved. It'll bring shame on the family."

"Okay." *Of course.* She had known her stepmother was going to say that.

"In my address book by the phone I have three numbers of drivers we've used in the past. Call them and see if any of them can take you now."

Florence knew that the chances of getting a driver at that short notice was remote, but she knew where there was a car and a driver available. "I'll see if the man next door can drive me there."

"*Jah,* okay, but hurry."

"Hope, make me a sandwich please while I get ready."

"Can I come too?"

"*Nee,* stay with *Mamm* and help her finish fixing dinner, please."

"Okay." Hope jumped up from her chair at the kitchen table, and then Florence ran upstairs taking them two at a time. Once in her room, she grabbed her thickest coat and her black over-bonnet to keep out the cold. When she got downstairs again Hope was coming out of the kitchen with her sandwich.

"It's only peanut butter."

"That's fine. Anything is better than nothing."

"Should I put it in something for you or will you just have it like this?"

"Like this." She grabbed it and yelled goodbye over her shoulder and then set off through the orchard hoping and praying that Carter would be home and that he'd take her where she wanted to go. It was late and she felt awful for asking him, but it was an emergency.

Florence was relieved when she saw his car outside and a light on in the house. She knocked on his door and he opened it.

He searched her face before she spoke. "Is she home yet?" he asked almost timidly as though he knew what her response was going to be.

"No, but my newly married sister called me because Honor called her and told her where she was going to be."

He sighed. "That was a big mistake on Honor's part if she truly didn't want to be found. Sounds like she wants to be found deep down. If she is with—"

"*Jah,* she is and they're heading to Hartford."

He slowly nodded.

She hoped he might've recognized the urgency of the situation and offered to drive her, but he hadn't. "I hate to ask this again, but it is an emergency. Could you drive me to the bus station at Hartford? They're going by Greyhound."

"Sure. Of course. Right now?"

"Yes, right now. It's okay if you can't. I do have the names of some drivers, but I just thought it would be quicker to ask you first since it's such short notice."

"Let's go."

He reached inside the house and pulled his coat off the hook by the door, flicked off the light, and then took keys out of his pocket and locked his front door. They then walked to his car and he clicked a remote control to unlock it.

"It's unlocked," he said.

Once again, she slid into the comfort of the black leather car seat.

When he was beside her with his belt fastened, he pressed some buttons on his navigation system. "Connecticut. It's three and a half hours away."

"Hartford, my sister said."

He pressed some more buttons. "Hmm, make that four and a half hours. There seems to be a bus and a train station combo. We'll make our way there."

She put on her seatbelt, happy he hadn't changed his mind when he saw how far away it was. "Thanks so much for doing this."

"I'm glad to be of some help. It's nice to be useful." He drove down the driveway.

· · ·

NOT FAR INTO their lengthy journey, the annoying side of Carter reared its head and reminded Florence that he was very much an *Englischer*.

He drummed his fingers on the console between them while he steered the car with one hand. "One of the bonnet sisters has fallen from grace, eh?"

"Don't say that; she hasn't. She's temporarily lost her way."

He raised both hands in the air. "Potatoes potahtoes."

"Please use both hands to drive." She was so worried about Honor that she felt her head would burst.

"They say the first few hours someone goes missing is the most vital. That's why I think you should go to the police."

"Please, I don't mean to be rude, but please don't speak."

"Sorry." Then he started whistling. After ten minutes of that, he made a suggestion. "Shall we stop and get coffee?"

She stared at him. Was he serious? It was going to be a long drive, she reminded herself, and perhaps he was tired. "Do you need one?"

"Not really. I just thought it would be nice."

"I'd rather just get her out of Jonathon's clutches as soon as possible. If we miss her by one minute or even one second, I'll never forgive myself."

"I'll make a few calls to see when the bus from Lancaster is expected."

"Yes, please do that." It was a good idea to see if they should hurry or whether they could take their time. Also, it would stop his whistling.

"What time did you say they left?" he asked.

"I really don't know, except that they missed the early one. I don't even know how many buses go there a day. Maybe only one or two. That's what I'm hoping."

In less than two minutes he was getting information from the station.

CHAPTER 17

Honor looked over at Jonathon, not sure of why he was angry with her. She wasn't going to put up with it.

"I can't understand why you called your sister. You already told me you couldn't trust any of them. Are you sure you can trust Mercy?"

Honor shrugged. "I don't know, but I didn't want anyone to think I'd been kidnapped."

He frowned at her. "What about the letter? I told you to write a letter."

"Calm yourself down. I did and I gave it to Joy."

"Good. How did you stop her from reading it?"

"I just told her not to."

"And, what else?"

"That's all."

Jonathon moved uncomfortably in his seat. "If someone gave me something like that I'd read it just as soon as they turned their back. I wouldn't be able to help myself."

"Joy's not like that. She always does what she says she's going to do. I told her she'd know when to give the note to *Mamm*."

"Didn't she ask questions?"

"Nee." Honor shook her head.

"Weird."

"She is a little weird. That's the word that best describes her. She's not like the rest of us sisters."

"I don't mean she's weird, I mean the situation. I thought you'd leave the note on your pillow or something. Joy could lose it or forget about it."

Honor frowned at him. He was already in a bad mood because she'd caused them to miss the first bus, by insisting to speak with Mercy, and now he was upset about the letter. If she wanted to be scolded, she needn't have left home. "I did what I believed was best. If you're unhappy with me I'll get on the next bus home. I don't need you, you know."

"I'm sorry, I've just got a lot on my mind. This is a big thing that we're doing and it's a lot of pressure. I'm doing it all for us. If we're found we'll both be in a lot of trouble, but especially me."

"Are you sure we'll be able to hide out for a whole year?"

"I don't know. We've got to give it a try. It's the only way we can be together until you're old enough for me to marry you. I'm pretty sure we have to wait until you're eighteen, and if you're younger than that you need a parent's approval."

"We're not going to get any approval now. Maybe I should've stayed at home and *Mamm* would've let me get married as soon as I could. I would've nagged her until she gave in."

"It's too far away. A year is too long. We can't deviate now from the path we've set out on. We've already burned our bridges. You with your family and me with your family and especially with Mark. I left the job without warning and left the place I was staying."

"Left your stable you mean." She giggled.

"We've both left everything and by now everyone knows we've gone. How long do you think it'll take them to figure out we're together?"

"Humph. They won't figure it out until they read my note."

"Let's just stick to the plan and stop looking back. I'll lease us a place to live. Firstly, I'll have to get a job. I've got a little money, but that'll be chewed up real fast."

"I can work."

"*Nee.* They'll want ID and a social security number."

"I'll work somewhere where they won't ask for that, or work for myself selling things at a stall. That's what I've always done."

"Maybe."

When another passenger turned around and looked at Honor, she pulled off her *kapp*.

"What are you doing?" he whispered.

"Everyone's looking at me. I want to blend in."

"I agree but wait until we stop and you can change into other clothes."

"You did bring *Englisch* clothes for me, didn't you?"

"*Jah,* I did." He patted his backpack that was by his feet.

She unbraided her hair and it fell down her back in waves. He ran his fingers through it. "Your hair is so beautiful."

"Is it?"

"It sure is."

CHAPTER 18

WHEN ISAAC and Joy had no success finding Honor, he took her home and then she collected Cherish and Favor from the markets.

Once they got home and unhitched the buggy, having no idea that Florence wasn't home, it was business as usual for Joy. "Give the money bag to Florence because she's got to put aside the rent for tomorrow."

"I will," said Cherish. "Give it to me, Favor."

Favor held the black money bag high in the air. "I'm older than you. I'll take it."

Cherish did her best to grab it out of Favor's hands, but she was too short. Favor giggled and then ran into the house with Cherish at her heels. Joy shook her head at them and started rubbing down the horse.

When Joy walked inside, she was met by her mother who was in tears. *Mamm* told Joy that Florence had gone to Connecticut to bring Honor home, and that Honor had run away with Jonathon.

Joy did her best to calm her *mudder*. "Leave it to Florence. She'll do it. I'm confident *Gott* has His hand on the situation." Over *Mamm's* shoulder, she saw Favor and Cherish roll their eyes, but she didn't care. They always did that when she talked about *Gott,* but she really was sure He would help them.

"Hope's got the dinner ready." *Mamm* sniffed.

"Great. I'm starving and it smells so good."

Once they sat down to dinner, the conversation was about Honor until it turned to the week's earnings.

"Florence isn't here so what happens to the earnings? Will you look after it, Joy? You're the next oldest."

"Hmm. I'm not too good with numbers."

"It's not numbers it's money," Cherish said. "Where did you put the bag, Favor?"

"You took it." Favor glared at Cherish. "As soon as we got inside you took it. You grabbed the bag out of my hands."

Cherish bit her lip. "I gave it to Joy."

"*Nee,* you didn't. I would've remembered that."

Mamm said, "Stop arguing. We're all upset about Honor." She turned to Joy. "Perhaps you don't remember that Cherish gave it to you?"

"Nee, she didn't. I was the one who told them to give the money to Florence. I didn't know Florence would be off somewhere."

"I remember Favor giving it to me but I can't remember where I put it."

"Nee! You snatched it from me," Favor said. "I didn't *give* it to you."

Joy sighed. "It's got to be in the *haus* somewhere. It'll turn up. As long as we find it by tomorrow morning it'll be okay, because Mr. Pettigrew will have to be paid."

Mamm said, "Just have a little break, Cherish, sit down and think where you put it."

"I am sitting down."

"I meant for you to relax and have a sit-down after dinner. Don't think about it for a minute and then try to remember where you were when Favor gave it to you and what happened next."

Favor shook her head and muttered, "What's the use? I might as well not speak at all because no one listens to anything I say."

Cherish nodded. "I'll do that after dinner, *Mamm*."

. . .

OVER THE AFTER-DINNER WASHING UP, Joy heard someone crying in the living room. She walked out to see Cherish crying and their mother comforting her.

"What's wrong?" Joy at first assumed Cherish was trying to take the attention away from Honor since Cherish thought everything should revolve around her.

"She can't find the money," *Mamm* told her while Cherish sobbed into her hands.

Joy sat on the other side of her. "You're getting yourself worked up. You're not going to remember when you're upset."

"My mind's just blank. I can't remember anything after when she gave me the bag. What if someone came into the *haus* and stole it?"

"No one would've done that. Someone would've seen them."

"That's the only answer I can think of because it's gone."

Now Joy was worried. With Florence and Honor absent, it was her job as the eldest in the house to look after the finances and if neither of them were back by tomorrow, she'd have to deliver the rent money. The only other way to get money was to draw money from the family's account, but for that to happen Florence needed to sign for it and she was halfway to Connecticut by now.

Joy said to Cherish. "I'll help you look all through the *haus*. Let's look through your bedroom first."

"I've looked there and Favor and Hope have even helped me."

"Have you looked through the clothes you were wearing today?"

"I was in these clothes and the bag isn't here." Cherish stood up and shook her dress and apron out. "Anyway, it was too big to be hiding somewhere, that's why I think someone has come in and stolen it."

Mamm shook her head. "No one's been near the place."

"They have." Cherish looked at Joy. "You came home with Isaac. You told us he helped you look for Honor here."

"Don't be ridiculous. Isaac didn't even come inside. Neither was the money here then because you weren't home from the markets."

"I don't think he took it. I don't, but I mean someone must've because it's not here. It couldn't have just vanished, could it?" Cherish sobbed again. "Everything's gone wrong for me. I can't believe Honor and Jonathon are together. They can't be. He liked me, not her. I was so sure of it."

Mamm frowned at Cherish and then looked at Joy who didn't know what to say.

Joy finally said, "Go to sleep, and we'll worry about the missing money in the morning."

Through tear-filled eyes, Cherish looked at her. "But don't you have to take the rent in tomorrow morning?"

"I do, but I'm confident it will turn up by then. We'll all pray, *jah?*"

"We will, Joy," *Mamm* said. "We will."

"Don't worry, Cherish, just go to bed."

"I don't think I'll be able to sleep. I'll be so worried and not only about the money."

Joy wasn't even going to ask what the other thing was that her sister was worried about. "Put it all out of your mind, say your prayers, and have a good night's sleep. You'll need all your energy for tomorrow when Florence brings Honor home."

After *Mamm* and the other girls went to bed, Joy sat alone by the fire. She had no idea where the money was and what Cherish had absent-mindedly done with it. Joy bit her lip and stared into the flickering flames in the fireplace. Would Florence be able to find Honor and bring her home?

Joy closed her eyes and thought about the positives of the situation. At least they knew that Honor was still alive and well because she'd called Mercy. And, Honor was with Jonathon and that was probably better than running away by herself—safer for her, at least.

CHAPTER 19

"Wake up. We're here."

Florence opened her eyes and with a jolt, realized where she was—in Carter Braithwaite's car. Then the horror of Honor having disappeared flooded back to her. "We're here already?"

"You've been asleep for hours. I stopped for gas and you still didn't wake."

"I must've really dozed off. I'm sorry." She blinked and when she saw he was staring at her, she said, "It's hardly fair on you for me to fall asleep."

"It's okay. I was entertained by listening to you snore." He chuckled and got out of the car.

She grimaced, then unbuckled her seat belt and opened the door. Her neck ached from falling asleep at a funny angle.

Rubbing her neck, she looked over the top of the car at him. "Are we on time?"

He glanced at his watch. "We're early."

Florence looked around. "Where to?"

He looked around and pointed to a sign. "Arrivals."

Once they were in the station itself, they had to walk through the food outlets to get to the arrivals.

"I'm starving. I've got to eat something." He headed to buy food and she hurried after him.

"But what if we miss them?"

He looked at his watch. "The bus isn't due for another fifteen minutes. Do you want anything?"

"No thank you." Her stomach churned too much to think about food. He ordered a large black coffee and a hot dog with mustard.

"The vegetarian thing didn't last long."

His mouth turned down at the corners. "I don't think there's real meat in these things."

Florence grimaced at that thought, and he laughed.

While they stood there waiting for the food, Florence said, "I hope they're on the bus and I hope they didn't change their minds and get off somewhere else." She held her stomach. "Or what if they just told Mercy they were coming here and it wasn't true?"

He drew his eyebrows together. "You mean we could've driven all this way for nothing?"

"It's possible." She'd feel bad for having him drive that long distance if Honor and Jonathon weren't on that bus, but all she could do was follow the lead she'd been given.

The server handed him his hot dog and at the same time his black coffee was ready down at the end of the counter.

He took hold of his food and then grabbed his coffee. "Let's go and wait somewhere for the bus." A few steps along, he said, "There's the bus from Lancaster. The one that's just pulled up. It's a few minutes early."

He took a large bite of his hot dog as they hurried over. Then Florence saw Honor step out of the bus in front of Jonathon.

Florence gasped.

"Is that her without her bonnet? The one with the really long hair?" Carter asked before he took his last bite.

"Yes, that's her." Florence sent up a prayer of thanks. It was devastating to see her sister with no head covering, but she was so pleased they'd found her. "Let's go." Florence felt like her legs were so heavy she couldn't move, and then she felt her chest constrict and couldn't breathe for a moment.

Carter threw his coffee away along with the hotdog wrapper. Then he held onto her arm. "Are you okay? You're as white as a sheet. You should eat something."

"I'm fine." Florence forced herself to take a slow deep breath, blew it out, summoned all her strength and stepped out.

Together they walked over and when Honor looked up and saw her, she froze to the spot and her jaw dropped open. When Florence stood in front of her, Honor gulped. "What are *you* doing here?"

"Bringing you home."

"I don't want to go anywhere. I'm going to stay with Jonathon." Jonathon stood beside her.

"That's right. We're together now."

Florence ignored Jonathon completely.

"No, you're not, you're coming home with me." Florence then stared at Jonathon and he looked away, looking dreadfully guilty. "What were you thinking, Jonathon? She's a child. She's only seventeen. I could have you arrested for kidnapping."

"Wait a minute. I didn't kidnap her. She wanted to come. We're going to get married."

Carter stepped forward and said to Jonathon. "Wake up to yourself, man. Do you know how much trouble you're in?" He shook his finger at him. "She's a minor. That makes—"

Florence put her hand lightly on Carter's shoulder. "Let's just get her out of here."

Jonathon said, "She's not a child. She's seventeen. Legally old enough to get married in some states."

Carter then shook his fist in front of Jonathon's face. "If I find you've laid one finger on her I'll come back and find you."

Jonathon hung his head. "I haven't touched her. It's not like that."

"You better be telling the truth." Carter turned to Florence and gave her a nod. "Let's go."

"I'm not going. I'm staying with Jonathon," Honor whined. She stamped her boot onto the asphalt.

Jonathon sighed. "They're right, Honor. We'll have to wait until you're older. Then we'll be together. There's no point if they're going to be so against us. Your mother would never give her approval."

"*Nee.* Let's just do what we were going to do. We can't let them stop us."

Carter said to Jonathon, "You'll be in big trouble if she doesn't come with us now."

"You'll have to go with them, Honor. We'll wait until your birthday."

"That's too far away," she whimpered, tears welling in her eyes.

Florence grabbed hold of Honor's arm and started walking.

Jonathon took a step forward and Carter gave a headshake and moved to block his way. Then Jonathon called out to Honor, "I'll be waiting for you, Honor."

"I'll see you soon," she called through her tears, looking back over her shoulder while being dragged away.

When they got to the car, Carter opened the back and the front passenger doors. Once Honor was in the back and had angrily fastened her seatbelt, Florence got into the front seat. Carter pushed a button on his door panel before starting the engine and driving away from the station. Florence realized the button was a child-safety feature that prevented Honor from opening her door.

Honor whimpered, "How did you find me?"

"I got a call telling me where you might be headed."

"It was Mercy, wasn't it? She's the only one who could've told you where I was going. I've gone all that way for nothing because of Mercy."

"You're the one in the wrong. Don't go making out someone else is to blame for this."

"I'm not, it's just that I know it was Mercy and I'll never trust her again."

"*Mamm* and I will never trust you again. Not after this. What were you thinking? You're a child." When Honor didn't answer, Florence turned around and saw her quietly sobbing into her hands. Florence looked over at Carter and he looked at her with an 'I don't know what to do either' look on his face.

Florence figured it was time to be silent. They'd gotten her back and now Honor needed to go home and stop thinking about Jonathon. The sooner the better.

A few miles along, Honor asked, "Why did you let the driver talk to Jonathon like that?"

"He deserved it and more. Anyway, he's not 'the driver,' he's our new neighbor. He's Carter Braithwaite. Carter, this is Honor."

"Pleased to meet you, Honor." Carter's voice was cheerful and Honor merely responded with a groan. Then Carter said, "I don't know about you two, but I'm starving."

"Me too. I think I can eat now," Florence felt better for Honor's sake and for Wilma's. Wilma would be thrilled to have her daughter home.

"I just want to go home," Honor said.

"That's too bad," Carter said. "We're going to stop for some food. Florence hasn't eaten for hours."

"Yes, that looks like as good a place as any. I'm sure you don't care what you eat, Florence, as long as it's something."

"That's right."

As Carter ordered the food at the window, Honor leaned forward over the seat and said to Florence, "Thanks for ruining my life."

Florence turned around and glared at her. "In a few months, you'll be thanking me for saving it. Be sure to put your prayer *kapp* back on before we get home."

Honor flopped back into her seat and the rest of the drive home was silent.

CHAPTER 20

CARTER DROVE UP THE BAKERS' driveway and stopped at the front door. Honor pulled on her door handle but nothing happened. She looked at it curiously. Carter subtly pushed the release button in his door panel and when she pulled the handle again, the door opened. She jumped out and hurried to the house.

Florence was pleased to see that Honor had braided her hair, pinned it up, and put her prayer *kapp* on at some point in the journey. She turned to Carter. "I can never thank you enough for doing this."

He blinked his bloodshot eyes. "Anytime—not too soon, though. I'll need a good sleep first if she runs away again."

"Sleep. What a thought. That's the first thing I'll be doing." She unbuckled her seat belt and climbed out of the car. "Thanks, Carter."

"You're welcome."

She walked to the door to hear *Mamm* say to Honor, "Why did you run off like that?"

"It's what I chose to do. That's all. I don't want to keep hearing about it. I'm back now. You got what you wanted."

"You sound like you don't even care how worried we've been."

"What's it got to do with you? It's my life. Florence keeps telling me I'm too young. I'm old enough to know what I want. Jonathon said I'm legally old enough to marry if we lived in a different state."

"Go up to your room now until you learn some manners." Florence overheard *Mamm* and knew she was doing her best to be firm. Honor charged up to her bedroom and then her mother walked to the bottom of the stairs and called out, "You're not old enough to know anything." She turned to Florence. "*Denke* for bringing her back."

"Of course." Florence collapsed into the couch. She felt like she hadn't slept for days.

"Where did you find her?"

"Getting off a bus in Connecticut, with Jonathon."

Wilma gasped. "So, it's true?" When Florence nodded, Wilma all but collapsed into the nearest chair.

"They say they're in love and want to be together." Florence didn't even like saying the words. What Honor was feeling wasn't love, not a mature ready-for-marriage love, and Jonathon

... Jonathon was so unprincipled that he needed some kind of discipline from someone. Perhaps his bishop needed to know what had gone on, or their own bishop, but she knew her stepmother wouldn't accept that because that would mean dragging Honor into it too. Wilma would prefer if it were all swept under the rug. Floating over the top of issues was how the woman coped with life.

Mamm said, "I can't believe that Jonathon didn't put a stop to the foolish girl's ideas."

"I'd say it was he who put the idea into her head in the first place. I wouldn't blame Honor too much. Jonathon's the older one and should've had more sense."

"Where is he now?"

"I don't know—and quite frankly I don't care."

"He won't come back here, will he?"

"He wouldn't be brave enough to show his face around here again after what he's done."

"That's mean, Florence." Honor's voice rang out from the top of the stairs.

"Go back to your room," *Mamm* said. "I can't believe you just ran off like that and left us worried. We had no idea what happened to you."

"I wrote you the letter so you wouldn't worry."

"What letter?"

Honor walked down two stairs and sat down on the top step. "I wrote a note and gave it to Joy to give to you."

Mamm and Florence looked at one another.

"That's the first time we're hearing about this," Florence said.

"We'll talk to Joy about that in the morning."

"It's morning now."

"Later this morning, after we've all had some sleep."

Then Joy came out of her bedroom. "You're home! Where were you?"

Honor didn't say anything.

"Joy," *Mamm* called out.

Joy walked down the stairs. "*Nee*. I haven't found it … um, yet?"

"What?" asked *Mamm*.

"The money. Isn't that what you were talking about?" Joy asked.

"Do you know anything about a note or a letter?"

"You mean the one Honor gave me?"

Honor ran down the stairs. "See? It's true!"

"Be quiet," *Mamm* told her. "Don't wake the rest of your sisters. Joy, why didn't you tell us about this note?"

"I couldn't. She said it was a secret."

Honor said to Joy, "I couldn't tell you I was running away, so I said, 'Here's a letter. You'll know when to give it to Mamm.'"

"I'm sorry. I didn't know I was supposed to give it to *Mamm* when you were missing. You should've been clearer."

All Florence could do was shake her head at all of them. At *Mamm* for telling Honor to go to her room and now saying nothing about her being in the living room, and at Joy for not realizing what an emergency was and for not giving *Mamm* the letter, and at Honor for doing what she'd done in the first place.

Feeling like she didn't fit into the family, Florence got a new burst of energy and jumped to her feet. She wanted to yell at the top of her lungs and tell everyone to wake up to themselves, but she held it together. Now she understood why Earl had just up and left after *Dat's* death. "I need some fresh air."

Mamm looked up at her in surprise, while the two girls stared at her, looking for all the world like a pair of owls. "But ... but ... It's dark outside," *Mamm* said.

"I'm not going far. I just need to get outside." Everything was so much harder for Florence because *Mamm* wasn't strict enough. Instead of being one of the girls, she'd had to step up and practically become the mother. That had resulted in her not having a sisterly relationship with any of her half-sisters.

If she'd had a different relationship with Honor, they could've talked and Honor might have told her what she had been thinking and feeling. Florence would've had a chance to help her see sense. It had been so 'over-the-top' wrong for her, a young unmarried girl, to run off with Jonathon.

Florence stepped off the porch and pulled her shawl higher around her shoulders. As she looked up at the stars in the dark sky, a gust of frosty wind bit into her cheeks. She knew she should be grateful to be part of the family, but she couldn't help feeling that if her father were still alive everything would be so much better. Honor wouldn't have dared run away.

Everything had changed when *Dat* died. Her world had turned upside down. She had lost not only him, but she'd lost her two older brothers as well. Earl had abruptly left for Ohio, and then Mark announced he was getting married. Mark had been on *rumspringa* when *Dat* died and Florence was sure that him marrying Christina right after was a reaction. There was surely no other reason Mark would have married Christina. She wasn't very pleasant.

Florence's biggest fear was that Honor would run away again. She'd shown no signs of repentance.

"Are you okay, Florence?" *Mamm* came outside with a flashlight.

"It's just too much, *Mamm* and I'm worried she'll try it again. We haven't been hard enough on her."

"I'll call Mercy and tell her we've found her."

"*Denke, Mamm.* I didn't even think of that. And can you call Mark and Christina as well? It's late, but they might be lying awake, worried."

"Sure. I'll call them."

While *Mamm* made the calls, Florence paced up and down, too worked up to relax. When *Mamm* came back out of the barn after making the calls, she said, "I told Mark and he was relieved."

"And what about Mercy?"

"Mercy said Jonathon arrived at his parents' *haus*. He's staying there for a few days and then he's going to go up north to get away for a while."

Florence let out a sigh of relief, but she knew that Honor would hate to hear Jonathon had made plans that didn't include her.

CHAPTER 21

FLORENCE ONLY HAD ABOUT two hours sleep and woke up at first light. She pulled on her apron, went downstairs and noticed the fire was still going. Her mother or one of the girls must've been up in the small hours and put on more logs. Once she'd rearranged the fire and added another log, she headed into the kitchen to make coffee. She was surprised to see Wilma sitting at the table sipping tea. "You couldn't get any sleep either?"

Her stepmother shook her head. "No sleep at all."

"Why don't you go back to bed now?"

"I feel sick with everything that's happened."

"I'm making *kaffe*. Do you want some, or would you rather have more tea?"

"I can't take any more hot tea. I'll try some *kaffe*."

When the coffee was made, Florence sat down with her stepmother.

"What you don't know is that there's another problem."

Florence sighed and couldn't believe her ears. "What's that?"

"The week's takings from the market is missing."

Florence stared at her stepmother, eyebrows raised almost to her hairline. "What on earth? How did that happen?"

"The girls had it when they got home—Cherish and Favor went to the markets yesterday and Joy drove them there and back. They had it when they got home. The money was in the usual black bag. It's somewhere here in the *haus,* but no one can find it anywhere."

Florence was relieved to hear that it was in the house, at least. "Well, if it's here we'll be able to find it. Has the rent been paid?"

"*Nee,* that has to be done today."

"I'll do that today after the girls have gone to the markets. I'll follow them in."

"Okay."

Cherish walked into the kitchen. "I see Honor's back."

"That's right. We found her where Mercy said she'd be and now—"

"What about Jonathon?"

"Mercy said he's staying with his family for a few days and then going up north for a bit."

Cherish tilted her chin upward. "Up north where?"

"I don't know. I didn't care enough to ask," Florence said.

Cherish frowned. "Are you sure he's staying with his family for a few days?"

"That's right."

Cherish walked over and poured herself some coffee out of the plunger pot and sat down with them.

Florence said, "About this missing money."

Cherish groaned. "Yeah, did *Mamm* tell you all about it?"

"*Jah*. You had it when you got home and then it disappeared?"

"That's right and I've looked everywhere."

"I'll help you look after breakfast."

"I really don't have anywhere else to look."

"It's obviously somewhere you haven't looked."

Cherish wrinkled her nose. "Obviously."

"Who's working on the stall today?"

"Not me. I refuse to go today. Hope didn't go yesterday so it'll have to be Hope and someone else."

Florence looked at *Mamm*, who said, "Hope and Joy can go today."

. . .

WHEN THEY'D FINISHED BREAKFAST, Honor was still asleep. Florence organized the girls to look through every inch of the house for the missing money. Her domain was the living room. She decided to start with the couch, picked up a cushion, and found the black bag. She looked inside to see all the rolled-up notes and called out, "I found it, as soon as I started looking. No one looked very hard."

Everyone hurried into the living room.

"Where was it?" Cherish asked.

"Under the cushion on the couch."

Cherish shook her head. "I don't even remember putting it there. I must've put it there as a hiding place."

"At least it's found now," Favor said.

FLORENCE WAITED for Joy and Hope to head out to the market stall, and then she traveled in a separate buggy to pay the rent to Mr Pettigrew. It was a little surprising that Cherish hadn't asked to come for the ride, but Florence figured she wanted to ask Honor about Jonathon as soon as she woke. Jonathon seemed to be Cherish's favorite subject at the moment. For the life of her, Florence couldn't figure out why her two sisters thought Jonathon was so great.

CHAPTER 22

ONCE THE RENT had been paid, Florence was tempted to stop and have a quiet coffee and a piece of cake by herself in a café before going home. What stopped her was the fear that an argument would break out between Honor and Cherish over Jonathon. She had to go home to be the peacemaker.

When she was about halfway home, she saw an *Englisch* girl a ways up ahead, hitchhiking with a bag slung over her shoulder and a small dog by her feet. The dog looked suspiciously like Caramel. And the girl …

The girl disappeared behind a tree. Florence drove until she was even with the tree, pulled the buggy over to the side and got out to take a look. She discovered Cherish hiding behind a clump of trees. Florence couldn't believe her eyes and kept staring at her in horror. Her long hair was braided and wound onto the base of her head and pinned in a messy clump, and she wore tight jeans and a loose white shirt. "What are you doing?"

"I'm leaving."

"No, you're not! Get in the buggy now."

"I won't. You can't tell me what to do anymore. I'm going and never coming back."

"Get into the buggy now!"

"No!"

Caramel jumped up on Florence, pleased to see her. Florence swooped down and lifted him into her arms and ran back to the buggy with him, knowing Cherish would never leave without Caramel.

"What are you doing? He's my dog and he's coming with me."

"If you don't get in right now I'm going back home to get *Mamm* and I'll bring her back."

"Florence, don't do this. I'm leaving and you can't stop me. If you take me home, I'm only going to leave again, and again and again. I don't want to be here anymore. I don't want to be Amish anymore. Just leave me be."

Florence drove off and her heart ached as though it was breaking. In the rear-view mirror, she saw Cherish's sad face, but what could she do? Her sister wasn't old enough to make the decision to leave.

Once Florence was home, she ran inside the house with Caramel tucked under one arm to tell her stepmother what was going on. It was another shock for her.

Then while *Mamm* got into the buggy, Florence figured they'd need backup so she called Mark from the phone in the barn. With Caramel safely inside the house, *Mamm* and she made their way back to Cherish.

"I hope she's still there," *Mamm* said.

"I did my best. She refused to get into the buggy."

"You should've dragged her."

Florence sighed and prayed that Cherish would be there. She couldn't go through with another search for a missing sister. She was already exhausted from the last one.

Fighting back tears, *Mamm* said, "I don't know where I've gone wrong with you girls. First Honor, and now Cherish. I don't know what I'm going to do."

Florence glanced over at her. "You've done nothing wrong. You've been a perfectly *gut mudder."* When Florence looked back at the road, she was delighted to see Cherish still there, sitting right where she'd left her. "There she is. Can you see her?"

"Look at what she's wearing!" her stepmother said in disgust.

"Er … *jah,* I forgot to mention that." Florence stopped the buggy close by and *Mamm* got out and hurried over to Cherish. Florence got out too and stayed by Wilbur, patting his neck and praying. She prayed her mother would be able to talk sense into Cherish and that her sister would get into the buggy without too many problems. After all, they couldn't physically force her into the buggy. Cherish had to see sense.

Florence heard her stepmother say, "What's gotten into you?"

"I'm leaving. And that's that."

"You can leave when you're old enough. If you want to leave us later, when you're eighteen, then that's your right to do so, but until then you have to come home with me."

Cherish then stared into the distance. "You called Mark?"

Mamm looked up to see Mark's buggy. "I didn't call him."

"I did," Florence called out.

"You should mind your own business, Florence."

"You are my business," Florence called back. "You're my *schweschder*."

Mark jumped out of his buggy and rushed toward Cherish. After a few minutes of him talking with Cherish, she agreed to go home. Florence said a silent prayer of thanks.

When they were home after an unpleasant silent trip, Cherish was sent up to her room. After Florence unhitched the buggy, she noticed Cherish's knapsack and took it into the house. When *Mamm* saw it in Florence's hands, she decided to look through it. She sat down on the couch and pulled everything out.

"Florence, look! It's make up." Her stepmother put a hand to her forehead and wept. Through tear-filled eyes, *Mamm* said, "I can't cope anymore. I think this is a job for Dagmar. She's always asking if one of you girls can come to stay with her."

Florence was shocked. Aunt Dagmar wasn't liked by any of her half-sisters. *"Dat's* older *schweschder,* you mean? Dagmar from Millersburg?"

"Jah."

"But she lives so far away and the girls aren't fond of her." When Wilma just stared at her, it clicked into place. "I see what you mean. You'd really send Cherish there? Or are you thinking about Honor?"

"Cherish needs to go. I think it's just what she needs. Can you call Dagmar and ask her if she can take her in?"

Florence was taken aback that her mother was sending Cherish away and not Honor, but at least she was disciplining someone for a change. "Sure. When do you want her to go?"

"I'll drive up there with her tomorrow if Dagmar agrees, or as soon as we can find a driver to take us."

"I'll make a few calls after I get some sleep. I'll arrange transport."

"And you'll call Dagmar?"

"Jah, sure."

"Gut. Could you do it now?"

Florence had hoped *Mamm* would change her mind. A little time would've given her a chance to think things through and maybe focus on a punishment for Honor. As far as she knew, Honor had no ramifications for running away. "Okay. I'll do it now."

"And if you can watch things here, I'll stay a couple of days with Dagmar to get Cherish settled in and then I'll come back. I'll tell Dagmar what's happened and I'll forbid Cherish to talk to Jonathon Wilkes ever again."

"It might be best not to tell Cherish what's happening until the car arrives—just in case she tries to run away again before we have everything organized."

Mamm nodded.

Florence headed to the barn and called Aunt Dagmar. She was delighted to have Cherish come to stay with her and even said yes to Cherish bringing Caramel. Dagmar also assured Florence she'd watch Cherish like a hawk and wouldn't let her talk to any man, let alone Jonathon Wilkes. As soon as Florence hung up the receiver from Dagmar, she arranged a car to take them tomorrow, and then made another quick call back to Aunt Dagmar to let her know what time they might arrive. Finally, Florence headed back into the house, drained of all energy.

When she saw Wilma asleep on the couch, she tiptoed up to her room to have a rest. Across the hallway, she heard Cherish sobbing, but had no sympathy. Every trace of emotion had been drawn out of her.

CHAPTER 23

THE NEXT MORNING, a car was due to arrive at any minute to drive them to Aunt Dagmar's farm in Millersburg.

Mamm walked down the stairs carrying a black fabric bag and set it by the front door.

"Going somewhere, *Mamm?*" Cherish asked.

"*Jah* and so are you. We're taking a little road trip."

Cherish rubbed her neck. "Where to?"

"To visit Aunt Dagmar."

"*Nee!* I'm not going there!"

"You're going to be staying there until you get over this silliness about being in love with Jonathon."

"What?" she screeched. "You're sending me away?"

"*Jah,* if that's what you want to call it."

Cherish shook her head. "I'm not going and there's no way you can force me."

Mamm nodded. "You are."

"I'm never going to change the way I feel about Jonathon."

Honor said, "Jonathon loves me not you. He's never been interested in you because you're a child."

Cherish's voice got louder. "Well, that's what *Mamm* and everyone say about you. If he really loved you he wouldn't have let you come back. Or, he would've come back too."

Florence heard the conversation from the kitchen and figured she needed to help Wilma. She walked out into the living room. "This is what's happening, Cherish. You're going upstairs and throwing clothes into a bag, and you're going to stay with Aunt Dagmar until *Mamm* says you can come home."

Favor and Honor sat at the table with their mouths open, listening to everything play out.

Cherish's lips turned down at the corners. "Can I take Caramel?"

"I did ask Dagmar about Caramel and she said he could come too, but if you don't get yourself ready right now, I won't allow you to take him."

Cherish pulled a face at Florence. "Okay. I'll go. I'll get out of going to the markets and doing so many chores. It won't be so bad. Probably better than here. It won't be so bad." She went upstairs and soon came back down carrying a bag over her shoulder and holding Caramel under one arm. "I'm ready."

At that moment, the car pulled up right on time. Cherish walked out of the house without looking back at Florence and without even saying goodbye. *Mamm* hadn't told Joy and Hope what was going on before they'd left for the markets. Then she quickly told Favor and Honor what was happening.

Honor stayed put, but Favor ran past *Mamm* to say goodbye to Cherish who was now in the car waiting. Florence moved out onto the porch and *Mamm* walked out the front door and heaved a sigh.

"*Denke,* Florence. I don't know what I'd do without you. These girls will be the death of me one day."

Florence hugged *Mamm*. "Have a nice couple of days with Aunt Dagmar and give her my love."

"I will."

"Will you be back before Christmas? It's only days away."

"I want to be back before then, if I can."

Florence walked Wilma to the car. "Bye, Cherish."

Cherish ignored her and looked straight ahead. It seemed Cherish thought sending her off to Aunt Dagmar was all her idea.

It was a relief when they drove away. It was going to be tough for Aunt Dagmar, but she'd said she was up for the task.

"Florence, *Mamm* said I could visit my friends today." Honor asked. "That's okay, isn't it?"

"Nee." Florence folded her arms across her chest. "You should be the one going to Dagmar's."

Honor's bottom lip quivered. *"Mamm* said I could go. I'm not grounded. Did she say I was?"

Florence sighed. In *Mamm's* haste to keep Cherish out of trouble, Honor's deed had gone unpunished. "Are you certain *Mamm* said you can?"

"Jah. I apologized for what I did. *Mamm* forgave me. She knows how sorry I am and I'd never do anything like that again. That's why Cherish is being punished and not me. Cherish might try to run away again. Who knows where she'd end up? At least I had a plan."

Florence had little strength to argue, or to enforce a grounding. Convinced Honor wouldn't do it again, she decided to take the easy way out for once. "As long as you're truly repentant and not about to do it again. *Mamm* wouldn't be able to cope with it and she might inquire if Aunt Dagmar has another bedroom for you."

"I won't. Believe me."

"Okay. Go visit your friends, but you will be getting extra chores starting tonight—for several weeks."

Honor nodded.

Favor came up beside them, and said to Honor, "It's weird that Cherish likes Jonathon and you do too."

Honor agreed. "I'm so upset with her. He's in love with me."

Florence was in no mood to listen to the girls. "Seems like you'll be on your own for a while Favor. You're old enough and I'll only be gone for a few hours."

"I'm plenty old enough. Older and wiser than Cherish."

"Being wiser than Cherish wouldn't be hard at all." Florence regretted her words, but it was too late to take them back. Her two half-sisters giggled.

"Will you be out the whole day?" Favor asked Honor.

"I'll be back in time to help with the evening meal and I won't leave for a couple of hours."

"*Denke.* That would be good," Favor said.

"I should thank our neighbor," said Florence. "It was so good of him to drive me there and back. We were nearly a whole day and most of the night driving." She stared at Honor. "You really should get more of a punishment for what you did."

"*Nee,* Florence. I've learned my lesson and I'll do those extra chores."

Florence pressed her lips together. "I'll think up some good ones for you."

The two girls walked back into the house and Florence headed to Carter's house through the orchard.

. . .

Today's walk was different. It wasn't the nice restful walk she took most afternoons. Her head was spinning from lack of sleep and her stomach still churned from the stress that Cherish had put her through.

When Carter's house came into view, she saw him getting into his car. He looked up, saw her and straightened up. He closed his door and walked toward her. "Hello."

"Hello. I thought you would've had enough of driving for a few days."

He chuckled. "That's true, but I had a good few hours' sleep and I'm ready to face the world again."

She walked a few more steps until she stood in front of him. "I've just come to say thank you."

"You already thanked me."

"Last night was a blur. Anyway, you did such a lot for someone you don't even know."

"I know you, and now I know Honor a bit more."

"My stepmother's sent my youngest half-sister to stay with an aunt. She was becoming a handful."

"Oh really? As punishment?"

"Kind of, and to keep her away from trouble of all kinds. She had a weird childish crush on Jonathon and she's only thirteen."

"Jonathon must have something going for him. I couldn't tell just by looking at him."

"Yeah, well I don't know what that something would be."

"It must be hard to be having problems with two of your sisters."

She nodded.

He stared at her more closely. "Would you care to see my renovations now?"

She took a step back. "I really should get back home. There's so much to do."

"Some other time?"

"Yes. Bye."

He smiled at her and gave her a nod before she turned and walked away.

CHAPTER 24

FLORENCE WAS COUNTING the days until *Mamm* was back. Ada had come to the house crying when she learned that Jonathon and Honor had run away. She blamed herself because Jonathon was her nephew.

Florence then learned from Ada that Jonathon had a reputation of being unscrupulous and a dreadful flirt. It would've been nice to know that before he'd worked in their orchard around her half-sisters, but still, she couldn't turn back the clock.

In the days that *Mamm* was gone, the girls had been unusually quiet.

Honor was understandably behaving well and keeping out of Florence's way.

Florence's afternoon walks around her orchard had been brief due to the chilly weather and also due to her decision to stay away from Carter Braithwaite. Staying away from his house though, wasn't keeping him out of her head.

On Christmas Eve morning, *Mamm* was back.

When the car pulled up, Florence's half-sisters ran out to greet their mother. Florence stayed back on the porch watching and waiting. She heaved a sigh of relief when it was clear Wilma was alone. She'd half expected Cherish would've talked her way out of staying with Aunt Dagmar. There was no doubt Cherish would've tried, but Wilma must've stayed strong and Florence was pleased. She stepped off the porch and joined in with the girls in greeting Wilma.

Florence took the bag from the driver and followed the giggling girls as they walked their mother into the house. After Florence took Wilma's bag upstairs and set it on her bed, she walked downstairs to see the girls gathered around Wilma in the living room. Two were sitting with *Mamm* on the couch, one to either side, and the others sat on the rug at her feet.

"Tea, *Mamm?*"

Wilma looked over at Florence and smiled. "Please, Florence."

"I'll boil the kettle."

"Then hurry back here so I can tell you what's been happening."

After Florence filled the kettle and lit the stove, she walked back into the living room. Hope had moved to the floor to allow her to sit on the couch next to *Mamm*. *"Denke*, Hope," she said as she sat down. "How's Cherish?"

"She's not happy, but then again I didn't expect she would be."

Florence was a little surprised to see a hint of a smile around *Mamm's* lips.

"Tell us everything," Favor said.

"As you know, Aunt Dagmar is very domineering and she always talks about when your *vadder* and she were young and how things were back then. They weren't allowed to get away with this and they weren't allowed to get away with that. And how their *Dat* used to beat them with a strap if they did the slightest thing wrong."

Florence nodded. "That's how things were back then for a lot of people."

Mamm said, "I've had quite an ordeal."

"Tell us."

"Cherish begged me to let her come back. I said she couldn't. Not until she got over this Jonathon nonsense."

"Jah, she should get over it," Honor said. "He'll be her *bruder*-in-law and that's all."

"Dagmar is not allowing her near a phone, and on the farm she'll only talk to people who visit, and the people at their bi-monthly meetings."

"Ach, she's going to hate that," Favor said.

"Serves her right. Jonathon loves me," Honor commented.

"Can't you let her come home?" Favor asked.

"*Nee.* Dagmar sews quilts and makes baskets and she's going to teach Cherish."

Florence nodded. "She'd like that. She's always asking me if she can sew."

"Now she can do that and make baskets all day except when she's doing chores on the farm," *Mamm* said.

Favor sighed. "I suppose she has Caramel with her, but when will we see her again?"

"Not for a while, I fear."

Joy sighed. "Now there's only the four of us. Oh, not counting you, Florence." Before Florence could comment, Joy kept right on talking, "I invited Isaac for dinner tonight. Is that all right?"

"*Jah,* that's okay. I might have a lie down to recover and then I'll find some more energy."

The kettle whistled. "I'll make you that tea first." Florence headed to the kitchen still listening to the girls talking.

"Do you want something to eat too?" Hope asked.

"*Nee.* I'm not hungry at the moment."

"Save it up for the nice dinner I'm cooking tonight," Honor said.

As Florence poured the boiling water onto the leaves in the teapot, she had a funny feeling about Joy and Isaac. They had been spending a lot of time together. What if they wanted to get married? *Mamm* was tired and ground down after the whole business with Cherish and Honor right on top of Mercy's wedding. Reminding herself not to cross her bridges before she got to them, she reached up into the cupboard for a cup and a saucer.

Florence put the tea items on a tray and carried them out to *Mamm*. She asked one of the girls to place the small table in front of her stepmother.

"Denke, Florence. I just realized … who's at the markets today?"

"Ada and Christina are at the stall for us. They said they'd do it because they knew you were coming home today."

Mamm smiled. "Bless their hearts. And they took their time to do that on Christmas Eve."

"They probably didn't have anything better to do," Favor said.

The other girls laughed.

"I'm sure that's not true," *Mamm* said.

Florence sat down next to her stepmother again. "I'm sure they'd have lots to do. They did it as a kindness to us."

"I'll pour the tea." Hope poured the tea for *Mamm* and then handed it to her.

Mamm had barely finished taking a sip when Joy told her that Isaac was now working in Mark's store and living in the room off from the stable where Jonathon used to live.

"Well," *Mamm* said, "things have worked out well for Isaac."

"Jah, and we heard that Jonathon has left the community," Joy said, shaking her head.

"He's heartbroken that's why," Honor said. "That's what I think, but he'll come back as soon as we can be together. He'll be back for me."

Mamm frowned. "Let's not talk about him."

CHAPTER 25

A FEW HOURS LATER, Florence found Honor in her bedroom, crying. She sat down beside her. "What's upset you?"

"*You* know. I'll never love anyone else and now he's left the community. What is wrong with everyone? I know people in the community who've married at seventeen."

"*Jah,* but they didn't run away to do it. They got permission and … and they chose a suitable person."

Honor pouted at Florence. "I knew you wouldn't allow it and *Mamm* would do what you said."

"There's no use discussing it. Jonathon's unsuitable."

"He just made one mistake, though. Where is the forgiveness in your heart?"

"He made many more than just one mistake, and he left his job suddenly and left Mark with no one on a day when Mark and

Christina had an appointment." Florence shook her head. "The man *Gott* has for you would not do these kinds of things."

"But Isaac's got the job now. Joy told me that. Jonathon always felt Isaac should've had the job anyway because he's Mark's *bruder*-in-law. He even told Mark to give him the job and he'd look for something else."

"We're not going to agree, Honor, so it's pointless talking about it. That just tells me he wasn't grateful for the job he had." Although she felt sorry for Honor, there was nothing more she could say. Time would heal her sister's heart. Florence walked back down the stairs and slipped some items into a basket for Carter—two apple pies, apple butter, chocolate cookies made from her grandmother's recipe and a large bottle of apple cider —and then announced she was going for a walk.

It was time to thank Carter properly. She'd been too short with him the other day and had brushed him off by refusing to see his renovations. He'd driven her around for hours in the daytime to look for Honor, and then he drove all the way to Connecticut and back in the night. It had been exhausting for her so she knew it would've been worse for him as the driver. It was Christmas time and she wanted him to know how much she'd appreciated his generosity.

As she approached his house, she knew he was home because she spotted his car.

She knocked on the door and when he took his time to answer, she walked to the window, looked in and smiled when she saw him playing on his computer with earphones in his ears. When she knocked loudly on the window, he looked up and then pulled off the earphones as he jumped up from the table.

He opened the door, smiling. "How's your sister?"

"Which one?"

"The one who was banished."

"Ah, she's good, I believe."

"You haven't talked with her?"

"I don't think she's talking to me. She thinks I was the one who sent her away. It was my stepmother's idea. Anyway, I think I told you that last time I was here."

"And the runaway sister?"

"She's doing okay. I'm hoping she'll forget about Jonathon." He slowly nodded and then she held out the basket. "These are for you. My way of saying thank you for all that you've done."

He took the basket from her and looked in it. "You have been busy. You did all this baking just for me?"

"Of course, especially just for you. Without you, I don't know what would've happened with Honor. We never would've found her in time."

"Things would've worked out. Now that you're here, come in and have a look at my renovations. I've been wanting to show them to someone."

"Sure. I'd like that." His words caused her to realize she'd never seen any of his friends there. No friends and no relatives—the man was a complete mystery.

He took the basket from her and led her through to the kitchen. She was impressed. A sparkling white and chrome kitchen had taken the place of the old one she remembered as a child.

"This is amazing. Truly beautiful."

He placed the basket down on the counter and took out all the contents. "Do you remember what it looked like?"

"Last time I was here the room was just a shell. I remember it as a child, but only vaguely. Before my father sold it he kept it ready for visitors, family and friends who came to stay."

He opened the cupboard and pulled out a little photo album. "This is what it looked like. I took these the day I moved in. The Graingers told me they never touched the place."

She picked up the album and flipped through it. Photos always reminded her of her mother. More than anything she would've loved to know what she looked like. Her only memories were vague impressions of holding onto her mother's dress and her mother hoisting her onto her hip. People had told her she looked like her mother now that she was an adult, but her father had never mentioned her mother. By the time Florence was old enough to ask questions, he was married to Wilma.

She put the photo book back on the table after she'd looked through. "You've certainly done a lot of work."

He placed his hands on his hips and looked around. "I don't know what to do with the rest of it. I was going to paint the living room a neutral shade because it looks so out-dated with the blue walls and the wood interior. I'll have to get rid of the wood."

"That's part of the charm, though. I think you'd destroy the place if you got rid of those features."

He smiled. "Do you think so?"

"I do."

"I'll show you the bathroom."

She followed him up the wooden staircase to a small bathroom. The ceiling was slanted.

"This was part of the old attic. It was remodeled at some stage, I guess when they went from outdoor to indoor plumbing." He pointed to the antique claw-foot bathtub. "I kept the same tub and had it sandblasted and re-enamelled."

"It's nice you've kept the lovely bathtub, and that's given the room so much appeal. It wouldn't be the same with a modern tub because the place is old."

He rubbed his neck. "I think you're right. But I couldn't live with the out-dated kitchen and I had to do something with this bathroom. I like a nice kitchen with all the mod cons."

She gave him a curious look.

"Modern conveniences."

"Oh. So, you like cooking?"

He chuckled. "I never cook."

She frowned wondering how he ate if he never cooked. "Never?"

"I don't cook, unless you count re-heating things, or thawing meals out and putting them in the microwave. That's the closest I've come to cooking. Or a frozen pizza in the oven."

"I see." She stared at him. From what she knew so far, he had no friends, no family and he couldn't cook. Add to that, he had plenty of free time, enough money even though he didn't have a job, and he was a self-confessed bad chess player. Maybe that's what she found appealing—the man was an enigma. When he smiled at her causing her heart to pitter-patter, she knew it was time to leave. "Anyway, Merry Christmas for tomorrow."

"Merry Christmas to you, Florence."

She turned away to walk down the stairs and when she was halfway down them, he said, "Are you going now?"

When she got to the bottom she turned around to see him on the last step. "Yes. We have guests for dinner. Well, one guest."

"A man?"

"That's right." She noticed the smile left his face as he ambled down the steps.

"Let me walk you to the fence. Wait, don't forget your basket." He got the empty basket from the kitchen and gave it back to her.

She giggled and then stopped abruptly when she sounded like one of her sisters, who often laughed at nothing at all. "Thanks."

He then opened the front door. "After you."

She walked past him and then stepped out into the chilly winter air.

As he walked beside her, he looked around. "I wonder if we'll get snow."

"I hope so. I love watching the snowflakes fall when I don't have to go out in it. If it snowed tomorrow it would be just perfect."

"You're not going to your church tomorrow for Christmas?"

"No. We don't do that. We celebrate at home with our friends and families."

He nodded.

"And, what will you do?"

"The same."

"You're having your family and friends come here when you don't cook? Are you going to microwave them a re-heated meal?"

He shook his head. "My friends are here already."

She frowned at him and he pointed to his cows. "Ah, yes, the cows you've adopted."

"I'll give them something special to eat—something Christmassy."

"I'm glad you won't be by yourself."

"A wise person once said that if you like your own company, you're never alone."

They'd reached the fence and he pulled up the wire for her and she bent down and slipped through to the other side still hanging onto her basket. When she straightened up, they held each other's gaze for a moment. There was something in those dark hazel eyes. She wanted to learn more about him—get to know him, but sadly that was out of the question. They could never be anything more than neighbors. "You're an interesting man, Carter." *A complete riddle is what she meant.* How did he get to this age and have no one with whom to spend Christmas day? He seemed nice and friendly, so surely, people didn't hate him. Was there something she wasn't seeing?

He was visibly shocked at her comment and that made her embarrassed. Like many of her comments, the words had rolled off her tongue before she'd thought about them. She hadn't meant it to sound like she was interested in him romantically. *Is that how he took it?*

As he stood there stunned, she said, "Bye. I have to go." She turned and walked away from him. This time, she was determined to stay away from him for good—at least for the rest of the year.

When Florence got home, she was ordered out of the kitchen by Joy, who had already told the others she was cooking the entire meal tonight since Isaac was coming. At least with Joy, Florence didn't foresee any problems.

Florence didn't mind in the least that someone was organizing the cooking and took the opportunity to have a much-needed nap.

Dinner that night, with Isaac as their guest, was pleasant especially since there was no talk of Jonathon.

CHAPTER 26

ON CHRISTMAS MORNING, Florence got out of bed early, pushed her feet into her slippers and pulled on her robe. Then she hurried downstairs to tend to the fire. This was always the job of the first person to wake.

When she got to the bottom of the stairs, she saw the embers were still glowing keeping the house warm to some extent. Carefully, she lifted more kindling onto the embers until they caught alight, then she carefully arranged more logs.

She stood back and watched the flames grow higher and folded her arms around her middle.

This was the first year the girls weren't awake before her, and it was also the first Christmas they'd be without Mercy—and now, without Cherish. Tomorrow, the girls would be up way before dawn. The day after Christmas was called Second Christmas, traditionally their 'gift-giving day.' She walked past the wrapped presents in the corner of the room and moved quickly across the gray linoleum flooring to light the stove. After she rinsed and refilled the kettle and placed it over the flame, she stayed by the stove enjoying the warmth.

Things were always changing. She had a feeling that, come next Christmas, things would be different again. Hopefully Mercy would be back, and maybe even Cherish too, if she got over her silly notion of being in love with a much-older and unsuitable man that her older sister also liked. There was never a dull moment in a household with so many teenaged girls.

When the kettle boiled, Florence took hold of the coffee canister and shook out some grounds. She was used to measuring coffee that way and saved herself the chore of washing a spoon. Then she filled the plunger with the boiling water. She gave the container a little swirl and then waited a minute before she pushed the plunger down. Once she'd poured herself a cup, she sat at the table pleased to have this quiet time before the others woke.

THE DAY WAS FILLED with visitors stopping by. Firstly, it was Levi Bruner and his daughter, Bliss. They brought with them a plum cake made by Bliss. Of course, *Mamm* invited them to stay for the midday meal. Florence could see what was happening. First the gift of a horse and now a casual visit on Christmas Day, with a cake. Levi Bruner was sweet on *Mamm*. Bliss was just happy to be with her friends, Favor and Hope.

. . .

LATER, Ada and Samuel arrived along with Mark, Christina and Isaac. It was fairly crowded around the dinner table as they shared coffee, tea, cake and cookies.

BOTH JOY and Honor opened the door expecting to greet Isaac. He'd gone home and was coming back again for the evening meal. He was to be the only guest for Christmas dinner.

The next thing Florence heard was Honor yelling out to her. Florence hurried over to her. "What is it?"

"It's a tree, and the note says, *Florence*. It's for you." Honor held it out to her.

Florence looked down at the small plant with the huge red ribbon and the tiny red envelope attached. Immediately, she recognized it as some kind of apple tree. She took it from Honor and sat down with it. She placed the tree in her lap and opened the note.

"So, what is it?" Hope rushed over.

"An apple tree." Florence could only laugh.

"Who's it from?"

"I'm trying to find that out." In her heart, Florence knew who it was from. She opened the note and read it to herself.

TO MY DEAR FLORENCE,

I happened to come across this and thought you might like it.

It's an already grafted Narragansett.

Your Secret Admirer

It was from Carter.

"Well? Who gave you that twig and spent so much time wrapping it up so fancy?" Joy asked with her hands firmly on her hips.

"No one. It's not a twig."

Favor grabbed the note and opened it. "A Secret Admirer! Florence has a secret admirer. Florence is in love! Who could it be?"

Florence jumped up and snatched the note back. The girls stared at Florence in disbelief.

Hope said, "It's Levi Bruner. He gave us the horse."

"Nee, he likes *Mamm,"* Favor said. "He's way too old for Florence."

Isaac stood there looking embarrassed. Then, in the midst of their noisy speculations, friends of the girls arrived unexpectedly to visit, and the girls turned their attention to them. Florence took her gift and the handwritten note upstairs and hid them in her room.

Where ever did he find such a plant? She knew it must've come from another collector. She hurried back down the stairs to help with the dinner and there she saw that Ada and Samuel had arrived and so it was two more people at their table.

AFTER DINNER, Florence was washing up with Hope and they were talking about Honor and how she'd laughed and joined in with the conversation. It was almost like she was back to her old self. Florence hoped that in time she'd forget Jonathon Wilkes. It didn't help that his brother Stephen was married to Mercy. He'd never be out of her life completely.

Ada walked into the kitchen and said to Florence, "I have a surprise for you. I've been talking to Wilma and she asked me something."

"What?"

"I won't talk about it today. I'll tell you soon, though."

"What is it? You have to tell me now." Florence shook the water off her hands and wiped them on a towel. She hated not knowing things. "You must tell me."

Ada chuckled. "Wilma asked me if I knew someone suitable for you."

"Ach nee! I told her not to do that."

"At first I said I didn't. But then I remembered Ezekiel Troyer."

Hope put down the plate she'd been wiping dry. "And you think he'd be a good match for Florence?"

"Stop it, Hope," Florence said, not wanting to prolong this conversation.

"Well, she was right about Mercy and Stephen."

Ada looked with eagle eyes at Florence. "Will you meet him?"

Florence frowned. "Where's he from?"

"Not too far away."

"She'll meet him," Hope said.

"Now wait a minute."

"What harm could it do to meet the man? Especially when Wilma has already arranged for him to come to dinner here next week."

"She what?"

Ada nodded. "That's right he's coming here for dinner next week."

Florence blew out a deep breath.

"What's he like? What does he do?" Hope eagerly asked Ada.

"He's a pig farmer."

That wasn't something Florence wanted to hear. That conjured an image of a large sweaty man wearing large knee-high boots and too-large overalls and smelling of pigswill. Hope must've thought something similar because she burst out laughing.

"There's nothing wrong with pigs," said Ada.

"I know. Piglets are cute," Hope replied smiling. "I'd love to have a pet piglet, but then they grow up and it wouldn't be so adorable."

Since he was coming for dinner, there was no way Florence could get out of it. "I'll meet him but only because he's already coming here. And please, Ada, don't do anything like this again. I don't care what *Mamm* tells you."

Ada nodded. "I didn't know. I thought you'd be pleased. That's why I was saving it as a surprise."

"*Denke.* I appreciate your efforts, but I did tell *Mamm* I wasn't interested in finding a man this way."

"Florence already has a secret admirer." Hope said. "He left a present at the door for her today."

Ada stared at Florence. "Is that so?"

Florence couldn't help but giggle. "It was just someone's idea of a joke. That's all." She didn't want rumors to start, so leaned over and whispered to Ada, "Just one of the girls having some fun."

CHAPTER 27

WHEN THE NIGHT was over and every one of the girls and Wilma were in bed, a weary Florence walked up the stairs. She pushed open her bedroom door and the light from the hallway lit her special apple tree. It seemed as though it was smiling back at her. Florence flicked on her light and turned off the gaslight in the hall. Then she sat at her window and looked out into the darkness in the direction of Carter's house.

Carter cared about her enough to find one of those apple trees she'd mentioned in passing. They weren't easy to come by and he would've gone to an awful lot of trouble finding a plant already grafted like that. He would've already had it when she was there yesterday. He'd planned all along to leave it on her doorstep for Christmas morning. For the first time in her life, she felt special.

Then an image of the pig farmer jumped into her mind. Was he the kind of man she would, or perhaps should, marry?

She closed her curtains and moved to the end of her bed. Nothing could ever come from her attraction to the *Englischer*. He was off-limits. The best thing she could do was put Carter Braithwaite out of her mind altogether. They lived next-door, but they were worlds apart.

When she'd gotten changed, she climbed into her bed and once her head hit the pillow, she reviewed how much had happened in a few short weeks. Mercy had gotten married, Honor had tried to run away with Jonathon, and then Cherish had tried to run away. Now there were two girls missing from the house, since Cherish was staying with Aunt Dagmar and Mercy was married.

Florence's life was disappearing into the lives of those around her. She knew she had to make a change somewhere, someway, so she could have a life of her own. Otherwise, she'd live her life worried about her half-sisters.

Would Honor ever forget Jonathon? For that matter, would Cherish forget him? Or would both girls liking Jonathon cause a huge rift to develop in the family?

Running the orchard, the household and now the market stall was enough for any one person. She didn't need all of these other worries.

Falling asleep, she could feel time ticking by. Her life was moving so fast and she was getting older by the minute.

Weeks ago, she'd realized God was using Carter Braithwaite as a sign there was a good Amish man somewhere for her. Could the one she'd been waiting for be Ezekiel Troyer?

Would the pig farmer be the answer to her having a life of her own?

HONOR HAD CRIED herself to sleep, and she woke up pining for Jonathon. Couldn't her family understand love? Surely *Mamm* knew what it was like to love because she'd loved *Dat*. She couldn't help being the age she was.

Since she'd been back she'd put on a brave face and had done the best she could to fit back in with the family, but she didn't want to be there. One thing she knew for a fact was that it made it worse for her that Cherish had a crush on Jonathon. It made it look like everyone was in love with him. The difference was that Cherish's love wasn't real and her's was.

Honor knew all she could do was pray. So she wouldn't fall asleep, she got out of her warm bed and kneeled down beside her bed and prayed that their love would find a way. She crawled back into her still-warm bed.

Soon, her sisters were squealing. It was Second Christmas and time to open the gifts. She changed into her day clothes, braided her hair, and after she placed her *kapp* on her head, she went downstairs. Her sisters were nowhere to be seen but her mother was in the living room talking to someone. Honor blinked twice, not believing her eyes. It was Jonathon.

He looked over and saw her and when he stood up, her mother pushed herself to her feet and walked over to her, smiling. "Jonathon has come here to explain everything. He's said he was sorry for running away with you."

Florence had walked down the stairs just a minute or so behind Honor and she did her own double take when she saw Jonathon. "What's going on?"

Mamm said, "Jonathon has come to say he's sorry. He's asked our forgiveness and I gave it. He's been here for nearly two hours and we've talked deeply and he's told me so much about himself."

Florence stood still, as stiff as a post.

Honor took another step forward. "Does that mean …?"

"You're still in trouble for doing what you did. You can't marry until you're eighteen, but if you still want to marry each other after that, we won't stand in your way."

This was what Honor had hoped for and she was thrilled Jonathon hadn't left her. He'd come back for her.

"You two can talk in the living room and we'll go to the kitchen." *Mamm* looked over at Florence. "Come along, Florence."

Florence was hugely upset. She'd done everything for the family and now on the important things *Mamm* completely overrode her—hadn't even asked for her opinion before she'd given 'their' forgiveness and blessing.

She kept her thoughts quiet, said nothing and walked into the kitchen with *Mamm* to join the rest of the girls.

Honor ran to Jonathon and threw her arms around him. "I'm so happy you came here."

"I had to. I couldn't be without you." He whispered into her ear, "We shouldn't get too close or I'll get kicked out."

She stepped away from him and then they sat down and he sat beside her holding both her hands in his. "I missed you so much I couldn't stay away. I thought your *mudder* would understand if I explained how we both felt. I've done so many things wrong, but there's always forgiveness."

"*Jah,* there is."

"We still have to wait a whole year."

"But we don't have to hide away anymore. You'll stay around here, *jah?*"

"I will. I've really learned some things. Some hard lessons. I should've stayed before, and talked to your mother and explained myself. It was impulsive to run away, and stupid. I'll get a job and I don't care where I stay as long as I can be close to you."

She giggled from sheer happiness.

"I want to be the best man I can be for you. I have nothing right now, no money, but I'll work hard and be a good provider. I'll have savings by the time we're married."

"I know you will and we'll get by." She put her head on his shoulder.

. . .

Once *Mamm* was in the kitchen, she peeped around the corner at Jonathon and Honor until Florence tugged at her sleeve.

"Looks like you've lost another *dochder* now. Is that what you wanted? To have her marry so young?" Florence was annoyed and it was hard to hide it.

"I said they'd have to wait until she's eighteen." *Mamm's* eyes grew wide. "Florence, I can't stop them. Not when she's this age. I haven't lost her, but I know I'd lose her if I told them they couldn't marry."

Florence placed her hands on her hips thinking about Cherish. "That also means that Cherish will have to stay at Aunt Dagmar's for longer or she'd surely get in their way while they're courting."

"You're right. That would be best. I hope Cherish is okay staying there."

"The question is how Aunt Dagmar is coping with Cherish." Florence and *Mamm* shared a giggle. Florence could see what a hard situation *Mamm* was in. "Did Jonathon tell you why I'm against him?"

"Jah, he told me what he did and he said he was sorry. Both his *bruder* and Mercy forgave him."

"He's family now so they kind of had to."

"He said he couldn't change his past and all the dumb things he'd done, but he'd learn from all his mistakes and not repeat them. I believe him. He said he'd talk to you too."

Florence nodded, hoping Jonathon meant every word. Words were easy, actions were harder.

While Florence's sisters were busy making breakfast, chattering away about when they'd open their presents, Honor walked into the kitchen. "Florence, will you talk with Jonathon?"

"He wants to talk to me?"

"*Jah*. I'll stay in the kitchen."

Florence wasn't in the mood. She looked at *Mamm* who gave her an encouraging nod. She walked out to see Jonathon sitting down and then he jumped to his feet as she approached. "I'm sorry about everything, Florence."

She sat down opposite and he sat down too. Before she could say anything, he said, "I know you don't like me, but—"

"If you want me to be frank with you, I liked you when I first met you—up until I started to see a side of you I didn't like. Then when you tricked Mercy, I didn't want you anywhere near any of my sisters."

"I'm deeply sorry about that and I've said I'm sorry already. I didn't mean it to happen how it turned out."

"I know that, but it was still designed to drive a wedge between the two of them."

He hung his head. "I was jealous of Stephen." He looked up at her. "All the girls have always liked him more than me. Then when he came here and I saw the same thing happen, I was more annoyed than ever. It was awful of me to do what I did, I can see that now."

"That's good."

"I can't change what I've done. People can only learn from their mistakes, they can't un-make them, and I've certainly learned from mine. I no longer want to be the trickster, or the manipulator. I just want to live a Godly life with Honor as my *fraa*. I'll wait as long as I have to or do whatever I have to do to prove to you all that I'm a good person."

"Well, Honor certainly believes that and I'd hate for her to be disappointed."

"She won't be. And, Honor just told me that Cherish tried running away, and I can sincerely say I never gave her any encouragement."

"I know. I believe that."

He gave a sigh of relief. "What about you, though? It seems you're acting like the girls' mother, when you're only a girl yourself. An older girl, but still a girl and your looks haven't faded completely."

Florence stared at him. "I'm none of your concern."

"I didn't mean to be offensive. I just meant that I would've thought you might have wanted to get out more and meet people or something. Instead of worrying about your sisters."

"Just when I was starting to find forgiveness in my heart you go and ruin it."

He stared at her, a worried expression crossing his face, and then smiled when he saw that she was smiling. "You had me concerned there for a minute. I've got this problem that I don't think too hard before I open my big mouth."

"That's one thing you and I have in common, then."

"I also want to say that I know I used to act on impulse, but now I've got Honor to consider. I'm working on changing my ways and my whole personality. I'm going to be that good and responsible man she deserves."

Florence knew in her heart that he was genuinely trying. "I'm glad we talked."

"I mean every word I said."

"I hope so." She stood up. "I'll help in the kitchen and send Honor back out. I'm sure you two have loads to talk about."

"We do."

"And..." She wagged a finger at him. "No running away again."

"No way!"

She smiled at him, and then walked to the kitchen. Honor's face was the first she saw. "You can go back to speak with him."

"How did it go?"

"Good. He told me a few things and I believe he's genuine."

Honor's eyes sparkled and she hurried out of the kitchen.

Mamm looped her arm through Florence's. *"Denke,* Florence. Your approval means everything."

"It's my reserved approval. I'll see how he does over the next few months."

"Ada and I have a surprise for you."

Florence grimaced before she could stop herself. "The pig farmer?" Neither could she prevent the image of the man coming into her mind.

"Jah. She told you already?"

Florence sank into a chair. "She did."

"It's your turn for something nice to happen for you." *Mamm* patted her on her shoulder.

Florence hoped that it was true. She turned away, closed her eyes and superimposed Carter's face over the image she held of the Amish pig farmer. It didn't quite fit. Even though she knew little about Carter, there was something about him that made her want to learn more.

Bishop Paul's words echoed in her mind. She had to stay on the narrow way—the narrow path. The more time she spent with Carter, the closer she'd get to the edge of that path. The Amish life was the only one she'd known and nothing and no one would cause her to leave. Being around Carter too much put her at risk of doing just that. He was a temptation and, like all temptations, he had to be avoided.

Florence turned around, looked at her mother and said the only thing a good Amish daughter could say. "When, exactly, do I meet this pig farmer?"

"Next week. I think he's arriving midweek. Did I tell you he's interested in apple trees?"

Florence could hardly believe her ears. "Why didn't you say that in the first place?"

"Whoops. That was Ada's special part of the surprise." Wilma put her hand over her mouth and giggled.

Someone with a common interest? He mightn't be too bad.

She wouldn't have long to wait to find out since he was coming to dinner next week.

JONATHON STAYED with the family for breakfast and then left to find himself accommodation. He'd said he didn't think he'd be welcome back at Mark's and Christina's, but since he was determined to mend his ways, he'd assured them his first stop would be their place to offer his apologies for letting them down.

THAT NIGHT, Florence walked into Honor's bedroom as Honor was getting into bed.

"*Denke, schweschder,* for accepting Jonathon."

She sat down on the end of Honor's bed while Honor slipped between the sheets. "He seemed sincere and I'm prepared to give him a second chance."

"I know, and I appreciate it."

Florence thought about her friend, Liza. She'd said she was in love with Simon and then the love soured after marriage. *Gott* had blessed them with rekindled love when their son was born, but Florence knew the discord could just as easily have gone on. "Take this next year to get to know him thoroughly. The good and the bad. You could be married for sixty years or even more and you have to make sure he's truly the right one for you."

"He is."

Florence shook her head. "With that attitude, you could find yourself making a mistake. I want you to have in your mind 'is he?' rather than 'he is.' Do you understand the difference?"

HONOR STARED at Florence's face. Her older sister's eyes were bloodshot and her skin was pale. Lines were forming around the edges of her eyes. She was getting old. "I do, but I love him."

When Honor giggled, Florence rolled her eyes. "What's the use?"

"Just be happy for me."

"I'm fearful that you'll marry him and then realize he's not who you thought he'd be."

"That won't happen because you and *Mamm* are forcing us to wait a whole year."

Florence nodded. "That's good."

Honor fluffed up the pillows behind her and then scooted to sit with them behind her back. "Have you ever been in love?"

Florence took a deep breath. "I've liked a couple of men in the past, but nothing came of it. I didn't get close enough to love them."

"Do you even want to marry?"

"*Jah*, I do."

Honor found that hard to believe. "You do?"

"*Jah*. Why do you say it like that?"

"It's just that I can't picture you with anyone."

Florence nodded. "Me neither, I'm sad to say."

"He'd have to be someone really special."

"*Mamm* and Ada think they have such a man and he's coming to dinner next week. He's a pig farmer and they think … well, Ada thinks we'd be a match."

"A pig farmer? Hope told me that but I thought she was joking." Honor put her hand to her mouth and giggled. "I suppose someone has to farm pigs."

"He might be okay. He might be my perfect match."

"I hope so, for your sake. But then, what would we all do without you? And what about the orchard? It can't run without you."

"I wouldn't leave the orchard."

"But how—?"

Florence shook her head. "That's way too far ahead, and it might never happen. Right now, I'm glad you're going to take what I've said into account."

"I'll remember. 'Is he,' rather than 'he is,' right?"

"*Jah.* You're only young yet, and there are lots of choices out there for you."

"Choices?"

"Lots of men."

Honor was a little annoyed with Florence for not understanding that Jonathon was the man she'd chosen. "I know you're only saying that because you're worried, but Jonathon is good. He's the man I love, and we know his family. When Mercy married Stephen, no one was so worried about that and they're brothers."

"Just pray about it and then after a year if you still want to marry him I'll be happy for you."

"Just be happy now, anyway."

Florence giggled. "Okay. I'll be happy."

"And stop looking for things to be worried about. In life, there are always problems, but we can't go around being gloomy."

"That's true."

"We all have to make our own decisions in life and all of us aren't going to make the decisions you'd make because we're not you."

Florence smiled, but still, the worry never left her eyes. "You're wise sometimes for someone so young."

"*Denke.* I try."

Florence leaned forward and kissed Honor's forehead. "*Gut nacht.*"

"*Gut nacht.*"

When Florence was gone, Honor flicked off the light on her nightstand and lowered herself further into bed. Everything had turned around to suit her. Jonathon had loved her so much that he'd come back and faced her mother and Florence. That had taken great courage.

I'm sure they still doubt him, but I don't. Not one little bit.

FLORENCE WALKED into her own bedroom feeling more at ease with the idea of Honor and Jonathon. Sure, he'd made mistakes, but he said he was willing to learn from them and she believed him to be sincere.

As she crawled into bed, she wondered why love had come so easily for others while for her it was just some far-off hazy notion. She wanted to love someone and be loved in return. Not just any man would do. She didn't want to marry for the sake of marrying. What she wanted was to be loved with deep abiding and unconditional love. That love though, had to come with one proviso. She had to be able to continue with the orchard because she couldn't imagine a life without her apple trees. It seemed implausible, but she knew that with God all things were possible. He'd make a way where there was no way.

With her mouth curving into a smile, the prayer on Florence's lips that night was to find such a love.

A SIMPLE KISS

THE AMISH BONNET SISTERS BOOK 3

CHAPTER 1

PULLING her woolen shawl snug around her shoulders to ward off the late afternoon breeze, Florence Baker made her way along the rows of apple trees in her orchard. It was wintertime, chilly but not bitter-cold today, and the trees' naked branches twisting toward the sky made a pleasant and artful sight.

No matter the season, she always found the trees beautiful. In the springtime, the trees woke from their winter slumber and sprouted the delicate, luminescent green leaves of new life. Then came the breathtaking show of white flowers that filled the air with sweet fragrance quite unlike any other. Spring was Florence's favorite season, but when blossoming season came to an end and the petals fell, they spread along the ground like a glorious blanket. As a child she had rolled around among the petals with one or both of her older brothers, and, even now as an adult she was often tempted to throw restraint to the wind and do the same.

It was pleasing to walk through the orchard every day and see so many changes take place.

Just witnessing so much beauty and grace filled Florence's heart to overflowing. Her daily walk was her escape from the struggles of life with six younger half-sisters and a stepmother who was weak—often in body and, more often, in mind. *Mamm* had never been the same since *Dat's* death two-plus years earlier. Neither had Florence, but someone had to run the household and the orchard. It had all fallen to her when her two brothers left shortly after the funeral. Even though the orchard was hard work, Florence couldn't imagine life without her trees. The orchard was her one connection to *Dat* and the times the two of them had walked here just as she did today, talking together about the trees and anything else that came to mind.

Today, Florence was finding it hard to let go of her troubles and soak in the beauty of the trees.

Every time she thought about Ezekiel Troyer coming to dinner tomorrow night, her stomach churned. Tomorrow evening was set to be memorable; she just knew it. Her stepmother and "Aunt" Ada had arranged Ezekiel's visit without her knowledge. They'd called it a surprise, but Florence considered the whole plot more of a shock. Especially when she found out Ezekiel was a pig farmer. That conjured up all kinds of images. There was no use protesting because—she soon learned—he'd already made plans to visit her community for a week. Who knew what *Mamm's* best friend, Ada, would've told him about her?

Would Ezekiel interest her more than her mysterious neighbor did? She hadn't seen Carter Braithwaite since he'd left her a gift of a grafted apple tree on her doorstep on Christmas morning. The note had said 'from a secret admirer,' but it had to have been from him. No one else knew she harbored the intention of looking for heritage varieties one day. She'd mentioned that very variety, and her intention of looking for it one day, only to him.

Since she'd received the gift, it'd played through her mind whether she should thank him or not... *But, if he wanted to be thanked, surely he would've used his own name—wouldn't he?* And if she did thank him, that would be clear and certain acknowledgment that he'd called himself an 'admirer' and was therefore fond of her.

She looked over at the setting sun, now a misty hazy ball glowing through the band of thin clouds at the horizon. It would be perfect and romantic—if only ... he wasn't an *Englischer,* and also if he wasn't slightly annoying at times.

Still, everything she repeatedly told herself about him being off-limits didn't stop her legs from taking her close to his property on each and every late afternoon stroll.

For the whole week, she'd stopped short of the fence line and lurked among the trees hoping to catch a glimpse of him to see what he was doing. His car was parked outside his cottage, but she'd not seen him. In the past, he'd come out of his house when he saw her nearby. Maybe if she stepped away from the trees ...

Why put myself in temptation's way? It will never be. She grunted, wondering why she felt such a pull toward him if nothing would come of anything.

She smiled to herself when she heard Joy's voice in her head saying it must be *Gott* testing her. Joy, her third oldest half-sister, thought she had the answer to everything. Joy's comments on most things said that they were either *Gott's* blessing or *Gott's* testing. Florence stopped at a tree that she'd stopped at many a time before. It was far enough away that she wouldn't be seen from Carter's place.

Florence had often been judgmental of those who'd left the community for love, considering they had some weakness or were lacking in faith. Now she could see how hard it must've been for them. Perhaps *Gott* was prompting her to soften her heart and not be so 'judgy.' She'd never leave the Amish or her family, so thinking too much about Carter Braithwaite was a complete waste of time and energy. There was no chance of him joining her community. She knew that was so by a few of the off-the-cuff comments that he'd made. Besides that, she wouldn't feel safe or secure with a man who joined the Amish community for love.

WHEN SHE SAW a car drive slowly up the driveway toward his cottage, she lowered herself even further.

He never gets visitors.

He'd said he had no family, and had even referred to the cows he'd inherited from the previous owner as his friends. He'd been alone over Christmas, so who would be visiting him now? Every conversation she'd ever had with Carter zipped through her mind before the car came to a halt. She decided it was someone coming to give him a quote for renovations. He'd upgraded the kitchen and bathroom, and he'd been talking about redoing the rest of the place.

CARTER OPENED the door and stepped onto the porch, and Florence's heart rate accelerated. Her heart pumped so hard she could feel it pulsating inside her head. Breathlessly, she looked on as Carter hurried to the car while pulling down the sleeves of his black pullover sweater. When he opened the driver's door, a dark-haired woman got out and they exchanged a quick embrace.

The woman's slim frame was hugged by a pencil-thin skirt that ended just above her knees, and that was complemented by a fitted jacket of the same fabric. Her hair, bluntly cut, stopped precisely at her shoulders, and even from her hiding spot Florence could see the generously-applied makeup defining the woman's eyes.

The two spoke a few words before they walked toward the house. It was then that Florence saw the high heels and tinted sheer stockings. Carter had to be attracted to a woman like that. For the first time in her life, Florence felt an emotion she'd never experienced—jealousy.

This woman was no stranger; the embrace had said that much. They had to know each other. Even though there had been no passionate kiss, and no other affection had been shown apart from that embrace, the appearance of the stranger bothered Florence immensely.

Why is she there?

She kept watching until the woman walked inside ahead of Carter. He turned toward the orchard and Florence ducked back, even further out of sight. After a moment, she looked up to see both of them gone and the front door closing.

In her heart, the closing of the door was symbolic. He was on one side and she on the other. A wide, deep chasm existed between them, and the possibility of anything happening between herself and Carter was ... well, impossible.

It felt so bad.

Florence huffed and lowered herself to the ground. She pressed her back into the tree trunk. She desperately did not want Carter to like that woman. Even though she—being an Amish woman—couldn't marry him, she didn't want anyone else to have him.

As she nervously looped the hem of her apron back and forth between her fingers, she tried to talk herself out of liking him. He was a good-looking man, but it was hard not to be attracted to his personality too. He was funny and kind. Kind enough to have driven her around locally, looking for her runaway sister. Compassionate enough that he'd next driven her through the night and all the way to Connecticut to find the escapee, and then turning right around for the drive to bring them back home. Sweet enough to find her that rare apple tree. That must've taken him a long time. She couldn't imagine where he'd found it.

She groaned. Even though he referred to her half-sisters and herself as the "Bonnet Sisters," she felt she could overlook that one annoyance. It didn't seem so big in comparison to all his positive points.

Then she reminded herself she knew nothing about the man. He was a closed book, and there were so many things about him she ached to know. The biggest thing was, how did he get his money since he didn't appear to have a job? The couple of times she'd visited him, he'd been on his computer playing chess. As far as she knew, he couldn't make money from that.

Forget about him, she told herself. *That's the only thing to do.*

When other questions about Carter flew through her head, she fended them off with the speed of one of their barn cats chasing after a mouse.

There was no point wasting her thinking-time on Carter. He'd shown some interest in her as a person, but he'd asked no questions about her faith. If he was seriously interested in a close relationship, then surely, he'd want to know about her beliefs.

She pushed herself to her feet, turned, and rather than finish her walk, she headed home dragging her feet. It was possible Ezekiel Troyer could be her dream come true, and cause her to stop thinking about Carter.

When she was nearly at the house, she saw her stepmother walking toward her wiping her eyes. Florence wasn't used to seeing her stepmother teary-eyed. She normally floated over the top of life's problems. Florence bunched up the sides of her long dress in her hands and rushed toward her. *"Mamm,* what's wrong?"

"It's just that I'm upset over everything that's happened and I didn't want the girls to see me like this."

Florence put her arm around her and pulled her close. Wilma was just the right height to rest her head on Florence's shoulder. "What is it exactly that's upsetting you?"

"I feel like I'm losing control."

Florence didn't want to share with *Mamm* that the woman had never really had any control since *Dat* died. Florence had been required to step up and become the disciplinarian and leader of the household. "With what?"

"The girls. Look at what Honor did running away like that, and Cherish …"

"Both Honor and Jonathon apologized. Cherish is safely tucked away with Aunt Dagmar until she learns some sense, and Mercy is happily married. What exactly has upset you?"

Mamm sniffed and stood up straight, taking her head off Florence's shoulder. "When you say it like that it makes me feel better. But … things would be nicer if Mercy was still here."

"She's a grown and married woman, *Mamm,* and anyway, they said they'd be coming back to live here after a while."

"I know. I just hope that Honor and Jonathon don't try to run away again."

Slowly, Florence shook her head. "I don't think they will. Not now that you've given your approval of them being together." Another thing Florence didn't approve of, but *Mamm* because she was the mother, had gotten the final say.

"You don't like him, do you?"

Florence swallowed hard—she wasn't going to be so quick to forget what he had done, running away with Honor like that and putting everyone through such a great deal of stress. "I'm not the one who wants to marry him." Florence giggled making a joke out of it.

Mamm smiled. "That's true enough."

Then Florence realized she didn't want to make light of it, so she added, "I don't trust him. Well, I am trying, but … let's just say I'm being cautious. You've told them they can't marry for a year. That should be long enough for us and her to see how he behaves."

"You're right as always."

"Is there anything else bothering you, *Mamm?*"

"I just hope Cherish forgives us for sending her away."

"It might take time, but I think we might've saved her from making a few big mistakes. Mistakes that might've ruined her life. She'll see that when she gets older."

"Do you think so?"

"I do. I know it. Now come on. Let's go back into the *haus.*"

"I always wonder how different things would be if your *vadder* were still alive."

Florence put her arm around her stepmother's shoulder. "Me too. Every single day."

Mamm put her arm around Florence's waist and together they walked back to the *haus*.

CHAPTER 2

THE NEXT EVENING, Florence was mentally preparing herself to meet Ezekiel Troyer as she cooked the dinner alongside her stepmother and Hope, her fourth oldest half-sister. They were unusually silent as each went about preparing her part for their simple dinner of roasted meats and vegetables.

"I've lost count of how many are coming tonight," *Mamm* said.

"Me too," Hope said. "I'll count them up before I set the table."

They'd found out that morning that Joy had invited Isaac, her special friend, without checking if it was okay. The two of them had become inseparable over the last few days. When Honor learned Isaac was coming, she'd insisted Jonathon be there too.

Jonathon had apologized profusely to *Mamm* and Florence for running away with Honor. He'd also made amends with Mark and Christina for leaving his job at their store with no prior notice. Now he was back living in their stable quarters, but the job he'd so irresponsibly abandoned had been given to Christina's *bruder,* Isaac, the same Isaac with whom Joy had become friends.

JOY LEFT Isaac in the living room and headed to the kitchen. She poked her head around the door. "Need any help?"

Mamm turned around from stirring applesauce on the stove. "We'll be fine. Go back and talk with Isaac."

Joy noticed Florence didn't look too happy about that but she didn't say anything. Joy took one step toward the door and then turned back. "Did I tell you I invited Christina and Mark?"

"Nee! You didn't, did you?" *Mamm* asked.

"It's alright, isn't it? I thought I had to ask them to come because Isaac and Jonathon are coming." Joy shrugged her shoulders. "They would've been upset if we'd had a special dinner without them."

"It's not a special dinner." Florence's vivid blue eyes flashed with annoyance. "We just have a visitor coming along with Ada and Samuel. That's all."

"Have I done the wrong thing again? I always try to do the right thing and then people don't like it. I don't like leaving people out of something. How would you like to be left out of something, Florence?"

Florence pressed her lips together, and then through almost gritted teeth responded, "It's not like that. Fine, they can come."

"That's good because they're on their way already. It's too late to un-invite them."

"There's plenty of food," *Mamm* told Florence.

"I know. It's just that I didn't want a crowd of people watching me when I first meet Ezekiel. It'll make me nervous."

Joy said, "They won't do that. They're smarter than that." After Florence nodded and went back to grating dark chocolate over the mint frosting that covered the chocolate cake, Joy walked back out to Isaac. She was pleased to see him bending over and stoking the fire.

He glanced at her as she sat down. "They don't need any help?" he asked.

"They said not."

He placed the poker down, dusted off his hands and sat down beside her. He stretched his arms over his head and then rested one arm on the top of the couch behind her. "I have some news to tell you."

"What is it?"

"Jonathon has agreed to move out with me."

"Really?"

He nodded. "Well, it's not official yet. We can't do it unless he finds a job this week. I found a cottage for us to lease and it's so cheap it won't last long."

"Oh, good. Is it close by?"

"Not far from Mark and Christina's. Just a little further away than their *haus.*"

"I hope he finds a job soon, then. How's he doing with his job searching?"

"He reckons he's got a few possibilities."

She smiled and nodded, but that didn't mean anything to her. From what the family knew of Jonathon so far, he was a big storyteller and that was concerning. *Mamm* had managed to forget how Honor and Jonathon had run away. She'd swept it under the rug, but Joy could tell Florence wasn't so sure they wouldn't do something like that again. "Do you think you should move out with him?"

"Sure. It'll mean you and I can see more of each other."

Joy knew she had to choose her words carefully. "I know, and that's good, ...but, do you think Jonathon is the kind of person who should become a close friend of yours?"

"He already is. We get along great and he's a fun person to be around. We laugh all the time."

She looked down at the subtle swirling patterns on the dark rug beneath the couch and coffee table, wondering if she should consider it an issue that Isaac thought Jonathon was suitable as a friend. She'd be happier if he found a friend who was more serious and Godly.

"What's wrong?" he asked.

She looked at him and saw genuine concern in his face. She had to be open and honest with him and not sugar-coat things the way most of her family members did. "It's just that I can't stop thinking about how he ran away with Honor. He's done some things that are not so good. And … you know what the Bible says about surrounding yourself with the righteous, don't you?"

The corner of his lips twitched as though he'd tasted something foul. "I thought everybody had forgiven him and moved past that."

"I know, but that's not what I'm talking about."

He breathed out heavily. "You're always saying what the Bible says, and doesn't *Gott* tell us to forgive? Even if we have to forgive someone over and over?"

She was pleased to hear him referring to the Bible. "That's true, but it also tells us that we need to choose our friends wisely. *He that walketh with the wise shall be wise: but a companion of fools shall be destroyed.* Are you doing that, Isaac?" She folded her arms across her chest. Didn't he want to be wise?

He withdrew his arm from behind her and stared at her open-mouthed. Then he slowly rubbed his jaw.

It was then she remembered someone had told her that men didn't like being told what to do. "Have I offended you?"

"You haven't, quite, but it sounds like you don't trust my judgement. Jonathon is fine and besides, it took two to run away. Why is it that the man always gets the blame? Your *schweschder* also ran away. Are you going to disown her—cast her out of your *haus?*"

"In this instance, it's because the man is so much older and should've known better. She's barely seventeen—not even legally 'of age' don't forget—and he's older than twenty."

Slowly, he nodded. "I guess that's true, but he told me he apologized and your mother accepted his apology."

She nodded. He was never going to agree. In a way, they were both right. She could see his point, just a little. "Let's talk about something else. How has it been, back living with your *schweschder* and *bruder*-in-law?"

When he chuckled, all the tension between them dissolved. "After living in the stable quarters for a few days, I kind of got used to being by myself and I'd like to do that again. It was hard to move back into the *haus,* but I figured that Christina would've been more comfortable with me moving back rather than—"

"Why couldn't Jonathon have moved in with his Aunt Ada and *Onkel* Samuel? They've got a big place."

"I guess he feels more comfortable around Mark. They do get along well together."

That made Jonathon letting Mark down even worse, in her estimation. Jonathon had suddenly left his job at the saddler store leaving Mark there by himself, but Joy considered it wise to leave that subject alone. "Why can't you get a place by yourself? Why do you need to move out with anyone at all?"

"I need someone to share the expenses. It'll be different living with a friend. He was ready to move out when he had a job, and now everything's reversed—I've got a job and he hasn't."

Joy giggled. "*Jah*, you got his job."

"That's right, and I'm keeping it!" He laughed. "I feel more than ready to live on my own now. When I say, 'live on my own,' I mean with someone my age but away from my *schweschder*. I can't wait to get out."

"If it's more money you need just ask Mark for a raise."

Isaac moved uncomfortably in his seat. "It doesn't work like that. He's only got a small business, remember, and I'm blessed to have a job there. There are plenty of people who'd love to have that job and would probably even work for less than he's giving me." He shook his head. "It's totally out of the question."

"Surely there's someone else you could move out with? Maybe someone who already has a job?"

"I don't know anyone else." He was quiet for a moment, and she could see something was bothering him. "Joy, why don't you trust my judgement? Jonathon is a perfectly fine and decent man. He made a couple of mistakes, but haven't we all? Your *Mamm* allowed your older sister to marry his *bruder*, Stephen, so doesn't that say something about the family he came from?"

"It says something about Stephen, but it doesn't necessarily say anything about Jonathon. The two of them are way different. Anyway, I'm sure Florence feels the same as I do even if *Mamm* doesn't."

They stared at one another for a moment, and then Isaac said, "Who's this 'special guest' who's coming to dinner? You haven't told me."

Joy knew he was trying to change the subject and she didn't mind. They'd never agree about Jonathon. She'd forgiven Jonathon already, since he'd apologized formally to *Mamm* and Florence, but that didn't mean she wanted the man she saw as a potential husband to be best friends with him. It was a recipe for disaster. "Just someone Ada and Samuel know. He's staying with them for a week or so."

When they heard a buggy, Joy was pleased for the interruption and jumped to her feet, hurried over, and looked out the window. "It's Honor and Favor home from the markets. I hope they had a good day. But not too good because I'll have to better it tomorrow." She giggled and spun around to face him while her long dress swished about her knees.

"Do you have competitions between yourselves?"

She sat back down next to him. "Not really, but I always like to have a good day of sales when I'm serving on the stall."

"I can understand that. I feel like that when Mark leaves the store for half a day. I try hard to make good sales—otherwise he'd maybe think I wasn't trying." He looked over toward the window. "Should I help them unhitch that buggy?"

"Nee, stay here and talk to me."

He chuckled. "Okay."

CHAPTER 3

ONCE THEY WERE all sitting in the living room, Joy returned to the kitchen to see how close dinner was.

"Is everyone here already?" asked Florence, looking a little anxious.

"Nee," said Joy. "I was just wondering. We're still waiting on about half of the people; Ada and Samuel, Ezekiel, Mark and Christina, and Jonathon too." Joy noticed how worried Florence looked. Fine lines appeared on her forehead, and then she noticed Florence's soiled apron. It wouldn't make a good first impression for Ezekiel to see Florence like that. "Do you want me to take over while you get ready, Florence?"

Holding a wooden spoon in one hand, Florence looked down at her clothes. "I was going to change my apron, naturally." She looked back up at Joy. "Is this dress okay?"

"I think you should wear one of your better dresses, don't you? This is just an everyday dress. It's a dress you'd wear to pin out the washing."

"*Jah,* you're right. I'll get changed now before the rest of them arrive."

"*Jah,* that's best."

Florence turned to *Mamm* and handed her the wooden spoon. "I won't be long. I was just about to make the gravy."

"Take your time. I'll do the gravy in a minute."

"And I'll help *Mamm* with that," Hope said, stepping forward.

"*Denke.*" Florence felt good that all the girls were coming together to help. That was what family did when it was needed, but sometimes her sisters needed prompting.

Florence briefly greeted Isaac in the living room as she hurried past to walk up the stairs. She hoped the night wouldn't be too dreadful. Now she was grateful for all the extra people who'd been invited. With more people, there was less chance of awkward pauses in the conversation at the table.

She pushed open her door and then with both hands flung open the double wooden doors of her closet. Her sudden burst of strength popped a nail and dislodged the top hinge and now the right-hand door was hanging down. Florence sighed. Another job to add to her list of things for tomorrow. With no man in the household, it was Florence's job to do all the fiddly mainte-nance work, and the list for those tasks had become never-ending. She'd become well-acquainted with her father's old tools and had taught herself to use them.

She turned her attention back to her clothes, and reached for the green dress. "*Nee!*" she said aloud. That was her best and she didn't want to look like she was trying too hard. If it turned out she liked him, she could wear her best dress at the Sunday meeting.

After she pulled off the 'pinning out the washing dress,' she took hold of the grape-colored dress—her second-best—and decided on that one. She'd been told the color made her eyes "light up."

As she stepped into her dress, she was filled with dread over the night ahead. There wasn't much chance of this man being everything for which she'd hoped. For one thing, he lived in the wrong location, and she doubted he'd willingly leave his farm to move closer. Leaving her orchard wasn't an option either. She'd rather stay single forever than do that. Amongst her apples she was at peace, contented. Surrounded by her trees, she felt close to her parents and the life she'd briefly shared when they'd both been alive.

Once she'd dressed, fixed her hair and placed on her *kapp*, she sat down on her bed and closed her eyes.

Dear Gott, *I'm ready for you to find me someone who suits me.*

That was her prayer and although it was brief, it said everything on her heart. Then she lay down on her bed thinking, as her head sank into her pillow.

The thinking soon turned into worrying, as it so often did. What if the man who suited her wasn't the one she wanted? God might think she needed trying and testing over things and the last thing she wanted was to face complications. She'd seen her best friend Liza struggle trying to make her marriage a happy one. Now, *Gott* had blessed her marriage with happiness, but Liza had been sad for years.

Florence would rather be tested in other ways. Being close to Liza and seeing what she'd been through was the main reason she'd cautioned her sisters into taking their time to make sure the men they married were just right for them.

It wasn't until Mercy got married that Florence thought about marriage as a reality for herself. Time had passed her by so quickly. The couple of men she'd liked in her younger days had not looked twice at her, neither one of them, and now they were married. After that, Florence had put love and marriage out of her mind.

Florence got up and moved to the window and stared out. In the distant semi-darkness, the lights of a buggy came into view. She watched as it came closer, and then she moved back so no one in the buggy would see her.

The first person out of the buggy was a man. Not Samuel, although it was Samuel and Ada's buggy. It had to be Ezekiel Troyer. He was tall, a little on the heavy side and from the distance she was to him, she wasn't repulsed at all like she'd expected. In fact, she was pleasantly surprised by the kindness of his face. Ada had done well. She'd chosen Stephen for Mercy and that had worked splendidly. Now, Florence only hoped Ezekiel's personality would be as pleasing as his looks.

Tying her *kapp* strings under her chin, she backed away and then hurried downstairs to be the first to meet him. By doing so, she'd feel less nervous.

When she reached the bottom of the stairs, her stepmother had her hand on the front door handle. She turned around and said to Florence, "Do you want to open the door?"

"You do it," Florence said, changing her mind on the spot.

Her mother flung open the front door before Florence could step aside, and the next thing she saw was Ezekiel smiling at her. Florence stepped forward and reached out her hand. "Hello. Ezekiel, is it?"

He took off his hat and offered his large hand for her to shake. It was delightfully warm. "That's me, and you must be Florence?" His accent was a little different from what she was used to. He spoke with slightly drawn-out words, almost sounding melodious.

Removing her hand from his, she said, "That's right. Florence Baker." To take the attention off herself, she introduced her stepmother and then Samuel and Ada joined them. Everyone else came out from the living room, eager to meet the visitor.

After all the introductions were done, Ezekiel said to Wilma, "How many girls do you have, Mrs. Baker?"

"Please, call me Wilma. I have six, but the oldest is married and has moved away. My youngest is staying with her aunt for a time." She lightly touched Florence's shoulder. "Seven *dochders* counting Florence. She's my step-*dochder.*"

Florence fixed a smile on her face. Why did *Mamm* always have to make that distinction? Why couldn't she just say she had seven daughters? Was it necessary to announce to all that Florence wasn't her biological daughter? Was she ashamed of her? It was something Wilma had always done and there hadn't been one time that it hadn't bothered Florence. It made her feel second-best.

"Can I help you in the kitchen, Wilma?" Ada asked.

"Nee. We're all done. Is everyone hungry?"

"I'm starving," Favor said, earning a glare from *Mamm.* "Well, I am."

Hope said, *"Mamm,* we're still waiting for Jonathon as well as Mark and Christina."

"Oh, that's right. They're not here yet," *Mamm* said looking around.

"Here they come now," Samuel said, looking out the still-open front door.

While they waited for the rest of the guests, Isaac and Joy talked to Ezekiel. Florence backed into the kitchen to start placing the food into the serving bowls. Whenever the family had many guests, it was always a help-yourself affair with the food placed down the center of their long table.

454

When the final guests arrived, another lot of introductions took place, and then Florence called everyone to their dining room, a room that was adjacent to their kitchen. With having no allocated seats for the guests, Florence was the one who suggested where everyone sat. Since *Mamm* and she were the ones doing the serving, they sat closest to the kitchen. When Florence was only halfway through her seating suggestions, Ada butted in and told Ezekiel to sit down right next to the chair where Florence was to sit. Florence had planned to put at least one person between them.

Once everyone was seated and their silent prayers of thanks for the food had been given, the bowls of food were passed around while everyone helped themselves.

Immediately, Florence noticed that Honor and Jonathon were talking exclusively to each other. It had been a mistake to seat them together.

"Did you have a good apple season this year? I mean, last year?" Ezekiel asked Florence, seeming to feel just as awkward as she felt.

"It was one of our best. We always try to do better than the previous ones, but that is dependent upon the weather."

"And *Gott,*" Joy butted in.

Florence looked over at Joy sitting to the other side of Ezekiel. She hadn't even realized Joy was listening. *"Jah.* And *Gott's* will," Florence agreed.

"That's something that normally goes unsaid," Ezekiel commented to Joy. "I'm sure Florence—"

"It shouldn't go unsaid. When we talk about *Gott* that brings Him into our presence, like He's sitting at the table with us. Matthew 18: 20 says, *where two or more of my people are gathered I am in their midst.*" Now everyone stopped their conversation and all eyes were on Joy. She lowered her head slightly. "That's what I think anyway."

Ezekiel said, "It's good to talk about Our Lord and Savior."

Florence smiled, pleased he was supporting Joy.

Isaac said, *"Jah,* and it's *gut* that we can all be free to have our say."

Favor snickered. "You don't know the half of that."

Everyone looked at Favor and Florence had no idea what she meant. Was it because Joy was constantly telling them all what the Bible said?

Suddenly Samuel's voice broke through the stunned silence, the second in less than three minutes. "These potatoes are delicious."

"They're just normal everyday potatoes," *Mamm* said.

"I think they taste creamier than usual."

"Nee. They're just the same."

Ada joined in. "I think they're good too and I love this crispy-skinned chicken."

"I've already given you the recipe for that," *Mamm* told Ada.

"Jah, and you've given it to me too," Christina said. "But I must remember to make it sometime. I've been too busy with other things."

Florence was grateful that everyone was talking now, rather than Joy dominating. It made things tense having to watch what she said around Joy every day.

Ezekiel rested his knife and fork against his plate, "I see you've got a shop down by the road. When does that open?"

Mamm said, "We open that in the warmer months. It does especially well at harvest time."

"I see."

"That's why we have the market stall in the colder months," Honor said.

"You don't have it all year?"

Florence explained, "We have been at the markets all year, but this has been the first year to try it, so we're not sure if we'll keep going with that. It needs two people, and it's a lot of travel there and back every day."

"We'll see what happens," said *Mamm.*

Ezekiel turned to Florence's older brother, Mark. "And you don't work in the orchard?"

He shook his head. *"Nee.* I have a saddlery store. Isaac works for me," he said with a nod toward his *bruder*-in-law. "Isaac's Christina's *bruder.*"

"Ah, now I'm making some connections." Ezekiel nodded, and then looked at Jonathon. "Where do you fit in, Jonathon?"

Florence desperately wanted to say that he didn't fit in at all, but unfortunately Mercy was married to his brother. That made Jonathon Mercy's *bruder*-in-law, and therefore as good as family to all the rest of the Bakers.

"The oldest Baker sister is married to my younger brother."

"That's Mercy and Stephen," Hope told Ezekiel.

"Hmm. It'll take me a while to remember all this."

Favor rolled her eyes. "Don't even try. I can't even remember it."

"That's because you don't care about anyone other than your-self," Joy told her.

Mark took on the older brother role. "I'd hate for any of you girls to have to finish your meals in your rooms..."

Favor looked down. "Sorry, Mark."

"Jah, sorry," Joy mumbled.

"I'm sure Joy didn't mean anything bad," Isaac said.

A few chuckles were heard around the table and no one made any further comment.

. . .

WHILE THEY WERE WAITING at the table for dessert, Joy leaned over and whispered to Isaac, "Thanks for helping me out before. No one understands me."

Isaac gave her a big smile. "Well, I do."

She looked at his flushed rosy cheeks and was glad. *"Jah,* you do, but no one else does."

"Will you be at the markets tomorrow?"

"Jah. I'll be there again tomorrow."

"If I get a chance, I'll come see you."

"That would be *wunderbaar.* I'd like that."

"I might get a half hour for lunch, but not if we're too busy."

"Okay. I'll keep an eye out for you."

Joy listened to Ezekiel and Florence over dinner. He was a plain man, pleasant mannered, and he looked like a good strong man —and that was perfect seeing as he was a farmer. From Florence's guarded expressions, Joy couldn't figure out what her half-sister thought about him. It wasn't ideal that he lived two hours away, but if they loved each other, things like that could be worked out.

CHAPTER 4

WHEN DINNER WAS OVER, everyone sat down in the living room while Joy and Honor made the after-dinner coffee.

Honor wrung her hands. "I hope Florence isn't going to be mean to Jonathon."

"Of course she won't."

"I know she doesn't like him—and he knows it too. She's still mad at us."

"She's trying to impress Ezekiel, so she wouldn't be mean to someone while she's trying to impress him."

Honor left off filling the kettle and peered around the doorway into the living room. Then she faced Joy. "Do you think Florence likes Ezekiel?"

"I do. He's perfect for her."

"I don't know if she'll ever marry anyone. I can't imagine her with him or anyone else."

"I think she'll take it slow."

Honor giggled. "Years even, from how she keeps telling us to slow things down."

"I think you're right."

Honor walked over to the sink and finished filling the kettle. "Sometimes I regret coming back here." She lit the stove and placed the kettle on the flame.

"*Nee.* You did the right thing. You would've had a dreadful life if you didn't come back. Jonathon mightn't have been able to find work and then you two would've been living as *Englishers* and might never have come back to the community—ever."

"I got the sweet taste of freedom when I was away. There're too many people looking over my shoulder." Honor grabbed the coffee container. "It's strangling me."

"It's called family. And people only keep an eye on you because they care about you."

"What's annoying about you, Joy, is that you have an answer for everything."

"And that annoys you?"

"*Jah,* it does." Honor shook the coffee into the plunger.

"Next time you ask me something, I'll say I don't know."

"*Gut.*"

Joy got the mugs ready to place on the tray. "Have we got any of that chocolate cake left?"

"*Jah,* um, *nee.* That one's gone. Florence made a fresh chocolate cake with mint frosting for tonight, and Favor made cupcakes this morning and candies, too." They prepared trays with plates of either cake or cupcake, and forks and napkins. They added a dish of the candies to each tray so everyone could help themselves.

The two girls took a tray each of the coffee fixings out to the living room and then Honor kneeled to pour while Joy passed a cup of coffee to each person. They went back into the kitchen after that, and brought out the cakes and the candies.

FLORENCE AND EZEKIEL were seated next to one another again, and when all of the others were talking in groups, Ezekiel smiled at her and said, "Would you have some spare time to spend with me tomorrow?"

"Of course. What would you like to do?"

He wrapped his fingers further around the white coffee mug, resting it on his knee holding it only by his fingertips. "What kind of things are there to do around here?"

"That's a hard one to answer because most of the time I'm here at home." She rarely went anywhere unless it was to go somewhere with Liza.

"When you go out, where do you go?"

"Mainly I visit people, go to the meetings, or go to the markets."

His face lit up. "Perfect—the markets. I wouldn't mind having a look around the markets." He took a mouthful of coffee.

"Really?"

He nodded. "Yes."

Jonathon called from across the room. "What caused you to visit us, Ezekiel?"

Everyone was silent and looked over at Ezekiel. Florence was embarrassed and wondered what he'd say. "It was Ada's fault," he joked. "She said I should visit them for a weekend and I've never been here, so I decided it was a good idea."

"Who's looking after your pigs."

Florence frowned at Jonathon. She could tell he was mocking Ezekiel.

"My two younger brothers."

"And what do you hope to do while you're here?"

Florence wanted to say something to silence the trouble-making Jonathon, but she couldn't think what. She saw one candy left on a plate and she was half inclined to toss it at him.

"Make new friends. And I had hoped to meet Florence, and now I have." Ezekiel looked over and smiled at Florence.

It was a good way to defuse Jonathon. He went quiet, apparently without a comeback, and then—to Florence's relief—went back to talking to Samuel.

AN HOUR LATER, Florence was standing beside *Mamm* waving goodbye to Samuel, Ada, and Ezekiel. Just before Ezekiel left, he made arrangements to collect Florence the very next morning.

When they walked back inside the house, Jonathon laughed loudly about something and that was the final blow that grated on Florence's nerves. Then and there she decided someone needed to talk with him about trying to embarrass Ezekiel. "Can I speak to you for a moment, Jonathon?"

He looked up at her, shocked. "Sure."

She nodded her head toward the door. "Outside."

He left his seat beside Honor and stepped out onto the porch with her. "What is it?" He looked sick with worry.

"I'm upset with you. Do you know why?"

He drew his eyebrows together and seemed confused. "No. Over what?"

She studied his face. There was no hint of amusement. "Well, you know Ezekiel came here to see me, don't you?"

He pulled a face. "No. No, I didn't know that. I'm sorry; now I feel like a fool. Honor never mentioned it. And I didn't think about it myself because I never thought you'd be interested in someone like him."

His comment jolted her. *Someone like him?* "Do you know anything about him?"

"No. I've never met him until today."

"What did you mean by your comment? You said, 'someone like him.'"

Jonathon said. "I'm sorry. I shouldn't have said that." He shook his head. "I keep putting my foot in it, don't I?"

"That's okay. I can't blame you for speaking your mind."

"I'm sure you're not interested in what I think about him or anything else."

She had to smile about that. Why was she worried what Jonathon thought about Ezekiel? She wasn't sure whether she did care to hear his opinion, but she would've liked to know how other people viewed Ezekiel. "Don't worry about it. You go inside now and spend some time with Honor."

"Okay, and don't worry, he seems a swell guy."

"*Denke,* Jonathon, and I'm sorry to blame you for what you said to Ezekiel earlier. I thought you were trying to embarrass him, or me, or maybe both."

"I hope you know now that I wasn't. It seems Honor doesn't tell me everything."

"It's okay, I believe you."

"I'd better get back inside before Honor gets jealous." He gave her a cheeky wink before he slipped through the doorway.

Florence stared into the night sky for a moment. Had Jonathon just used his charms and talked his way out of trouble? She sighed in dismay at her iffy people-reading skills.

Not yet ready to return to the noisy house, she lingered in the crisp night air. Looking into the still night, she leaned against the porch railing thinking some more about Ezekiel.

He was nice.

She blew out a deep breath. It was far too soon to know if there was a future with him. They'd have to spend more time together to allow their relationship to bloom. And, like a carefully tended plant, perhaps love would grow between them.

It was times like these Florence missed the guidance of her mother. It wasn't something she could bring herself to discuss with Wilma.

CHAPTER 5

IT WAS nine o'clock Friday morning, the time that Ezekiel had arranged to collect Florence. She already felt like she'd done a day's worth of chores. Besides making breakfast for everyone, and organizing the cooking for the day, she'd hammered the nail back into her closet door, put the sliding door of the utility room back onto its track, and found some left-over paint in the shed to re-paint the back door of the house. The painting itself was a project for another day.

Having done enough work so she wouldn't feel guilty for the free-time she was taking today, she sat nervously next to *Mamm* in the living room hoping the day would go well. She was so anxious that she found it hard to sit still.

Honor and Joy had gone to the markets while Hope and Favor were in the kitchen starting the first lot of cooking—a batch of applesauce—before Hope headed to the store at the front of the family home at nine thirty. After that, Favor and *Mamm* would cook the remainder of the items on Florence's list.

"You look so nervous," *Mamm* commented to Florence.

Florence swallowed hard. "Do I?"

Mamm nodded.

"I am, more than a little." Florence smoothed down her dress and then spread her apron out to cover it. *"Denke* for helping Ada arrange this."

"I didn't do anything at all. It was Ada who did everything. I didn't even know him. It's good that he wants to go to the markets because you'll be able to keep an eye on the girls."

Florence didn't want to worry about having to check on her sisters today of all days. "I'm sure they'll be okay, and if not I can't do anything about it. I just want to concentrate on Ezekiel and get to know him."

"And you should." *Mamm* patted her on the shoulder and then she glanced at the clock on the mantle. "Oh dear, it's two minutes after. I hope he's not one of these tardy people." *Mamm* disliked it when people were late.

"I don't think so. He doesn't know the area. He could've taken a wrong turn, or something could've gone wrong with the horse. Anything could've happened."

"Well, l suppose we'll soon find out. I do like him. I think he'll suit you fine. You have several things in common."

Florence screwed up her nose. "Like what?"

"His father has gone home to *Gott* leaving him to run his farm and so has yours."

"My *vadder?*"

"Jah. Yours has gone to be with *Gott* too."

"That's true, but we don't have a farm." Florence kept a straight face. She knew she was being difficult, but she couldn't help it.

"I'm sure running an orchard and a farm are very similar."

"I guess so."

"And he's helping his *mudder* just like you're helping me."

Florence was certain she had things tougher. "He's only got two younger brothers, and I've got all our girls to worry about. I wonder if he'd trade places?"

Mamm put her hand up to her mouth and giggled. "You've only got four to worry about now and next year you might only have three. But by then, you might be married to Ezekiel." Her step-mother's eyes twinkled.

Florence knew *Mamm* hadn't even considered any ramifications a marriage to Ezekiel would bring. What would become of the orchard if she moved away? "Let's not get ahead of ourselves. I want to make sure he's right for me."

"Of course, I wasn't suggesting anything else."

Florence leaned back in the couch and closed her eyes. There was no reason he wouldn't be suited to her. He was the right age, and he seemed even-tempered and polite. On top of that, he was hard-working, a trait that was important to Florence.

Favor flew out of the kitchen. "He's coming, he's coming!"

Florence bounded to her feet. "Shush. He'll hear you."

Amidst peals of laughter, Favor ran back into the kitchen.

Florence exchanged anxious looks with Wilma. It seemed a lot hinged on this day. Perhaps her entire future. While Florence was in the middle of wrapping her shawl around her shoulders, there was a loud knock on the door. *Mamm* pushed past her to open it.

"Ezekiel, this is a nice surprise," Wilma said.

"Didn't you know I was coming? I arranged with Florence last night to take her out for the day. I hope it hasn't slipped her mind."

"Of course it hasn't. Come in."

Before he had a chance to move, Florence appeared from behind the door. "Hello."

"Hello, Florence." He looked down at his feet. "Are you ready? I don't want to come in because my feet are muddied from all the rain we've had."

"I'm ready." She gave her stepmother a quick kiss on the cheek before she accompanied him out of the house and down the porch stairs.

"Do you always get this much rain here?" he asked.

"No, not really." She stepped carefully avoiding the puddles. "We do need the rain, though."

Once they were in the buggy and traveling down the driveway, she hoped the conversation would flow easily. "I guess your brothers will be missing your help on the farm by now."

"They'll be fine as long as they work a bit harder. I'd like to get my mother a gift from the markets today. Do you think they'll have anything suitable there?"

"They should. They sell all kinds of things there, not just fruit and vegetables. I'll enjoy this. I haven't been shopping for some time. Looking at all the pretty things will be nice. What did you have in mind?"

She looked over at Carter's house as they rode past. There was no one about.

Ezekiel looked over at her. "I thought you might be able to give me some ideas."

She laughed. "Me?"

He nodded. "You're a woman, so you know what women like."

"I guess so, but that's a big responsibility. Tell me a bit about your mother."

"You remind me of her."

Florence stared at the road ahead. That wasn't what she wanted to hear. Did she look like an old person to him? His mother had to be at least fifty, and she was only in her mid-twenties.

She had to ask, "In what way do I remind you of her?"

"The way you're always making sure that others are okay."

Immediately, she was relieved. He didn't think she looked much older than her years like Mercy's husband had thought when he first met her. Stephen had presumed she was Mercy's mother, at first, rather than her half-sister. "You could tell that just from last night?"

"I'm a pretty good judge of people and I know what it's like to be the eldest. We are both the oldest in our families."

"I'm not the eldest. I have two older brothers. You met Mark last night, and then there's Earl. He's moved away to Ohio."

"But you're the oldest living at home, aren't you?"

"That's true. Well, I hope I'll be able to steer you in the right direction to find a suitable gift."

"I'm sure you will."

"It'll be a lot of pressure." She giggled.

"When I said you reminded me of my *mudder*, I didn't mean you're as old as she is or anything." He chuckled. "I meant she's the nicest person I know."

"Oh, I'm glad to hear it. I was a little worried." She smiled at him.

"I wasn't talking about looks. For starters, she doesn't have your amazing blue eyes. She has the same boring brown eyes as I do."

"Brown eyes are lovely. They're not boring at all."

"I guess it's a matter of opinion. They serve me well to look out from. I'm pleased I don't have to look at them. I'd rather look at yours."

She couldn't help smiling at the corny compliments. She was reminded of the first time she met Carter. He too had commented on her eyes.

When Ezekiel kept smiling at her, she pushed Carter Braithwaite from her mind. Today was about getting to know Ezekiel Troyer and not to think about someone who was *verboten*.

"It's been awhile since I've been away from the farm, and I must say I'm enjoying it." He cast a sidelong look at her.

She nodded and did her best to stay focused on Ezekiel and him alone. "I can imagine how that would feel."

"When did you last take a vacation?"

"Hmm, let's see now." The last time she'd been away from the farm was when Carter Braithwaite drove her overnight to bring Honor home when she'd run away with Jonathon, but that probably didn't count. It certainly hadn't been any fun. "I can't remember. I think the last time was when *Dat* was still alive and we went visiting."

"And how long has it been?"

"Over two years now. Vacations aren't that important to me. I'd rather stay at home with my apple trees." He might as well find out early on that she was devoted to her orchard. That was how she'd been raised. She'd loved the orchard as much as her father had, which was just as well because her two older brothers hadn't been the least bit interested in taking it on after *Dat's* funeral.

"That's exactly what I used to say as well until I started taking little trips away. A couple of days here and a couple of days there. Now, a week here."

"Maybe one day I'll take a vacation."

"Perhaps you might come to my farm to visit me?"

She glanced at him again to see him smiling at her. "Maybe." She had to change the subject. It was too soon to commit to visiting him. "It's mostly food there."

"What's that?" Confusion wiped the smile from his face.

"At the farmers markets. Sorry. It's mostly food."

"I thought it was an arts and crafts market. Where I come from, the markets have food in one section, and the other section sells all kinds of wares."

"*Nee,* this one is mostly foods, some flower vendors, too, but I can take you to one of those if you want."

"*Jah,* please. Can we go there after the farmers market? I'd like to see your stall."

"Okay, but don't expect too much. Many others have built-in shelves and countertops. We only have trestle tables because we don't know for how long we'll keep the stall. We already have the shop at the front of the *haus,* so …"

"I'd like to take a look none the less."

"Sure. It's not very far from the other markets where you'll be able to find a gift."

"Okay, looks like we're having a market day."

Florence smiled. "It seems like it."

"Are you going to see how the market stall turns out? See if it's worthwhile?"

"That's exactly right. We're comparing it to the roadside stand we had up until recently—until the cold weather arrived. There's no rent for that, of course. But it's too cold in the winter for the girls to stand out there without shelter or heat."

"That's true about the rent, but there'd also be less traffic to bring customers."

"That's it, exactly. Years ago, when we were younger, my *vadder* put our fruit and vegetables on a table on the roadside with an honesty box. Turns out, people weren't that honest—a lot of them. So, when we got older, two of us were there all the time. We sold a lot more that way, and it stopped the losses, too. And just this winter, we decided to see how a market stall would do."

"Has it been worth it?"

"It has so far, but it's a lot of extra work and the extra traveling time, so we have to weigh it up." She shook her head. "With two of my sisters gone now, we're feeling the extra work."

"I understand. Our main method of sale for our pigs is through our local farmers market."

"Is that so?"

"That's right. *Mamm* runs it, along with a couple of girls she's hired from the community. Our pigs are grass fed and there's a lot of demand for that nowadays."

"That's good for you, then."

He chuckled. "Yes, it is. We do alright."

"It sounds like your *mudder* works hard with running the household and the stall."

"That's also how you remind me of her. From what I heard over dinner last night, you're just as busy."

"And that's the way I like it."

"Same with my mother, and she does charity work as well."

While Florence was smiling on the outside, she wasn't happy about being compared to his mother. "We do charity work as a family sometimes, too."

When they walked through the market stalls, he showed great interest in the meat section, and even stopped to ask the operators questions.

"Getting ideas?" she asked when he finished.

He chuckled. "They do have good displays. This market is a little nicer than ours." He chuckled. "Ours is a lot smaller besides." He looked along the row of stalls. "They just go on forever."

"I know. And our stall is right at the back. Follow me."

They strolled along one of the rows until they came to Honor and Joy. They were busy serving, so they just waved at them while Ezekiel had a quick look at the stall. Then they kept moving.

"I wonder if Ada needs anything. I should've asked before I came here."

"It's not likely. Ada and *Mamm* trade fruit and vegetables between themselves. What one wants, they just take from the other, and Samuel gets meat from his *bruder.*"

"I didn't know Ada and your mother were so close."

"They've been best friends ever since I can remember."

"It seems that Ada is one of those people who knows everyone."

"She and Samuel travel to other communities a lot. Samuel doesn't work every day now that he's older and it gives them the time to do it."

After they walked up and down more of the aisles, Florence was getting a little bored, but Ezekiel seemed to be enjoying himself. "Are you ready to go to the other markets now?" she asked, giving him a gentle hint.

His attention was taken by something else. "Feel like a bite to eat first?"

She suddenly realized how hungry she was and followed his gaze to one of the two cafes at the entrance of the markets. "Okay. That'd be nice."

"Will this place be okay, or do you know somewhere else that's better?"

"I believe the food's nice here, although I've never tried it myself."

He sniffed the air. "The smell of the coffee is what got to me."

"Let's try it." They both walked into the cafe that was near the front of the markets. They sat down and he passed her one of the two menus on the table.

"Order anything you like, my treat."

"Denke." She scanned down the menu. "I think I might have a toasted cheese and bacon sandwich."

"Is that all?"

"That's all I feel like. And maybe a coffee. Since that's what pulled us into this place." She finished looking at the menu and looked across at him. "What will you have?"

"I think I'll have the spaghetti Bolognese."

"That sounds nice."

"Do you want to change your order?"

She shook her head. *"Nee."*

They stayed at the cafe for another hour, talking and eating, and ended up having a second cup of coffee.

They both finished their last swallow at the same time and then stared at one another, smiling.

"Are you ready to go?" he asked

"I am, but I'm still nervous about picking out a gift for your *mudder.*"

He laughed. "Also, Ada. I'll get something for her allowing me to stay at her place."

As Florence rose to her feet, she said, "*Ach!* Even more pressure."

Ezekiel laughed. "I'm sure you'll be okay. You'll do fine. And selecting something for Ada should be easier since you know her."

"I'll try my best."

CHAPTER 6

SOON AFTER JOY had spotted Florence and Ezekiel as she looked up from her stall, Isaac appeared. Joy quickly turned around looking in all directions for Florence, but she'd gone.

Fortunately for Joy, the number of customers had lessened, so she left Honor by herself and went to speak with Isaac. He wore his usual grin.

"I don't have long," he told her.

"Neither do I, or Honor will complain."

"I just saw Florence and Ezekiel. They didn't see me. They were sitting down eating and looked pretty cozy."

"That's interesting. I saw them too about five or maybe ten minutes ago. I don't know what they were doing here. Probably keeping an eye on us. Florence would've been, anyway."

His face lit up with mischief. "She doesn't need to do that, does she?"

Joy shrugged. *"Nee,* but it's just strange for them to be here."

Isaac's eyes sparkled with humor. "They looked like they were getting along."

"Did they?"

"Jah, they look like an old married couple."

Joy giggled and shoved his arm slightly. "I'll tell her you said that."

He chuckled. "You'd better not. I don't want to end up on the wrong side of Florence like Jonathon is."

"Yeah, I know what you mean, but she's just trying to protect Honor."

"I know that's the reason, but still …"

"Let's not waste time talking about anyone else. I couldn't wait to see you today."

His grin got wider. "Me too."

"I was hoping and praying you would come to see me. How did you get the time off?"

"It's my lunch break."

"It's a little late for that, isn't it?"

"We were busy, so I waited to take my lunch when it got quieter. Now, I have to hurry back."

Joy pouted. "Do you have to go already? You only just got here."

"I have to. I really should stay in the back room to eat. Normally I would, but I just had to come see you." He took her hand and squeezed it and her heart melted. "What time should I collect you tomorrow?"

"I'll be doing chores until twelve, so, any time after that."

"One minute after twelve." He raised his eyebrows and she giggled again.

"That's fine by me. Wait!" She shook her head. "I'm working here again tomorrow."

"But it's my day off and we planned—"

"I know. I'm sorry. Come for dinner tonight instead?"

"Tonight?"

"*Jah.*"

He smiled broadly. "I'll be there." Slowly he placed her hand back down by her side, released it, and then turned and walked away. She stood and watched him leave. A few steps later, he turned around and gave her a wave. She waved in reply, and then hurried back to the stall.

"You're in love," Honor said when Joy got back.

"I think I am. I can't imagine feeling more for anyone than I do for him. I feel so good when he's around. I feel as though I come alive, and when he's gone I feel as though I'm not really living. Is that crazy?"

"Jah. It is. Now you know how I feel about Jonathon."

"Nee, it's nothing like it. The difference between you and me is that I wouldn't run away."

"I know that—because you're perfect." Honor rolled her eyes.

Joy didn't want to start an argument and she already regretted what she'd said. "I didn't say I was perfect, but I do try to do the right thing as much as possible." Joy flipped her *kapp* strings over her shoulders as though she was shrugging off her earlier words.

"What if running away was your only option to stop you from losing Isaac forever? What would you do? Choose your family or Isaac?"

Joy scoffed. "It was more like, choose the community or go with your boyfriend. No, wait a minute. You *did* leave the community to go with your boyfriend."

"Stop it." Honor glared at her and then her fingertips quickly covered a yawn.

"Ha! You're tired because you spent most of the night speaking with Jonathon. I heard you. It was like one o'clock in the morning when he left."

"Nee. Was it that late?"

"It was. I know it because I couldn't sleep with the two of you talking. You should've told him to go because of us both having to wake up at four to get here in time."

"I couldn't do that. I'd miss sleep anytime to be with him for another moment."

Joy shook her head. "Just think of others, though."

"I can't help it if you're a light sleeper."

"You're lovesick," Joy said.

"So are you."

Joy rolled her eyes and just then some customers walked over to the stall and they had to end their conversation.

FLORENCE RARELY FOUND the time to wander through stores looking at what was for sale. There were always more important things to attend to. Now she and Ezekiel were at the crafts markets, and they were stopping to look at so many different things—jewelry, leather handbags and shoes, and all manner of handcrafted toys, and clothing, and candles ... the variety seemed endless.

Ezekiel couldn't make up his mind and after half an hour, Florence was tiring. "Do you have any idea at all what you're after?"

"Not really, I was kind of hoping you would know."

"I don't know what your mother would like, but I think Ada would like something practical. Something she could use rather than something pretty to look at."

"Okay, well, that's a good start." They came across boot-cleaning kits in wooden boxes. "What about this?"

She took a step closer. "You've got brown polish there, and black polish, leather cream, brushes—everything you need. Who are you thinking of for that?"

"I don't know."

"It is practical."

"That's what I was thinking," Ezekiel said.

"I'm not sure who does the boot cleaning, though. It might be Samuel rather than Ada."

He put the kit back on the shelf with the others and looked at her. "Who does it in your family?"

"Mostly, we do our own."

He picked it back up. "I like it and if she likes practical things, she'll like this."

"Okay. That's one gift down."

He paid for it and it was handed to him in a large paper bag with string handles. "Where to now?"

"We'll keep going up and down the aisles until something jumps out at you for your *mudder*."

"Or something jumps out at you, since you're helping me."

"You were the one who spotted that present for Ada."

He chuckled. "I know, I quite surprised myself. What about this?" He reached out and took hold of a needlework cushion kit. "I like this." He held it up. It had the design already marked on the fabric and had needles and threads to go with it. "What do you think?"

"I like it too. The red and the green in the flowers will be quite striking. Do you think it'll be too bright for your *mudder?*"

"*Nee.* Everything else in the house is gray. This will brighten the place up and she loves this kind of thing."

She took a closer look and saw it was cross-stitch. "Are you positive?"

"Yes."

She laughed at the concentration on his face. "Get it, then."

"Okay, I will."

He paid for it and soon after that he got presents for his two brothers and a bunch of flowers for Wilma.

"How come Wilma got flowers?"

"Because she's a lovely lady and I'm thanking her for dinner last night."

"You don't have to do that."

"I like buying things for people. What about you? Anything look good to you? I'll get you whatever you want."

"I don't need anything. In fact, I'll be quite upset if you get me anything. You bought me lunch, so there you go."

"Okay. I don't want you to get upset with me or you mightn't go out with me again."

She giggled at his comment. It made her feel good.

On the way out of the markets, he said, "Would you like to?"

Florence looked up at him. "Would I like to what?"

"Go out with me again?"

"Oh. *Jah,* I would. I'd like that." She surprised herself that she genuinely meant it. She wanted to see him again.

CHAPTER 7

WHEN THEY GOT to Florence's house, he pulled up the buggy and looked over at her.

"Thank you for coming out with me today, Florence. Would you be free to do something with me tomorrow?"

"Sure."

He rubbed his chin. "I gave my word I'd help Samuel with rebuilding a chimney at Simon Miller's house, but that might not take long."

"Simon? His *fraa*, Liza's my best friend. I'd love to come along. I didn't know there was anything wrong with their chimney."

"It's stone and it's crumbling away in pieces. How about I collect you around nine and we can go together?"

"Nine in the morning sounds perfect. I'll call Liza from the phone in the barn and make sure she's going to be home."

"Samuel said she'd be supplying us with refreshments."

"Wunderbaar. I don't even need to call."

He smiled at her. "I better get Wilma's flowers out and give them to her."

"She'll be delighted. She loves flowers in the house when our garden is in bloom."

Florence climbed out of the buggy and together they walked up to the house. She pushed open the front door and then looked around for her stepmother. "I'll have to look in the kitchen."

Right then, Wilma came out of the kitchen wiping her hands on a towel. "Oh! I wasn't expecting you home quite so early."

"Is it early? It feels like we've had a long day." She quickly added, "I mean, because we fitted so much in," not wanting him to think she'd been bored.

"It's only four o'clock," Wilma said.

He held the flowers out to her. "These are for you, Wilma. "

"For me?"

"Yes."

"Oh, that's very kind." She took the bunch from him, and stared at the daisies mixed with pink and burgundy lilies, and a scattering of deeper pink roses. "I can't remember the last time anyone brought me flowers." She took them from him. *"Denke.* I'll just put these in some water. Come into the kitchen and I'll make you both *kaffe.*" They followed her in and sat down and then she turned to face them with the teakettle in her hands. "You will be staying for dinner, won't you, Ezekiel?"

"I can't tonight, I'm sorry. Ada has the bishop and his *fraa* coming for the evening meal. It's a good chance for me to meet him before the meeting on Sunday."

"Jah, quite right." Wilma turned back and put the kettle on the stove.

Then she sat down with them. "Tell me, what have you been doing today?"

"I wanted to get a few things. Florence has been so kind as to show me around the markets."

"Oh, that's good. Is that all you did?"

Florence could tell Wilma liked Ezekiel by the way she was talking. "We also had lunch at one of the cafes and I think that's all." Wilma's obvious approval made Florence more comfortable with him. Now she felt like she was one half of a couple. It was a nice feeling to have. "Where is everyone?" Florence noticed the absence of Favor and Hope.

"I've got them working upstairs cleaning the windows."

"That's good. Does that mean everything on the list is finished?"

"All the cooking that needed to be done has been done. And we can always do more after dinner if the girls come home and tell us they're short of something."

"Of course."

"Sounds like you've got a highly organized team here, Wilma."

"We have to be highly organized. Otherwise nothing would get done," Wilma said.

"That's right." Florence agreed. "The girls would just stand around talking to each other and laughing all the daylong if we didn't have a plan and a routine to follow."

"It's good that they all get along so well."

Florence and *Mamm* exchanged smiles. "Most of the time they do," Florence said.

Once he had finished his coffee, Ezekiel was ready to leave. Florence walked him out to his buggy. As she stood watching him drive away, she realized if she'd written down a list of the qualities she needed in a man, he would've fulfilled every one of them.

CHAPTER 8

NOW THAT HER big day with Ezekiel was over, Florence figured she had about twenty minutes of daylight left. She walked back into the house, took hold of her warm hand-knitted shawl, threw it around her shoulders, and then skipped down the porch steps. It had been a big day with Ezekiel and she'd enjoyed it, but at the same time being with one person all day had been a little overwhelming.

When she reached the first row of trees, the soft outline of the moon had already appeared in the pale gray sky. As she walked between the rows of apple trees, many scenarios about her potential future with Ezekiel played out in her mind. Then her thoughts turned to her parents. What guidance would they have given if they'd been alive?

"Florence."

Florence was jolted from her daydreams. It was Carter's voice. She was nearly at the border of her property and his.

"Hello," she called out to him as he leaned on the wooden fence post that held five strands of wire to keep his cattle on his side of the property line.

"How are you?"

"Fine." She walked closer, knowing he wanted to talk.

When she was a few feet away, he began, "I was sitting in my kitchen—my *new* kitchen—and when I looked out the window I saw you."

She frowned when he stopped at that. "You saw me where?"

"In a buggy. But, it wasn't your buggy. I know the two horses you use and it wasn't either of those. A man was driving it, which also led me to the conclusion it wasn't your buggy."

"Ah, that would've been Ezekiel."

He stood up straight, and now one hand rested lightly atop the post.

She wished he wasn't so handsome. Even in old jeans and a pullover he looked good. His hair had been cut short—which, she noted in her musings, particularly suited him.

"A friend of yours?"

"Yes. A new friend. He's a farmer."

"What kind of a farm does he have?"

She had been so hoping he wouldn't ask that question. "A pig farm."

"He's hardly suited to be your friend since you don't have any pigs. Does he have anything to do with apples?"

"I don't think so, apart from liking to eat them. I met him recently."

"Yes, you said that already."

"He's from another community. It's not too far away."

He slowly nodded while not taking his eyes from hers. "Are you going to marry this man who spends his day with pigs?"

She tried not to laugh at the expression on his face. It was half disgust and half shock. "It's a bit soon to think about things like that."

His eyebrows rose. "Is it? One of your sisters married someone not too long ago and then there's Honor, the escapee. We both know she fled the scene when she wasn't allowed to marry the man she loves. Even though he was a jerk, I'm sure her feelings were real."

Secretly she was pleased he held the same opinion of Jonathon as her own. "It wasn't that she 'wasn't allowed.' She will be allowed when she's older."

"I'm not talking about them, I'm talking about you." He shook his head. "Tell me you're not in love with a pig farmer." His lips were open just slightly as though he was about to say something else.

Was he jealous? It didn't matter. It couldn't matter. There was no point stringing him along. She could never be with a man like him, so whatever was between them had to stop. This seemed like a *Gott*-given opportunity to end their friendship in case it developed into more. "Who knows? I might end up marrying him. We're very similar in many ways."

He tilted his head to one side. "How so?"

"He works with his family on his farm just as I work with my family on the orchard. His farm is as important to him as my orchard is to me."

"And that's a basis for marriage? If that were the case you'd be suited to every unmarried farmer in the whole countryside and beyond."

"Well ... he's Amish, too."

He ignored that comment, which was—in all honesty—her main point, and looked over at his cows placidly eating their hay. "How can someone be around animals and then slaughter them for food?" He shook his head and looked down.

"He treats his pigs humanely. They wander the fields and ..."

He raised his hand to stop her there. "I'd rather not think about it."

"It's because you're from the city. If you'd been raised in the country, you wouldn't think twice about it. It seems you city-folk don't even know where your food comes from. You wouldn't survive a day if you were suddenly thrust into the wilds of a forest."

He pressed his lips together hard. "How would it work if you married him? Would you have to be subservient and leave your apple trees?"

That was a concern. It would've been much easier to find a man in her area, so if she couldn't live on the land of the orchard, she'd maybe still have the chance to be there every day. "If it's God's will, He'll work things out."

"You're leaving your future to *chance?*"

From his comment, and from his aghast expression, she knew he had no belief whatsoever in God. Her mouth opened, and then she closed it. She had words, but they were many and all jumbled up, and there was no point getting into a discussion with him. He was too opinionated and, she guessed, narrow-minded.

Then he waved a hand in the air dismissing their previous conversation. "All that aside, why have you been avoiding me?"

CHAPTER 9

"I HAVEN'T BEEN AVOIDING YOU." Her tongue made the denial before she had a chance to realize she wasn't being honest.

"I never see you anymore."

Feeling she was choking, she loosened her prayer *kapp* strings underneath her chin. "I've been busy."

"With what?" he shot back.

"Oh, just the usual things that need to be done around the place." He often talked about them having no man there, so she used that. "As you know there's no man around the house, so I'm the one who has to do all the odd jobs and there are a lot of those."

He grinned, softening his face and, she hoped, his mood too. "Is there anything you can't do?"

She relaxed a little. "There are many things I can't do."

"But I'd reckon you'd learn pretty quickly if the need arose. I can see a lot of determination in the startling depths of those blue eyes."

Another compliment. It pleased her, but she wasn't going to allow him to see it. "What have *you* been doing lately?" She hoped she'd find out about that woman she'd seen there the other day. Nodding toward his house, she added, "Have you done any more renovations?"

"After talking to you about that, I decided to put things on hold. I agree with you about keeping the old character of the place. They say every house has a soul and each person who lives in it contributes a little piece of themselves."

Slowly, she nodded at his ramblings. That ruled out the woman being any kind of consultant for the renovations, or an interior designer. "What part of yourself have you contributed?"

He chuckled. "I've added some soul of the city. Physically, a little bit of modernization, and in turn it's breathed new life into it so it can keep breathing new life."

She frowned wondering if that made sense. *He's adding physical things and calls that a soul?*

"How's your wayward sister?" he asked, before she could respond about his house.

Florence giggled. "Which one?"

"The one that was sent away in disgrace. Not the runaway."

"Oh, Cherish—she's fine, I think. She writes to Mom every other day, pleading to come home."

The smile left his face. "That's heart-breaking."

"No, it's not!" She shook her head. "If you knew her you wouldn't think so."

"It seems harsh. Why can't the girl come home if she's having such a miserable time?"

"She did some things she shouldn't have done and would've gotten herself into big trouble if we didn't do something drastic. She tried to run away. It seems she had a crush on the same man as Honor and she was on her way to find him."

He threw his head back and laughed. "You've had two runaways?"

"We have."

"It must've been a hard decision—which one to send away. The thing you must be concerned about, though, is why they don't want to stay."

Her fingertips flew to her mouth. She'd never considered that. Was home-life so dreadful for her sisters they saw marriage as their only escape? "There's a simple answer. They want to grow up too fast. Oh, and something else you don't know. Jonathon is back and he's apologized."

"That's the one I met when I drove you to get Honor?"

Florence nodded.

"Just like that, everything's okay? He's been forgiven, just like that?"

When Florence nodded, confusion covered his face and she was pleased that he felt the same as she. "Well, my mother has now said they can marry when she turns eighteen. They have to wait nearly a year."

He shook his head. "Is that your stepmother?"

She nodded. "Yes, that's right."

"Hmmm. Seems odd that she'd reward them for what they did."

"It's not like that. She figures when Honor's eighteen, she won't be able to stand in their way so it's better to give her blessing, with that limitation. By telling them they're approved of, they won't feel the need to run away again. At least, I'm sure that's what she's thinking."

"How old were you when your mother died? If you don't mind me asking."

"I was only two, and she died from heart inflammation caused by some kind of virus. My father was left with me and my two older brothers."

"I'm sorry. That's terribly sad."

"I don't remember much about her, which is also sad. Two years later, my father married Wilma."

"And they went on to have six girls together," he said.

"That's right. I remember I was pleased to have a mother because I wanted to be carried all the time." She smiled at the hazy memory. "Wilma carried me around on her hip and that kept me happy."

He smiled as he once again leaned on the wooden fencepost. "She wouldn't have been able to carry you for long though, because those bonnet sisters would've been arriving thick and fast if there are six of them."

"Don't call us that."

"I was calling them that, not you."

She sighed.

"Okay. I'm sorry."

She realized it was happening again. He was making her talk about herself and she still didn't know anything about him. "You haven't told me anything about your family."

The smile left his face and he took his arm off the fence. "There's nothing to tell."

"Oh really? So, you just appeared in the vegetable patch one dark and stormy night? Maybe a beanstalk dropped you?"

"That's right. Dropped me from a great height and I landed on my head." He tapped his head with his knuckles.

She giggled, and then said, "Seriously, Carter, tell me about your family. I've told you lots about mine."

He shrugged his shoulders and then his lips slightly curved upward. "Okay, I've got nothing to hide. I was an only child and never saw much of my parents. I told you that before."

"I don't think so. You only said you were by yourself and that could mean many things. Anyway, why didn't you see much of your parents?"

"It's a long story." He grinned. "I might even tell you about it one day."

"There's a saying that I like. Never put off till tomorrow what you can do today."

He ran a hand over his cropped dark hair. "I don't want to bore you."

"Unfair. You know everything about me and I know very little about you."

His eyebrows raised. "You'd like to know more about me?"

"Well, you live next door and we're neighbors, so yes. I'd like to know who's living in the house my father once owned."

"What do you want to know?"

"Do you have a job?"

"Not a job as such. It's difficult to explain."

"I'm sure I'll understand. I do read the newspapers sometimes. I'm not totally cut-off from what's happening in the world. I know there are jobs people do off-site without turning up to an office every day." She took a stab in the dark. "Do you do something from home on your computer?" Out of the corner of her eye, she saw movement. A car was coming up his driveway. He looked around and saw it too.

"I have a visitor, it seems," he mumbled, looking none too happy to see the car.

Florence stared at the car's occupant. She was certain it was the same woman from the other day. "A member of your family?"

"No. Excuse me, Florence, I'll have to speak with her."

"Sure. That's fine."

He took two steps away and then swung around. "Will you come back tomorrow?"

She shrugged her shoulders. "I walk most days. It just depends which way I go." He kept glancing over his shoulder, preoccupied rather than listening to her. "Bye, Carter."

He faced her and gave her a quick smile. "Bye, Florence."

She walked back to the safety of her apple trees grumbling about the bad timing of that woman. He'd been just about to tell her what he did for a living. When she reached the first tree, she looked back. The woman was out of the car and they were talking. He said something to her and then they walked into the house. If she wasn't someone to do with his renovations, and she wasn't a relative ... hmmm ...someone from his work, perhaps?

CHAPTER 10

MEANWHILE, Joy and Honor were driving home from the markets in the buggy.

"I think I forgot to ask Florence if Isaac can come to dinner tonight."

"It'll be fine. I can't see why it wouldn't be. I won't be there, so there'll be one less place at the table." She giggled. "One less mouth to feed."

"Where are you going?"

"Out with Jonathon. Where else would I go?"

"Do Florence or *Mamm* know that?"

"I'm not sure. I told *Mamm,* but I never know if she's paying attention. Why? Do you think Florence will mind?"

"It's hard to say. I don't know what she'll be mad at any more. I don't think she's ever been mad at me." Joy giggled.

"That's because you always do what they want you to do."

"No, I do what I want to do and it just so happens to be that they don't mind me doing that."

"You wouldn't do anything wrong anyway. So no one will ever be upset with you."

"Good. Because that's the way I like it. Why would I want to upset anyone?"

Honor shook her head. "Don't worry. There are some things that you just don't understand."

"What kind of things?"

"The kind of things like, how it feels to be in love."

"I like Isaac a lot."

"*Jah,* but are you in love with him?"

"You were the one who said I was earlier today. How would I know the difference?"

"If you have to ask that you're not in love with him."

"How can you say that? You don't know what's in my heart."

"Sounds like you could live without him. That means it's not the same love that Jonathon and I have. Ours is so strong."

Joy didn't want to get into an argument over whose relationship was better, so she changed the subject. "What do you think about Ezekiel?"

"I think he's lovely. He'll suit Florence fine."

"But what'll happen if Florence leaves? We need her around. *Mamm* needs her, everyone needs her. She runs the place."

"She won't leave, silly. There's no way she would."

When they got to the bottom of the driveway, they saw Jonathon standing beside his buggy next to their barn.

"What's he doing?" Joy stared at Honor.

"We're going somewhere."

"Oh, right now? Why didn't you tell me that? I thought you meant later on."

"Sorry. *Mamm* said it was okay, if that's your next question, so I hope she remembers it. Can you do me a favor and unhitch the buggy so I can leave sooner?"

"Sure."

"*Denke.*"

FLORENCE CAME HOME from her walk just in time to see Honor riding off with Jonathon. She walked over to Joy, who was rubbing down the horse.

"Where are they going?"

Joy looked up and then glanced over her shoulder at the fast-disappearing buggy. "I don't know where they're heading, but I do know *Mamm* said it was okay."

"And Honor's left you to unhitch the buggy?"

"I don't mind. Truly I don't."

"I'll help you." As Florence moved closer, she asked, "You're not planning to run away too, are you?"

"Of course not. Can Isaac come for dinner tonight?"

"Of course."

"Good. I invited him already."

Florence giggled. They often had people stopping by for dinner, so one extra wasn't ever an issue. They always cooked plenty.

When they had put the buggy undercover and finished caring for the horse, they walked into the mudroom together. They changed their shoes and washed up, and headed through to the kitchen. "

Florence thought it best to check Joy's story with *Mamm*. "*Mamm*, did you say it was okay for Honor to go somewhere with Jonathon?"

"I did. Why, is there something wrong?"

"I suppose not. If you said it was all right."

Mamm softly laid a hand on Florence's shoulder. "We have to trust them."

"Do we?"

Joy knew she wasn't part of the conversation, but still she couldn't help butting in. "If you allow them freedom they won't feel they have to run away."

Florence shot her a look that told her to be quiet. "Do you want help with dinner, *Mamm?*"

"Favor and Hope have already done that."

"Great, what is it? I'm starving."

"Joy, you completely butted in and I wasn't finished with what I was saying."

Joy huffed. "I'm sorry."

"*Mamm,* don't you think there should be some restrictions placed upon them?"

Mamm stared at her without blinking. "Do you think so?"

"I do."

"Okay, we'll talk about it after dinner."

"We can't because Isaac will be here," Joy said.

Mamm looked up in shock. "I thought it was just us tonight! He's coming again?"

"*Jah,*" Florence and Joy chorused.

"When will Honor be home?" Florence asked *Mamm.*

"They're going to have dinner at Christina and Mark's house."

That made Florence feel a little better.

"I don't know why they invite her over all the time. What about us?" Joy asked.

Mamm nodded. "I know. Christina has always gotten along well with Honor."

Joy tilted her head upward. "I don't know why she can't get along with all of us and treat all of us the same."

Florence yawned. "I might have a little lie down before dinner. Is that okay with everyone?"

Mamm's eyes opened wide as she looked at Florence. "You're not getting sick, are you?"

"Nee. I'm not used to all the shopping I've done today. I'm exhausted."

Joy giggled. "You can work from sunup to sundown at harvest time and you're exhausted over a little shopping?"

Florence shrugged her shoulders. "I guess it does sound funny."

"I'll fetch you when dinner's on the table," *Mamm* said.

"Denke."

Florence climbed the stairs feeling pretty awful. The trouble was, she liked everything in her life to be organized and that meant having a fair idea about her future so she could plan. Now, her future was uncertain.

Carter was right, how could she have a future with Ezekiel when they lived so far apart? And even if there wasn't that problem, she wasn't in love with Ezekiel.

She pushed open her bedroom door with the edge of her boot. Was she only attracted to Carter because he brought some excitement into her life, along with a hint of the unknown? Maybe she liked the danger that being fond of an *Englischer* brought.

CHAPTER 11

AFTER THEY'D HAD dinner and Isaac had gone home, Joy made use of the time before bed to make taffy apples for the next day. They were completely sold out of them at the markets.

Joy was in the midst of warming the toffee when Jonathon brought Honor home. Jonathon came inside with her, and then Joy heard him ask to speak with *Mamm* and Florence. Hope and Favor were upstairs and with the quiet surrounding her, she was able to hear every word of the conversation that was happening in the living room.

"The problem is, he hasn't been able to find work around here," said Honor.

Joy frowned at his excuse. He hadn't been looking for long.

"I wouldn't worry. Something will happen soon," *Mamm* said.

Florence wasn't so placid. "How long's it been? Only two weeks? Surely there's something out there you could do. It doesn't have to be your ideal job."

Joy covered her mouth to stifle a giggle; Florence had said exactly what she'd thought.

"Believe me, Florence, I don't like having time on my hands. I've done everything I can and left my name at so many places. Samuel and Mark have been asking around for me too."

"Tell them what we talked about, Jonathon," Honor urged.

There was a moment of silence. Joy stopped skewering the apples so she would be able to hear Jonathon better.

"I've been offered a job near my folks' place. This job is secure —it's with one of my uncles. I've talked with my parents and they said they'd love to have Honor stay there. Even though Mercy and Stephen are there. There's still plenty of room."

"Wait! Wait a minute. What are you suggesting?" Florence asked.

Joy put down the apple that was in her hand. She never imagined he'd ask such a thing. Before he could answer Florence, *Mamm* spoke.

"And where will *you* stay if we allow Honor to board with your parents?"

Joy couldn't resist it. She tiptoed over to the doorway of the kitchen and peeped around the corner.

Florence stared at *Mamm* in disbelief. Was *Mamm* going to allow them both to leave just like that? After everything that had just happened?

Joy shook her head, sympathizing with Florence. She had no real say when Mamm overrode any of her decisions.

"I was thinking that I'll stay with friends. There are plenty of people I can stay with."

Joy knew exactly what Florence was thinking. As she sat in stunned silence, Florence was hoping *Mamm* wasn't seriously considering the option of Honor leaving to be close to Jonathon with only his parents to supervise.

Mamm then stared at Florence. "What do you think?"

WHEN ALL EYES were on her, Florence had to say what she thought. *"Nee!* I don't think it's a good idea." She looked directly at Jonathon. "I'm a little shocked you've asked us something like this, Jonathon, after everything you've put us through already."

"Why, Florence?" Honor asked.

"It's simply out of the question. Both of you ran away and I don't trust either of you now."

Joy knew they'd be short another pair of hands if Honor left. It was more difficult with two of her sisters gone, and it would be harder still if they were down a third.

"Mamm?" Honor asked through tear-filled eyes.

"We'll have to think about it."

"There's no time to think."

"It's okay, don't get upset." Jonathon patted Honor's shoulder. Tears flowed down Honor's face and she bounded to her feet and left the room. Jonathon stood up and stared after her as she ran up the stairs. Then, he slowly sat down. "Florence, I have a job there and she'll be perfectly safe with my folks. They're even stricter than you."

"All the same, I've given my answer."

He looked at *Mamm.* "Mrs. Baker? You said you'd think about it."

Joy hoped her mother would back Florence up.

Mamm stood up. "Just one moment. I'll talk to Honor and see how she's feeling."

Mamm was going to be talked into allowing it. Joy just knew it. She always caved under pressure.

"I'm not the way you think I am," Jonathon told Florence now that they were left alone.

"Would you like a cup of hot tea?"

Joy frowned at Florence's strange response. What did tea have to do with anything?

"I wouldn't mind a *kaffe,"* he answered.

"Sure." She stood and then he got up to follow her into the kitchen. *"Nee.* You sit down."

"I thought we could talk."

"Nee. I've said all I have to say about the matter."

"We could talk about something else then."

She stared at him and shook her head, and then he slowly sat back down.

Joy ducked away, turned down the stove, and then sat down and pretended to continue skewering the apples even though she'd finished.

Florence saw her and stopped, then walked to the teakettle and filled it with water.

"I'm making taffy apples."

"So I see." Florence then lit another burner on the stove and placed the teakettle on it, next to the pot of toffee.

Joy rushed over to her and whispered, "I heard everything. I wasn't deliberately listening—I was kind of stuck in here. What's your main objection to what they asked?"

Florence sighed. "She was told that she couldn't marry him until she was eighteen. It only feels like they've been back days from running away. We might never have seen them again, and now they want us to forget everything and trust them. *Nee,* trust must be earned. Especially with having done what they did."

Joy placed her hands down by her sides as she wandered back to the kitchen table and played with her apples. "Part of me agrees, but the other part doesn't. What about forgiveness?" She looked back at Florence.

"Let's get these apples dipped while we're waiting for the kettle to boil."

"Okay, *denke*. But I'm serious. What about forgiveness—shouldn't that mean we let go of it?"

"There is forgiveness, and there's bringing up a child correctly. You can forgive, but you still have to give guidance. Do you see what I mean?"

"Sort of, but Honor isn't ten-years-old. She's an adult and she told me she's old enough to get married if she has a parent's permission, so why not let *Mamm* give it if they love each other? Their love must've been strong to feel the need to turn their backs on both of their families just so they could be together." Joy could see both sides of the issue.

Florence shook her head. "I'm not about to forget what they did. She can't just say she's sorry and then all is forgiven and forgotten, and the same with him. You'll know what it's like when you have your own *kinner* to raise."

"So might you. None of us is your *kinner,* Florence. You're our *schweschder.*"

"Half-*schweschder,* as I'm so often reminded."

"And I know you do pretty much everything around here, but the end decision lies with *Mamm.*"

Joy saw Florence's face change, and she regretted her words. "I'm sorry. I didn't mean that like it came out."

"That's okay. You're right—I'm just frustrated. *Mamm* could very easily give in and allow Honor to do whatever she wants. We'll just have to wait and see what *Mamm* says."

Joy quickly turned away. It couldn't have been easy for Florence, trying to get all the girls in the family to behave well. "How are things between you and Ezekiel?"

"We're doing okay. Getting to know one another. I can see the two of us will be good friends."

"And that's good, isn't it? Don't friends make the best husbands?"

"Well, that's something I can't really say because I have had no experience with that."

"I can see the two of you together having lots of *bopplis*."

Florence smiled. "Well, that's fine. As for you, don't think you have to rush in just because Mercy and Honor have made their choices early in life."

"Why? Don't you like Isaac?"

"I do. Very much. I think very highly of him, but at your age, you have all the time in the world. Use it wisely."

By the time *Mamm* came back downstairs, the apples had been finished and Florence had just served Jonathon his cup of coffee.

"Here's a hot tea for you, *Mamm,*" Joy said.

"*Denke,* Joy. Um ... Joy, do you mind if Florence and I have a talk alone with Jonathon?"

"Sure. I mean, no, I don't mind. I was just going to bed anyway." Joy took her own cup of hot tea upstairs while Florence sat down on the couch next to Jonathon and opposite *Mamm.*

"Have you made a decision yet?" Jonathon asked.

"*Jah.* I've decided she can go with you, but I'll have to speak to your parents first to make sure it's all going to be okay."

Florence stared at Jonathon in shock. He'd gotten just what he wanted and he smirked as though he was pleased with himself.

"*Denke,* Mrs. Baker."

Florence stood.

"Where are you going?" *Mamm* said.

"I'm following Joy. I'm going up to bed. Good night, all."

"But aren't you going to stay and talk about this?" *Mamm* asked, staring up at her.

Florence sighed. "There's nothing more to say."

Florence leaned forward and picked up her cup and saucer and then balanced them carefully while walking up the stairs to her bedroom.

As she sat on her bed sipping her tea, she decided she should worry less about the girls and start thinking more about herself. Tomorrow, she was going to seriously consider Ezekiel Troyer as a potential husband, even more so than she had thus far.

CHAPTER 12

THE NEXT MORNING, Florence rubbed her eyes trying her best to forget a lost night's sleep due to worry over what might become of Honor. She'd done pretty poorly at sticking to her resolve to worry less about her half-sisters.

Florence had to wait until after breakfast to be alone with *Mamm* so she could tell her what she thought. No one had mentioned anything about Honor and Jonathon the entire morning. Both Honor and *Mamm* had avoided eye-contact with her.

"I honestly can't believe you, *Mamm*. You're rewarding them for running away."

Mamm nodded. "I know you're upset."

"I am, and it all started when Honor ran away. You left with Cherish without even bothering to punish Honor properly. It was left up to me to give her extra chores. If Honor had been given a harsher punishment, she might've seen things clearly. Now Jonathon's weaseled his way around the situation and gotten his way."

"What you don't know is that something else might've happened. That's why I didn't punish her for returning. If she's punished for coming home, she might not come home the next time."

Florence frowned wondering which way was right.

"We've had a win. She's stayed here and they've asked permission rather than doing things their own way like last time. Now, don't get upset, but there's something else I haven't told you. I told all the girls this morning but I told them that I wanted to tell you myself."

Florence stared at her stepmother. Had someone died? "What is it?"

"After you went to bed last night, I had a more serious talk with Jonathon and I gave them permission to marry. So, they'll marry before he leaves to take that job."

At first, Florence thought she hadn't heard correctly. "What?" She put her hand over her heart to calm herself as she wrapped her mind around the shocking news. While her stepmother repeated it, Florence pulled out a chair and sat down. "I can't believe what I'm hearing. This was everything I was trying to avoid." She shook her head. "Now I feel I wasted my time bringing her back. I should've just let them run away."

"*Nee*, you did the right thing. Now they're staying in the community and they would've left if you hadn't brought her back here."

Florence rounded her shoulders in defeat. "I'm shocked, but still, I know it's not my decision to make." It was deeply upsetting that her opinions were so disregarded by *Mamm*. She felt like she truly *was* wasting her time. All she wanted to do now was get far away from the house so the news could sink in. "So, you're serious about this? They're actually getting married?"

"*Jah*. They're visiting the bishop today to arrange a date for their baptisms and for their wedding, as soon as he'll permit."

With a hand over her stomach, mentally fighting the nausea, she looked at the half-made apple pies. "Once these pies are in the oven, I'll visit Liza."

"I can do the rest if you want to go now."

"*Denke*, but Ezekiel is collecting me at nine to take me there. He's volunteered with some other men to fix Samuel and Liza's chimney."

Mamm nodded. "You look over-worked. You probably need some time with your friend."

"*Denke, Mamm*."

FLORENCE COULDN'T WAIT to leave all her problems behind her. Liza was a good listener and she always agreed with

Florence's way of thinking. Complaining to her best friend was all that she'd need to make her feel better.

When she saw Ezekiel's borrowed buggy coming toward the house, she hurried out to meet him. The first thing she noticed was his big smile.

"*Wie gehts?*" he asked.

"I'm good, and you?"

"Fine, on such a beautiful morning."

The sky was gray and a chilling wind swept through the orchard. It was anything but beautiful. She climbed into the buggy next to him. "Are you looking forward to the day ahead?"

"I am. I helped work on a chimney not long ago, so I do have some experience."

As the horse clip-clopped along the road, their relaxed conversation continued, allowing Florence to release some of the tension her home-life so often brought.

When they pulled up at Liza and Simon's house, Liza was waiting at the door. Florence stepped down and walked to meet her while Ezekiel secured the horse.

"I'm so pleased you're here because I've been wanting to tell you this for days." Liza then glanced across at Ezekiel. "Oh! Hello. I didn't see you there."

Florence noticed Liza was unusually flustered.

"I'm here to help with the chimney," Ezekiel told her.

"Liza, this is Ezekiel Troyer."

"Pleased to meet you. *Denke* for coming to help. That's *wunder-baar*. The men are around the back."

"I hope I'm not late."

"*Nee*. They've only been here five minutes. I'll take you to them."

After they accompanied Ezekiel to where the men were just getting started, Liza looped her arm through Florence's and pulled her into the house through the back door.

"Now, what's this news?" Florence stared into her friend's face as they stood facing each other in the center of the kitchen. The glowing skin, her big smile and those sparkling eyes could only mean one thing. "You're having another *boppli?*"

She giggled. "I am"

The two women hugged. Florence was so overjoyed for her friend that it felt like something good had happened for her. This wasn't the right time to unburden all her worries. She'd hold them in for now. "That's so soon."

"I know. The two will be close together and we're hoping for another boy to be close in age with Malachi. Simon had Michael, and they were only a year apart."

Florence nodded as an image of Michael came into her mind, reminding her of his rejection of her.

"I'm sorry, I shouldn't have mentioned Michael."

"Nee, that's okay. I'm over that now. I was over that a long time ago, believe me."

"I'm sure he didn't know you liked him. You should've let him know."

Florence shook her head. "That would've only made the inevitable rejection harder to bear."

"Oh, Florence, you shouldn't say that."

"That's all in the past. I'm so pleased for you. Your life's turning out just perfectly."

"I know, it is. Can I fix you some *kaffe?*"

"Please. I'd love a cup."

THE NOISE from the banging and hammering in the living room was too loud, so Liza closed the door of the kitchen and they sat down with their coffee mugs at the kitchen table.

"Now, tell me about Ezekiel?"

"I spent the whole day with him yesterday."

"And, what do you think of him?"

"He's nice."

"Oh." Liza's shoulders dropped.

Florence laughed. "Nice, in a good way."

"Are you interested in him?"

Liza knew her better than anyone. "I haven't really gotten to know him yet. That's what I'm doing in the week that he's here." She sipped her hot coffee.

"That's good."

Florence placed her mug carefully down on the table. "He's very easy to be around."

"That's what you need. You need to marry someone who's also a friend."

"I guess so."

"I mean, most people go through rough patches in their marriage. It's mostly at the beginning when you're adjusting to one another."

Florence screwed up her nose. That part didn't sound like much fun.

"But, it's so worth it when you get through that bit," Liza added.

"Is that the same for everyone?"

"Most people. It's not easy sometimes."

"It should be easy. I want a love that's no effort whatsoever. A love where I don't have to work at it."

Liza laughed. "I hope you find it. You always complain about your sisters being unrealistic and now I know they get that from you."

Florence grimaced. *"Nee.* I'm a very practical person." She leaned forward and whispered, "I'm just hoping it works out with Ezekiel. It would be nice to have someone special in my life."

"And no one deserves it more than you. You're always doing everything for everyone else."

"When Earl and Mark moved away after *Dat* died, I had to assume the role as the oldest. Naturally, there's not much time to think about myself with running the orchard and everything."

"The orchard, the shop, the household and everything else. I hope they appreciate you."

Florence wasn't doing it for appreciation. She was doing it because that was what needed to be done.

"If Ezekiel's right for you, it'll happen." Liza took a mouthful of coffee.

"That's true. Oh, Liza, I'm so pleased for you. You waited long enough for your first *boppli* and now to have another one straight after, you must be thrilled."

"I am. It's *wunderbaar,* and Simon's … well he just doesn't have words to express himself, but he cried when I told him."

Florence laughed. "I hope they were happy tears."

"Most definitely, tears of joy." The two of them shared a little chuckle. "I have something to ask you."

"What's that?"

"Will you be there at the birth, to help me?"

Florence was delighted she asked. "Really?"

"*Jah,* I'd love it if you would."

"I'd love to."

"*Denke.* I was going to ask you last time, but my *schweschder*-in-law pushed her way in and volunteered. I didn't want too many people there. This time, I'm getting in first with you, and I'll tell her no."

"I'd be truly honored to be there to share your special moment. I can't think of anything I'd like more. I'd love it." Liza felt closer to her than any of her own half-sisters did.

WHEN FLORENCE LEFT LIZA'S, she rode homeward in the buggy beside Ezekiel, her mind full of mixed feelings. She'd gone there to unburden her woes. She wasn't expecting Liza's good news – news that brought home to her what her own life had become.

She glanced over at Ezekiel who seemed much quieter than usual. "Are you tired?"

"Very. It was hard work."

That was all he said. He seemed to be in a funny mood and Florence couldn't work out why. Perhaps he was just tired.

CHAPTER 13

ACROSS TOWN, Joy and Hope were serving at their stall at the farmers market. Hope left to get a mid-afternoon take-out coffee, leaving her sister at the stall alone.

Joy was busy serving a customer. She took the money and then handed her customer a bag containing two jars of pickles and a jar of apple sauce. Once the customer left, she noticed her friend Bliss Bruner was standing close by. There was a quiet moment between customers, so she waved Bliss over.

Before even saying hello, Bliss said, "Did you realize my *vadder* likes your *mudder?*"

Joy'd had her suspicions about that ever since Levi Bruner had gifted their family Wilbur—a fine gelding. If her mother felt the same about him, Joy wasn't sure how she herself would feel about a stepfather. "Really? He likes her?"

"*Jah*. He didn't admit it, but he talks about her an awful lot and what a *wunderbaar* woman she is." Bliss laughed. "Do you think they'd make a good pair?"

"I don't know, I have to think about it a bit more."

"I've been thinking about it."

Joy laughed.

"What if we arrange something where they could spend some more time alone?"

Joy winced. She didn't want to interfere. Her mother had never shown any interest in men apart from *Dat*. Still, she didn't feel she could say no. Bliss seemed so excited. "What did you have in mind?"

"Maybe, a dinner. What if just your *mudder* comes to my place for dinner, and then I'll leave them alone?"

That sounded awful. "That would be a little obvious, don't you think?"

"*Nee*."

"I don't think she'd like it. It'd make her feel awkward, and she might think your *vadder* arranged it."

"Does she even want to get married again?"

"I don't think so, Bliss." Joy shook her head. "She's never talked about it." Joy didn't know if she or any of her sisters was ready to have a stepfather. "I really don't think we should do anything.

If it's meant to be, and if *Gott* wants it to happen, it will." She smiled at Bliss, hoping she'd see the sense in that.

Bliss giggled. "Yeah, but it won't matter if we help it along a bit, will it?"

"I'm not comfortable with that," Joy said.

"Why not? You were a moment ago."

"Now I've had time to think about it, though, and I'm not interested in interfering."

More customers approached the counter, and Bliss stepped back. Once the customers left, Bliss carried on talking. "It will affect their lives, Joy, but only for the better. Aw, come on. You used to be more fun than this."

"Fun? I am fun. But this doesn't sound like fun to me."

Bliss blew out a deep breath. "I should've asked one of your sisters."

"Maybe it was just as well you didn't. I can't believe you think I'm not fun. I'm just the same as I always was."

"Don't you think it would be good if my *vadder* and your *mudder* got married?"

"Sure, if that's what they want. It would be great, but she's never spoken about marrying again." And then she had to know about Bliss's father. "Has your *vadder* mentioned anything about a second marriage?"

"Not so much. I mean, he talks about your *mudder,* but he doesn't talk about marrying her." Bliss leaned forward. "Does she talk about him?"

"Nee, not really. Not like that." She couldn't remember her mother ever talking about him at all.

"Ach." The smile left Bliss's face.

"That could be because we've had so much going on with Mercy getting married and then Cherish going away. Now there's the Honor and Jonathon saga. Every day there seems to be some drama or other playing out."

"At least it sounds interesting." Bliss sighed. "Nothing ever happens at my place. It's boring with just me and *Dat."*

"'Boring?' You mean peaceful. Give me boring any day."

Bliss laughed. "I suppose it's all in the way you view it."

Joy nodded. "Anyway, it's interesting to know your *Dat* is sweet on *Mamm."*

"Don't you tell anyone. He'll be so upset with me."

"I won't say anything to *Mamm,* but I might tell one of my sisters—if that's okay? It's hard to keep things from them. Keeping any kind of a secret is not easy in our house."

"Okay."

"Here comes Hope now. About time. I can't do all this by myself. We're going to have the after-work crowd soon."

"I'll go. Bye now." Bliss hurried away before Joy could even say goodbye.

"What did she want?" Isaac frowned looking at Bliss striding away.

Joy was startled. She hadn't seen Isaac approaching from the other direction. "She just had some silly things she wanted me to be a part of."

"Like what?" Hope took a careful sip of her take-out coffee as she joined them.

Joy was now focused on coffee. She had thought Hope might've bought her one too. "Where's mine?"

"I thought you'd like to stretch your legs and get your own."

Joy grumbled.

"Take a walk with Isaac, but don't be too long."

"Unlike you, I won't." Joy took hold of her purse from under the counter and then Isaac and she walked away from the stall.

"Was Bliss talking about me?" he asked.

His question took her by surprise. "What? *Nee*, of course not. It wasn't about you. What makes you think that?"

"She left when she saw me coming. She's your friend and she probably doesn't think I'm good enough for you." He glanced over his shoulder, and then looked back at Joy. "Did she say something like that to you?"

She stared at Isaac. She'd never seen this side of him. "Why are you saying these things?"

"Things have never come easy for me, Joy. My size has always been an issue." He looked down at himself.

"There's nothing wrong with your size." He was only a little larger than others, and Joy liked the way he looked.

He patted his stomach. "I'm overweight. And when people see that, they think I'm lazy and not a hard worker. I've always been this way."

"She was talking about her *vadder* and my *mudder*, if you must know. I didn't want to say it, but she had the idea she and I should push them together."

Slowly, he nodded while studying her face. "If that's true, it sounds like meddling to me."

"Meddling ... yes, that's a good word. Sounds like it to me too. Hey, what do you mean by 'if that's true?' Of course it is. Why would I say something untrue to you?"

"I'm sorry."

"It's okay. I guess you've heard the news about Honor and Jonathon? The shocking news, I should say."

"*Jah*, Jonathon mentioned they're getting married. I was there when he told Mark and Christina."

"I'm a little shocked, but anyway, that ruins your plan of moving out with him. They're moving away, too. Heading back to Wisconsin. I forget what the Amish community there is called."

"Jah. He told me all that—but I don't recall the name of their community either." He rubbed his chin. "Do you want coffee?"

"Not now. Let's just walk around. Talking about Honor getting married has made me feel a little sick. I've gone from five sisters to two in just a couple of months. Not counting Florence, that is."

"Big changes for you."

She sighed. "It makes me feel uneasy somehow."

"In what way?"

"I just want things the way they were before Stephen appeared. He took Mercy away. It was only supposed to be for a year, but there's no sign of them returning."

Isaac nodded. "That's the thing about life, things never stay the same. Everything is always changing and there's nothing much we can do about it."

"I guess."

"Do they have a date for the wedding? Jonathon didn't say."

"I don't know, but I think it's going to be soon because Jonathon has to start work back home." She shook her head. "I can't believe *Mamm* allowed this."

"Aren't you happy for Honor?"

"Not really, if I'm honest."

He opened his mouth in shock. "Why not?"

"I think she should've waited to see if someone else came along that she'd like better."

He stared at her in disbelief and then looked down. When they had walked another couple of paces, he asked, "Is that what you're doing with me?"

"We'll just have to wait and see what happens."

"I need some kind of assurance of your feelings. Can't you give me that?"

Joy didn't like being put on the spot. Was he asking if she intended marrying him? That was something she'd think about in a few years, not now. "I'm way too young to get married now and I don't think I'll be ready to marry when I'm seventeen or even eighteen. I want to be fully grown up and ready to make a responsible decision." That's what Florence was always telling her and her sisters and she wanted to do the right thing. After all, among the Amish, marriage was for life.

He slowly nodded. "So where do things stand with us?"

"I like you, otherwise I wouldn't be spending so much time with you. I'm just being honest right now."

He shook his head. "I know what the problem is. And it's a problem I can't do anything about." He stopped still, and then left her there and walked away in the other direction.

"Wait!" She caught up with him and touched his arm and he stopped. "What's the matter?" When Isaac turned to face her, she saw how upset he was. "Why are you acting so strange today?"

He frowned and took a step away from her. "Because I don't like wasting anyone's time."

"Well if you're asking me if I want to marry you at some future date, how can I say yes or no? It'll depend on how I feel then. If I knew how I'd feel then I'd say so, but I don't."

"Okay, I won't pressure you."

She pointed her hands on her hips. "Good, because I don't like being pressured."

They both stared at each other for a moment. Joy hoped that would be the end of this topic and they could go back to being how they were. Then, Isaac walked away leaving her standing there. This time, she made no attempt to stop him. She had no patience for his sulky attitude. What she did regret was forgetting to buy her take-out coffee.

CHAPTER 14

AFTER A WEEK of Florence seeing Ezekiel nearly every day, the time came for him to leave. She'd gotten to know him as the strong quiet type. He saw humor in little things and was even-tempered. She saw nothing bad in him, and from what she knew of him, he seemed like a good choice for a husband.

They were alone on Florence's porch after he'd said goodbye to Wilma and the girls. It was just on dusk as they said their personal goodbyes. A car was coming to collect him from Ada and Samuel's house early the next morning.

"Florence, what I want to say to you is that I've enjoyed getting to know you."

"So have I. It's been really enjoyable."

He cleared his throat. "And there's something else I need to say."

She looked up at him. "And what's that?" She didn't want him to propose and she hoped that wasn't what he was about to do. If he did, she'd have to turn him down, but she didn't want to hurt his feelings and neither did she want to close any doors with him. Anxiousness caused her to bite down on the inside of her mouth.

"Would you write to me?"

That was it? Instead of heaving a large sigh, she contained it and nodded. "Of course, I'll write."

The serious look hadn't left his face. "I'm hoping there's something good in our future for the both of us."

"Me too. Time will tell."

His face softened when he laughed. "Not too much time, I hope. Might we see our friendship as something a little more while we write?"

"*Jah*. I thought that's what we were doing by agreeing to write to one another."

He nodded. "Good, I just wanted us both to be clear. Communication is very important in a relationship."

She wondered how often he'd write and what she'd write in return. Lots of things happened at the orchard, but most of it wasn't very interesting. He wouldn't want to know the latest dramas with the girls. Maybe she could tell him about the orchard and he could write to her about his farm.

Florence liked the way he got to the point about things. A man like that would love her and cherish her. That was how she wanted to be treated by her husband and in return, she'd be a good wife.

She watched him get into the buggy. Once he'd picked up the reins, he moved them into one hand, and gave her a wave before he steered the horse and buggy down the long driveway.

Wilma hurried out to join her. "Well? Did he mention marriage?"

Florence put a hand over her mouth and giggled. *"Nee,* he didn't. But we're going to write to each other."

"He didn't discuss marriage at all?" *Mamm's* eyes opened wide.

"Nee, but I know he likes me. I think he knows me well enough to know that I'm not the kind of person who'd rush into something."

"Like Cherish?"

It wasn't only Cherish it was Honor, and possibly Joy as well, but Florence didn't want to say it. "I wasn't speaking about anybody. I think there could be something special between us. It's not a crazy kind of love at first sight or anything, it's more of a dependable kind of love."

"I agree, and he'd make a fine husband. Now, do you forgive me for allowing Honor to get married?"

"It's your choice. There's nothing to forgive. I wouldn't have allowed it, but that doesn't matter."

"When we have a moment alone, I'll tell you exactly why I allowed it and then you'll see there are at least two sides to a thing."

"*Jah,* there are. The right side and the wrong side."

Mamm shook her head. "What about the inside and the outside? We'll have that talk as soon as we're alone. Maybe when the girls are in bed."

"I can't wait to hear what you've got to say."

Mamm chuckled. "I'm so pleased you met Ezekiel. Ada's done well choosing men for you girls."

"She didn't choose Jonathon, or come to think of it, Isaac."

"Well, it's two out of four. And we didn't ask her to find anyone for Joy or Honor."

"Let's get in out of the cold," Florence suggested.

CHAPTER 15

OVER BREAKFAST THE NEXT DAY, *Mamm* announced they needed Cherish back to help with the wedding preparations.

Honor groaned. *"Nee, Mamm.* You know how she thinks she's in love with Jonathon? How can I have her around at my wedding?"

"She's your *schweschder.* You can't leave her out of it."

"Nee! You can't do this to me."

Florence said, "How about she comes back just a day or two before. That way, everyone will be so busy it won't matter."

Honor shook her head. "I've got a better idea. How about she doesn't come back until the day, or even better, the day after."

"I'll arrange for her to come back two days before, and I hope Dagmar can come with her. She'll have to find someone to look after her farm—I hope she's able to."

"Please, don't have a lot of attendants if you want me to sew," Florence told Honor.

"*Nee,* I'm only having Joy."

Everyone looked at Joy, who looked delighted.

"I knew you'd choose her," Favor said.

"She's the next closest in age, that's all. I'm not choosing favorites."

"That's fine by me."

"And, the men already have suits. Jonathon has the one he wore to Stephen's wedding and he's happy to wear that one again."

That was good news to Florence's ears. "You don't mind him not being in a new one?"

"*Nee,* it's a waste. It's money we can put toward our home when we get one."

Mamm and Florence exchanged smiles.

When Honor and Joy went to work at the markets, Florence sent Favor and Hope to clean the laundry room. She was anxious to hear what *Mamm* had to say about allowing Honor and Jonathon to marry. It sounded like Wilma had a story to tell. After Florence made two cups of coffee, she settled down with *Mamm* in the living room.

"*Mamm,* now we're alone …"

"I can see you're still annoyed, Florence. Do you want to talk about it, or wait a bit?"

"Jah. Please begin. You said you'd tell me more when we were alone, and now we're alone." A wave of emotion came over Florence. It was awful having to discipline the girls when *Mamm* had the final say. "First Mercy and Stephen got married, which I suppose is fine because we all know they get on great. But now you've given Honor permission to marry Jonathon. Jonathon, of all people. And next, before we know what will happen, Joy will marry Isaac." She paused, drawing a breath.

"I know, but you like Isaac."

"That's not the issue. I'm worried that they're all getting married too young."

"They're marrying when they fall in love."

"But, are they old enough to know what love is?"

A small smile hinted around the edges of *Mamm's* lips. "Florence, let me tell you what I know. There was a woman I knew very well."

"Before you tell me a story, let me tell you one. There is a woman I know very well and she thought she was in love. After she married in haste, she had years of misery before *Gott* turned it around. I just don't think those years of misery were worth it. People say marriage takes work, but does it have to be that hard? And, perhaps it wouldn't be so much work if one chose one's husband more carefully. Those are some of my thoughts from what I've seen."

Mamm's eyebrows rose. "Florence, if you will listen to me, you'll see why I haven't put my foot down to stop your sisters from marrying."

"Go on."

"There was a woman who was very much in love with a man in the same community, but her parents thought she was too young."

"How young?"

"She was sixteen and the young man was eighteen. Their parents refused to allow them to marry. He went on to marry someone else years later."

"What happened to her?"

"Ah, that's a totally different story. Heartbroken that their parents wouldn't allow them to see one another, she left the community thinking that would make their parents agree to the marriage. It didn't happen. She got in with the wrong crowd, and became pregnant, or she might've already been pregnant before she left. That's my guess. Away from her friends and family and as an unmarried mother, she faced many struggles and her life was ruined."

"Who was it, *Mamm*?" Many scenarios ran through Florence's mind. She couldn't have been talking about herself, could she?

"I might as well tell you. To you, she'd be your step-Aunt Iris."

Florence tried to make sense of everything. She knew there wasn't an Iris on her father's side and she was sure her stepmother only had one *bruder, Onkel* Tom—and his wife's name was Ruth.

"I have a step-aunt, Aunt Iris? Is she your *schweschder?*"

"*Jah.* My younger *schweschder.* I haven't seen her for many years. She stopped by one day when I was pregnant with Mercy, and I told her she should leave. Something that I regret to this very day."

"You can't blame yourself. You thought you were doing the right thing."

"It doesn't matter what I thought. I've learned since then that closing my heart off to others doesn't help them. I mean, how could it?"

"Don't be so hard on yourself."

"I've never heard from her again. I think about her every day, hoping she'll find the courage to knock on my door."

Florence swallowed hard. That explained why *Mamm* was so soft on everyone. She'd been hard on her own sister and, as a result, lived with not knowing where Iris was or whether she was okay. And, *Mamm* had to wonder what had become of the *boppli.*

"I don't know what might happen, but do you see now why I am not standing in their way?"

Florence nodded. "I do. You're afraid if you stop them, they'll do something drastic."

"Well, also, imagine her heartbreak to learn that the man she loved and probably still does to this day is married to someone else."

Florence thought about that for a moment. "I wouldn't want any of my sisters to leave the community over a man."

"Honor very nearly did."

"I guess there are two different ways of looking at these things, aren't there? There is the story of my friend, and then there's Iris."

Mamm nodded. "And they're both true."

"And we're both trying to do the best we can for the girls."

"That's true. But I truly think at their ages they know their own minds."

"I'm sorry, *Mamm,* but I know when I was sixteen, I would have chosen a very different man compared to the one I'd choose today. Sixteen is not old enough."

"I must disagree with that."

"*Denke* for telling me about your sister. It's a sad story when you're not in love with the person you marry. You were in love with *Dat,* weren't you?"

"From as far back as I can remember." She giggled.

"Only after my *mamm* died though, right?"

"Of course."

Florence smiled. She'd only remembered her father with Wilma. From what she remembered, they'd been in love. They were always talking to each other, and they always agreed on everything.

"Our coffees have gone cold."

Florence giggled. "I'll make us more." She stood up, and leaned over and hugged Wilma. "I hope one day we'll find out what happened to your *schweschder.*"

"If *Gott* wills it, we will."

CHAPTER 16

THE WEEKS FLEW by and Florence was so busy organizing the household and the wedding, she hadn't had any time for herself. Now just two days remained before the wedding and it was time for Cherish to come home.

At five in the evening, Wilma excitedly yelled out, "She's here!"

Florence went to the kitchen window and looked out. Caramel, Cherish's dog, was out of the car first, and then Cherish stepped out looking none too happy. The expression on her face was exactly the same as the one she had worn when she left. Florence was immediately filled with dread. With so much left to do they didn't need any more complications.

The girls raced out to greet her and Florence was the last one. A tiny smile met Cherish's lips as her sisters hugged her in turn. Then Caramel charged at Florence pulling the leash out of Cherish's hand.

Florence bent down to pat him as he jumped up at her. "How have you been, boy?"

"It seems like you're more pleased to see Caramel than me."

She looked up to see Cherish right there. What she said was true, but Florence couldn't admit it.

"It's so nice to have you home," Florence stood up and hugged her, while Caramel ran onto the grass.

"I've got your bag, Cherish. I'll take it up to your room."

"*Denke,* Favor."

All the girls ran after Cherish to hear about her stay with Dagmar. That left Florence and *Mamm* standing at the bottom of the stairs.

"I know we haven't talked about this, but do you intend for Cherish to stay?" Florence asked.

"I've made no promises to her. Aunt Dagmar's pleased for her to go back to her. She's pleased for the companionship."

"So, you will send her back if she hasn't changed?"

"*Jah,* I don't want her to get into any kind of trouble."

Florence nodded as she recalled the conversation they'd had recently about Wilma's long-lost sister.

THAT NIGHT, when everyone was seated around the dinner table, Cherish began with the stories. "Aunt Dagmar has this tiny bird that she keeps in a cage. His name's Timmy. And all I hear all day is, *Timmy, Timmy, Timmy.* She's trying to teach him to talk."

The girls giggled.

"I can't tell you how annoying I find it. 'Timmy, Timmy,'" she tried to mimic Dagmar's voice and all the girls laughed louder.

"You should be grateful she's welcomed you with open arms," *Mamm* said.

"If she hadn't wanted me, where would you have sent me?"

"Somewhere really bad," Florence chipped in.

Cherish's eyes grew wide as she stared back at Florence. "It *is* really bad, Florence. Haven't you been listening to what I've been saying?"

"*Nee,* all I've heard is you being rude about a person who's been kind. It wouldn't hurt you at all to develop some patience and gratitude."

That kept everyone quiet for a few moments, until Cherish started once more. "I feel like a prisoner there. I don't have to go back there again, do I?"

"I told you, you can stay here as long as you behave."

Honor said, "And don't imagine that Jonathon likes you, please don't think that he does. He's marrying me. Anyway, you're far too young."

Cherish's face screwed up. "I didn't like him. Not like that," she insisted, but everyone knew she was making that up. Florence took a large drink of water, and when she put the glass down, Cherish said to her, "I hear you have a boyfriend."

Florence hadn't thought about Ezekiel as a boyfriend, but perhaps that's what he was. "Maybe I do."

"I heard he's a pig farmer. I bet he smells awful, a bit like a pig, or pig swill, or even pig manure."

Amongst a flurry of giggles, *Mamm* said, "Cherish, you shouldn't say such things."

"He does smell—he smells nice," Florence said, trying to make light of things.

Cherish's eyes danced with mischief. "Ah, so you've been close enough to smell him, have you?"

Mamm shook her head at her youngest. "No more, Cherish, or you'll be sent to your room."

Hope whispered in Cherish's ear, but it was loud enough for Florence to hear, "Don't say any more or they'll send you right back."

Cherish put her head down and then looked back up at *Mamm* and then Florence, as though summing them up. "I believe it," she muttered back.

"I hope everyone is ready to do a lot of work tomorrow," said *Mamm*. "We've got a big day ahead of us. All the ladies are coming to give the *haus* a going-through. Then the day after, we'll concentrate on the food."

"I was hoping to have a rest. Can't I have a rest?" Cherish whined. "I'm tired from all the traveling."

"You'll get a good sleep tonight and you'll be okay," *Mamm* said.

Cherish played with her food. "At least I know how to make baskets now."

"You should've brought some with you," Joy said.

"I'd like to know how to make baskets," Favor said.

"I can show everyone, if I get to stay here."

Favor leaned forward. "Was it really that bad?"

"I like Aunt Dagmar. I didn't at first, but then I got to like her. When she's not talking to Timmy, that is. The thing I don't like is, she lives out in the middle of nowhere and I feel like a prisoner. When I'm feeling sad, Dagmar starts talking to her stupid bird, trying to make him talk and that makes me feel worse."

Mamm smiled a little, and then coughed to cover it up. "What did Caramel think of the bird?"

"Nothing, nothing at all. He just ignored him." Cherish sighed. "I can't believe that there's just four of us left now."

Favor giggled. "Joy will be marrying Isaac next."

Florence suddenly realized they'd have to close down the stall at the farmers market. It wasn't practical for them to keep it going.

Joy shook her head when everyone stared at her. "That won't be happening. Not for years and years. Not for a couple of years, anyway. I'm in no rush, not like the rest of you."

"We aren't," Favor said. "I'm not."

"Neither am I," said Hope. "Maybe if there was someone I liked, I might be in a hurry, but there's no one for me."

"Well, if Florence can find someone, anyone can," said Cherish.

"Denke, Cherish." The comment was said to upset Florence, but she wasn't going to let what Cherish said bother her.

Mamm glared at her youngest. "It's not a very nice thing to say."

"Oh, I didn't mean it like that. I'm so sorry, Florence."

Florence smiled at her, figuring it was the best thing to do. "The ladies will be arriving early in the morning. We've got a busy day of cleaning ahead of us."

"The place is already clean, if you ask me," Favor said.

Mamm smiled. "It'll be cleaner than clean by the end of the day tomorrow."

CHAPTER 17

THE DAY AFTER NEXT—THE day before the wedding—a crowd of women gathered at the house to cook, just as they had for cleaning the previous day. Even Jonathon came to see if he could be of any help. Wanting to keep Jonathon and Cherish far apart, Florence knew she'd have to keep him busy with jobs far away from Cherish.

For his first task, Florence asked him to go to the building that they operated as a shop, at the front of their property, to count the cakes that they'd stored there. Florence knew exactly what was there and how many of each, but Jonathon didn't know that.

When she went back to her own task, she noticed Cherish was leaving the cleaning task she'd been given, assisting with dishes for the cooks.

Florence quickly asked Favor to temporarily take over Cherish's task. When she stepped out onto the porch, she saw Cherish hurrying down the path that led to the shop. She was deliberately following Jonathon. This wasn't good.

Florence hurried to stop a disaster from happening. When she reached the door, she hovered to listen in.

"Hello, Jonathon."

"Hi, Cherish. It's a long time since I've seen you."

"I've just been visiting some relatives. I thought it was time I came home."

"*Gut*. In time to see your *schweschder* and I get married."

"Um, *jah* … about that."

Florence froze as she listened.

Cherish continued, "It's not too late to change your mind. Other people have done it. No one will think badly of you. People will respect you for making your own decision instead of being pushed into something."

"Now wait a minute. No one's pushing me into anything. I love her with all my heart, and we belong together. There's not one single solitary doubt in my mind. There's no reason to change anything."

"Really?" Cherish asked.

"*Jah*. What are you doing here anyway?"

"Florence sent me to count the cakes."

"You sure about that? It doesn't take two, and she asked me to do that. I think you should go back. I'm not sure why we're even talking like this, and ..."

Florence was pleased to hear his response and was just about to save him from Cherish, when she heard Cherish's next comment.

"But I'm in love with you, Jonathon."

Florence couldn't believe her ears. She waited to hear what Jonathon said.

"I'm sorry to hear that. That's something you should keep to yourself considering the situation."

"*Nee*, that's exactly why I must tell you; because you're making a big mistake."

"I'm not!"

Florence moved into the building, and Cherish turned around, shocked to see her. "I thought you were in the kitchen, Florence."

"I was, but we need you to keep cleaning up after the cooks as they work. Why did you leave?"

Cherish shook her head. "I'm talking to Jonathon."

Jonathon kept his head down. "You'd better go, Cherish."

Florence was livid that Cherish was so arrogant toward her. She grabbed her by the arm. "Back to the kitchen, now." Once they were out the door and halfway to the house, Florence said to her, "I heard what you said in there. I can't even believe my own ears. How could you say something like that? Are you trying to ruin your *schweschder's* life? What were you thinking?"

"I was doing nothing wrong. I just thought he might've been pushed into it and that's not fair."

Florence shook her head. "You're definitely going back to Aunt Dagmar's."

"Nee, Mamm won't allow it."

"If it's the last thing I do, I'll see that she's in full agreement with me."

"You wouldn't."

"Just watch me."

Once Cherish was back in the house, Florence took *Mamm* aside and told her what had happened. *Mamm* was greatly upset. "I think she'll have to go back."

Florence nodded. "I agree."

"I'll talk with her and make sure she behaves herself until she goes back to Dagmar's."

"And when will that be?" Florence asked, hoping it'd be soon.

"I'll talk with her now. I'll take her up to her room, so no one will hear us. I don't want Honor being upset over this. It's better she doesn't know, for now. Can you call Aunt Dagmar and make sure it's okay that she goes back there?"

"Sure. I'm happy to do it. Do you want me to call a driver and find one who can drive her there soon?"

Mamm nodded, and then sighed. "It's all too much for me, Florence. Please find someone who can drive her back there the next day after the wedding."

"Okay." From where they stood in the living room, Florence looked at all the workers in the kitchen. "I'll stay here until you talk with her. One of us should stay. When you come back, I'll go to the barn and make some calls."

"Denke, Florence."

EARLY THAT AFTERNOON, Florence walked out of the barn ready to deliver the news to *Mamm* that a driver would be arriving at nine the morning after the wedding. That would mean Cherish would miss the big clean-up day after the celebrations, but Florence was certain her youngest half-sister wouldn't have made much of a contribution to that anyway. Dagmar was pleased with the news that Cherish would return.

While walking up the porch steps that led to the house, Florence spied a bundle of letters left on a chair. She picked up the half dozen letters and leafed through them for Ezekiel's familiar handwriting. Then she spotted it.

Florence was distressed to get a letter from him so close to the wedding. In her heart, she knew what that meant. She sat on the porch chair, and then, with the other letters in her lap, she ripped open the envelope.

In his letter, Ezekiel explained his mother wasn't well and he wouldn't be attending the wedding. Dropping the letter into her lap, she looked out over the orchard. She'd been counting the days until she would see him, so they could continue their courtship. Even though she was against rushing into a relationship, neither did she want it to drag out for an eternity.

When would something ever go right for her?

There was no time to feel sorry for herself. Not with the wedding tomorrow. She picked herself up and fixed a smile on her face before she headed back into the house.

CHAPTER 18

JOY WAS EXCITED to be participating in her sister's wedding, wearing the exact color medium-blue dress as Honor. As she sat behind Honor, who was standing in front of the bishop with Jonathon, it almost felt like her own wedding in a way. Especially with Isaac there looking so handsome in the dark suit that his older sister, Christina, had made him.

While the bishop gave his talk, she couldn't help looking over at Isaac. Each time she glanced at him, he smiled even wider. And then she noticed someone else's eyes upon her. It was Jonathon's younger brother, Luke, who was sitting behind Jonathon as his wedding attendant.

When their eyes met, he beamed her a smile and she turned away. Now she couldn't look at Isaac because Luke might think she was looking at him. So, she concentrated on the bishop's words as he spoke on the topic of *Gott's* plan for marriage.

. . .

HONOR GLANCED at her husband-to-be as they stood in front of the bishop in the family's living room. Just as it had been for Mercy's wedding, all the furniture in the house had been exchanged for wooden benches. Now every one of those benches was full, leaving people to stand on the sides of the room.

It felt good that so many people had come to see them get married. And that no one had said anything about her getting married so young. People seemed to like the idea she and her older sister would be married to brothers. Jonathon had even teased his young brother, Luke, that he'd have to marry Joy. Honor knew that was very unlikely because Joy only had eyes for her half-brother's wife's brother. It was confusing, but many relationships within the community were like that.

This marriage was what Honor and Jonathon had wanted more than anything, and against all odds Jonathon had made it happen. He convinced her mother that the timing was right. With all that they'd been through together, Honor knew he was the perfect man for her. They'd also be moving close to Mercy. She glanced over her shoulder to look at Mercy, and after they exchanged smiles, she saw Florence staring at her disapprovingly. Quickly, she faced the front. In time, Florence would learn that Jonathon was a good man, and when she did, she might even apologize for ever doubting him.

Once they were finally pronounced married, it was time for the festivities. Everyone moved from the house into the annex that covered the area between the house and the barn.

· · ·

THROUGHOUT THE CEREMONY, Joy had kept a close eye on Isaac. When he didn't gravitate to her when the ceremony was over, she walked over to him. He saw her coming and then he deliberately moved away. Joy had no idea what had gotten into him. When she finally caught up with him, she saw from his face that he was upset.

"Is everything okay?"

He pressed his lips together. *"Nee."*

"What's wrong?"

"I saw you looking at someone else just now."

Joy laughed. "Don't be silly. I was looking at you."

"Not all the time."

Joy stared at him. Was he joking? When there was no hint of a smile on his face, she knew he wasn't. Being a no nonsense kind of a person, she wasn't in the mood for drama. Not on such a special day for her sister. "Find me when you get over the mood you're in." She turned and walked away from him. He must've been talking about when she had noticed Luke staring at her. Isaac was being immature and she wasn't going to be drawn into his silliness. Pushing him out of her mind, she walked amongst the crowd determined to enjoy herself and help the many guests enjoy themselves.

MEANWHILE, Florence was working in the kitchen supervising the ladies who were helping with food for the three hundred or so guests. Florence wasn't bothered by the huge task on her shoulders. She helped out so often at weddings. Years ago, her father had set their kitchen up with two large ovens and there was loads of countertop space for working.

Once the first course of the food had gone out, Florence was able to slow her pace. Yet, her mind never stopped working— never stopped thinking about the orchard and her family's finances. Their savings had taken a hit with Honor's wedding coming so close behind Mercy's. *Mamm* hadn't taken that into consideration when she'd allowed them to marry now rather than having them wait for a year.

With Cherish going back to Aunt Dagmar's, and the two oldest half-sisters now married, that only left five of them. As much as the money coming in from the farmers markets was a great help, she didn't see that they could continue that especially with the harvest approaching. Between the orchard and their shop, that was probably all they could manage. She made a mental note to cancel their stall at the farmers market.

A flushed-faced Christina hurried into the kitchen. "Florence, what's going on between Joy and Isaac?"

"I'm not sure I know what you mean."

"It seems they had a tiff. He barely talks to me and he keeps looking at Joy. She seems to be ignoring him."

"I'm sure they can work things out between themselves. In the meantime, can you take these napkins out and put them on the table?"

"Don't you care?"

"I'm too busy to even think about it now, Christina."

Florence held out the white napkins toward Christina. Christina snatched them from her. "You're the same as the rest of your family. Only thinking about yourself." She stomped away leaving Florence shocked. Her life was consumed with looking after others.

Ada was one of the ladies working in the kitchen and she'd overheard what Christina had said. "Don't worry about her, Florence."

"I don't know what I did to upset her."

"She's very highly strung." Ada shook her head. "Two years married and no *kinner*."

"Is that what's upsetting her?"

"*Jah*. Mercy or even Honor might give birth before her. That's what she'd be thinking."

"Hmm, they both seem like *bopplis* themselves. Do you think that's really what's upsetting Christina?"

"I can't see what else it could be."

As far as Florence remembered, Christina had always been standoffish towards her family. Maybe one of them had done something to offend her. When two ladies walked in with stacks of dirty dishes, Florence's attention was back on the job.

. . .

JOY HAD BEEN successful in avoiding Luke Wilkes. Every time she looked over at Isaac, he avoided eye contact. Just as she was considering walking over to talk with Isaac to sort things out, someone tapped her on her shoulder. She turned around to see Christina, Isaac's sister.

"What's going on with you two?" Christina asked.

"Me and your *bruder?*"

"Jah,"

"Just a small misunderstanding. It's okay. I'm just giving him a bit of time to work a few things out."

"Don't you know he's leaving?"

It couldn't be true. "What?"

"Jah, he's leaving and I'm not talking about him leaving the wedding. He will be leaving. He was only staying here for you."

"I didn't know."

"Couldn't you figure that out? Now we've lost him working in the store just like we lost Jonathon. You girls have got a lot to answer for. That's another worker we've lost from our store because of you girls."

Even though she was sad about Isaac leaving, she wasn't going to let an opportunity go by. "I could work for you."

"Denke, but no thanks. I don't think you'd be reliable enough to work six days a week and do all the heavy lifting needed."

"I am reliable. Ask anyone, and I do heavy lifting at home. You'd be surprised how strong I am. I lift all the bags of horse feed."

"Your *mudder* and Florence need you at home, at the market stall, and to do the cooking and what not."

"Okay." Joy shrugged her shoulders. "At least I offered to help out."

"Hmm. I'm not sure if it was a genuine offer or not."

Joy could now see the side of Christina that her sisters so often talked about. She wasn't very pleasant. She was always nice to Honor, and even more so since Jonathon had stayed with them. "I hope you find someone for the store." She wasn't going to beg Isaac to stay if he wanted to go.

"There's a shortage of jobs, so it won't take long for us to find someone, but Isaac is my *bruder,* so I'm not happy. He wasn't just a worker."

"I know that's upsetting for you, but it's not my fault. If you want him to stay, just ask him."

"You should be the one asking him. He might stay if he knows you want him to. Aren't you the least concerned that he's leaving?"

"I am, but there's not much I can do if he wants to go."

Christina looked over her shoulder at Isaac and then looked back at Joy. "Do what you want. You girls always do. Wilma hasn't disciplined any one of you." Christina walked away from her.

Joy wasn't going to leave things at that. She hurried after Christina to have her say. "She doesn't need to discipline us if we never do anything wrong."

Christina's eyes blazed. "You do plenty wrong."

Joy knew she couldn't protest, not with both Honor and Cherish having tried to run away. "Well, everyone does wrong things, but I think it's a bit harsh to say that we're not disciplined. You're being disrespectful to my *mudder*."

"That's a matter of opinion."

"I'll talk to Isaac." She was going to do that anyway.

"*Denke,* that's all I was asking."

When Christina walked away, Joy headed in the direction she'd last seen Isaac. When she got there, she saw him sitting down by himself eating a piece of cake. She walked up and sat beside him. "Why are you sitting down by yourself?"

"I don't know these people very well."

"You know them well enough, don't you?"

"*Nee.*"

"When I first met you, you didn't seem shy at all. You were bold and led the conversations and now you're sitting here quietly filling your face with food."

"I like food, can't you tell?" He pushed a huge piece of cake into his mouth.

"It seems you like cake. I can tell that much." Scriptures ran through her mind, as they so often did, and she wondered if he had a problem with gluttony. *For the drunkard and the glutton shall come to poverty: and drowsiness shall clothe a man with rags.* But, who was she to judge someone? It did make her cautious about him. It wasn't his size that was a problem, though, it was his bad attitude.

When he finished his mouthful, he said, "I made the decision I'm going back home."

"I don't want you to go. I want you to stay."

Without answering her, he pushed the last piece of cake into his mouth and with his finger, gathered the last of the frosting and popped that into his mouth also.

"My, you're really enjoying that cake."

"I know exactly what you mean by that. You can have any man you want and you don't want someone like me. I'm overweight. I know it's a problem, but the more I think about it the more I eat."

"Forget about it, then. Problem solved."

"It's not so easy."

"You're not fat at all. I like the way you look. You have a large frame and there's nothing wrong with that."

"I appreciate you trying to be nice, but there's no point anymore." With his plate in his hand, he rose to his feet, and then she watched him walk back to one of the food tables. At that point, she decided he was in a strange mood and nothing she could say would bring him around. With Honor leaving early tomorrow morning, she decided to spend the rest of the day as close to her as she possibly could.

HONOR LEFT with Jonathon the very next day. Cherish was picked up at nine that same morning for the return trip to Aunt Dagmar's, and one week after that, Isaac was gone. Isaac and Joy had not spoken once after the wedding.

The Baker household was quiet.

IN TRYING to make things work with Ezekiel, Florence had deliberately kept herself away from Carter, but that didn't stop the aching in her heart. She longed to be loved by one special person and for now, Ezekiel was falling way short of the mark.

When the sun was low in the sky, loneliness and frustration led her through the orchard and toward Carter's house. All she intended to do was catch a glimpse of him. When the house came into view, she saw his car there but there was no sign of him.

Florence walked close to the fence. Maybe she should knock on his door and just see him one last time? Where was the harm in that?

Before she lost her sudden courage, she slipped through the five-strand wire fence. Halfway to his house, she stopped still as doubts crept into her mind.

He's an outsider, she reminded herself. Ezekiel Troyer was the kind of man she should marry. Ezekiel was the sensible choice, but she'd come this far.

As she stared through one of his windows, she knew she had to close the door of her heart once and for all. It would be hard, but then she brought to mind the suffering of her forefathers and what they'd endured in the name of God. Just staying away from a man was no comparison. She wasn't being tortured or killed. She sighed, summoned the courage, and walked away from his house.

Getting to know Ezekiel would keep her mind busy and put a stop to her thinking about Carter.

"Hey."

Her heart raced when she recognised his voice. She turned around but she couldn't see him.

"Over here," the voice said. She followed the sound and saw him coming toward the fence from the orchard. "It seems we both had the same idea. I was looking for you."

She hurried over to him, horrified. "You didn't go to the house?" What would her stepmother think if an *Englischer* knocked on the door looking for her? Besides that, it would be a dreadful example to her half-sisters. They met as they always seemed to, at the fence.

"I was looking for you." He gave her a smile, flashing his white teeth. His cheeks were slightly pink blending nicely with the hue of his maroon knitted scarf that hung casually around his neck.

He looked so good. Coming to see him was a huge mistake. They needed more than a wire fence between them. "Look, this is your side of the fence and that is my side. Stay on your own side and everything will be fine." She pulled up one of the wire strands to slip through and he tried to help her. "I can do it," she snapped.

He frowned. Now they were both on her side of the fence. "Why the anger?" he asked.

"I can't keep talking to you like this—all friendly like." Her whole body trembled.

He grinned. "Why?"

"I just can't."

"You can't be friends with someone of a different faith? Or someone who has no faith at all?"

"No, I mean, that's right."

He rubbed the back of his neck. "I see Amish people talking to non-Amish people all the time."

"Talking yes, but we're not close."

It annoyed her that she'd never found out more about him, but that might've been the attraction. If she knew everything about him maybe he wouldn't seem so interesting. She had to know more, and then she'd finally have the courage to forget him.

He carefully ran his fingers along the top row of barbed wire. "I saw you with a man the other day. You both looked happy."

"We're just friends." That was her chance. She could've pretended things were serious between her and Ezekiel. Now was also her chance to know about that woman. "I've seen a woman here a few times while I've been on my afternoon walks."

"She's just a friend."

"You're only saying that because I said the man was just a friend."

"No." He shook his head. "She's truly just a friend."

"I thought you didn't need friends."

"More of an acquaintance." He laughed. "It's not like that. I know what you're thinking."

"I'm not thinking anything."

"Anyway, all that aside, I'm glad he's only a friend of yours."

"Why's that?" She knew she should walk away, but she couldn't. Besides, he'd been so good to her when Honor had run off with Jonathon. He'd driven through the night and that was after spending the whole day driving around locally looking for her.

"He doesn't suit you at all." He wagged a finger at her. "You're scared of getting to like me too much, aren't you?"

"No!" Her nervous fingers straightened her *kapp*. "Of course not! I would never—"

He smirked. "But you've thought about it."

She shook her head and annoyance took over before she got a chance to ask more questions. "It's best that you stay on your side of the fence and I'll stay on mine."

"Is that what you want?"

"Yes."

"Come on. I'm sorry if I've upset you."

She walked away leaving him standing there. The only way she could finally end this was to do it this way. If they parted amicably, it would leave the door open.

"Florence."

She ignored him.

"I'll be here when you've gotten over whatever's bugging you," he called after her.

Just put one foot after the other.

Once she was far enough away among the safety of her apple trees, she slowed her pace. As she walked, she looked up through the high branches at the gray sky above. In her youth, she'd expected to grow up and marry. It seemed a simple thing.

It was irritating that love was happening so easily for her sisters. It wasn't that she was envious, it just left her with so many unanswered questions.

If she could fall in love with Ezekiel Troyer, her life would be wonderful. To have *kinner* of her own would be a dream come true. She quickened her pace, determined to write another letter to Ezekiel before the evening meal.

CHAPTER 19

I<small>T WAS</small> months after Honor and Jonathon's wedding and everything had returned to normal—a new version of normal—in the Baker household. Another apple harvest had come and gone—this time, without three of Florence's half-sisters. They no longer had the stall at the farmers markets and concentrated their efforts on their shop down by the road. Florence had kept her word and sent regular letters to Ezekiel Troyer, but his letters were fewer than what she would've liked. It was hard to develop a meaningful relationship without regular contact. In his letters, he'd asked more than once if she'd come to see him. It would be difficult to leave the orchard, but Florence was starting to realize she had to make some effort.

Her best friend Liza now had her second baby—another boy—a brother for Malachi.

It was the best moment in Florence's life to witness a baby coming into the world. First off in the labor, came Liza's suffering leaving Florence utterly helpless, not knowing what to do other than look on. Nothing gave Liza comfort until the hours of those first-stage contractions passed. When the urge came to Liza to bear down, it wasn't long before the baby boy slithered out. Everyone was in tears. Florence hadn't been prepared for the miracle to be so impactful. It was a moment she'd remember for ever, and was grateful her very best friend had shared that special moment with her. It was a true gift. She hoped Liza would be at her own baby's birth—one day.

Florence had some serious catching up to do with Liza, who was two children and one husband ahead of her. But for that to happen, she needed her own man. That was another reason to make the effort to visit Ezekiel.

It was late one night when she was sewing with *Mamm* that she raised the subject of Cherish. If she'd learned her lesson, there would be another pair of hands to fill in for her when she visited Ezekiel. "When do you think would be a good time for Cherish to come home?"

Mamm jerked her head up from her sewing. "I was thinking about her just now! It's like you heard my thoughts. She hasn't been writing those pleading letters for a while now, and that's making me nervous."

"*Jah*, I noticed her letters had stopped."

"Why don't you call Dagmar and find out how Cherish's been doing?"

"We can both call her tomorrow and say happy birthday to Cherish. That is, if they hear the phone in the barn from the *haus.*"

"That's right. It'll be her birthday. How could I have lost track of that? I guess because she's not here ..."

"I know Cherish will be upset that she won't make it back for Joy's birthday and for hers." Joy's birthday was the day after Cherish's. They were one day off being born exactly three years apart.

"She should've thought of that before she started chasing someone far too old for her."

Florence nodded in agreement as the words brought the memories back. As they sat quietly by the toasty crackling fire, her thoughts turned to Carter. She hadn't seen him for months. He still lived there. She knew that because she often saw his car there.

"What are you thinking about with that faraway look in your eyes?"

"Nothing. Well, I was thinking how peaceful it is tonight."

"I wonder if it will ever be like that again once Cherish returns?"

Florence giggled. "Let's enjoy it while we can, shall we?"

Mamm smiled and nodded.

. . .

THEY CALLED Aunt Dagmar the next morning, but there was no answer. It wasn't until the night-time that they spoke to Cherish. Nothing was discussed about when she'd be allowed home. Dagmar had arranged a special birthday dinner and Cherish was only interested in getting back to the guests.

The whole day Florence had waited anxiously for the mail to be delivered. When it finally came, there was only one letter in the box. It had come from one of Favor's many pen pals. There was nothing from Ezekiel.

ON NOVEMBER 5, the morning of Joy's seventeenth birthday, Joy stayed in bed tossing and turning. Every night was the same. She couldn't sleep for thinking about Isaac and wondering if they'd ever be back to how they once were. He'd been so easy to get along with, and then he had changed.

In her mind, she'd analyzed every conversation, every glance, every action, wondering what had upset him. She must've done something. She'd written to him and even asked his sister, Christina, many times how he was. All Christina did was give a little smile and then change the subject. And she didn't want to get her half-brother Mark involved. He would be uncomfortable talking about the matter. She tried not to worry about it and to leave it in *Gott's* hands, but it wasn't as easy as she thought. Every time she managed to push it out of her head, it was there again five minutes later.

Luke Wilkes, her sort-of brother-in-law hadn't helped matters with Isaac. Isaac was jealous and for no good reason. She couldn't help it if Luke had shown her attention at Honor and Jonathon's wedding. His interest was certainly not returned. He was too immature, not serious about much of anything.

Maybe everyone was right and she would be like Dagmar, and remain a spinster forever. Passed by, overlooked, and forgotten about. At least she'd have memories of Isaac and the times they once shared. If only he'd stayed the confident, carefree man she'd first met.

Then it occurred to her that he might have a girlfriend by now. Her stomach churned. Surely, she would've heard about it if he'd gotten married.

There was nothing she could do but trust *Gott* that He had a plan for her life. For all her preaching at others over the years, she was failing dreadfully in the trusting department. Why was such a simple thing as trusting so hard to do?

JOY HAD TAKEN over Mercy's old bedroom and she just happened to look out the window to see Isaac getting out of Christina and Mark's buggy. She could barely believe her eyes.

He's back!

Her heart felt like it had stopped for a moment. She put a hand to her chest and then sat down, as though frozen.

"If he's here that means he doesn't have a girlfriend and he's not married. Or is he coming to tell me he is getting married?"

Surely not on my birthday.

No, he was there to make up for lost time. To make amends. Maybe to apologize because he realized she had done nothing wrong.

She already had on her best dress for her birthday and one of Christina's specially sewn *kapps*.

She blew out a deep breath and walked down the steps in just enough time to hear Christina say, "We had an unexpected visitor today so we thought we'd bring him along. I hope that's okay."

"Isaac, it's nice to see you again," *Mamm* said.

She paused on the steps and he looked up at her and then everyone else faded into the background. "Joy," he said as he stood there staring.

"Hello, Isaac." She continued walking down the steps feeling like she was floating.

"Happy birthday,"

"*Denke*. You are staying for dinner, aren't you?"

He nodded. "That's why I've come." He handed her a slip of paper.

"What's this?"

"Read it." She slowly opened it and read it.

. . .

I'm sorry for what I've done and I'm sorry for the time that we've been apart.

HER HEART MELTED. In one moment, all the heartache was gone. She folded the note over. "I'm sorry too."

"Why don't we make a new start of things?" He grinned.

She stared at him. Why was he back now all of a sudden? Had he been dating another girl and she'd rejected him? That would explain Christina's behavior and the way she always avoided answering questions about him.

"What do you say?"

She realized she hadn't answered. *"Jah,* a fresh start."

"I can't change my weight. For starters, I've got big bones."

"Why would you want to change your weight?"

"For you."

"Nee. I l … like you just the way you are." She nearly said the word *love,* but wasn't prepared to say that word unless he said it first. She'd been disappointed by him once and didn't want a repeat.

"I've been miserable for months. Just ask my whole family."

She was pleased to hear it. "Are you feeling better now?"

When Isaac smiled at her, she knew everything would be okay.

"I'm fine. I just feel funny sometimes because I'm so overweight."

"You're not overweight, you're just perfect. I keep saying the same thing. Please, let's stop talking about it."

"I'm sorry for before."

"That's fine, forgiven, and there's no need to ever feel anything like that. To me, you're perfect just the way you are."

"I don't know about that, but thanks for saying so."

"Good. Now we can forget about all that and go back to how things were."

"Sure. I came to the conclusion it was all in my head." He held out his hand and she put her hand in his. "You'll have to catch me up with what you've been doing."

"I will, and it'll take all of five minutes because I've just been doing the same old thing over and over again."

Joy was relieved he was back. If he had been dating another girl, he wouldn't have said what he just had. Even though they'd never made promises to one another, it would've been awful if she had lost him. She couldn't imagine herself with anyone else and she wanted him to feel that way too.

"I remember when I reached seventeen. Do you feel any older?"

"Not a bit."

They walked into the dining room where they found everyone had gathered. Ada and Samuel, *Mamm's* close friends were there. They came to all the birthday dinners and family celebrations.

FLORENCE WAS fearful now that Isaac was back. Would Joy think she could also get married at seventeen just because her older sister had?

Half of her was worried, the other half really liked Isaac. And he was Christina's brother, and they'd known him for a long time. It was nice how he had surprised Joy by coming to her birthday dinner.

Once dinner was over and everyone was in the living room, Ada and Florence went into the kitchen to make coffee.

"Now come here and talk to your Aunt Ada."

Florence laughed. She wasn't her aunt, but her stepmother and Ada were so close she felt like her aunt. "All right. I'll just light the stove." When she had put the kettle to heat on the gas flame she sat down next to Ada.

"I think we should have a talk about something."

"What is it?"

"It's about Ezekiel."

"He's alright isn't he?"

"He's fine. But … I asked him how things were going with both of you and he said you were still writing."

"*Jah*, we are."

"I haven't finished yet."

"Oh, I'm sorry. Go on."

"He said he has invited you to the farm several times and you find a reason why you can't go."

"And the reasons are real. I'm not making them up. I'm thinking of going soon. Really I am."

"You should. He's a good man and you don't want to let him get away."

I know."

"Wilma tells me our Cherish might be coming back."

Florence nodded. "We have talked about that."

"That will give you more free time."

"No, it won't because I will have to keep an eye on her. Nothing ever runs smoothly when she's around. I first thought it would be good to get her back before I go away, but I just don't know."

"That's only because everyone is reliant on you now. If you didn't check on everything people would check on themselves." She leaned closer and whispered, "even Wilma has become too reliant on you. Once you're gone, they'll realize exactly how much you do."

"I will go to visit him, Ada. *Denke* for prompting me. I think I just needed a little push."

Ada put her arm around Florence's shoulder. "You deserve a lot of happiness, Florence. Your father and your mother would be pleased to see how lovely you've grown up to be."

She stared at Ada. Her mother was so rarely mentioned by anyone. "Were you close with my *mudder?*"

Right at that moment, the kettle boiled and Wilma walked into the room. "Florence, why don't you talk to our guests while I help Ada in here."

"*Nee, Mamm.* That's fine."

"I insist."

"Okay." Florence left the kitchen and headed to the living room. It felt strange having someone else do the work in the kitchen. The only seat left was one next to Christina, so she sat down next to her. There was no reason why they couldn't get along together and Florence was determined to make a special effort. Talking to Christina would also take her mind off what happened in the kitchen just now. Obviously, *Mamm* had overheard them talking about her birthmother. Was she jealous of even the memory of *Dat's* first wife?

CHAPTER 20

Two days later, Florence had booked into a bed-and-breakfast, for one week in mid-December, close to Ezekiel's farm. She knew he'd complain and insist on her staying at the house. She intended to refuse since his mother hadn't been well and she didn't want to put any undue stress on the poor woman. In a letter, she sent him all the details and all the dates.

Two weeks later she had a reply. She took it into the living room to read, unable to keep the smile from her face as she ripped open the envelope, but that smile fled from her face when she read what he had written. She looked it over again, hoping she'd somehow read it wrong.

Dear Florence,

I'm sorry to say that my mother has had a small relapse. It wasn't helped by one of my brothers suddenly moving away leaving me busier than ever. I was hoping you might be able to delay your visit.

I have made some attempt over these past months to have someone look after the farm so I can come to see you. Each time, something gets in the way.

Perhaps this is God's way of telling us something?

I still think about my visit to you and I have pleasant memories of you, your family, and your apple orchard.

Look after yourself Florence.

Yours faithfully,

Ezekiel Troyer.

IT WAS JUST SO SHORT. It was a goodbye letter. There was no doubt about it.

"What's that you've got?" Wilma walked into the room with a basket of clean clothes that needed to be ironed. Florence was so upset she couldn't speak. All she could do was pick up the letter and extend it toward her stepmother.

Mamm put the basket of clothes down on the couch and took hold of the letter.

Once she was finished reading it, she looked at Florence. "Are you going to cancel your vacation?"

"I have to. I can't really go there now after that letter. Do you think he was saying goodbye?"

Wilma licked her lips and looked down at the letter. "It seems he thinks everything is against you two being together. It's hard with you both living so far apart."

Florence felt she would burst into tears. In faith, she'd turned her back on the *Englischer* from next door and put all her energies into the possibility that she might one day be Mrs. Ezekiel Troyer.

The problem was, she wasn't good enough for him to make the required effort.

She felt fat, ugly, old, tired, and used up. No wonder no one loved her.

All she wanted was to be happy and feel loved. Was that too much to ask?

Mamm handed her back the letter. Florence took it and tossed it into the fire. Her quick actions shocked even herself. She could feel that Wilma was also amazed.

Wilma then picked up the basketful of clothes and continued on her way to the kitchen, where the clothes were normally ironed.

Then Florence heard her call out, "Don't forget to cancel the booking at the bed-and-breakfast."

"I'll remember." Florence sniffed back her tears. She's been so looking forward to meeting Ezekiel's family, helping his mother around her house, and looking around the pig farm. Now that door was firmly closed. No, it had been slammed in her face. Her letters had outnumbered his by three to one. There was no excuse for that because she was just as busy, or even more so.

Yet, she had continued to convince herself that all was okay. He had certainly given her the impression that he was interested before he left and she had no idea why he so suddenly lost interest.

IT WAS times like these she needed the comfort that only a mother could give. She knew she'd been loved by her birth mother. If she had something tangible, like a pillow or a blanket that used to be hers, she could put it on her bed at night, and feel her close.

She remembered the attic where her mother's and father's things were stored. While her stepmother was busy in the kitchen, and her sisters were out with friends, she opened the small door of the attic and climbed up the stairs.

It was semi-dark and smelled so musty. The only light shone from a small window in the roof.

The place was lined with boxes, all piled one on top of the other. She and Earl were the ones who'd placed their father's belongings up here and she remembered where those had been placed. The rest of the boxes must've belonged to her mother.

The first box she opened was full of letters. Curiosity got the better of her when she saw an envelope with her name on the front, and two other envelopes named for each of her brothers.

When she opened *her* letter, she looked at the date. It was dated a month before her mother had died. She stood up and taking the letter with her, she walked closer to the window so she could read it more easily.

MY DEAREST FLORENCE,

If you're reading this letter that means I'm no longer around. I've asked your father to give you this letter when you're an adult, the same as the letters I have for Mark and Earl.

Life is so uncertain.

I've learned nothing is forever. I want to be there always, guiding you and your brothers, whispering in your ears. If I can't be there, pay attention to my following words and keep them in your heart.

Always be kind to others.

Try to see the other person's point of view. It's just as valid as your own.

You must follow your heart rather than your head sometimes.

Don't make my mistakes.

No matter where I am, I will always love you, your father and your brothers.

Always be there for your family.

Your loving *Mamm*

HER MISTAKES. *What were her mistakes?*

She looked at those many letters. Perhaps in that box lay the answer?

Folding the letter carefully, she set it on the windowsill to collect later and sat down on the floor in front of the box to sort through the letters. After fifteen minutes of skimming through all the correspondence, she saw there was nothing helpful. At the bottom of the box she found a key. She held it up in the half-light—it was a small key, not big enough to open a door. Then her eyes traveled to a small wooden box wedged between the cardboard boxes. She pulled it out, admiring the beauty of woodgrain and workmanship as she turned it to find the lock, and then tried the key. It opened and there were more letters. Perhaps these were personal letters between her parents when they had been courting.

When she picked up the first envelope she turned it over and saw the last name of Braithwaite. She was sure her eyes were playing tricks on her, so she took it over to the light. Sure enough, the last name was Braithwaite and the first name was Gerald.

With her heart pounding in her head, she took out the single-page yellowed letter. Scanning the words, she saw it was a heartfelt plea. The man was pleading with her to come away with him and to leave the community. Florence dropped the letter and her hands covered her mouth. Her own mother must've been in love with someone before she married *Dat*.

She clutched her throat. Braithwaite. That was Carter's last name and it wasn't a common one, as far as she knew.

Then she recalled that Carter had once specifically asked her about her mother. What did it all mean?

She peered out the small attic window. On her tiptoes, she could just make out the roof of Carter's house peeping above the trees. Could she, or should she ask him questions?

Follow your heart. Don't make the same mistakes as me. The words rang in Florence's head and that was all she needed. Despite the other voices in her head that told her not to do anything in haste, she put everything back where it had been, and climbed down the stairs. She found Wilma in the kitchen.

"I'm going for a walk." Before Wilma could respond, Florence had grabbed her shawl and was out the door heading to Carter's house as she swirled it around her shoulders.

She had been so horrible to him last time and he had done nothing to deserve it.

Was it possible for people from two different worlds to come together and find some common ground? She couldn't see herself in his world, and she knew he wouldn't fit into hers, but her mother's letter must've meant something. Didn't it?

She knew there was a scripture in the Bible that said anything was possible with God. Joy would know the exact words and exactly where in the Bible it was.

This morning she'd felt sadness, but now all she had in her heart was the happiness of many possibilities. Perhaps it was possible, while putting God first, to follow your heart and find your dreams.

She slid between the wires of the fence, ever mindful of the barbs, and then walked quickly to Carter's door before she changed her mind. She knocked on the door and was pleased that he answered it when he did, before her courage left her.

"Florence." He looked her up and down as though he was taking it all in. "You came back."

"I never left."

"I haven't seen you for several months."

"That's an exaggeration." She inhaled quickly, then said, "I've come to say I'm sorry. I think we parted on bad terms. I'm here to say that I'm sorry for how I acted and the things I said."

"I don't remember who said what. I only know that after it was said, you hurried away and wouldn't stop when I called you back. I waited and then went through the orchard looking for you, but couldn't find you."

"Did you?"

"Yes. After I got over the shock of being spoken to like that." He grinned.

"So, do you forgive me?"

"There's nothing to forgive. I'm pleased you're here now."

"I want to ask you a question."

"Fire away."

"You've asked me about my mother a couple of times."

"Yes, and you asked me about my family. What of it?"

This wasn't going to be easy. "This may sound totally crazy and maybe it is, but did you or anyone in your family know my birth mother?"

He stared at her blankly. "I'm not sure what you're asking."

There was no way around it—she had to tell him. "I was going through my mother's things today, something that I've never done before. Well, I made an attempt years ago, but it was a bit more upsetting than I could handle then, so I stopped. Anyway, I found some interesting things. There were letters from someone with the last name of Braithwaite. Those letters were addressed to my mother."

"Ah, now the penny drops. Is that the only reason you're here?"

She suddenly felt giddy and light-headed, but she couldn't stop asking or she might never again have the courage to ask. "No, I am here to apologize, but also to find out if there's any connection between someone with the last name of Braithwaite and my mother."

"There obviously was since you said they wrote her a letter. Are you asking me if there's anyone I know of in my family who wrote to your mother?"

"Yes. That's what I'm asking. His name was Gerald Braithwaite."

He blinked slowly, a few times, showing no recognition of that name. "What kind of letters were they?"

"I didn't read all of them but they appear to be love letters." When he smirked, she quickly added, "From before my mother married my father."

"That's interesting. Braithwaite is not an Amish name."

"That's right, I don't recall any Amish person having that name. Or anyone marrying into the Amish, but it's not impossible." Then it hit her like a bolt of lightning on a summer's day. Her mother had been in love with a non-Amish man. She turned her back on him and all that he represented to stay within the community and ended up marrying her father. That had to be the mistake her mother referred to since it followed the advice to follow her heart.

Joining the dots, that meant her mother regretted marrying her father. She'd always imagined her parents had an idyllic marriage and the perfect life. It wasn't so. The real love story never happened because her mother's heart belonged to Gerald Braithwaite.

Everything around her faded, and she collapsed into Carter's arms.

CHAPTER 21

WHEN FLORENCE OPENED HER EYES, she was lying on Carter's couch, in his living room, and he was kneeling beside her.

She tried to sit up.

"Stay there." He held up his hand. "You fainted. I'll get you a glass of water."

Her heavy eyelids closed, and then he was back. He helped her sit up and plumped up some cushions behind her back. She brought the glass up to her lips and took a couple of sips.

"I'll take you to the hospital to get checked out."

"No. I'm fine." She wasn't really. She felt weird and drained of energy. Her fingers wrapped around the cool glass.

"People don't faint unless there's a problem. Has it happened before?"

"Only once. When I heard my father had died." She took a deep breath.

"What brought it on?"

She looked up at him standing there with his hands on his hips. "It was the shock of going through my mother's things. I'm sure of it. It brought a lot of things up from the past."

"Bad things?"

"Not really. It's hard to explain. I should go home." Leaning forward, she put the glass on the coffee table.

If she got away by herself, she could think things through. She stood up, took a step and then her foot caught on the edge of the rug and she fell toward him. His arms encircled her as she leaned into the hardness of his chest.

She looked up into his unusual colored eyes. They weren't brown or even a typical hazel; there were flecks of green and gold, and gray—light gray and charcoal, and ...

"You're beautiful, Florence."

She wanted to believe his words. She wanted him to kiss her, and just like that, his gaze traveled from her eyes to her mouth.

Florence's mother had given her the permission to follow her heart and, in that micro-second in time, that was what she wanted. She clung to him wanting him to kiss her and just before it happened, she moved her head. He pulled her into him instead, and she rested her head against his shoulder.

Suddenly, she couldn't let this madness continue. "I'm sorry. I tripped." She put her hands on his chest, pushing as she stepped back.

His hands moved to her shoulders and lingered as though he didn't want to let her go. "That's the stupid rug. I only just bought it yesterday. I'm sorry about that."

"It's okay. I have to go."

"Stay awhile."

"No. They'll come looking." It was a lie. There was no one who'd be looking for her, and the only place she wanted to be was here with him.

"Let me walk you home."

She shook her head, knowing there'd be too many questions from her family if they saw her with an *Englischer*.

"Partway, at least. I insist."

"Okay, if you insist."

"I do. I just said so." With a hand lightly on her arm, he guided her out of the house. "Are you warm enough?"

"Plenty." She glanced at his smiling face and adjusted her shawl. "I'm sorry about fainting."

He laughed. "You were determined to be in my arms one way or another today."

"I didn't do it deliberately. And your rug … I tripped on it."

"I'm not complaining, believe me."

While she was with him, she never wanted to leave. She never felt anything like this with Ezekiel. They reached the border of their two properties far too soon. "I'll be alright from here."

"No. I'll take you further."

"I'll be okay."

He pressed his lips together and shook his head. "Well, don't leave it so long next time. Will you come and see me tomorrow? Tomorrow morning? I'll be home all day."

"Those chess games on your computer sure must be interesting. Do you still do that all day?"

"Not all day. I do other things. I might even tell you one day, but you'll never know if you don't come back."

"I will."

Then there was a silent moment as their eyes said goodbye. Then he took a step closer, causing her heart to flutter like a butterfly just emerged from her chrysalis and finding her wings for the very first time. With his hand on the small of her back, he pulled her into him. Their bodies nearly touched as he lowered his head to hers. This time she stayed still. As soon as their lips touched, she pulled away.

"I have to go."

He released her. When she reached for one of the wires, he separated them so she could slip more easily through the fence.

Once she was on the other side, she thanked him and bid him goodbye.

"Bye, Florence," he called after her as she hurried away into her orchard.

Florence made it to the first line of trees and looked back. He was out of sight, so she stopped and leaned on a tree. She felt different—everything did. As she looked above, she saw the sky was bluer, the white clouds fluffier, and she could even smell the crisp air.

Happiness flooded through her, her heart took wing, and she became fully alive.

A light had been shone into the darkness of her life.

Is this what it feels like to be loved and wanted?

Florence gulped and lowered herself to the cold ground beneath her and leaned back onto the friendly trunk of the apple tree.

The last thing she wanted to do was ruin this delightful giddy moment by being practical, but Carter wasn't from her world.

As much as she wanted to be close to him and learn everything about him, it was *verboten*.

She sighed loudly.

If only they'd had just one last kiss.

Just one.

That kiss would've lasted her a lifetime.

"Florence!"

She looked over at the sound of Carter's deep voice and saw him running toward her.

"Are you okay?"

"I am."

He crouched down beside her. "What are you doing on the ground like this?"

Here was her chance for just one kiss—a proper kiss.

The memory of which would last a lifetime.

What would the harm be in just one simple kiss?

She could be practical tomorrow, and in time, she'd marry someone suitable—a sensible man. Then she'd go on to have a sensible family with many sensible children. Or not ... Maybe she'd be like Aunt Dagmar, running the orchard as an unmarried businesswoman.

This kiss would be her one indulgence—something that would be hers and hers alone to remember when times got tough. She could close her eyes and remember her first kiss with the man her heart wanted.

If and only if, he wanted to kiss her again.

"I was just thinking." She held out her hands, and just as she knew he would, he stood and as he did he pulled her to her feet with him. Once they faced one another, they stared into each other's eyes.

Because she'd twice rejected him, she knew she had to make the first move.

She took a step to him and turned her face upward. He wasted no time in lowering his head until their lips met. The warm, gentle and love-filled kiss was everything she'd hoped it would be.

His lips were soft and loving—his arms, strong, manly, and reassuring.

In that moment, she felt loved like she'd never felt before.

"Oh, Florence." He hugged her to himself. "There are so many things you don't know about me."

It was dangerous to get too close and she hoped with that kiss that he hadn't taken it as something more than it was.

Summoning all her strength, she said, "I have to go."

"Don't!" He leaned down and kissed her forehead.

"There's always tomorrow."

"I'll be waiting. Just like I've waited for the last few months."

Her mouth dropped open in shock and then she had to know more. "Who's that woman I saw at your house that time?" It was twice, but she didn't want him to know she'd been counting.

"She's someone involved with my work. You don't need to worry about her, or anyone else. I'm a one-woman man." He shook his head. "You'll never need to be concerned about that."

A giggle tumbled from her lips. Any other time, she would've probed more about his work. She had so many questions to ask, but it scared her that he was talking like they were on the border of starting some kind of relationship.

It was nice to be wanted.

"Would you ever consider joining the community?"

At that point, she was certain he'd run away. Instead, he said, "My life's motto is, *never say never.*"

Was there a spark of a chance for them?

This was something she'd never seriously considered. All she could do was stare at him.

"Would you ever leave?" he asked.

"Never," she answered without hesitation.

He chuckled. "Tomorrow then?" he asked.

Happiness bubbled within her to overflowing. "Yes, tomorrow." *And the day after, and the day after that,* she wanted to say, because that's what her heart wanted.

They stood there smiling at one another until she turned and walked away feeling as though she was gliding, flying.

Deep in her heart, she knew she was dancing with danger.

Yet, she'd never felt so alive.

Thank you for reading this Box Set.

THE NEXT SET IN THE SERIES

Find out in what happens next for Florence and the girls in the next box set. (Books 4-6).
You will get some surprises.
(Includes: Amish Joy, Amish Family Secrets, & The Englisher).

ALL BOOK SERIES

Amish Maids Trilogy
A 3 book Amish romance series of novels featuring 5 friends finding love.

Amish Love Blooms
A 6 book Amish romance series of novels about four sisters and their cousins.

Amish Misfits
A series of 7 stand-alone books about people who have never fitted in.

The Amish Bonnet Sisters
To date there are 28 books in this continuing family saga. My most popular and best-selling series.

Amish Women of Pleasant Valley

An 8 book Amish romance series with the same characters. This has been one of my most popular series.

Ettie Smith Amish Mysteries
An ongoing cozy mystery series with octogenarian sleuths. Popular with lovers of mysteries such as Miss Marple or Murder She Wrote.

Amish Secret Widows' Society
A ten novella mystery/romance series - a prequel to the Ettie Smith Amish Mysteries.

Expectant Amish Widows
A stand-alone Amish romance series of 19 books.

Seven Amish Bachelors
A 7 book Amish Romance series following the Fuller brothers' journey to finding love.

Amish Foster Girls
A 4 book Amish romance series with the same characters who have been fostered to an Amish family.

Amish Brides
An Amish historical romance. 5 book series with the same characters who have arrived in America to start their new life.

Amish Romance Secrets
The first series I ever wrote. 6 novellas following the same characters.

Amish Christmas Books
Each year I write an Amish Christmas stand-alone romance novel.

Amish Twin Hearts
A 4 book Amish Romance featuring twins and their friends.

Amish Wedding Season
The second series I wrote. It has the same characters throughout the 5 books.

Amish Baby Collection
Sweet Amish Romance series of 6 stand-alone novellas.

Gretel Koch Jewel Thief
A clean 5 book suspense/mystery series about a jewel thief who has agreed to consult with the FBI.

A NOTE FROM SAMANTHA

I'm often asked how my stories come about and how I come up with the ideas, so I'll share my inspiration for The Amish Bonnet Sisters series.

I grew up listening to my mother's memories of her childhood. Her favorite ones were of staying at the family's dairy farm. She was often sent there for her aunts to look after when she was a young girl.

A few years ago, my mother started telling me about her Aunt Florence.

Florence was the oldest of thirteen girls (no boys), and she did everything for the family. They lived on a large dairy farm and had a reasonably tough life. While Florence's mother was busy having babies, Florence ran the household, looked after her younger sisters, and worked, milking the cows by hand alongside her father. I was amazed by Florence being the backbone of the family at such a young age. She was the real-life Florence that inspired Florence Baker of the Amish Bonnet Sisters.

I do hope you will enjoy spending time at the Baker Apple Orchard as much as I have.

Much love & blessings.

Samantha Price

www.SamanthaPriceAuthor.com

Made in the USA
Middletown, DE
05 October 2023

40322754R00373